"A splendid collection from the field of fiction that is the widest-angled lens of the imagination"

Such was the comment of one reviewer about last year's annual. Such will be the comment around the country for this year's, even as it has been for the decades past. For the 1985 anthology of the best of the year's science fiction marks the beginning of the third decade of this series!

Here you can keep up with the best of the old writers and the best of the new writers. Here you may encounter the award winners of 1985 and of years to come. Here meet Lucius Shepard and Gary Shockley, John Dalmas and Stephen Donaldson, Ian Watson and Tanith Lee, and more. Let your imagination soar!

Anthologies from DAW

ASIMOV PRESENTS THE GREAT SF STORIES
The best stories of the last two decades.
Edited by Isaac Asimov and Martin H. Greenberg.

THE ANNUAL WORLD'S BEST SF
The best of the current year.
Edited by Donald A. Wollheim with Arthur W. Saha.

THE YEAR'S BEST HORROR STORIES
An annual of gooseflesh tales.
Edited by Karl Edward Wagner.

THE YEAR'S BEST FANTASY STORIES
An annual of high imagination.
Edited by Arthur W. Saha

TERRA SF
The Best SF from Western Europe.
Edited by Richard D. Nolane.

WOLLHEIM'S WORLD'S BEST SF
Edited by Donald A. Wollheim

THE 1985 ANNUAL WORLD'S BEST SF

Edited by

DONALD A. WOLLHEIM

with Arthur W. Saha

DAW BOOKS, INC.
DONALD A. WOLLHEIM, PUBLISHER

1633 Broadway, New York, NY 10019

Cover art by Frank Kelly Freas.

DAW Collectors' Book No. 630

First Printing, June 1985

1 2 3 4 5 6 7 8 9

PRINTED IN U.S.A.

CONTENTS

INTRODUCTION

Recently there arrived in the mail a copy of the magazine *Soviet Literature* (No.2/ 1984) which was entirely devoted to the topic of Science Fiction of Today. This edition was in English, published in Moscow by the Writers' Union of the USSR. In this journal, the editors had sent out letters to various science fiction writers asking them, among other questions, this: What do you consider to be the social mission of science fiction? What role can it play in the contemporary world?

We think it would be of interest to quote some of the replies. Defining science fiction and its value has always been a topic of controversial interest among readers, writers and academics. So let us see first what Isaac Asimov answered:

"The social mission of science fiction is to accustom the minds of human beings to the inevitability of technological change. The role it can play is to to encourage human beings to make use of technology in such a way as to improve society and increase human happiness, and *not* the reverse."

Arthur C. Clarke wrote this: "It is the gravest mistake to ascribe to science fiction the role of some kind of prophet . . . Its role is to *develop* people's imagination, to educate people capable of thinking in categories of the future . . . Science fiction is able to *warn* people about the dangers that lie in store for them, and it can do this much more effectively than it can make utopian projections. I would call it an advance warning system about forthcoming catastrophes."

James Gunn is quoted: "Science fiction has taught me to be optimistic . . . Science fiction—even its most gloomy examples—presupposes the existence of a future, and therefore, it may prove a very effective means in fighting lack of will-power and faith."

Harry Harrison stated: "Good SF writers can give their readers some idea of how science works, that this is a world of change—and that we can change change itself, not accept it blindly for the betterment of mankind."

Joe Haldeman: "Science fiction offers a way of intellectually testing the ways that life might change in the future—harmless testing, like the fledgling pilot's flight simulator. It can provide early warnings for future pitfalls and offer possible solutions to present-day problems."

Frederik Phol: "The social mission of science fiction (setting aside that large fraction of science fiction which has no mission but to entertain) is to allow us to examine the possible consequences of all sorts of technological, social and cultural changes, so that we can better decide now which ones we want to see become reality."

Soviet science fiction writers participated and much of what they wrote agrees broadly with the above comments. Dmitry Bilenkin wrote: "Any idea, before it becomes an action, must ripen in one's mind. Science fiction, just as any other form of literature, can influence man's mind and feelings. It is of no great importance that SF is sometimes regarded as entertainment; on the contrary, it may be considered an advantage, for it becomes accessible to a broader circle of readers."

Kir Bulychev: "Science fiction, as distinct from realist literature, deals with probabilities; it is interested in the problems not only of individuals, but of society as a whole . . .

Science fiction is addressed primarily to young people, to those who tomorrow will be reponsible for the destinies of the human race."

Yeremei Parnov: "The social mission of science fiction lies first of all in detecting and incarnating people's anxieties and expectations. It prepares society, if I may put it so, for new achievements and radical changes and warns against possible dangers."

Vadim Shefner: "Even non-science fiction writers inevitably become writers of fantasies when they try to take a look at Tomorrow. The power of science fiction lies not only in its ability to visualize the world of tomorrow but also in its ability to influence the Future and even, to some extent, to shape it. Negative prognoses are as appropriate here as positive ones . . . Science fiction writing has still another task, or to be more precise, a super-task: to teach people to be kind. In my opinion this goal is best achieved when science fiction is neither purely scientific nor technological but when it is something like a fairy-tale or parable. I repeat that this is *my* opinion, and I certainly may be mistaken."

In a long article in that same issue, the Soviet SF critic and editor, Vl. Gakov, wrote: "The time for science fiction arrived as soon as man needed images of 'what had not been', pictures of what one would like to believe, no inhabitants of our planet will ever see with their own eyes.

"It is not a matter of gratifying idle curiosity, but of a vital necessity. No one, of course, is going to present mankind with a peaceful future on a plate. We have to build it, and therefore we must all protect it. As soon as the question of preserving the future arises, then we are under obligation to know something about the dangers that threaten it.

"Scientific foresight is a matter for the scientists. The SF writers can only train advance human thought like radar on the targets of imaginary antiworlds. The sifting out of undesirable and even deadly dangerous variants is a responsible task. Science fiction, to give it its due, excels at this job."

Surveying the current crop of science fiction in view of the above comments one must note the insight of the writer Vadim Shefner to what is actually being mainly produced—more of a not quite scientific or technological nature but rather of a more imaginative social nature or even parable. Fairy-tales for grown-ups, now generally labeled Fantasy, are appearing in ever greater quantity and such books in America seem about to overwhelm the book racks. Yet perhaps Shefner is right—this form of parable or entertaining adventure, too, is based on the moral principles of good versus bad—and bad, even in the farthest-out fantasies, is still that which kills and maims and destroys the hope of the future.

You will find in the ten stories selected here as the most memorable and unusual of the past year something of what all these writers have spoken of. Stories which warn, stories which possibly scare, stories which enhance the imagination and spark the concepts that may shape our world's future; they are all present.

—DONALD A. WOLLHEIM

THE PICTURE MAN

by John Dalmas

Knowing the immediate future could be very profitable—if we could act upon such information. Particularly if it was like tomorrow's newspaper available today. But there are problems and catches . . . and the human element cannot be ignored.

I put down my copy of *Ecological Review* and walked over to the TV. I generally liked to catch the ten o'clock news. The picture popped out to fill the screen; the last moment of the opening commercials was just flashing off.

I sat back down to watch, all by myself in my three-bedroom, one-and-a-half-bath, near-campus, 1950-model house. It got a little lonely at times since Eydie had "dear John'ed" me with Barney Foster, but it was certainly quieter and less irritating. For example, the house wasn't dominated night after night by game shows, situation "comedies," and TV dramas.

I'd learned the hard way that marrying the best-looking girl in the class and living happily ever after weren't necessarily the same thing.

Several female faculty and staff members had demonstrated an interest in filling the presumptive hole in my life, and there had been some interesting evenings. Maggie Lanning in particular combined looks and physical interest with remarkable level-headedness in every area we'd talked about. Plus, she was willing to hike in the rain, played a great forward in couples basketball (she was an assistant professor in phys. ed.), and even had a collection of old John Campbell editorials cut from years of *Astoundings* and *Analogs*.

Not that she was old. She was thirty-three—two years younger than I.

But marriage? We could already talk and romp at our mutual convenience, and she had one major drawback: ten-year-old Lanny. Lanny was a good kid, we got along fine, and he kept dropping hints that I'd make a good dad and Maggie would make a good wife. But he was going to be a *teenager* in less than three years.

And I was still enjoying my new independence. I should, I decided, write a thank-you note to Barney, now that the divorce was final. I wouldn't, though. It would be a cheap shot, and I wouldn't feel good about it afterward.

The weatherman joggled me out of my reverie with mention of a sunspot storm. So when the basketball and hockey scores were over, I put on a jacket and went to the door. Sunspots might mean an aurora display, and watching northern lights was one of my favorite spectator activities.

If I'd turned on the porch light before I went out, I might not have seen what I did. A stocky, square-looking man was digging in my plastic trash can that sat by the curb waiting for morning pickup. Two steps, and he could have been out of sight behind Chuck Ciccone's privet hedge. He'd dug in to the armpit, setting some contents on the sidewalk for better access, straightened for a moment, then tidily put everything back in the can and replaced the lid, clamping it down. There hadn't been anything edible or valuable in the can.

"Hey!" I said. Slowly he looked toward me, then lowered his face and started to walk off.

"Just a minute!" I called. "Come on in. Do me a favor; help me eat some leftovers."

The dim face looked at me again for a few seconds, then he walked toward the house, hands stuffed in the pocket of his denim work jacket. For a moment I had a feeling of strangeness as, hunched against the cold and night, he approached. Not a feeling of threat. Just strangeness.

The square, high-cheekboned face, grimy and stubbled, was lined with the track record of late middle age. He looked like someone who'd ridden into town on a freight train, probably headed south. I held the door for him—it was that or wash the knob—and headed him for the bathroom.

"Why don't you shower down while I cook?" I said, then pointed out the guest towel and washcloth and left him there.

Being fresh out of leftovers, I put eggs and wienies on to boil, set a can of beans over a low flame, and put the teakettle on for hot chocolate. When everything was under way, I resurrected an old pair of jeans and a baggy sweatshirt and put them on the bathroom rug. The place was full of steam, like a Turkish bath; he must have a remarkable tolerance for hot water, I thought. I announced to the shower that I was going to run his clothes through the washer and dryer, that I was leaving some of mine he could wear, and, getting a faint acknowledgment, went and started the washing cycle. I even threw his black stocking cap in; I'd have to remember not to put it in the dryer.

What in the hell, I asked myself, *are you doing? This guy could be a psycho. He could murder and rob you.* But there'd been nothing deadlier than a small jackknife in his pockets.

On an impulse, and feeling uncomfortable about it, I checked his wallet. It had no money. A merchant mariner's certificate identified him as Jaakko Savimaki, of Calumet, Michigan.

Fireman, oiler, water tender. Dated 1951—thirty-two years back. The square face in the picture was a youthful version of my man's, the hair blonde and crewcut. His driver's license address was Ironwood, Michigan; I'd heard about the mines up there being shut down.

Opening the bathroom door, I peered into the clouded interior. "You'll find a razor and shaving cream in the medicine cabinet," I said, and turned on the exhaust fan so he could find the mirror.

When he came out, he looked a lot better, although on him, my jeans were a couple of inches too long and a couple too tight. He'd made do by folding cuffs into them, leaving the waistband open, and keeping them up with the elastic belt.

"My name's Terry," I said, "Terry O'Brien."

"Mine is Jake," he answered. "Jake Hill."

Even in those few words, I detected an accent.

"Mr. Hill, I took the liberty of looking in your billfold for identification. It said your name is Savimaki."

He didn't blush or look angry or embarrassed. The strange, soft blue eyes just gazed at me as if examining the inside of my head.

"Savimaki is a kind of hill in Finnish," he said. "Away from home, it's easier to just tell people 'Hill.' "

I nodded. "Got it," I said. "All right, Mr. Savimaki, supper is on the counter."

As hungry as he must have been, he didn't bolt his food. When he'd finished, he thanked me and took his dishes to the sink before I realized what he was doing. Then he turned to me, and again his eyes were direct. I got the feeling that he saw more than other people did. "How do I pay you back?" he asked.

"Forget it. It's on me."

He didn't shake his head—simply said, "It's not all right for me to take something for nothing."

Well, I thought, *that's a refreshing viewpoint.* I wasn't sure I totally agreed with it, in a country where the system was so screwed up that some people found themselves backed up against the wall. But if everyone had his attitude, things would be a lot better.

"O.K.," I said, "what do you do?"

The pale eyes shifted to the fireplace. "You got any wood to split?"

"No. Sorry. I buy it already split."

"Any carpentry you need done? Windows fixed? Locks repaired?"

I looked at the possibilities. "You hit me at a bad time. I've got nothing like that. Why don't we defer payment? There'll be snow to shovel a little later in the fall."

His eyes withdrew for a moment; he didn't plan to be around Douglas long. "Tell you what," I suggested, "why don't you pass it on? Help someone else out when you have a chance."

He nodded slowly. "O.K.," he said. "I guess that's O.K." Then he turned to the sink and began to run water for the dishes while I transferred his clothes to the dryer, remembering to hold out his stocking cap. He seemed to think slowly, but he washed dishes fast. They were clean, rinsed, and in the drainer in about two minutes.

When he was done, he followed me into the living room and stood uncomfortably. I could see he still wasn't happy about not exchanging anything for the bath, meal, and laundry. Then he noticed the pictures on my wall, mostly wildland photos. When Eydie had taken her prints from the house, I'd mounted some scenic photographs on mat and hung them to handle the bareness. He walked over and looked at them.

"You got a camera?" he asked.

"Three of them. A 35-mm Pentax for slides, an old Rollei 4 × 5, and a Polaroid 680."

"A Polaroid." He considered that for a moment. "How would you like if I gave you some interesting pictures?"

"What do you mean?"

"Let me show you. Get the Polaroid."

Feeling mystified, I got it reluctantly. When I came back to the living room, he was sitting in a chair.

"Is it loaded?" he asked.

"Always," I said.

"Then aim it at my face." He closed his eyes tightly, his brow clenched with concentration. "When I say 'now,' shoot it."

Feeling foolish, I raised the camera.

"Now," he said. I touched the shutter release, lowered the camera, and waited. He was on his feet beside me when I removed the print. It wasn't a picture of Savimaki. It was a house, somewhat blurred, an old, frame, two-story house with a steep roof, no front porch, and an upstairs door that opened out onto thin air. A ladder was built on the wall up to the strangely placed door.

"Let's do another one," he said. "That one ain't very good. I can get something more interesting than that."

"Wait a minute," I said. "How come it isn't a picture of you?"

Actually, I thought I knew why. Years before, I'd read a book about the detailed, if somewhat ambiguous, studies done on Nick Kopac, the psychic photographer. This looked like the same kind of thing.

"I don't know," he said. "It's just something I can do."

"Strange-looking house. Where is it?"

"In Calumet, Michigan. It's the house I grew up in. It looks like that because they get so much snow there. Some winters you get in and out through the upstairs door."

"My god! And didn't you know that's what the picture was going to be of?"

"No. I haven't learned how to know yet." He sat down

again. "Usually I get something I never even seen before. But it's always a house or a ship. So far. Actually, I only ever did this about ten or twelve times before. I found out about it last winter, by accident, when a guy tried to take a picture of me and I didn't know it. I was reading a magazine, and all he got was a picture of a lighthouse."

"Are you ready now?" he asked.

I nodded. "Yep."

He closed his eyes, I aimed, he said "now" again, and I shot. Together we looked at the print. This one was sharper, hardly blurred at all, showing a square house that looked stuccoed. It reminded me of pictures I'd seen of French farmhouses, but in the background was a broadly naked landscape with what looked like a high, cliff-faced plateau behind it. As an ecologist with a strong interest in biogeography, I was willing to be it was an Afrikaner farmstead in South Africa, and told him so.

He shrugged. "Could be."

We took a couple more, then called it quits, and I showed him the guest bedroom. But my mind was racing. I didn't have a class the next day until two in the afternoon, and I could always cancel my morning office hours, although I didn't like to. I thought I knew where I could get Jake a job. After he sacked down, I went to the phone and called Herb Boeltz.

I didn't actually know Boeltz very well, although as well as I wanted to. We were both in the faculty jogging club. He was a faculty politician, if you know what I mean, reputedly handy with a knife to the back, a full professor in psychology at thirty-two; and a man who always seemed to have access to grant money.

And he was said to be interested in parapsychology.

It was 11:15, and apparently I had wakened him; he didn't sound terribly friendly. So as soon as I'd identified myself, I put it to him this way.

"I think I've got something that can get you a lot of good publicity. Remember the studies on psychic photography at the University of Nebraska? . . . That's right, Nick Kopac.

"Well, I've got a guy staying here at my house that does the same sort of thing. I took four shots with my Polaroid; got two houses, a church, and what looks like a commercial fishing boat. . . .

"No, I just met him today. Seems like a good enough guy. Kind of quiet. He needs a job, and I knew, or at least I heard, that you had some grant money that might be available. It looks like a good opportunity for research with some media appeal, if it's handled right."

When I hung up, we had an appointment for eleven the next morning.

At 11:07 we walked into the Education Building, which also houses the psych department. I prefer to be on time, but Herron's Men's Wear doesn't open until ten, and we needed some presentable but inexpensive clothes for Jake—slacks, a shirt, shoes, sweater, jacket. . . . Actually, on my salary there isn't such a thing as inexpensive clothes. Some just cost less.

The meeting wasn't long. Boeltz admitted to eight hundred dollars in an account for exploratory research, which these days suggests he had something on someone. It wasn't enough to put Jake on the payroll. He agreed to pay him a ten-dollar allowance for "cigarettes and socks," as he put it. Jake was to stay with me, and Boeltz would pay me thirty dollars a week toward his room and board for any week in which Jake's services were used, plus ten dollars for each additional session, which we could split as we saw fit.

I was also to transport Jake to and from local sessions, as the studies would be done at Boeltz's home on the other side of town. Starting that evening at 7:30.

Boeltz had a bad reputation, so I wrote it all down and the

three of us signed it, and afterward I got it photocopied. I was surprised that my wanting it in writing didn't annoy Boeltz, but he was genial and cheerful throughout. I told myself he ought to be. He was getting a very promising research project, journal articles, personal publicity, and speaking engagements—all at damned little expense. And none of the expense was his personally.

I, on the other hand, would be an unpaid cook and chauffeur. But it did promise to be damned interesting. We hurried home, I grabbed a quick snack, and left Jake there while I rushed off to handle the Thursday afternoon lab in Plant Science 101. It occurred to me that it wasn't ideal, leaving a stranger alone in my home while I went off to work, but somehow I didn't feel concerned.

I took time to phone Maggie that afternoon; I needed someone to tell all this to, and she was the closet thing I had to a confidante. She said she'd be at my place about 5:30 to meet Jake and fix us supper; she sounded almost too cheerful to be real. Then I phoned home. Jake sounded sober and had started reading Churchill's memoirs. I told him Maggie would be coming by to fix supper and might get there before I did.

She drove up just as I was opening the garage door, and we went in together. To find supper on the table! Jake had hunted through refrigerator and cupboard, and had fixed pork chops, rice, sweet potatoes, and corn-bread. He'd walked to the store and bought the cornmeal out of a five I'd loaned him. When I came out of shock, I introduced him to Maggie.

"*Hyvää iltaa,* Mr. Savimäki," she said grinning. I stared at her.

"*Hyvää iltaa,* Mrs. Lanning," he said back. "*Mitä kuuluu?*"

She laughed. "I just used up all the Finnish I remember. When Terry told me your name, I thought, 'Hey! That sounds like home!' I'm from Duluth."

"So that's where you learned to say *Hyvää iltaa.*"

"Right. My mom is Finnish-American, but my dad wasn't,

so I didn't learn much at home. I learned more from the neighbors." She turned to me. "What a treat this is going to be." She gestured at the table. "If I'd fixed it, we'd be having hot dogs and beans."

I knew better than that. After supper, when Jake insisted on washing the dishes, I decided this arrangement was going to be a lot better than I'd thought. And after I took Jake to Boeltz's, I could hurry back to spend an hour or two alone with Maggie.

But that wasn't the way it worked, because Maggie wanted to go along and stay to watch.

That was fine with Boeltz; he liked to play to an audience. He had his own Polaroid, new that day, and took quite a few exposures. The first couple were "whities"—no picture. Not even of Jake. They looked as if they'd been shot into a floodlamp, which was remarkable enough in itself. The third was a blackie—it was as if it hadn't been exposed at all. But Boeltz and I were prepared for that; according to the literature, Kopaç used to get whities and blackies a lot.

Boeltz looked at Jake, then, with this knowing smile, went over to a cabinet and poured a whole glass of bourbon. "Would you like a drink, Jake?" he asked. But how it came across was, *'kay, you cunning boy. I know why you're holding out on me.* It irritated me—I felt insulted for Jake—but whether the whiskey had anything to do with it or not, the next picture was of the Taj Mahal, sharp and clear. Then Jake threw down the whiskey like ginger ale.

The next was of a Hilton hotel somewhere. Without saying anything, Boeltz nudged me and pointed at a part of the picture. On the sign, the name Hilton was spelled wrong!

"Jacob," said Boeltz, "how do you spell the name 'Hilton'?"

Jake's quiet eyes fixed on Boeltz. "H-I-L-T-E-N," he answered.

What in the hell, I thought to myself, *does this mean?*

By the time we left, at 8:30, Boeltz had poured a second glass of whiskey down Jake and had half a dozen pretty fair shots—four of them buildings, one a pyramid buried in tropical jungle, and one of a three-masted schooner in a storm.

Jake didn't even seem a little tight when we walked out, although he wasn't saying much. I decided he must have a thing for booze—in his generation that was apparently why most drifters became drifters, although it might have been the other way around. And Boeltz was using it as a way to keep Jake around and performing.

That was how it looked.

When we got home, I asked Jake how the evening had been for him. His answer was concise and unambiguous: "I don't like Professor Boeltz," he said. He also said he was tired, and went to get ready for bed. Maggie and I watched television until he retired, then moved together on the sofa.

There were three more sessions scattered over the next ten days, semipublic in that Boeltz invited several other faculty members and Bea Lundeen to them. Bea was the owner/editor of the local paper, the *Douglas Clarion*. As chauffeur, I was welcome to sit in, too. It was interesting as hell, although Boeltz didn't try anything that hadn't been tried fifteen years earlier with Nick Kopac.

Under his direction, Jake found he could do things he hadn't tried before. To start with, all he got were seemingly random shots of buildings and ships, pretty much like Kopac had gotten—almost nothing but buildings and statues. But Jake had a lot better batting average—he got a picture about two times out of three, and most of them pretty clear.

Frankly, I was surprised he did that well, because Boeltz was really unpleasant to work for. He continued to use booze in a very obvious way as a carrot on a stick. But I noticed that Jake never asked for it; he didn't even say yes when

Boeltz asked if he wanted some. He just accepted it when Boeltz handed it to him.

He certainly knew what to do with it then, though.

Another thing Boeltz did was to talk to Jake as if he were some kind of retard. "Now Jacob, I'm going to ask you to make us a picture of a cathedral. Can you do that for us? Let's try. Do you know what a cathedral is? Good. Very, very good." And, "Oh, that's *good,* Jacob. You're doing very, very *well* tonight."

Maybe that's why Jake kept accepting the whiskey. Not really, though, because I'd swear I saw a sort of amusement in those pale eyes. Maybe he enjoyed seeing Boeltz unwittingly irritate everyone around him and in general make an ass of himself.

The article Bea wrote for the *Clarion* was all about Jake, Boeltz was mentioned only once.

Then there was a lapse of a few days before the fifth session, which was a big one, a Saturday night affair. We'd been written up far beyond the *Clarion* by then, and interest was spreading. More people had been invited than there was room for at Boeltz's, and it was held in the home of Professor Tony Fournais, chairman of the physics department. Fournais was wealthy, had a big house outside town, was cautiously interested in the project—and made for good positioning: physics had a lot more status than psychology.

Everyone who'd been invited was there. And relatively on time: no one was more than twenty minutes late, even though the streets were snow-packed and slippery and the temperature was about ten degrees. Professor Alfred Kinglsey Kenmore had flown in from Virginia—the Kenmore of "Herz-Kenmore-Laubman Clairvoyance Studies" fame. And Marty Martin, the award-winning science writer from the *Trib*.

Maggie went with us.

It started out like a circus, or at least a drawing room comedy. Fournais announced that his assistant was going to film the whole procedure, and had a 16-mm movie camera at one side of the room, on a high tripod, to shoot down at Jake over people's heads. The film would later be examined in slow motion for any sign of hokey-pokey. Then Martin announced that he was going to match every shot of Boeltz's with his own camera and film, to provide a second, independent print. Finally, when Boeltz was ready to begin, Kenmore, who was a psychiatrist and therefore an M.D., had Jake lie down, and examined his eyes, pulling out the upper and lower lids, peering under them with a little light. I haven't the slightest what he was looking for.

Then we got started. Boeltz was on his good behavior for a change: he didn't put Jake down, and no booze was in evidence, confirming that his previous bullshit was deliberate.

He warmed Jake up by letting him do whatever he came up with. He started with an oblique aerial view of a beautiful landscaped home, with city spread out in the midground against a backdrop of mountains. Not Denver, I decided. Maybe Calgary. The next looked like Hong Kong. The third was a double row of tar-papered shacks with deep snow piled all around and forest close behind. A guy wearing what looked like a leather apron was caught in midstride between two of them. When it was shown to Jake, he identified it as the Axelson-Peltonen logging camp in Baraga County, Michigan, about 1948. He'd worked there. The guy in the apron, he said was Ole Hovde, the blacksmith. I could tell that Jake was really pleased with that one, and I got a notion that just maybe he'd gotten it deliberately.

Boeltz didn't take any of the pictures himself. Each of them was taken by a different person standing directly in front of Jake and about six feet away. The camera had been bought new by Fournais. The film packs were taken from their sealed wrappers right there in front of us.

Each shot was passed around before the next was taken. Then it was laid on a table, available for further examination.

Martin was off to one side with his camera, and didn't pass his shots around. But after the third, he arranged them on the table with Boeltz's, making matched pairs.

Boeltz beamed. "Ladies and gentlemen," he announced, "we have something very interesting here: Mr. Martin's photographs. Come and see!"

I was already there. In each instance, Martin's picture was of the same scene, but as if seen from an angle of about ninety degrees to the right, higher, and farther away.

Everyone crowded around talking, except Fournais's assistant, who stayed by his camera. A couple of them shook Jake's hand as he came over to look. The way the pictures matched up, it was as if the actual scene, the physical scene of each pair, had occupied the location of Jake's chair, in three dimensions. And it was something that hadn't come up in the work with Nick Kopac.

Boeltz was ready now to attempt something he'd tried with equivocal results the two sessions just previous. He had Bea Lundeen and me go into Fournais's library to find a picture of a building or ship—any building or ship—in the encyclopedia. Maggie went with us. Bea pulled out volume 14—KI to LE—and turned to "Kremlin." And there was the great Russian fortress looming above Red Square, the towers of its buildings showing above the massive wall. I nodded, we all looked at it, concentrating, and Bea called out, "O.K., we got one!"

Nothing more happened for about half a minute, and I got pretty fidgety, but we all kept looking at the picture. Then someone called, "Come on out. It's done."

We did. Bea took the encyclopedia to the table and laid it down open, weighting it with an ashtray. Boeltz removed his print, marked it with black grease pencil, and laid it down next to the book.

What was there made my scalp crawl. Jake had given us the Kremlin, all right, but not at all like the picture in the book. There was no broad paved parade ground. Instead, small log buildings were backed up against the fortress wall. The ground was mud, with logs laid in it as a sort of rude and partial paving. There were rows of market booths, and hundreds of people stood or walked around, some mostly naked, a few wearing long coats.

It was a photograph of the Kremlin centuries ago! A photograph of life, not of a painting!

There were some brief, quiet comments, but actually not much was said as people crowded up to look. Everyone seemed to realize the basic significance of it: Jake Savimaki could give pictures from the past, from before photography. This was not a picture of a photograph or thing he'd seen. We were in the presence of something much further beyond the limits of known science than we'd realized—a whole dimension further.

Martin crowded his way to the table and looked without comment, then silently laid his own print beside the other. Again it showed the same scene from maybe twice as far away. And here the apparent elevation was conspicuous. Boeltz's shot might have been taken from forty or fifty feet above the ground. Martin's was an oblique aerial shot, as if from a low-flying airplane. Except, of course, it wasn't.

Jake had come quietly over, and now he took a look. His eyes didn't change. People looked at him and he didn't seem to notice. It was as if he'd just dropped in and wanted to see what was going on.

My eyes found Boeltz; he was murmuring something quietly to Fournais. Fournais then called a break. In a minute or so their cook appeared with hors d'oeuvres, and the lid was removed from the punch bowl. Something for people to handle without getting tight. Almost everyone soon had a glass in their hand except Jake. He stood apart, watching the effects he'd caused, and caught my glance with a smile and a nod.

Fournais and Boeltz talked quietly in a corner, then Martin joined them, and Kenmore. I started over to join them too, but some out-of-towner stopped me and asked if I hadn't come in with Mr. Savimaki. By the time I was free, the four of them had left the room.

I felt a hand on my arm, and it was Maggie. "What does he do for an encore?" she asked.

"God knows," I said; *or the Devil,* I added silently. But that was unfair; if anyone around here had a devil, it was Boeltz, not Jake. Jake was as clean as anyone; we went over to him.

"*Kuinka se menee,* Mr. Savimäki?" Maggie asked him.

He grinned. "Pretty good, *tyttö*. How about you?"

"I'm impressed," she said. "Do you know how you did that?"

"Not exactly," he told her. "I just kind of—open myself up. I still don't know what a picture's going to be, but this time I decided I wanted something that would startle people."

"You want to do any more tonight?" I asked him, "or are you tired? We can go home if you'd like."

"No, I feel real good. This gets easier every session. I'd like to see what else I can do. Those last pictures look like something from the past; maybe I can get something from the future next."

I felt my gut give a little twist.

"You know what?" he went on. "I never felt this good before. In my whole life, and most of it ain't been bad." He put his full attention on me then, and called me by my first name for the first time. "Terry, I never thanked for you calling me in that night. I'd hit bottom, and you pulled me back up. I want you to know I appreciate it." He held out a hand big enough for an NFL tackle, and we shook. Then he turned to Maggie with a big grin, and she grinned back, and they shook, too.

We were interrupted; Boeltz, Fournais, Martin, and Kenmore had come back in, Boeltz practically rubbing his hands in anticipation. "Excuse me everyone, if you please," he called, and conversations stopped. "We'd like to continue now."

People quieted down and shuffled themselves into a loose circle. "Do you need to warm up with something easy, Mr. Savimaki?" Boeltz asked. *Courtesy yet!* It was the first time he'd called him "Mr. Savimaki." But his eager eyes were like ice picks.

Jake shook his head and said he was ready. Fournais had his wife take over Martin's camera, and he, Boeltz, and Martin left for the library. Kenmore picked up Boeltz's camera and positioned himself in front of a slightly smiling Jake.

It was a couple of minutes before we heard a voice call, "All right, we've got one."

Jake closed his eyes. No longer was there any effortful concentration, no tightly shut lids. He looked relaxed and confident. "Now," he said. Kenmore clicked his shutter, and so did Liz Fournais, and someone went to get the three from the library. Martin came in with a large book and laid it open on the table. I looked at it while Liz and Kenmore brought their prints over.

It wasn't an encyclopedia, but a book entitled *Weapons in the Sky: Military Applications of Space Technology*. The chapter it was open to was "Soviet Programs." There wasn't even a picture on the page.

Jake had outsmarted them, though. I didn't realize it at the time, but he had. Kenmore laid down his photo, and it was not of some satellite or anything like that. Instead, I saw a car, unidentifiable to me in the darkness, lying on its top in the snow. Liz's photo was the same, from another angle. In hers, I could see a body pinned underneath.

That was the end of the performance. While people donned coats and caps, I took Boeltz aside and collected. He didn't even look irritated with me—"not there" would describe him—then pulled on his gloves and left.

On the way home, nobody talked for the first mile. "Whose car do you suppose that was?" I said at last.

"I don't know," Jake answered. "I just know I didn't want to show them what they wanted, so I just decided to do a picture from the future. And that's what I got."

No one followed up on that until we got home. When we'd hung up our coats and sat down, Maggie decided she needed to know. "Jake," she asked, "could you have shown them? . . . What they wanted?"

His eyes were sober. "Get your camera," he told me.

The first picture was of an orbiting space station, like nothing yet built, I'm sure. It was hard to judge size and distance, with nothing familiar as a reference, but it might have been a hundred feet in diameter, bright against black space, from a viewpoint of maybe a hundred yards away. A red hammer and sickle vivid on its side.

"Holy God!" I said. A whole panorama of potential events began to shape up for me: the CIA moving in, Jake held in some secluded place doing God-knows-what kind of spying for them—and Boeltz, of course, handling Jake. Boeltz would love it; how important he'd feel!

"Take another one," Jake said. "I can see this one, too."

So he was seeing them in advance now. I aimed, he said, "Now," and I shot. It showed Jake strapped down on something like an operating table. He didn't even take the trouble to look at the photo. Maggie's hand found mine.

"You see why I did it," he said, and we both nodded.

The first thing I saw in the *Clarion* the next morning, right on the front page, was a picture of an overturned car. I'd seen one like it the night before. It was Bea Lundeen's. Kenmore and Martin had been with her, and Kenmore was dead.

There was nothing in either the *Clarion* or the *Trib* about the session, that day or any other. It was as if they were afraid of it, pushing it out of sight, out of mind, unable to confront what was there.

We didn't hear anything from Boeltz, either, on Sunday. Or on Monday, or for most of the week. Meanwhile, Jake got a job cooking at the Douglas Hotel. He also arranged to move into a room there, but for some reason I talked him out of it.

On Monday evening Maggie came by with her mother, Anna Lahti, who'd driven down from Minnesota to stay a week. She was a good-looking woman about fifty or fifty-five, and she and Jake hit it off right away, talking Finnish. She turned to us and laughed—said she knew he was from Savo as soon as he opened his mouth because he rolled his r's. As if she didn't; when they talked Finnish, it sounded like two chain saws.

It was Friday when Boeltz phoned. He wanted Jake again in half an hour—said I wouldn't need to bring him, that he'd come by and pick him up. I told him he'd have to talk to Jake, and put my hand over the mouthpiece, remembering the picture of Jake strapped down.

"It's Boeltz," I said. "He wants to come and get you in half an hour, for another session. He obviously doesn't want me to be there. I don't trust him; tell him to go to hell."

He smiled and took the phone. "Hello, Dr. Boeltz," he said. "I'm busy tonight, but if you want to make that for tomorrow evening at eight, that will be fine. . . . At eight, then, I'll be ready." He hung up.

"Jake!" I said, and he grinned. His eyes weren't soft anymore. They looked darker, and bright.

"It's O.K.," he said. "And what you're worried about, it's not going to happen."

"Something's fishy with him," I insisted. "He's hiding something, or I'm not Irish."

He nodded. "It's nothing to worry about, though."

"Do you *know* that?" I asked. "Do you know what he has in mind?"

"I don't know what he has in mind, but it's not dangerous. Not to me." He grinned again then. "And you told me you're only half-Irish. The other half is Dutch."

"And you're half-Swede," I said, trying to insult him. He just laughed; maybe I should have said Russian. Then Anna Lahti drove up. They had a date for supper and an evening at the ice rink.

I watched them drive away; it looked like a romance in the bud. I hoped nothing bad would happen the next evening.

The next night Boeltz was there five minutes early. After he and Jake drove away, I put on my jacket and cap, got in my car, and headed after them for Boeltz's place.

I parked half a block away, then chickened out. I couldn't think of any excuse for going up and pounding on his door, and I didn't want to get arrested for window peeking. So I got the Black Hawks pregame show on the radio and waited. At two minutes into the first period, Marcel Dionne scored on a breakaway. A couple of minutes later, Jake walked out of Boeltz's and started down the sidewalk. I rolled down the window as he approached.

"Want a ride?"

He grinned and got in.

"Care to tell me what happened?"

"Nothing much," he said. "We talked a little bit. But you don't have to worry about my going back."

"Yeah?" I said encouragingly.

"Yeah," he answered cheerfully.

I started the car and pulled away from the curb. "Yeah *what?*" I demanded.

He laughed. "He wanted me to make a picture showing someone dead. His father. He said the old man is dying slowly of an incurable cancer, in terrible pain, and that he'd be grateful to die. He thought if I made a picture of it, it would happen.

"I asked him what his father did for a living, and he said he'd been a banker. You can see what he's after."

"So you told him to go to hell."

"No, I told him I'd see what I could do."

I almost drove up over the curb. "You *what?*"

"Then I gave him a picture of his father as he was at that moment. Playing golf." Jake laughed again. "There were palm trees in the background. Hawaii, I suppose; it's daylight there now."

"What did he say to that?"

"He got all excited, said I'd made a mistake and got something from a year or two ago."

It was six minutes into the first period. Esposito stopped a Mark Hardy slapshot and fell on Dave Taylor's rebound. Charley Simmer fell on top of Eposito. Hutchinson shoved Simmer.

"Are you sure it wasn't the past?" I asked.

"Positive."

"Then what happened?"

"I told him I'd try once more." He wasn't smiling now. "Maybe went a little bit too far then."

"What do you mean?"

"Pull over and I'll show you."

He opened his jacket while I pulled off on the shoulder, tires crunching on frozen slush, and handed me a Polaroid color print. There was Herb Boeltz, in a coffin. He didn't look a day older than he had that night at eight o'clock.

"God!" I said. "You wished him dead?"

He shook his head. "I wouldn't do a thing like that," he said soberly. "I just decided to show him a picture of himself dead. I never thought about it looking like it could be next week or something. I just wanted to see how he liked it with the shoe on his own foot. He turned white as a sheet and just kind of fell on the chair. He sat there staring at nothing and never said another thing."

"Do you think it'll come true? This picture?" I asked.

"I don't know," Jake said. "I don't think so, but I'm not sure."

I shifted back into drive again and pulled onto the pavement, half my attention on driving and the other half on the power of suggestion. Boeltz seemed susceptible. He had at least half-convinced himself that Jake could control, as well as predict, the future.

It turned out that Jake's pictures do not fix the form of the future, or even necessarily predict it closely. Though we learned later that they tended to be quite accurate.

But the picture he showed me wasn't correct, any more than Hilton has an e in it. Because the coffin was covered. About four o'clock the next morning, Herb Boeltz put a .38 pistol barrel in his mouth and pulled the trigger, and there wasn't much the mortician could do to make him presentable.

Jake got a room in the hotel, after all. He said he'd been cramping my style, but maybe I'd been cramping his. He remained as cheerful and friendly as ever. Anna Lahti went back to Duluth, put her property up for sale, and moved down, taking an apartment in the same building as Maggie lived in. A couple of months later, she and Jake got married. Maggie and I took a bunch of wedding pictures, and all they showed were Jake and Anna.

I mentioned that to Jake, jokingly, and he said he wasn't doing pictures these days.

They really are a nice couple, and we went out with them fairly often, despite the age difference. Mostly to dance halls or the ice rink. I even learned to skate, though nowhere nearly as well as all three of them did.

With their example, Maggie and I decided to tie the knot, too. So Lanny was only two and a half years short of his teens; I'd been a teenager once myself. And frankly, he was more likable than I'd been. Jake took a bunch of wedding pictures; he had a brand new Polaroid 680. I couldn't help but wonder. That summer they bought a restaurant and fixed it up really nicely with a Scandinavian motif, bringing a Swede down from Duluth to help with the cuisine. I figured Anna must have had a lot of money, but Maggie said not so far as she'd even known.

Then, one day they asked if we'd like to go to the races that weekend. I supposed they meant at Rockston Downs, only fifty miles away, but instead we *flew* to Maryland! And Jake bought the tickets and rented a car there!

I bet on the same horses he did, and talk about a kick in the tax bracket! We had nothing but winners. A lot of things became clear to me then.

It felt like strange money to me, but the bank was happy with it.

Last evening we celebrated the anniversary of Jake's and my meeting. At their place, a little farm they'd bought just outside town. They'd fixed it up really nicely.

When we got there, I noticed a big book on the table—a folio-sized book on astronomy for the informed layman. Beside it was a brand-new video camera. He told me he had an interesting project going, and asked if we'd care to take a little tour.

CASH CROP

by Connie Willis

Colonies of Earthfolk planted on alien worlds must find some way to pay for the necessities they will have to import from Mother Earth for the hundred or so years of their colony's founding. Such was the case with the colonization of the Western Hemisphere by the Eastern back long before spaceflight and such will be the case in times to come. But what can they find to export worth anything like the stuff they must import? Consider also the question of simple adaptation to an empty alien land. . . .

"Oh, Haze," Sombra said. "Aren't you excited about tomorrow? Our new dresses and the school all decorated with flowers?"

"Yes," I said, trying to see down the hill to the peach tree. Francie always waited by the peach tree after school, triumphant that she had made it home before the downer. But this morning Mother had come to take her home, and I could not see any figure standing beside the stunted tree.

"I can hardly wait to see the flowers!" Sombra said.

"Mamita says they always bring yellow roses. And red carnations. Do you know what carnations look like, Haze?"

I shook my head. The only flowers I had ever seen were my mother's greentent geraniums.

Earlier today the district nurse had talked to Mother for a long time. I had heard the words "scarlet fever" and "northern," and the nurse's face had become flushed and angry as she spoke. "Flowers!" she had said angrily. "They buy us off with flowers and antibiotics when they should be sending us a centrifuge so we can make our own antibiotics. They take our grain and give us flowers!" And Mother had hurried Francie home.

"Just think," Sombra said, looking up at the dusty haze, "right now the *Magassar's* orbiting. Floating up there in space with its hold full of flowers." She was shivering, hugging her arms across her chest. We had ridden the dustdowner home, clinging to the narrow seat under the sprinklers, and both of us were wet from the spray.

Dirty downers, my father called them. "They buy us off with the downers when they could be doing climate control, when they could be eliminating the strep altogether." All I seemed to be able to think of today were angry words against the government. There shouldn't be, with graduation coming. The government had sent a special ship just for the occasion of our first graduating class. They had already sent fabric for graduation clothes with the last grain ship, and although Sombra's romantic notions about the ship floating overhead with its hold full of flowers were not quite right and the *Magassar* was instead already filling its massive hold with compressed grain and alcohol from the orbiting silos, when it did land tomorrow there would be gifts and special foods from earth, fresh fruits and chocolate, and Sombra's flowers. Yet all I heard were angry words.

Father had threatened to dismantle the dustdowner that circled our stead daily and build a cannon out of it. "Then when the government men tell me they're doing all they can about the strep, I can tell them what I think." The government's argument was that the strep outbreaks were being caused by the dust, so they sent the automated sprinklers crawling up and down the adobe-hard roads between the steads, wasting Haven's already scarce water, and stirring up dust with their heavy wheels that their sprinklers didn't even touch. The quarantine and sterilization regulations the first steaders set up did more to keep the strep under control than the downers ever would.

The steaders made their own use of them, hitching supplies and messages on the back to send them between the steads. During quarantines the district nurse sent antibiotics that way and sometimes a coffin. And all the kids caught them on the way to and from school, if they could time it, arriving damp and disheveled at their angry mothers, who told them they would get a chill and catch the strep, who forced the government-supplied Schultz-Charlton strips into their mouths and wrapped them in blankets. I had seen Mamita Turillo do it to Sombra and Mother to Francie. Not to me. I was never chilled. The breeze on my wet shirt and jeans today was cool, but not cold.

"Oh, you're never cold," Sombra said now, her teeth chattering. "It isn't fair."

Even in winter I slept under a thin blanket and forgot my coat at school. Even in Haven's sudden intense summer that was nearly here, my dust-colored cheeks didn't flush like Sombra's red ones. Sweat didn't curl my dust-colored hair as it did her black hair. Sombra looked like a greentent flower, her body tall and narrow, her cheeks and hair bright splashes of color. I only came to Sombra's shoulder, and I looked more like the flowers Mother tried to plant outside the greentent, dusty and pinched and they never bloomed.

I was not the only one. A few of the first-generation steaders, like Old Man Phelps, were short and hardy, and more and more of the new hands Mamita boarded fresh off the emigration ships looked like me. I looked out across our stead and Sombra's with the bare hard road and low mud fence dividing the pale sweeps of winter wheat, and the pinkish-brown haze in the sky above them. Maybe the emigration people had decided to send people as colorless and dusty as Haven itself in the hope the strep would overlook them.

I could see Father's peach tree at the corner of our stead, where Sombra would turn to go another quarter-mile to her house, but no Francie. Only one thing would have made Mother come and get her, somebody sick here in western.

"Sombra," I said, "do you know of anybody sick in this district?"

"Yes," she said, unconcerned. "Old Man Phelps. I heard the district nurse tell your mother."

"Scarlet fever?" I said blankly, but it could not be anything else. It was always scarlet fever. Stray streptococci brought by the first steaders had taken to Haven's dry, dusty climate like cherrybrights to a tree. It was always there, waiting for a shortage of antibiotics. There had been a heart-stopping outbreak in northern three weeks ago, seventeen reported, mostly children, and a local had been slapped on the district by the district nurse. It shouldn't have spread to western. What was worse, Mr. Phelps brought us within two of a planetwide quarantine. Mr. Phelps, one of the oldtimers who never got the strep, down with scarlet fever.

"The district nurse told your mother there was nothing to worry about. Mr. Phelps lives alone, and she said she could stop an outbreak with the antibiotics the *Magassar's* bringing."

"If the *Magassar* lands," I said. A faint scratchiness of fear was beginning behind my throat. Two more reported cases and the *Magassar* would go back to earth without even landing. There would be no graduation.

Sombra said, "Mamita says there's no reason for them to

quarantine us without antibiotics. She says they could drop the antibiotics from orbit. Do you think that's true?''

The scratchiness became almost an ache. ''No, of course not. If they could, they would. They wouldn't leave us without any antibiotics if there was any way to get them to us.'' But I was remembering something from a long time ago, when little Willie died. Mother telling me to get out of the house, out of her sight, and Father saying, ''Don't take it out on Haze. It's the government that's left us to the wolves. Blame them. Blame me—I brought you here, knowing what they were doing. But not Haze. She can't help being what she is.'' The ache was worse. I swallowed hard, and when it didn't go away, I pressed the flat of my hand against the hollow space between my collarbones and swallowed again. This time it went away.

''Of course not,'' I said again, feeling much better. ''Don't worry about Mr. Phelps. He won't stop our graduation. There's got to be an incubation period, and by the time it's up, the *Magassar* will already be on the ground. The local's probably already got it stopped.''

We were nearly down the long hill to the corner, and I didn't want to leave her thinking about a possible quarantine. I said, ''Mother finished our dresses last night. Are you going to come over to try it on?'' Sombra's flushed cheeks darkened. ''To make sure about the hem,'' I said hesitantly. ''To see how we're going to look tomorrow.''

Sombra shook her dark head. ''I'm sure it'll be all right,'' she said uncomfortably. ''Mamita has a lot of chores for me today. With the *Magassar* coming in tomorrow. She's taking the new hands to board again, and so she said she wanted me to bring in everything ripe from the greentent for the supper tomorrow night. I wish Mamita had made our dresses,'' she finished unhappily.

''It's all right,'' I said. ''I'll bring it over tomorrow morning. We'll get dressed together.''

It had been a mistake to mention the dresses, and a worse one to have had Mother make them for us. I had been to Sombra's house countless times, with Mamita bright and cheerful as a cherrybright, feeding us vegetables from the greentent and asking us about school, reaching up on tiptoe to pull Sombra's curls away from her face and, no taller than me, hugging me goodbye when I left. Mother was rigid and erect as one of the tallgrasses that shaded our porch when Sombra came home with me. She had not spoken a dozen words to her during all the fittings. We should have had Mamita make the dresses.

Yesterday Sombra had tried on her dress timidly. I had not seen it so nearly finished before, with the red ribbons pinned where they would be threaded through the bodice. "Oh, Sombra, you look so beautiful!" I had blurted out, "Oh, Mama, it's the loveliest dress I've ever seen."

Mother had turned on me with a look that made Sombra gasp. "I will not allow you to call me that," she had said, and slammed the door behind her. Sombra had shimmied out of the dress and into her jeans so fast she nearly tore the thin white cotton.

"It's because of the babies," I had said, helplessly. "She had seven babies that died between Francie and me. Little Willie lived to be three. I remember when he died. It was a planetwide and there wasn't anything to give him and he laid upstairs in the big bed crying, 'Mama! Mama!' for five days."

Sombra had her shirt buttoned and her books scooped up. "She lets Francie call her Mama," she said, her cheeks flaming with anger.

"That's different," I had said.

"How is it different? Mamita lost nine babies to the strep. Nine."

"But she has you and the twins left. And all Mother has is Francie."

"And you. She has you." I had not known how to explain to her that Francie, with her blue eyes and yellow hair, made her think of San Francisco, of earth. Francie and the geraniums she tended so carefully in the hot damp air of the greentent. And when she looked at me, what did she think? She had found me that day after Willie died, hiding in the greentent, and had switched me. What was she thinking then? And what did she think this morning when the district nurse told her Mr. Phelps had scarlet fever and we were within two of a planetwide? The scratchiness had returned, this time as a dull ache. I knotted my hand into a fist and pushed against it, but it did no good. I wondered if I'd better take a strip when I got home.

"You're worried about them imposing a quarantine, aren't you?" Sombra said. We were nearly down the hill, and I had not said anything the whole way.

"I was wondering if they'll have pink carnations tomorrow," I said. "I was wondering if they'll give us some to wear in our hair?"

"Of course. Mamita said so. You'll have red roses. You'll be so pretty." The long walk down the dusty hill had dried us off. She looked hot now, the sweat on her forehead curling her dark hair. "Let's sit down a minute, all right?" She sank down on the low mudbrick fence and fanned herself with her books. "It's so hot today."

I looked over her head at the peach tree. It was no taller than me and folded in on itself so that it barely gave any shade at all. Its leaves were narrow and so pale a green the dust made them look the same color as the wheat. There were little pinkish-white specks between the leaves. I squinted at them.

"Don't you think it's hot?" Sombra asked.

This was the only one of Father's trees that had lived past the ponics tanks. It had lasted five years now, though it had never borne fruit. And now there were the pale specks all over it, which could be moths or sorrel ants. The ache pressed dully against the hard bone of my sternum, bending me forward under it. I put the edge of my fist against the pain, pressing hard into the bone, willing myself to straighten. Mother was always telling me to stand up straight, to try to look at least as tall as I could, not like some hunched dwarf, and I would straighten automatically, my whole body responding. I willed myself to hear her voice now. My shoulder blades pulled back, stretching the ache with it till it had pulled out to nothing. I stood still, breathing hard.

"I can't sit down," I said breathlessly. "I have to go right home."

"But it's so hot! Do I feel hot to you?" She pulled me onto the wall with her and pressed her cheek against mine. It was burning against my chilled face.

"A little," I said. I must take a strip when I get home. And tell Father about the tree.

"You're not getting sick, are you?" she said. "You can't get sick, Haze, not for graduation. You go right home and go to bed, all right? I don't want you sending us under a planetwide."

"I will," I promised her, climbing over the fence and into the field for a closer look at the tree. The specks were larger than I had thought, almost the size of . . .

"Oh, Sombra," I shouted after her delightedly, "we won't go under a planetwide, and I'm not getting sick either. I've had a good omen. There'll be flowers for graduation."

"How do you know?" she shouted back.

"I thought the tree had something wrong with it," I said. "But it doesn't. It's in bloom!"

She grinned a happy surprise. "You mean blossoms?" She was over the low fence in an easy step and peering eagerly at the tiny tight blossoms. "Oh, they're just starting to come out, aren't they? Oh, Haze, think how pretty they'll be!"

A red cherrybright whizzed through the air over our heads

and lighted unafraid on the top of the tree, shaking the branch in our faces. The folded blossoms bowed and dipped.

"The pink blossoms are for my ribbons," Sombra said happily, "and the cherrybright's for your red ribbons!" She put her arm around my waist. It felt warm through my thin shirt. "And you know what they mean?"

"That we'll be beautiful tomorrow! That nothing can possibly go wrong because we're going to graduate!"

"Oh, Haze," she said, hugging me, "I can hardly wait." She ran back to the road. "Bring my dress over first thing in the morning and we'll get ready together. Everything's going to be perfect," she shouted to me. "The day is full of omens."

No one was in the house but Francie, sitting at the kitchen table, dawdling over her lessons with a strip in her mouth.

"Papa's in the greentent. With Mama," she said, taking the strip out of her mouth so she could talk. It was the bright red of a negative reading. Active strep blanched the strips like a person going white from fear. "Are you scared?" she said.

"Of what?"

"Mama says two more and they'll call a planetwide. There won't be any graduation."

"There will so, Franie. There hasn't been a planetwide in ages."

"How do you know?"

"I just know," I said, thinking of the peach tree and what Father would say when he saw it was in bloom. He would think it was a good omen, too. I smiled at Francie and went out to find Father.

He stood in the door of the greentent, blocking it with his bulk. Mother stood across the ponics tanks from him, holding on to one of the metal supports. Through the thick plastic, she looked as if she were drowning. Her hand clutched the strut so hard I thought she would pull the whole tent down.

"It's what they want," Father said. "It ties us to them. We'll be doing just what they want."

"I don't care," she said.

"It will take away every chance of a cash crop. You know that, don't you?"

"Mr. Phelps died this morning. There have been seventeen cases in northern."

"The *Magassar* will be landing tomorrow. We don't have to . . ."

"No," she said, and looked steadily at him. "You owe it to me."

His hand on the doorframe tightened until I could see the veins stand out on his hands.

"The peach tree's in bloom," I blurted, and they both turned to look at me, Father with blank drowned eyes, Mother with a look like triumph. "It's a good sign, don't you think?" I said into the silence. "An omen. It means the *Magassar* will land tomorrow and everything will be all right . . . anyway, it has to have some kind of incubation period, doesn't it? People can't just catch it in one day."

"It's a new strain," Mother said. She had let go of the strut and was pushing dirt around the base of a geranium. "The district nurse said it appears to have a very short incubation period."

"She doesn't know that," I said earnestly. "How could she know that for sure?"

She looked up, but at my father, not at me. "Mr. Phelps had taken a strip that morning. It was negative. You would not have expected Mr. Phelps to get it at all, let alone so quickly. Maybe others you wouldn't expect will get it, too."

The call box, attached to the plastic feederlines above the ponics tanks, barked suddenly. The sharp, short signal that called the district nurse. The signal that meant our district. Mother looked at me. "What did I tell you?" she said.

My father let go of the doorframe, and took a step toward her. "Move your geraniums to ponics," he said, "I need the plaindirt to plant more corn in." He turned and walked away.

I helped Mother move the geraniums into the tanks, my body tensed for the alerting bark of the box, but it did not ring again. After supper we stayed in the kitchen, and when we went up to bed, Father carried the little box with him, trailing its wires like ribbons, but the box did not sound again. Oh, yes, the day was full of omens.

The pale pink haze was gone in the morning, replaced with the clear chill to the sky that meant night frost. I took Father down to the tree before breakfast to look at the peach blossoms. They dropped like scraps of paper at his feet when he put out his hand to a branch. "The frost got them," he said, as if he didn't even mind.

"Not all of them," I said. Some of them, crumpled and tight, like little knots against the cold, still clung to the branches. "The frost didn't get all of them," I said. "It's supposed to be warm today. I knew it would be warm for graduation." He was looking past me, past the tree. I turned to look. A cherrybright fluttered on Sombra's fence. Our good omen.

"No!" Father said sharply, and then more gently as I turned back to him in surprise, "the frost didn't get them all. Some of them are still alive." He took my arm and steered me back to the house, keeping himself between the tree and me, as if the frozen blossoms were my disappointment and I could not bear to see them.

At the greentent I stopped. "I have to take Sombra her dress," I said, barely able to keep the excitement of the day out of my voice. "We have to get ready for graduation." He did not let go of my arm, but his hand seemed to go suddenly lifeless. I patted his cold hand and ran into the house to get Sombra's dress and down the steps past him with it over my arm, fluttering pink ribbons as I ran. He still stood there, as if he had finally seen the frozen blossoms and could not hide his grief.

It was not a cherrybright. It was a quarantine sticker, tied to one of the distance markers. I stood for a moment by the peach tree looking at it as my father had done, the dress as heavy on my arm as my hand had been on his. "No!" I said, as sharply as he had and took off running.

I could not even let myself think what breaking quarantine meant. "I don't care," I told myself, catching my breath at the last corner of the fence. "It's graduation," I would tell Mamita. "The *Magassar* will be landing with all those flowers. We have to be there."

Mamita would look reluctant, thinking of the consequences.

"One of the hands has it, doesn't he? The new ones always get it. But this is our *graduation!* You can't let him spoil it. Think of all the flowers," I would say. "Sombra has to see them. She'll die if she doesn't see them. Give her a strip. Give us both one. We won't get it."

I climbed over the fence, careful of the dress. Even folded double, it almost dragged on the ground. The gate would be locked. I cut through the field at a dead run and came up to the house the back way, past the greentent. The door stood open, but I could not see anyone through the plastic. Sombra must have hurried through her chores to get ready and left the door open. Mamita would kill her. I could not stop to shut it now, because someone might see me and turn me in. I had to get to Mamita and convince her first.

I knocked at the back door, leaning against the scratchy stalk of a tallgrass, too breathless for a moment to say any of the things I had planned to say. Then Mamita opened the door, and I knew I would never say any of them.

I could hear a baby crying in the house. Mamita passed her hand over her chest, pressing as if there were a pain there.

Then she put her hand up to her forehead. There were brilliant scarlet creases on the inside of her elbows. "Why, Haze, what are you doing here?" she said.

"I brought Sombra's dress," I said.

A sudden, hitting anger flared out of her black eyes, and I stumbled back, raking my arm against the tallgrass. It came to me much later that she must have thought I brought the dress for Sombra's laying out, that she had felt the same anger as Mother did when she saw me standing and still healthy while the babies died, one after the other. I did not think of that then. All I could think was that it was not one of the hands, that it was Sombra who was sick.

"For graduation," I said, holding the dress out insistently. If I could make her take it, then it would not be true.

"Thank you, Haze," she said, but she didn't take it. "Her father's already gone," she said. "Sombra's . . ." and in that breath of a second, I thought she was going to say that she was dead already, too, and I could not, would not let her say that.

"The *Magassar* will be landing this morning. I could go over there for you. I could catch a downer. I'd be back in no time. The *Magassar's* bringing a whole load of antibiotics. I heard the district nurse say so."

"He died before the district nurse could get here. He wouldn't let me call until we found Sombra in the greentent. He didn't want to spoil her graduation."

"But the *Magassar* . . ."

She put her hand on my shoulder. "Sombra was the twentieth," she said.

I still could not take in what she was saying. "There was only one call. That makes nineteen." One call. Sombra and her father. One call.

"You should go home and take a strip, dear," she said. "You'll have been exposed." She put her hand to my cheek, and it burned like a brand. "Tell your mother thank you for the dress," she said, and shut the door in my face.

When Francie found me, I was sitting under the peach tree with Sombra's dress across my lap like a blanket. The last of the blossoms fell on the dress, already dead and dying like the flowers aboard the *Magassar*.

"Papa says for you to come up to the house," Francie said. Mama had curled her hair with sugar water for graduation. The curls were stiff against her pink cheeks.

"There isn't any graduation," I said.

"I know *that,*" she said disdainfully. "Mama's been making me take strips all morning long. She thinks I'm going to get it."

"No," I said, my cheeks burning from the brand of Sombra's cheek, Mamita's hand. The pain pressed against my sternum and would not go away. "I'm going to get it."

"I *told* Mama I didn't even sit near her. And how you never let me walk home with you two, how you always ride the downer. She sent for me as soon as she found out about Mr. Phelps, and Sombra wasn't even sick then. But she wouldn't listen. Anyway, you never get sick. She probably won't even make you take a strip. And Sombra wasn't sick yesterday, was she? So you probably weren't exposed either. Mama says the incubation period is really short." She remembered why she had been sent. "Papa says you're supposed to come *now*." She flounced off.

I stood up, still careful of the white dress, and followed Francie through the field of scratchy wheat. They don't know about my breaking quarantine, I thought in amazement. I wondered why Father had sent for me. Perhaps he knew and wanted to talk to me before he turned me in. "What does he want?" I said.

"I don't know. He said I was supposed to come and get

you before the downer came. There's been one already, with a coffin. For Mr. Turillo."

I stopped and looked back toward the road. The downer rattled past the peach tree, spraying water over the scattered blossoms, wetting the coffin it pulled behind it. Sombra's coffin. He had at least tried to spare me that. And now I would have to try to spare him my dying, as much as I could.

I imposed my own quarantine, sneaking a strip as soon as I got back to the house. I had been afraid that Mother would make me take one, but she didn't, although Francie was already sitting at the kitchen table when I came in, protesting the bright red strip Mother held in her hand. I held the strip I had stolen behind my back until I could get out to the greentent. I took it there, huddled under the ponics tank in case it took a long time. It blanched white as soon as the paper was in my mouth. I did not need the strip to tell me I was getting sick. Sombra's cheek, her mother's hand, burned on my face like a brand.

No one reported me. I did not doubt that Mamita, much as she loved me, would have turned me in. This was more than a planetwide. It was a local, too. The *Magassar* had already broken its orbit and was heading for home. We were on our own, and the only way to stop it was to keep the quarantine from being broken. Which meant Mamita had the fever, too, that maybe all the people on the Turillo stead were dead or sick with it and no one to help them.

I tried to stay out of everyone's way, especially Francie's. I talked with my head averted and asked to do the wash and the dishes so I could sterilize my own things. I picked a fight with Francie and called her a tagalong, so that she avoided me as carefully as I did her. Mother paid no attention to me. She had eyes only for Francie.

* * *

Three weeks after Sombra died, Father said at supper, "The local's off at Turillos'. Mamita's over it. The district nurse cleared her this afternoon."

"The twins?" Mother said.

He shook his head. "Both of them died. But none of the hands came down with it. Six months here and not one of them has had so much as a white strip."

"It was an unusual strain," Mother said. "It doesn't prove anything. They could all die tomorrow."

"I doubt it," he said. "The incubation period was very short, as you said. But none of the hands got it." He put a subtle emphasis on the word 'none.'

"Yet," Mother said. "I'm sure Haven isn't through coming up with new strains. We're still without antibiotics." The fear I had expected was not in her voice.

"They intercepted the *Magassar* halfway home and told them we'd had no new cases in a week. They're holding where they are for a week, and then if there are no other reporteds, they'll come back." He smiled at me. "I'm full of good news today, Haze. The peaches didn't freeze after all. We're getting some fruit starting."

He turned and looked at Mother, and said in the same cheerful tone, "You'll have to move the geraniums out of the ponics."

Mother put her hand up to her cheek as if he had hit her. "I talked to Mamita," he said. "She said she'll buy all the corn we can give her. Cash crop."

"Can I move the flowers back to plaindirt?" she asked.

"No," Father said. "I'll need to put the corn wherever I can."

She looked at him across the table as if he were her enemy, and he looked just as steadily back. It was as if a bargain had been struck between them, and the price she was paying was her precious flowers. I wondered what price Father had paid.

"If the peaches aren't frozen, they could be our cash crop,

Father," I said urgently. "They'll ripen almost as fast as the corn and you know how hungry everyone will be for real fruit."

"No," Father said. His eyes never left her face. "We need the cash from the corn. To pay for something. Don't we?"

"Yes," she said, and pushed her chair back from the table. "You have your cash crop and I have mine."

"I want to put the corn in tomorrow," he shouted after her. "Pull your geraniums out this afternoon." Francie was staring at him wide-eyed. "Come on, Haze," he said more quietly, "I'll show you the peaches."

They did not even look like fruit. But they were there, hard little swellings like pebbles where the tight blossoms had been. "You see," he said, "we'll have our cash crop yet."

The quarantine sticker was gone from Sombra's fence. My strip had been white again this morning, and the ache that never quite left me was deeper, into my lungs now.

"First-generation colonies don't have cash crops," Father said. "They're too busy hanging on, too busy trying to stay alive. They're abjectly grateful for what the government gives them—greentents, antibiotics, anything. Second-generation aren't so grateful. The wheat's doing well and they start noticing that the government's help isn't all that helpful. Third-generation colonies aren't grateful at all. They have cash crops and they can buy what they need from earth, not beg for it. Fourth-generation stop growing wheat altogether and start manufacturing what they need and to hell with earth."

"We're fourth-generation," I said, not understanding.

Father had carried down a bucket of lime-sulphur and water and a wad of cloth rags to paint the peaches with. He dipped a rag in the bucket and pulled it out dripping. "No, Haze," he said. "We're first-generation, and if the government has its way, we'll be first-generation forever. The strep keeps us down, keeps us fighting for our lives. We can't develop light industry. We can't even keep our children alive long enough to graduate them from high school. We've been here nearly seventy years, Haze, and this is our first graduation."

"They could drop the antibiotics without landing, couldn't they?" I said. Little Willie upstairs in the big bed, crying for Mama. "They could wipe it out altogether if they wanted to." Father was bending over the sulphur-smelling bucket, dipping the rag in the liquid. "Why aren't you doing something about it?"

I expected him to say there was nothing they could do, that it was impossible to manufacture antibiotics without filters and centrifuges and reagents, which the government would never ship us. I expected him to say that the only manufactured goods they shipped were those guaranteed not to be vandalized for parts and that the main virtue of the dustdowners as far as the government saw it was that they could not be turned into equipment for making antibiotics. But he wiped industriously at a peach and said, "We will be second-generation yet, Haze. We'll have our cash crops, and the government won't be able to stop us. They're shipping us the one thing we need right now, and they don't even know it."

I knelt by the bucket, dipping the worn cloth in the sulphur-smelling liquid.

"When I first tried to grow peaches, Haze, I used ordinary peach seeds from back home. I started them in the ponics tanks and some of them lived long enough to bloom and I crossed them with others that had survived. Do you remember that, Haze? When the greentent was full of peach trees?"

I shook my head, still kneeling by the bucket. I could not even imagine it. Now there was no room for anything, not even Mother's geraniums.

"I bred for what I thought they needed—a thick skin to

stand the sorrel ants and a short trunk to stand the wind, but I couldn't do any genetic engineering. There isn't any equipment. I could only cross the ones that did well, the ones that lived long enough to bloom. I knew what I was breeding for, but not what I would get. I never thought it would be so . . . stunted and turned in upon itself . . ."

He was not looking at the tree. He was looking at me. The rag he held was dripping whitish water on the toe of his shoe. "We have people working in emigration, some of them colonists, some of them not, looking at the gene prints and deciding on the emigration permits. We all thought your mother . . . her genetic prints were almost exactly like Mr. Phelps', and he'd never had the strep. I've only had it twice in all these years. If it was a few points off, still it would be close enough, we thought. You cannot do the same things to people that you do to peach trees. Because it matters when they die.

"All I have left is this one pale and stunted tree," he said, and squeezed out the rag on the ground and began painting the fruit again. "And you."

The next day we trenched the tree, filling the narrow moat with dried mud and straw to keep the sorrel ants away. Father did not say anything more, and I could not tell anything from his face.

The day after that I had a negative strip, and I looked at it a long time, thinking about how I was never hot, never cold, how I had never had strep as a child. But Mr. Phelps had died of scarlet fever. Mr. Phelps, who looked like me and never felt the cold. And Mother's gene prints were almost like Mr. Phelps'.

I ran down to the tree, almost tripping in the tangle of ripening wheat. Father was standing by the tree, examining one of the peaches. It was no larger that I could see, but it had lost a little of its greenish cast.

"Do you think we should put a moth net on?" he said. "It's a little early for moths."

"Father," I said, "I don't think anything we do will help or hurt it. I think it's all in the seed."

He smiled, and his smile told me what I had been afraid to see before. "So I've been told," he said.

"I'm immune to strep, aren't I?"

"Her prints were almost exactly those of Mr. Phelps. I had only had the strep twice. We thought it would be close enough, and after you were born, we were sure it would." He looked through me, as he had done on that day when he saw the sticker on Sombra's fence. "I have done the best I can for her. I have tried to remember that it was not her fault, that I brought her here to this, that it is my fault for thinking of her as I thought of my peach trees. I have let her turn Francie into a greentent flower that cannot possibly survive. I have let her treat you like a stepchild because I knew you could survive no matter what she did to you. I have let her . . ." He stopped and passed his hand over his chest. "There is a cache of blackmarket penicillin in the greentent for Francie. It took the cash crop to do it. It will save her once." He looked away from me toward Turillos'. "I think it's time to send you to Mamita's. She's got all the hands to do for. She'll need you."

He sent me back to the house to pack my things. The day was very hot. Halfway across the field I put my hand up to my forehead, and I could feel the damp sweat curling my hair. It will be cooler under the peach tree, I thought, and started back toward the tree. But halfway there the haze seemed to thicken almost to clouds with a fine pink tint, and the temperature to drop. It will be warmer in the greentent, I thought, shivering. I turned back the way I had come.

I hit one of the supports in the greentent when I fell. Francie will see that it's down, I thought, Francie will find me. I tried to pull myself up by the edge of the ponics tanks, but I had cut my hand when I fell and it bled into the tanks.

Mother found me. Francie had seen the greentent sagging heavily on one side and run to the house to tell her. Mother stood over me for a long time, as if she could not think what to do.

"What's wrong with her?" Francie asked from the doorway.

"Did you touch her?" Mother said.

"No, Mama."

"Are you sure?"

"Yes, Mama," she said, her bright blue eyes full of tears. "Shouldn't I go get Papa."

And at last she knelt beside me and put her cool hand on my hot cheek. "She has the scarlet fever," she said to Francie. "Go into the house."

They put me in the big bed in the front bedroom because of Francie. I tried to keep the covers on, but it was so hot that I kicked them off without meaning to, and then I shivered so that they had to bring more blankets off Francie's bed.

"How is she?" Father said.

"No better," Mother said. "Her fever still hasn't broken." Her voice was less afraid than it had been in the greentent. I wondered if the planetwide had been lifted.

"I called the district nurse."

"Why?" Mother said, still in that quiet voice. "She doesn't have anything to give her. The *Magassar* won't come back again."

"There's the penicillin." I wondered if they looked as they had looked that day in the greentent, each clutching the frame of the bed as they had held onto the supports of the greentent.

Mother put her hand to my cheek. It felt cool. "No," she said quietly.

"She'll die without it," he said. I could hardly hear his voice.

"There isn't any penicillin," Mother said, and her voice was as still as her hand on my cheek. "I gave it to Francie."

Something worried at the edge of my mind. I tried to get a hold on it, but my teeth were chattering so badly I could not. The pain in my chest burned like a flame. I thought if I could press with my hand against it, the pain would lessen, but my hand felt muffled, and when I tried to look at it, it was as white as a positive strip.

Mamita had told me to take a strip when I got home. I did and it was white. But that could not be right, because the incubation period was very short, and I had not gotten sick for nearly a month. But I already had it, I thought. That day Sombra had asked if I was getting sick and there had been that pain behind my sternum that nearly doubled me over by the tree, I had already been getting sick.

I was edging closer to the worrisome thing, but it was so cold. I never felt the cold. Or the heat. Sombra had leaned forward to me on the wall and said, "Don't I feel hot?" and the pain had almost doubled me over. She was already getting sick, but so was I. I had been getting sick that day, and I had gotten over it.

I pulled my hand free of the blankets, and that started me shivering again. The hand was still white and clumsily heavy. I put it over the hollow space between my collarbones and pressed and pressed, my whole body straightening, tautening with the pain until it stretched to nothing.

Then I got up and put on my graduation dress, fumbling over the buttons with my bandaged hand, a little weak from the fever, but better, better.

Father was standing by the peach tree, throwing the peaches at the road. They bounced when they hit the hard mud and rolled against Turillos' fence.

"Oh, Papa," I said, "don't do that."

He did not seem to hear me. The dustdowner was kicking up its little trail of dust far down the road. He picked a hard peach off the tree, covered it with his big fist in a grip that should have smashed it, and pitched it at the distant downer.

"Papa," I said again. He whirled violently as if he would throw the peach at me. I stepped back in surprise.

"She killed you," he said, "to save her precious Francie. She let you die up there crying out her name. Putting her hand on your cheek and tucking you in. She murdered you!" He flung the peach down violently. It rolled to my feet. "Murderer!" He turned to wrench another peach off the tree.

I put my hand up in protest. "Papa, don't! Not your cash crop!"

He dropped his hands and stared limply at the dustdowner rattling down the road toward us. It was pulling a coffin behind it. My coffin. "You were my cash crop," he said quietly.

I remembered Mamita's face when she thought I'd brought the dress for Sombra's laying out. I looked down at my white shroudlike dress and my hand wrapped in the white bandage. "Oh, Papa," I said, finally understanding. "I didn't die. I got better."

"She gave the penicillin to Francie," he said. "While you were still in the greentent. Before she even let Francie come to get me. Your hand was bleeding. She gave her the penicillin before she even bandaged your hand."

"It doesn't matter," I said. "I didn't need the medicine. I got over the scarlet fever by myself."

It was finally coming to him, bit by bit, like it had come to me in the big bed. "You were supposed to be immune," he said. "But you got it anyway. You were supposed to be immune."

"I'm not immune, Papa, but I can get over the strep myself. I've been doing it all along, all my life." I picked up the peach at my feet and handed it to him. He looked at it numbly.

"We were breeding for immunity," he said.

"I know, Papa. You knew what you were breeding for, but you didn't know what you'd get." I wanted to put my arms around him. "Haven will always be coming up with new strains. It would be impossible to be immune to all of them."

He took a knife out of his pocket, slowly, as if he were still asleep. He cut into the peach in his hand, sawing through the thick, dusty skin to the sudden softness underneath. He bit into it, and I watched his face anxiously.

"Is it all right, Papa?" I said. "Is it sweet?"

"Sweet beyond hope," he said, and put his arms around me, holding me close. "Oh, my sweet Haze, we bred to fight the strep, and look, look what we got!"

He held me by the shoulders and looked down at me. "I want you to go to Mamita's. You can't help here. But the hands all have gene prints like yours." His eyes were full of tears. "You are my cash crop after all."

"Now run," he said and walked away from me, back through the field toward the house. I stood for a minute, watching him, unable to call to him, to shout after him how much I loved them all. I climbed over the fence and stood in the road, looking at the litter of unhurt peaches. The downer was finishing its determined circuit at the top of the hill. If I hurried I could ride my own coffin to Mamita's and not even get my graduation dress wet. It seemed to me suddenly the most joyous chance in the world—to ride my own coffin, triumphant in my white dress with its fluttering red ribbons.

I stopped the catch my breath at the top of the hill and looked back at the peach tree. Francie was standing by it, with her hand raised almost in a question. Mama had done her hair in sugar curls for some occasion, and they did not move in the dusty wind that fluttered the red ribbons on my dress. She seemed as still as the brown haze that surrounded her, hugging her thin arms against her chest. I was too far away to see her shivering. Perhaps I would not have known what it meant if I had: I was not bred to read omens.

"I'll bring you some penicillin," I shouted, though she would have no idea of what I was saying. I shouted past her to Papa, who was too far away already to hear me. "I'll bring you some if I have to walk all the way to the *Magassar*."

"Don't worry!" I shouted. "They'll lift the planetwide. I know it." The dustdowner rattled past me, drowning out my words, and I ran to pull myself up onto the splintery edge of the coffin. "Don't worry, Francie!" I shouted again, putting my bandaged hand up to my mouth and holding on tight with the other. "We're all going to live forever!"

WE REMEMBER BABYLON

by Ian Watson

In legend and song people have always thought of the Golden Ages of time gone by. We tell of Jerusalem the Golden, and of the Glory that was Greece, of Nineveh of the Dragon Gates, and of the red-stained pyramids of Tenochtitlan. Who marched the terra-cotta soldiers of ancient Xian? What banners flew over the sunken towers of the lost Atlantis? Now let me rebuild and reenter these wonders of our own past. Come with Ian Watson back to the Hanging Gardens aided by the archeology of the centuries to come.

We cross the Arizona desert awakening from a daze, our minds buzzing with *koiné*, the common tongue, the universal language, Greek.

Our brains still froth and simmer from all the speed-teaching: with receptivity drugs, hypnosis, computer interface, recorded voices squeaking at high speed like whistling dolphins. By the time we arrive at Babylon, they have told us, our heads will have cleared. A deep sediment of Greek words, phrases, syntax will have settled to the bottom of our minds; our ordinary consciousness will be lucid, clear and Attic. And so we will try to come to terms with the future which is written in the past.

A few saguaro cacti flash by: probably the last native American vegetation we shall see. Ahead, the desert is stripped bare, a buffer zone between America and Babylon.

We cross this denuded desert in a hovercraft, following the concrete ribbon of the road which once gave access to the construction site. No wheeled vehicles are allowed to use it now. It is closed; no longer a modern highway. We fly a few inches above it, the gale of air supporting us beneath and the wind from our tail fans sweeping it clear of sand. Yet we do not touch it. We are disconnected; disconnected, too, from the America we have left behind. The voices babbling in our brains disorient us, too; but already as promised they are becoming quieter, dropping beneath the horizon of our awareness.

"Alex—" Deborah is saying something to me in ancient Greek—Greek with an enriched vocabulary. I nod, but pay little attention. Nothing we can say at the moment means anything. We are still in transition.

Besides, I don't really wish to pursue a relationship with her. Not yet. Not as the people who we were when we first met. Which was only a matter of ten days ago, the two of us coming from opposite points of the compass to the gleaming hypermodern township south of Casa Grande: the so-called University of the Future, the University of Heuristics.

I, Alexander Winter, from the foundering ecotopica of Oregon with a fairly useless degree in social studies. She, Deborah Tate, from New York—which perhaps gave her something of a prior lien on Babylon—and a background as computer programmer and hopeful actress; but already that dream had died, to be replaced by the desire to live a role at last.

Deborah. Quite tall, quite graceful. Curly raven hair, dark

eyes. Maybe she will go promptly to sit in the Temple of Love in Babylon waiting for any stranger to come along and toss a coin into her lap. Old man, young man, ugly or handsome, skinny or fat, clean or filthy: she must go with him, and lie with him. That is the custom. A custom inconvenient to some homely women; they can spend months on end waiting in the temple. The prospect seemed to fascinate Deborah.

But maybe she only spoke of this back at the University in the hope that the stranger might be me? So that she could experience the frisson of excitement and trepidation, and then avoid the reality? Already I know that it will not be me who throws that coin to her with the head of Alexander stamped on it. Not me; not yet. I hope she understands this. It would be untrue to Babylon.

Though later on, assuming that our visit is a success both in our own eyes and in those of the University—and presuming that we both become Babylonian citizens—later on maybe I will bid for Deborah before the auction block in the Marriage Market of Babylon. (For that is also the Babylonian custom.) Maybe.

I've little doubt that we will both become citizens. Babylon still needs some extra population; and there must, I suppose, be a turnover of citizens who leave of their own choice. I suppose; though I have not met any ex-Babylonians to my knowledge. But then, the city has only been finished for four years.

Yes, I will be a citizen. I will grow my hair long, wear a turban and perfume, and flourish a jaunty walking stick.

"Look," she says in Greek. (Everyone in Babylon speaks Greek to begin with. Presently we will learn Babylonian. But Greek is the world language, used by travelers. It is the English of its day. For this is the epoch of Alexander the Great; and these are the last days of his reign. My namesake lies dying of fever in the Palace of Nebuchadnezzar.)

"Look!"

Some way ahead, to east and west, in a glint of water and the green of irrigated farmland. The desert will soon narrow into a great V, cutting through toward . . .

I spy the walls of Babylon, far off.

Our whole party disembarks at the Ishtar gate. Soldiers watch us idly, leaning on their spears. They pay no attention to the hovercraft as it re-inflates its skirts and swings round, roaring, to head back the way it came. It does not belong. The wind from its fans whips us with dust so that, having already arrived neat and clean, 20th-century-style, we suddenly become travel-stained in our Greek garb.

The brickwork of the gate towers is gorgeously enameled, with beasts in high relief standing out one above the other: a white and blue bull with yellow horns and hooves; a creamy white composite dragon—part viper, part bird, part lizard, part lion—against a turquoise background; its forked tongue, mane and claws are golden brown. . . .

My thoughts are sharp and clear now. They are as luminous as that brickwork. I feel as though I should perform a sacrifice of thanksgiving to some long-forgotten god. To Shamash, perhaps, whose sun beats down on us. It would only be polite.

"Rejoice," says Deborah. "We have come." She sounds like Pheidippides after the long run from Marathon to Athens, when the tide of the Persians had been turned—a hundred and sixty-odd years ago, now.

Much has happened since then; and so we band of Greek travelers walk peacefully into the Babylon of the Chaldeans, who came before the Persian rulers of the city, who in turn came before Alexander, who now lies dying within. . . . Once again, it is the last days of a world.

The walls of the street beyond gleam with lions and tigers, boars and wolves pictured in colored, enameled brick. And already the smells assail our noses: of dung, fishcakes, charcoal, offal, urine . . . and of the aromatic gums, musk, sandalwood, patchouli and fragrant oils of the inhabitants. Perhaps we too shall have to visit the perfume vendors before long!

Our original group soon splits up, to go its various ways. Presently Deborah and I are alone together in a crowded thoroughfare.

We need to find lodgings. In Greek I address a barefoot beggar squatting in a bundle of rags. I choose him more out of curiosity than perversity; he was, after all, recently an American. "Greetings! Could you direct me to—?"

He grins evilly, yellow-toothed; and he sticks out an upright palm. Like a monkey, for peanuts. The motion briefly reveals a knife stuffed in a band of cloth round his waist.

Deborah drags on my arm, pulls me away hastily deep into the crowd. And she's right, of course.

A chariot clatters down the street; the crowd scatters.

Synchronicity rules in Babylon. And I need hardly add that synchronicity is not an Assyrian king. Like Sennacherib. Here in Babylon, the great buildings of several different epochs all occur together. They co-exist in time.

A little history, then . . .

Babylon the Magnificent, the Babylon of Hammurabi the law-maker and builder of canals, fell to the pugnacious, greedy, uncultured Kassites who let the city fall into neglect. After a while, that first Babylon was totally destroyed by the Assyrian Sennacherib. His soldiers killed every man, woman and child in the city, smashed the houses down, and even diverted a major canal to flood the ruins.

But less than a hundred years later the Chaldeans—who destroyed the Assyrians with Persian help—rebuilt Babylon as their own capital. Before long, under Nebuchadnezzar, the city was even more splendid than ever.

Yet curiously these Chaldeans failed to quite live in the present. The intelligentsia—the priests and scribes—failed to. Amidst sumptuous new palaces and temples, and even while building observatories to study the planets and the stars, they were also digging nostalgically in the old ruins for clay books and record tablets. With these as a guide, they began to copy the past affectedly in dress and custom and speech.

Presently their former allies the Persians attacked and destroyed the Chaldean empire; and slowly Babylon crumbled away again into ruins and wreckage.

And presently Alexander of Macedon overthrew the Persians. But then something new in history happened. Alexander conceived the dream of ruling the whole world. He unified the Macedonians and the Persians; and the first world empire was organized with a common language and a common economy, centered upon Babylon. Babylon rose again, as capital of the known world.

Briefly, briefly. For in the palace of Nebuchadnezzar—which of course had decayed long before Alexander's birth, yet which is still here as pristine and perfect as ever—my namesake lies a-dying. At the age of thirty-three.

It is the end of Babylon, yet again. The last days of rekindled glory. Rise and fall. Rise and fall. And fall. It is all here, co-existing: the Babylon of Hammurabi, of Nebuchadnezzar, of Alexander. And ahead, dust and ashes; and the unknowable future.

The future of Rome—currently a tiny village. The future of Byzantium. The future of the Holy Roman Empire. Of the Spanish Empire. The British Empire. The Third Reich. The Stars and Stripes.

Dust and ashes. Buried monuments. Bones. Amnesia.

Meanwhile what rough village, in the Congo or the South Seas, slouches toward the future to become the new capital of human life? When there is no room left in the world for new golden hordes to gather, or for barbarians sweeping down from the hills?

Where is the new incarnation of power and splendor? Can there be such a thing? Must the latest Babylons, of Moscow and New York, Tokyo and Peking, make way in their turn? What are the dynamics of decline and fall? Where is the elixir of longevity? How, as the years roll by, can the present be perpetuated into the future so that change does not sweep away what we know? Whence permanence? Whence mutability? What does the social psyche know, which the futurologists know not?

To answer such questions is Babylon rebuilt synchronously, and rekindled with life in the Arizona desert, gloriously poised on its final precipice with Alexander forever dying of a fever in the palace.

For Babylon is no Disneyland, no "park of the past." It is no "ancient-world," where tourists can spend vacations. Nor is it a utopian arcology, or an experimental community which willfully turns its back on the 20th century in pursuit of an ancient lifestyle. If it were merely any of these, would the U.S. Government have underwritten the huge initial cost, equivalent to that of a manned space station? Or exempted Babylonia from State and Federal law?

Babylon is the most ambitious, most important project regarding the future of civilization as we know it.

Perhaps. And perhaps the University of Heuristics is a monstrous folly—and its Babylon a different sort of folly: more akin to the follies built by rich Englishmen in their landscape gardens in the 18th century? Though much vaster; and not merely a facade, either, but a fully functioning ancient city.

And why? Is the autumn of a culture marked by vast, fanciful building projects? By exercises in architectural metaphysics, designed to stem the tide of time? Schemes reeking of immortalist religious yearnings, masquerading as something else? (Call this the Ozymandias syndrome . . . !) Is Babylon the psychic salvation of the American dream, or the very symbol of its decay? I do not know. I hope to find out.

Here is the temple of Marduk, god of victory. Broad ramps slope steeply upward, zigzagging, bisecting one another, circuiting the temple's many towers. A stream of worshipers mounts; others descend. Can they really be intent on prayer—or only on admiring the view from the summit? Vendors sell incense and oil and bleating lambs, bowls of imported Greek wine, and rissoles, on the vast forecourt.

I accost one departing worshiper: a bearded, turbaned man. "Excuse me, Sir. I'm a visitor. Do you *really* worship the God of War?"

Who worships war these days? However, this is the year 323 B.C. . . .

The man flushes.

"Fool!" he snarls, and pushes me aside.

Another, older man has heard this exchange. He approaches, smiling wryly and apologetically, and stands twiddling his ornamental walking stick.

"Perhaps it is purer to worship gods that don't exist?" he offers cryptically. "But perhaps worshiping them *causes* them to exist? On the other hand, where else can you innocently worship war in these late days? Perhaps these worshipers are simply searching for their own lost innocence—the innocence of the beast, which does not ask whether the sun will rise tomorrow. Or whether tomorrow will exist. For the beast knows nothing of tomorrow. And yesterday is already erased. All is now, the present, the moment. So the moment repeats itself forever. Thus the beast and his kind endure for a million years. In place of history, they have instinct. But perhaps Greek gods of war destroy empires with all their records and monuments every so often—otherwise the weight of memory would cripple us beneath its burden. We wouldn't have the energy for new enterprises; which are really the same old enterprises, forgotten then rekindled."

What am I to make of this? Is he a philosopher, a fantasist, a fool? Or a futurologist? Is he saying that the world must be destroyed, so that the world can carry on? That America must fall into decay, so that the kingdom of Amazonia or Ashanti can arise? Surely he's forgetting all the nuclear missiles poised in their silos? But could it be that society could simply collapse, and the missiles stay where they were, rusting, unfirable?

He executes a little skip around his walking stick.

"And perhaps, foreigner," he says, "Marduk isn't God of War at all. Don't assume that you're wise, because you are a Greek. You're here to *discover* Babylon. But then, so are we!"

He winks, and strides off in sprightly style.

"Wait!"

He will not wait.

We buy fish rissoles and wine.

Here is the river Euphrates flowing through the heart of Babylon, giant coracles afloat on it, bearing produce and passengers and goats downstream. Even with oars fore and aft, these perfectly round boats tend to spin in the current like the waltzer cars at a funfair.

We stand on the stone bridge which Herodotus so much admired, leaning on the balustrade watching the river traffic. From stout pier to stout stone pier stretch rows of planks which can all be lifted up and hauled back on shore, rendering the bridge uncrossable. Every night all the planks are lifted and stacked; every morning they are put back. You do not build a bridge for your enemies to cross! Yet this is in the very heart of Babylon. Is the heart sick, divided against itself? Is this the corpus callosum, the bridge between the two hemispheres of the Babylonian brain? Every night when the city sleeps does it dream two separate dreams, the dream of the past, and the dream of the future?

Beyond the city walls the Euphrates flows on through irrigated farmland for half a dozen miles. Then it runs back through a subterranean tunnel to an equivalent distance upstream of the city. The Euphrates is a closed loop two dozen miles around. The Corps of Engineers constructed it. A buried geothermal spike provides the power for the mighty pumps at the upstream end which raise the river back up from the depths. Downstream, there hidden sewage works cleanse the polluted water before it flows back underground.

Sleep. And dreams.

We had found lodgings in a tatty inn, with a courtyard where horses and camels pawed and snorted, coughed and nickered. A caravanserai.

Debroah and I had taken separate rooms: tiny brick chambers with straw-stuffed mattresses and raggy bedding, but quite clean. To our surprise there was no infestation of bugs.

Deborah and I do not sleep together because since we entered Babylon we are increasingly strange to each other. We can only come together if we first travel all the way to strangeness—and at last meet each other there. If indeed we recognize each other then. Or wish to recognize each other.

We have the same lodging place, and we even go about together. But not like lovers, which we never were, nor yet like brother and sister who only reflect each other's familiarity back at one another.

I dream: that the missiles have all flown, the bombs have all fallen. Russia and America are no more; Europe and China have been wiped off the map. Man-designed plagues rage elsewhere. It is the collapse, the end of technological culture, of global government.

But Babylon survives. Here in the loneliest corner of the American desert—though there is no longer an "America"—

Babylon remains intact, entire. Untouched. And continues to be Babylon.

It's as though the mega-power released by all the warheads has rent a hole in the continuum of space and time, has scrambled the clock of the sun and the calendar of the earth, and has pulled this ancient city out of a previous era and deposited it in the future. As the only future which remains.

Babylon thrives. The Euphrates flows around and around. Seasons pass; decades. Eventually the Babylonians begin to colonize what was once America. But they know nothing any longer of the customs or speech of dead America, or the dead 20th century. They only know Babylonian ways. Long hair and perfume; Marduk and Ishtar; coracles and ziggurats.

But elsewhere, far away, is a new Assyrian wolf of another Alexander marshaling his forces in Angola or Argentina, to collide with Babylon once more?

We shall see.

No doubt there are oneiromancers, dream-diviners somewhere in the city who could see the meaning of this dream.

Days pass by.

The images of animals are everywhere in Babylon, in bright wall reliefs and statues. Largely of animals destined for slaughter. Stags, bison, lions, bulls and rams. And dragons.

With Deborah I visit the Wonder Cabinet of Mankind in a corner of the palace: the first museum in the history of the world, opened to the general public by Nebuchadnezzar. I had wondered whether it would be full of animals, exotic animals stuffed or modelled.

It isn't. It is full of antiquities. There are clay tablets and cylinders. There is a diorite column inscribed with ten thousand cuneiform letters: the laws of Hammurabi. There are inscriptions from Ur. stone bowls and figurines of Aramaic weather gods, Kassite clubs, Mesopotamian statuary, foundation stones of antique temples, reliefs, stelai, Theban obelisks, mace-heads and cudgels, jewelry, breastplates, bric-à-brac. And so on, and on.

The curator intones at us, "Here is the whole span of time, Greeks." For a moment I believe him. Gone is the Rome of the Caesars, and the Rome of the Popes. Gone is the crucifix, gone is the mosque. Gone, the Renaissance; gone, the space age. They are *not*, yet. So they have never been.

Deborah must feel this deeply too. "Isn't it strange?" she murmurs to me. "There's so much that isn't here. In fact, almost *everything* isn't here, that we ever thought important! And yet, for them the world was just as full—with all this ancient history stretching way behind them.

"And the future . . . Us. What we think of as the culmination of the past—which had hardly even *started* when this museum was opened: it seems such a fantasy, a fever dream! Of men like Gods flying through the sky, and space, and wielding bolts of lightning, and sending their thoughts and pictures from place to place in an instant—as though mythology lies *ahead*, not behind!"

"The *whole* span of time," repeats the curator, with emphasis.

"Yes," she says to me. "And in another thousand years the 20th century will seem such a partial, provisional, restricted thing. Because X hadn't happened yet. Or Y, or Z—which is so goddam important, so crucial to history that it changes everything. Creatures from the stars, immortality, I don't know what. Then a thousand years later X, Y and Z will have been totally dwarfed by A, B or C. . . ."

She stares wildly around the Wonder Cabinet. "To believe that this is the whole span! To know it in your heart. Why, this could free us from the treadmill of time! Then time might not sweep us away. Or else . . . we might expect it to sweep us away—and fashion our world accordingly. And so survive through the changes. We could swim with the flood of years instead of being drowned by them. Yes, I see. Our culture is trying to learn how not to drown—by sending us here, where *it is not*, and never has been."

Wonders? These? Here, in this first museum? Clay and stone? Bronze and gold? Rather than steam engines, Saturn rockets, microcomputers?

Yes, perhaps. To enter a frame of mind where such things as rockets, satellites, wrist computers and heart transplants are simply equal to obelisks and pots and breastplates—to look at the 20th century through the other end of the telescope of time—is to enable one to comprehend the future. . . .

We have built an alien city, as though on Mars, to alienate us from the big dipper of the present, which seems about to fly apart. As soon as Babylon is no longer alien to us we can begin to redeem the future, purging it of its threat, knowing it. Not by Delphi methods or computer projections, world models or algorithms based in the present. Not by reason. But emotionally.

Then Deborah and I, too, may begin to understand our own emotions. Whatever they may be.

Here is the Tower of Babel: tallest of all ziggurats, a skyscraper, even though the sky it scrapes here is a cloudless desert blue, so it is difficult to set an upper or a lower limit to that sky.

A single spiraling ramp winds upwards, around and around, so that each tier is of less girth than the one below. And the tall walls of each tier are indented with doors and windows—if unwound into a ribbon, the corkscrew helix of the tower's height would reach right across the city and into the countryside beyond. It's a very long walk to the top, and many people dwell up there inside the belly of Babel: a miniature city within a city, with its own inns, shops, workshops and homes. Some people may never bother to descend; others must be occupied full time in trading supplies and craftwork between the different levels, and between Babel and the ground below.

In design this tower is far from being an angular ziggurat of straight lines and sharp corners; visibly it owes more to Breughel, though it is slimmer than his tower. Perhaps there are structural reasons for this; or perhaps Breughel's vision of Babel was too compelling to ignore, even though it would not be pictured for another two thousand years. . . .

I'm not sure whether a hundred foreign languages really are spoken up around those tiers: Akkadian and Egyptian, Persian, Aramaic. But secure in the Attic clarity of Greek, I set off boldly toward the base of the great access ramp.

"Alex!"

Deborah has hung back.

"I'm not going up there. It could take all day. Two days, even . . . You go, though."

"So where are you going?"

"To the Temple of Ishtar. I feel it's time to."

To the Temple of Love. Of sacred prostitution. Obligatory, once in every Babylonian woman's life. More than once is optional.

Probably Deborah's right. It's time. This will alienate her from her 20th-century-American self more effectively, more viscerally, than climbing Babel.

So we part, with a curiously formal handshake followed by a quick kiss. She walks away; and I watch her go. But not even when she has disappeared do I carry on toward the ramp of Babel.

I stand, I crick my neck, I contemplate the tower. Presently I buy a bowl of wine, and a handful of ripe figs. I while away an hour.

And finally I follow her.

In the tree-shaded courtyard of the Temple of Love some forty women wait, each on a separate woven mat, cross-legged or with their knees drawn up, the laps of their dresses forming for each a begging bowl.

Men come and go: inspecting, choosing, commanding with a coin. Walking with their chosen woman into the temple. Departing later, they go separate ways.

Deborah isn't anywhere in the courtyard; and I realize that I'm glad of this. Glad that the affair has already been settled? Glad that she has been spared the humiliation of a long wait? (But is that considered a humiliation here?) Glad that she has not seen me follow her here? Glad for whose sake: hers or mine?

Better that she should not know I came! I wonder whether, by coming here, I am trying in some way to get even with her? But I cannot do that; because I am a man. Deborah submits to Babylon today; but it will simply be one individual woman of Babylon who submits to me.

I walk about, fingering a coin; not too large, so that I seem like a naïve tourist unable to believe my luck, or like a fool—nor too small, so that I seem insulting, mean and disrespectful.

Whom shall I choose? The women wait politely, patiently. They do not ogle or flash seductive smiles, eager to be done with it, and gone; eager, perhaps, for Alexander Winter rather than for someone with acne, warts or bad breath. They wait dispassionately, gracefully. They neither drop their gaze, nor fix me with it.

This young tanned blonde?

This comely, freckled redhead?

This negress, with cheeks and arms of polished ebony?

Or shall I choose this homely dumpling? Or this angular, bony lady with a face like a horse? These two may have been here all week, all month, all year. Lying with one of them might prove an alien, disconcerting experience for both her and me. After all, there's a certain familiarity about the joining of bodies accustomed to such maneuvers—and I do not seek the familiar. And besides, the dumpling or the horse may be wiser in the ways of Babylon, if not in the arts of love. Or contrariwise the ugly woman may be far more sensual; the beauty may be frigid. . . .

When I make my choice, it is by accident. Out of the corner of my eye I catch a glimpse of Deborah emerging from the doorway of the temple, accompanied by a tall, robed, bearded man, who inclines his head, smiles faintly, and walks off.

The woman I'm standing before: she's mousy. A little mouse. Short brown hair. Small, ordinary features. Neither beautiful nor otherwise.

I drop my coin into her lap. "You," say I.

And she rises smoothly, holding the piece of silver.

Let Deborah (who is heading away across the courtyard) make what she will of my choice. If she notices. She seems preoccupied. Or perhaps she is taking pains not to stare at me.

Inside the temple light filters softly through high clerestory windows. Private chambers, like a row of confessionals, occupy each side of the "nave." Richly brocaded curtains are drawn across those which are occupied. In those which are open and empty, waiting, I see a couch, an ewer of water, a bowl, a towel, wine and fruit, and a little oil lamp burning. But first we walk down to the altar to deposit my coin in a great silver bowl full of other coins, beneath a statue of Ishtar, with rubies studding her hair. A old woman is sweeping the floor and whistling. Another old woman is replenishing clean towels and water. Are there any priestesses as such? Perhaps every woman who enters with a coin becomes a priestess for a while. My mouse kneels and prays briefly, whispering in Babylonian. What does she pray for? Gentleness, on my part? That she will not become pregnant or the contrary?

She walks before me to an open booth. We enter; I close

the curtain. Facing each other in the lamplight we undress, ignoring the wine and fruit. For just a moment I imagine her at a PTA meeting; or in church, in Smallville, USA. Instead, she is the whore of Babylon. Then I forget those things as our bodies meet.

Later: "What did you pray for at the altar?" I ask.

"For you," she answers. "For you."

And when eventually I leave, and walk off across the leafy courtyard, I realize that this Temple of Love teaches us of ourselves: of our mixed emotions, our false chivalries, sham and sanctimonious, our egotisms and illusions; so that we may at last learn love, affection, joy.

It isn't the lesson I had expected to learn; yet I suspect nonetheless that this disordering of our emotional routines is a necessary way stage to that future, which we must grasp emotionally before all else.

In my brief absence Deborah has moved out of the inn, leaving no forwarding address or message. But perhaps the absence of any message for me is in itself equivalent to one: saying silently that there is no need of any message, since we both know what is happening. We have to proceed along diverging routes, which will lead perhaps to the same destination. Such feelings cannot be written down in a scribbled note; to do so would make them a lie, an evasion.

Time flows on; but now I no longer know which way it is flowing: forward, or back into the past. Perhaps, like the river Euphrates, time really flows in a circle. Though I suspect not.

Here am I back once again at the Palace of Nebuchadnezzar, with its long pillared tiers draped in the Hanging Gardens. I had thought I would explore these gardens in Deborah's company, each of us thinking our own green thoughts in the green shade. But as it is, of this palace together we only visited the dusty antiquities of the Wonder Cabinet down at street level at the northern end, chambers full of clay and stone.

This palace is a prodigy even for the 20th century. What was it like twenty-six centuries ago? Perhaps in reality the palace was only a rather large ziggurat with a few trees planted on it, and potted palms and shrubs. But no: this is how it was, exactly, because this is how it is, now. Besides, consider the Great Hall of Karnak. Or the Pyramids. Obviously there were giants living in those days; even though compared with us no doubt they were pygmies.

As I gaze up from the street at the seven terraces, once again time reverses and twists; and the 20th century which I have left becomes a distant epoch which simply led here, to this achievement, all of our future ambition and skill culminating—in a 6th century B.C. palace.

A broad flight of marble steps leads up to the first terrace, of giant ferns and fountains. Some Macedonian and Persian soldiers guard the way aloft, but hinder no one. A party of fine ladies in rich array are gossiping halfway up, while servants hold plume-fans over their heads. A trio of bearded men in black robes and conical caps descend, deep in conversation. Astronomers, astrologers?

I climb. I wander up and along one terrace after another: through palm trees, fig trees, bays, orange and avocado, thickets of jasmine, a miniature forest of cypress and smaller conifers, a garden of succulents. Watercourses run everywhere, plashing in waterfalls from level to level, sparkling skyward in fountains. Here is a statue of a sphinx, there of a winged bull, or elephant. And at the back of each terrace columned arcades give access to the palace proper.

To be a gardener in Babylon, upon the Hanging Gardens! I have passed several at their tasks. Here is another, an old frail man, sprinkling the flagstones of the fifth terrace to still any dust.

We fall into conversation. And all the while we're talking I'm thinking to myself, "He has emigrated to Babylon as an old, tired man! Doesn't he care that he'll die the sooner here? Doesn't it worry him that the medical facilities are those of the marketplace? Consisting of folk wisdom, quack diagnosis by passers-by, herbal potions? No surgery, no antibiotics, no real medicine! Does Babylon represent for him a death wish? Yet amid this riot of growth—here in these gardens which are the very antithesis of decay? How can that be?"

He has, of course, noticed me assessing his wrinkles, the bend of his shoulders, the slowness of his hands, the liver spots upon the skin. ("Grandad, shouldn't you be resting in a rocking chair on some back stoop with a rug over your knees, instead of laboring in Babylon?")

He starts to cough: a dangerous, wheezing noise.

"Are you all right?"

He spits, scrapes the sputum away with his sandals, then grins.

"Everyone dies, lad. The young king himself lies dying within, and he's just thirty-three. But that's from fever . . .

"Listen: the cells in any body only replace themselves so many times—there's a limit, isn't there? And a city or kingdom is just a body writ large. What if there is some natural limit in the *polis*, the State, just as there is in any animal body? The *polis* that I left," and I suppose he must mean America, "it seemed to have reached a limit. Its limit as a body. . . . Think on that."

Is this right? Is this what he learned here in Babylon: this insight so vital to the University of Heuristics, namely that any society has an inbuilt limit to how long it can perpetuate itself?

Or is that what he came here determined to learn, and so console himself for his own imminent departure from the world?

Strange things are happening in this city; strange tides of

consciousness are being drawn up, as if by an ancient moon which once shone over the original Babylon.

"Alexander's dying," he mumbled, "but that's just fever . . ."

Far away down the leaf-clad terraces, beyond parapet after parapet, I think I spy Deborah walking. Really, the figure is too far away to be sure; and now a Banyan tree eclipses her.

"Why don't you visit him, then?"

"Visit? Who?"

"Alexander, of course."

"But . . . he's the King! You don't just visit a King. And anyway, he's dying."

The gardener winks. "He's been dying for long enough. Must get boring. He might appreciate a visit from a compatriot. Anyway, you Greeks are supposed to be such a democratic lot. Well, that was once upon a time . . . Now you have to grovel and prostrate yourself and make obeisances."

"Do you mean I can really visit Alexander?"

"S'pose so. You can always ask. Me, I'm only one of his gardeners."

This is incredible. Alexander the Great lies dying in this very palace, maybe only a hundred paces distant . . . I knew this. Of course I knew it. But I had never imagined that he was *really* here.

Does he actually exist? Or is this old man just playing a joke on me?

"If you don't believe me, lad, go up to the next terrace. Ask a guard."

"I will!"

Yes. Yes. And Yes.

I am searched, for daggers. I am clad in borrowed cloth of gold, in case my clothes themselves are poisonous, or lest I offend Alexander's fevered eyes. I'm instructed how to throw myself down and approach on my knees.

Flanked by two guards (one Persian, one Macedonian) armed with short spears, a chamberlain leads me toward the presence. Rich vases are everywhere in this part of the palace, polished ivory and carved jade, lootings of India and beyond.

A staff is stamped before double doors of carved teak. They open upon a large, airy room. Filmy curtains of gauze ripple across the stone window frames; yet the sweet smell is not of flowers, but of sickness and incense. Or perhaps it is simply the incense which smells sickly. His bed is great and golden, with claw and ball feet, and a canopy above.

I prostrate myself on the Persian carpet; I crawl.

"Stand up," says a voice wearily.

And I behold Alexander the Great, plumped up on soft pillows, wearing a silken gown embroidered with dragons, jeweled rings on his fingers. The ruler of Babylon.

He doesn't *look* fatally ill. But then, hasn't he been sick of this same fever for the past four years? He doesn't look thirty-three—more like forty—nor a dashing, muscular conqueror, either. But then, he is only an avatar of Alexander. He's stout and jowly with long ringletted hair and dark sad eyes, glinting nevertheless with a sharp intelligence: an intelligence imprisoned in pillows and sickness. Does he have rouge on his cheeks—and on his lips too?

Bowls of ripe fruits and candies, and flasks of wine surround the bed; incense sticks burn. I'm reminded of Nero, of Aubrey Beardsley's drawings, of Oscar Wilde, of some Borgia Pope—phantasms from the future. Alexander, it seems, has succumbed to Persian luxury. Scrolls lie on his bed: maps of empire? No, graphs, doodles, charts of cryptic symbols. Alchemical diagrams and horoscopes? Perhaps. Or perhaps exercises in heuristic futurology.

What is he? What is his fever? The fever of the dying 20th century seeking the elixir of immortality?

I wonder whether he is drugged, like a seer or sibyl.

I wonder whether he will eventually be killed by his guards—given an overdose—and replaced with someone younger, likewise to be kept abed in a semi-drugged state. For a moment the frightening, presumptuous thought crosses my mind: am I the next Alexander?

Yet if this king's body seems half paralyzed and comatose, what of his brain?

He stares at me. His rouged lips move.

"Few come to visit the maggot in the apple . . . Wine!"

A serving woman bows, pours, sips from a cup; then, since she isn't now writhing on the floor in agony, she holds the cup to Alexander's lips, tipping it up for him. Gulping, he drains the cup. Several dribbles run down his chin to be mopped up by the woman with a napkin.

"Ambassadors, petitioners, magi with their cures . . . What's yours, Greek? What's your cure for the world?"

"Babylon," I say. "Babylon is the cure." For I believe this. Even more so, paradoxically, now that I have seen him.

And now, as though the wine—or whatever was in it—has inflamed the sinews of his vision, the muscles of his mind, he speaks again in a sing-song voice:

"We have heard tales of the morning of the Earth—and of its golden afternoon, which we presume must be the twentieth century or the thirtieth or fortieth or the hundredth. And we have heard tales of the long, long evening of decay. Perhaps with assorted rises and falls in between: new barbarism, trips to the stars, who knows?

"But this is all nonsense. For it's still the morning, now; and in a million years it will be the morning of the planet, still. And in a million more. Even the early afternoon is unimaginably different—and may be inhabited gloriously by creatures that are only a few inches long now: voles, shrews. Or by dogs that walk erect, or by birds, or by creatures we can't even imagine, because their ancestors haven't happened yet . . .

"Who can ever *feel* time? Who can really sense its vast arcades? Ah, but we have performed a clever conjuring trick.

"For the ancient world is obviously older than ours. It is an old man, to our brash youth—even if we live longer than anyone lived then. It is the evening, to our morning, because it is ancient.

"So by recreating it—by reviving the dawn of civilization, which is now dust—we take a giant leap into the afternoon of life, and even perhaps into the evening, in our psyche, in our soul. And so we reach beyond our callow ten a.m. of time—to other, later hours of the future. . . ."

A scribe takes this down, scratching quickly with a stylus. Will they post these sayings in the marketplace? Will they read them aloud in the Temple of Marduk? Will they convey them up the ramp of Babel?

Why else copy down his words? Since surely there is a microphone listening somewhere in this room, and a hidden camera watching. Surely in the King's room, if anywhere!

Yet perhaps there are no hidden cameras or microphones anywhere in Babylon. Even with the latest semi-aware, fuzzy logic computer to screen the flood of input, how could any team of observers cope?

Perhaps the University simply samples Babylon by sending observers in directly (and I am one right now). But perhaps everyone in Babylon—every citizen, that is—is an observer; and it is the stream of newcomers whom they observe, the applicants for citizenship, the visitors, for changes in their behavior—for signs of bewilderment, acceptance, spiritual crisis, illumination.

And perhaps, in its arbitrary yet wholehearted adoption of ancient alien customs, Babylon has become the first self-aware *polis* in the history of the world: self-aware beyond time and space. As nowhere else. A communal brain. Maybe it is Babylon itself that is the computer, built of human beings.

Alexander slumps further back into his pillows, exhausted, drained. He shuts his eyes; I see there is kohl on his eyelids. The chamberlain tugs my sleeve, forcing me down. The audience is at an end. Together, we back out of the room on our hands and knees.

My thoughts buzzing, my brain burbling to itself—uncertain whether I have been witness to a profound truth in my namesake's bedchamber, or to a wild folly, a grandiose gesture of despair. I blunder out of the palace, escorted politely but firmly by the guards back to the gardens of the sixth terrace.

Eventually, days later, a messenger—a fat fussy little man—rouses me in the inn.

"It's time," he says. "Today."

I stare at him, non-plused. "Today? But of course it's today. It's always today. It could hardly be tomorrow, or yesterday!"

"It's *time*," he says again.

"Time for what? I'm going to climb Babel today."

"The rest of your group checked in at dawn, by the gate. You're keeping them waiting. The woman Deborah said you might still be here. You've forgotten." He hesitates, then whispers in an alien tongue, English: "The hovercraft. To take you back to the University. For debriefing. Decisions." A dead tongue. Dead, because it hasn't yet been born.

But I go with him.

As we walk through the early morning streets of Babylon toward the Ishtar gate, I wonder: should I have changed my lodgings? Did I somehow lack initiative? But obviously I have to return to the University. To learn Babylonian. To be speed-taught, force-fed with the true language of the city. Otherwise I would be forever a foreigner here, a visiting Greek.

Is that why they teach us Greek to begin with? To ensure that we first arrive as strangers, and always retain at least a memory of our strangeness? Otherwise we might be totally submerged as soon as we stepped through the gate. Like long-lost kin who have come home at last, like amnesiacs who have suddenly regained their memories. Or like the insane, from whom the veils of madness have abruptly lifted . . .

Once on the hovercraft, I sit down by Deborah.

"After you checked out of the inn," I ask her, "where did you go?"

At first her voice is cool, remote. "Me? I went to live on Babel. Up the Tower of Babel."

"The one place I missed!"

"One always misses something, Alex."

"I might say that I'd missed you—"

She frowns, and I hasten to add, "But how could I? I didn't know who you were—till you found out for yourself." It sounds insulting, but it isn't; nor does she take it so.

"And did you find out too, Alex? Who you are?"

"I think so."

Now she smiles.

I'm sure we have a real relationship at last. But it is a relationship by virtue of Babylon.

"One day," I promise her, "I'll bid for you at the auction block."

"If you're rich enough, Alex."

"I will be. I'll be rich in something, even if it isn't coin."

"Won't it be interesting," she remarks, "as more and more children are born in Babylon, whose first language is Babylonian? Kids who only learn a smattering of Greek, the hard way? Kids who have never even heard of English?"

And I suppose this is some kind of promise on her part.

With a roar the hovercraft lofts itself smoothly above the ground, and turns to head north in a billow of dust. The notch of wasteland which abuts the Ishtar gate widens rapidly. Soon we are speeding through the Arizona desert, along the abandoned road.

When I see the first Saguaro cactus, I shall know we are somewhere else. Somewhere anonymous.

For no name can match the name of Babylon the Great.

WHAT MAKES US HUMAN

By Stephen R. Donaldson

The author is known for his bestselling fantasy novels of Thomas Covenant, but this novelette demonstrates his capacity in the realm of straight science fiction projection. Here then is a colonized planet which sets out to return to its roots—and encounters the riddle of the title.

Aster's Hope stood more than a hundred meters tall—a perfect sphere bristling with vanes, antennas, and scanners, punctuated with laser points, viewscreens, and receptors. She left her orbit around her homeworld like a steel ball out of a slingshot, her sides bright in the pure sunlight of the solar system. Accelerating toward her traveling speed of 0.85c, she moved past the outer planets—first Philomel with its gigantic streaks of raw, cold hydrogen; then lonely Periwinkle glimmering at the edge of the spectrum—on her way into the black and luminous beyond. She was the best her people had ever made, the best they knew how to make. She had to be: she wasn't coming back for centuries.

There were exactly 392 people aboard.

They, too, were the best Aster had to offer. Diplomats and

meditechs, linguists, theoretical biologists, physicists, scholars, even librarians for the vast banks of knowledge *Aster's Hope* carried: all of them had been trained to the teeth especially for this mission. And they included the absolute cream of Aster's young Service, the so-called " 'puters" and " 'nicians" who knew how to make *Aster's Hope* sail the fine-grained winds of the galaxy. Three hundred ninety-two people in all, culled and tested and prepared from the whole population of the planet to share in the culmination of Aster's history.

Three hundred ninety of them were asleep.

The other two were supposed to be taking care of the ship. But they weren't. They were running naked down a mid-shell corridor between the clean, impersonal chambers where the cryogenic capsules hugged their occupants. Temple was giggling because she knew Gracias was never going to catch her unless she let him. He still had some of the ice cream she'd spilled on him trickling through the hair on his chest, but if she didn't slow down, he wasn't going to be able to do anything about it. Maybe she wasn't smarter or stronger than he was, better trained or higher-ranking—but she was certainly faster.

This was their duty shift, the week they would spend out of their capsules every half year until they died. *Aster's Hope* carried twenty-five shifts from the Service, and they were the suicide personnel of this mission: aging at the rate of one week twice every year, none of them were expected to live long enough to see the ship's return home. Everyone else could be spared until *Aster's Hope* reached its destination; asleep for the whole trip, they would arrive only a bit more mature than they were when they left. But the Service had to maintain the ship. And so the planners of the mission had been forced to a difficult decision: Either fill *Aster's Hope* entirely with 'puters and 'nicians and pray that they would be able to do the work of diplomats, theoretical physicists, and linguists; or sacrifice a certain number of Service personnel to make room for people who could be explicitly trained for the mission. The planners decided that the ability to take *Aster's Hope* apart chip by chip and seal after seal and then put her all back together again was enough expertise to ask of any individual man or woman. Therefore, the mission itself would have to be entrusted to other experts.

And therefore, *Aster's Hope* would be unable to carry enough 'puters and 'nicians to bring the mission home again.

Faced with this dilemma, the Service personnel were naturally expected to spend a significant period of each duty shift trying to reproduce. If they had children, they could pass on their knowledge and skill. And if the children were born soon enough, they would be old enough to take *Aster's Hope* home when she needed them.

Temple and Gracias weren't particularly interested in having chidren. But they took every aspect of reproduction very seriously.

She slowed down for a few seconds, just to tantalize him. Then she put on a burst of speed. He tended to be just a bit dull in his lovemaking—and even in his conversation—unless she made a special effort to get his heart pounding. On some days, a slow, comfortable, and just-a-bit-dull lover was exactly what she wanted. But not today. Today she was full of energy from the tips of her toes to the ends of her hair, and she wanted Gracias at his best.

But when she tossed a laughing look back over her shoulder to see how he was doing, he wasn't behind her anymore.

Where—? Well, good. He was trying to take control of the race. Win by tricking her because he couldn't do it with speed. Temple laughed out loud while she paused to catch her breath and think. Obviously, he had ducked into one of the rooms or passages off this corridor, looking for a way to shortcut ahead of her—or maybe to lure her into ambush. And she hadn't heard the automatic door open and close because she'd been running and breathing too hard. Very good! This was the Gracias she wanted.

But where had he turned off? Not the auxiliary compcom: that room didn't have any other exit. How about the nearest capsule chamber? From there, he'd have to shaft down to inner-shell and come back up. That would be dicey: he'd have to guess how far and fast, and in what direction, she was moving. Which gave her a chance to turn the tables on him.

With a grin, she went for the door to the next capsule chamber. Sensing her approach, it opened with a nearly silent whoosh, then closed behind her. Familiar with the look of the cryogenic capsules huddled in the grasp of their triple-redundant support machinery, each one independently supplied and run so that no system-wide failure could wipe out the mission, she hardly glanced around her as she headed toward the shaft.

Its indicators showed that it wasn't in use. So Gracias wasn't on his way up here. Perfect. She'd take the shaft up to the outer-shell and elude him there, just to whet his appetite. Turn his own gambit against him. Pleased with herself, she approached the door of the shaft.

But when she impinged on the shaft's sensor, it didn't react to her. None of the lights came on: the elevator stayed where it was. Surprised, she put her whole body in front of the sensor. Nothing. She jumped up and down, waved her arms. Stil nothing.

That was strange. When Gracias ran his diagnostics this morning, the only malfunction anywhere was in an obscure circuit of foodsup's beer synthesizer. And she'd already helped him fix it. Why wasn't the shaft opening?

Thinking she ought to go to the next room and try another shaft, find out how serious the problem was, Temple trotted back to the capsule chamber door.

This time, it didn't open for her.

That was so unexpected that she ran into the door—which

startled more than hurt her. In her nearly thirty years, she had never seen an automatic door fail. All doors opened except locked doors; and locked doors had an exterior status light no one could miss. Yet the indicators for this door showed *open* and *normal*.

She tried again.

The door didn't open.

That wasn't just strange. It was serious. A severe malfunction. Which didn't show up on diagnostics? Or had it just now happened? Either way, it was time to stop playing. *Aster's Hope* needed help. Frowning, Temple looked for the nearest speaker so she could call Gracias and tell him what was going on.

It was opposite her, on the wall beside the shaft. She started toward it.

Before she got there, the door to the chamber slid open.

A nonchalant look on his dark face, a tuneless whistle puckering his mouth, Gracias came into the room. He was carrying a light sleeping pallet over one shoulder. The door closed behind him normally.

"Going somewhere?" he asked in a tone of casual curiosity.

Temple knew that look, that tone. In spite of herself, she gave him a wide grin. "Damn you all to pieces," she remarked. "How did you do that?"

He shrugged, trying to hide the sparkle in his eyes. "Nothing to it. Auxcompcom's right over there." He nodded in the direction of the comp command room she had passed. "Ship motion sensors knew where you were. Saw you come in here. Did a temporary repro. Told the comp not to react to any body mass smaller than mine. You're stuck in here for another hour."

"You ought to be ashamed." She couldn't stop grinning. His ploy delighted her. "That's the most irresponsible thing I've ever heard. If the other 'puters spend their time doing repros, the comp won't be good for alphabet soup by the time we get where we're going."

He didn't quite meet her happy gaze. "Too late now." Still pretending he was nonchalant—in spite of some obvious evidence to the contrary—he put the pallet on the floor in front of him. "Stuck here for another hour." Then he did look at her, his black eyes smoldering. "Don't want to waste it."

She made an effort to sound exasperated. "Idiot." But she practically jumped into his arms when he gave her the chance.

They were still doing their duty when the ship's brapper sounded and the comp snapped *Aster's Hope* onto emergency alert.

Temple and Gracias were, respectively, the 'nician and 'puter of their duty shift. The Service had trained them for their jobs almost from birth. They had access, both by education and through the comp, to the best knowledge Aster had evolved, the best resources her planners and builders had been able to cram into *Aster's Hope*. In some ways, they were the pinnacle of Aster's long climb toward the future: they represented, more surely than any of the diplomats or librarians, what the Asterins had been striving toward for three thousand years.

But the terms themselves, " 'nician" and " 'puter," were atavisms, pieces of words left over from before the Crash—sounds that had become at once magic and nonsense during the period of inevitable barbarism that had followed the Crash. Surviving legends spoke of the 'puters and 'nicians who had piloted the great colonization ship *Aster* across the galactic void from Earth, light-years measured in hundreds or thousands from the homeworld of the human race. In *Aster*, as in the great ships that Earth had sent out, striving to preserve humankind from some now-forgotten crisis, most of the people had slept through the centuries of space-normal travel while the 'nicians and 'puters had spent their lives and died, generation after generation, to keep the ship safe and alive as the comp and its scanners hunted the heavens for some world where *Aster*'s sleepers could live.

It was a long and heroic task, that measureless vigil of the men and women who ran the ship. In one sense, they succeeded; for when *Aster* came to her last resting-place, it was on the surface of a planet rich in compatible atmosphere and vegetation but almost devoid of competitive fauna. The planet's sun was only a few degrees hotter than Sol; its gravity, only a fraction heavier. The people who found their way out of sleep onto the soil and hope of the new world had reason to count themselves fortunate.

But in another sense the 'nicians and 'puters failed. While most of her occupants slept, *Aster* had been working for hundreds or thousands of years—and entropy was immutable. Parts of the ship broke down. The 'puters and 'nicia[illegible] made repairs. Other parts broke down and were fixed [illegible]. [illegible] *Aster* began to run low on supplies and equipme[illegible] [illegible]he [illegible] that broke down were fixed at the expense of other parts. The 'nicians and 'puters kept their ship alive by nothing more in the end than sheer ingenuity and courage, but they couldn't keep her from crashing.

The Crash upset everything the people of Earth had planned for the people of *Aster*. The comp was wrecked, its memory banks irretrievable, useless. Fires destroyed what physical books the ship carried. The pieces of equipment that survived tended to be ones that couldn't be kept running without access to an ion generator and couldn't be repaired without the ability to manufacture microchips. *Aster*'s engines had flared out under the strain of bringing her bulk down through the atmosphere and were cold forever.

Nearly nine hundred men and women survived the Crash, but they had nothing to keep themselves alive with except the knowledge and determination they carried in their own heads.

That the descendants of those pioneers survived to name their planet Aster—to make it yield up first a life and then a future, to dream of the stars and space flight and Earth—was a tribute more to their determination than to their knowledge. A significant portion of what they knew was of no conceivable value. The descendants of the original 'puters and 'nicians knew how to run *Aster*; but the theoretical questions involved in how she had run were scantly understood. And none of those personnel had been trained to live in what was essentially a jungle. As for the sleepers: according to legend, a full 10 percent of them had been politicians. And another 20 percent had been people the politicians deemed essential—secretaries, press officers, security guards, even cosmeticians. That left barely six hundred individuals who were accustomed to living in some sort of contact with reality.

And yet they found a way to live.

First they survived: by experimentation (some of it fatal), they learned to distinguish edible from inedible vegetation; they remembered enough about the importance of fire to procure some from *Aster*'s remains before the wreckage burned itself out; they organized themselves enough to assign responsibilities.

Later they persisted: they found rocks and chipped them in order to work with the vegetation; they made clothing out of leaves and the skins of small animals; they taught themselves how to weave shelter; they kept their population going.

Next they struggled. After all, what good did it do them to have a world if they couldn't fight over it?

And eventually, they began to reinvent the knowledge they had lost.

The inhabitants of Aster considered all this a slow process. From their point of view, it seemed to take an exceptionally long time. But judged by the way planetary civilizations usually evolved, Asterin history moved with considerable celerity. A thousand years after the Crash, Aster's people had remembered the wheel. (Some theorists argued that the wheel had never actually been forgotten. But to be useful, it needed someplace to roll—and Aster was a jungle. For several centuries, no wheel could compare in value with a good ax. Old memories of the wheel failed to take hold until after the Asterins had cleared enough ground to make its value apparent.) A thousand years after the wheel, the printing press came back into existence. (One of the major problems the Asterins had throughout their history to this point was what to do with all the dead lumber they created by making enough open space for their towns, fields, and roads. The reappearance of paper offered only a trivial solution until the printing press came along.) And a thousand years after the printing press, *Aster's Hope* was ready for her mission. Although they didn't know it, the people of Aster had beaten Earth's time for the same development by several thousand years.

Determination had a lot to do with it. People who came so far from Earth in order to procure the endurance of the human race didn't look kindly on anything that was less than what they wanted. But determination required an object: people had to know what they wanted. The alternative was a history full of wars, since determined people who didn't know what they wanted tended to be unnecessarily aggressive.

That object—the dream that shaped Asterin life and civilization from the earliest generations; the inborn sense of common purpose and yearning that kept the wars short, caused people to share what they knew, and inspired progress—was provided by the legends of Earth and *Aster*.

Within two generations after the Crash, no one knew even vaguely where Earth was: the knowledge as well as the tools of astrogation had been lost. Two generations after that, it was no longer clear what Earth had been like. And after two more generations, the reality of space flight had begun to pass out of the collective Asterin imagination.

But the *ideas* endured.

Earth.

Aster.

'Nicians and 'puters.

Sleep.

On Aster, perhaps more than anywhere else in the galaxy, dreams provided the stuff of purpose. On Aster evolved a civilization driven by legends. Communally and individually, the images and passions that fired the mind during physical sleep became the goals that shaped the mind while it was awake.

To rediscover Earth.

And go back.

For centuries, of course, this looked like nonsense. If it had been a conscious choice rather than a planetary dream, it would have been discarded long ago. But since it was a dream, barely articulate except in poetry and painting and the secret silence of the heart, it held on until its people were ready for it.

Until, that is, the Asterins had reinvented radio telescopes and other receiving gear of sufficient sophistication to begin interpreting the signals they heard from the heavens.

Some of those signals sounded like they came from Earth.

This was a remarkable achievement. After all, the transmissions the Asterins were looking at hadn't been intended for Aster. (Indeed, they may not have been intended for anybody at all. It was far more likely that these signals were random emissions—the detritus, perhaps, or a world talking to itself and its planets.) They had been traveling for so long, had passed through so many different gravity wells on the way, and were so diffuse, that not even the wildest optimist in Aster's observatories could argue that these signals were messages. In fact, they were scarcely more than whispers in the ether, sighs, compared to which some of the more distant stars were shouting.

And yet, impelled by an almost unacknowledged dream,

the Asterins had developed equipment that enabled them not only to hear those whispers, sort them out of the cosmic radio cacophony, and make some surprisingly acute deductions about what (or who) caused them, but also to identify a possible source on the star charts.

The effect on Aster was galvanic. In simple terms, the communal dream came leaping suddenly out of the unconscious.

Earth. EARTH.

After that, it was only a matter of minutes before somebody said, "We ought to try to go there."

Which was exactly—a hundred years and an enormous expenditure of global resources, time, knowledge, and determination later—what *Aster's Hope* was doing.

Naturally enough—people being what they were—there were quite a few men and women on Aster who didn't believe in the mission. And there was also a large number who did believe who still had enough common sense or native pessimism to be cautious. As a result, there was a large planet-wide debate while *Aster's Hope* was being planned and built. Some people insisted on saying things like, "What if it isn't Earth at all? What if it's some alien planet where they don't know humanity from bat dung and don't care?"

Or: "At this distance, your figures aren't accurate within ten parsecs. How do you propose to compensate for that?"

Or: "What if the ship encounters someone else along the way? Finding intelligent life might be even more important than finding Earth. Or they might not like having our ship wander into their space. They might blow *Aster's Hope* to pieces—and then come looking for us."

Or, of course: "What if the ship gets all the way out there and doesn't find anything at all?"

Well, even the most avid proponent of the mission was able to admit that it would be unfortunate if *Aster's Hope* were to run a thousand light-years across the galaxy and then fail. So the planning and preparation spent on designing the ship and selecting and training the crew was prodigious. But the Asterins didn't actually start to build their ship until they found an answer to what they considered the most fundamental question about the mission.

On perhaps any other inhabited planet in the galaxy, that question would have been the question of speed. A thousand light-years was too far away. Some way of traveling faster than the speed of light was necessary. But the Asterins had a blind spot. They knew from legend that their ancestors had *slept* during a centuries-long, space-normal voyage; and they were simply unable to think realistically about traveling in any other way. They learned, as Earth had millennia ago, that c was a theoretical absolute limit: they believed it and turned their attention in other directions.

No, the question that troubled them was safety. They wanted to be able to send out *Aster's Hope* certain that no passing hostile, meteor shower, or accident of diplomacy would be able to destroy her.

So she wasn't built until a poorly paid instructor at an obscure university suddenly managed to make sense out of a field of research that people had been laughing at for years:

C-vector.

For people who hadn't done their homework in theoretical mathematics or abstract physics, "c-vector" was defined as "at right angles to the speed of light." Which made no sense to anyone—but that didn't stop the Asterins from having fun with it. Before long, they discovered that they could build a generator to project a c-vector field.

If that field were projected around an object, it formed an impenetrable shield—a screen against which bullets and laser cannon and hydrogen torpedoes had no effect. (Any projectile or force that hit the shield bounced away "at right angles to the speed of light" and ceased to exist in material space. When this was discovered, several scientists spent several years wondering if a c-vector field could somehow be used as a faster-than-light drive for a spaceship. But no one was able to figure out just what direction "at right angles to the speed of light" was.) This appeared to have an obvious use as a weapon—project a field at an object, watch the object disappear—until the researchers learned that the field couldn't be projected either at or around any object unless the object and the field generator were stationary in relation to each other. But fortunately, the c-vector field had an even more obvious application for the men and women who were planning *Aster's Hope*.

If the ship were equipped with c-vector shields, she would be safe from any disaster short of direct collision with a star. And if the ship were equipped with a c-vector self-destruct, Aster would be safe from any disaster that might happen to—or be caused by—the crew of *Aster's Hope*.

Construction on the ship commenced almost immediately.

And eventually it was finished. The linguists and biologists and physicists were trained. The meditechs and librarians were equipped. The diplomats were instructed. Each of the 'nician and 'puter teams knew how to take *Aster's Hope* down to her microchips and rebuild (not to mention repro) her from spare parts.

Leaving orbit, setting course, building up speed, the ship arced past Philomel and Periwinkle on her way into the galactic void of the future. For the Asterins, it was as if legends had come back to life—as if a dream crouching in the human psyche since before the Crash had stood up and become real.

But six months later, roughly 0.4 light-years from Aster, Temple and Gracias weren't thinking about legends. They didn't see themselves as protectors of a dream. When the emergency brapper went off, they did what any dedicated, well-trained, and quick-thinking Service personnel would have done: they panicked.

But while they panicked, they ran naked as children in the direction of the nearest auxcompcom.

In crude terms, the difference between 'nicians and 'puters was the difference between hardware and software—although there was quite a bit of overlap, of course. Temple made equipment work; Gracias told it what to do. It would've taken her hours to figure out how to do what he'd done to the door sensors. But when they heard the brapper and rolled off the pallet with her ahead of him and headed out of the capsule chamber, and the door didn't open, he was the one who froze.

"Damn," he muttered. "That repro won't cancel for another twenty minutes."

He looked like he was thinking something abusive about himself, so she snapped at him, "Hold it open for me, idiot."

He thudded a palm against his forehead. "Right."

Practically jumping into range of the sensor, he got the door open; and she passed him on his way out into the corridor. But she had to wait for him again at the auxcompcom door. "Come on. Come *on*," she gretted. "Whatever that brapper means, it isn't good."

"I know." Leftover sweat made his face slick, gave him a look of too much fear. Grimly, he pushed through the sensor field into the auxcompcom room and headed for his chair at the main com console.

Temple followed, jumped into her seat in front of her hardware controls. But for a few seconds neither of them looked at their buttons and readouts. They were fixed on the main screen above the consoles.

The ship's automatic scanners were showing a blip against the deep background of the stars. Even at this distance, Temple and Gracias didn't need the comp to tell them the dot of light on the phosphors of the screen was moving. They could see it by watching the stars recede as the scanners focused in on the blip.

It was coming toward them.

It was coming fast.

"An asteroid?" Temple asked, mostly to hear somebody say something. The comp was supposed to put *Aster's Hope* on emergency alert whenever it sensed a danger of collision with any object large enough to be significant.

"Oh, sure." Gracias poked his blunt fingers around his board, punching readouts up onto the other auxcompcom screens. Numbers and schematics flashed. "If asteroids change course."

"Change—?"

"Just did an adjustment," he confirmed. "Coming right at us. Also"—pointed at a screen to her left—"decelerating."

She stared at the screen, watched the numbers jump. Numbers were his department; he was faster at them than she was. But she knew what words meant. "Then it's a ship."

Gracias acted like he hadn't heard her. He was watching the screens as if he were close to apoplexy.

"That doesn't make sense," she went on. "If there are ships this close to Aster, why haven't we heard from them? We should've picked up their transmissions. They should've heard us. God knows we've been broadcasting enough noise for the past couple of centuries. Are we hailing it?"

"We're hailing," he said. "No answer." He paused for a second, then announced: "Estimated about three times our size." He sounded stunned. Carefully, he said, "The comp estimated it's decelerating from above the speed of light."

She couldn't help herself. "That's impossible," she snapped. "Your eyes are tricking you. Check it again."

He hit some more buttons, and the numbers on the screen twisted themselves into an extrapolation graph. Whatever it was, the oncoming ship was still moving faster than *Aster's Hope*—and it was still decelerating.

For a second she put her hands over her face, squeezed the heels of her palms against her temples. Her pulse felt like she was going into adrenaline overload. But this was what she'd been trained for. Abruptly, she dropped her arms and looked at the screens again. The blip was still coming, but the graph hadn't changed.

From above the speed of light. Even though the best Asterin scientists had always said that was impossible.

Oh, well, she muttered to herself. One more law of nature down the tubes. Easy come, easy go.

"Why don't they contact us?" she asked. "If we're aware of them, they must know we're here."

"Don't need to," Gracias replied through his concentration. "Been scanning us since they hit space-normal speed. The comp reports scanner probes everywhere. Strong enough to take your blood pressure." Then he stiffened, sat up straighter, spat a curse. "Probes are trying to break into the comp."

Temple gripped the arms of her seat. This was his department: she was helpless. "Can they do it? Can you stop them?"

"Encryption's holding them out." He studied his readouts, flicked his eyes past the screens. "Won't last. Take com."

Without waiting for an answer, he keyed his console to hers and got out of his seat. Quickly, he went to the other main console in the room, the comp repro board.

Feeling clumsy now as she never did when she was working with tools or hardware, she accepted com and began trying to monitor the readouts. But the numbers swam, and the prompts didn't seem to make sense. Operating in emergency mode, the comp kept asking her to ask it questions; but she couldn't think of any for it. Instead, she asked Gracias, "What're you doing?"

His hands stabbed up and down the console. He was still sweating. "Changing the encryption," he said. "Whole series of changes. Putting them on a loop.'' When he was done, he took a minute to double-check his repro. Then he gave a grunt of satisfaction and came back to his com seat. While he keyed his controls away from Temple, he said, ''This way, the comp can't be broken by knowing the present code. Have to know what code's coming up next. That loop changes often enough to keep us safe for a while.''

She permitted herself a sigh of relief—and a soft snarl of anger at the oncoming ship. She didn't like feeling helpless. ''If those bastards can't break the comp, do you think they'll try to contact us?''

He shrugged, glanced at his board. ''Channels are open. They talk, we'll hear.'' For a second he chewed his lower lip. Then he leaned back in his seat and swung around to face her. His eyes were dark with fear.

''Don't like this,'' he said distinctly. ''Don't like it at all. A faster-than-light ship coming straight for us. Straight for Aster. And they don't talk. Instead, they try to break the comp.''

She knew his fear. She was afraid herself. But when he looked like he needed her, she put her own feelings aside. ''Would you say,'' she said, drawling so she would sound sardonic and calm, ''that we're being approached by somebody hostile?''

He nodded dumbly.

''Well, we're safe enough. Maybe the speed of light isn't unbreakable, but a c-vector shield is. So what we have to worry about is Aster. If that ship gets past us, we'll never catch up with it. How far away is it now?''

Gracias turned back to his console, called up some numbers. ''Five minutes.'' His face didn't show it, but she could hear in his voice that he was grateful for her show of steadiness.

''I don't think we should wait to see what happens,'' she said. ''We should send a message home now.''

''Right.'' He went to work immediately, composing data

on the screens, calling up the scant history of *Aster's Hope*'s contact with the approaching ship. "Continuous broadcast," he murmured as he piped information to the transmitters. "Constant update. Let Aster know everything we can."

Temple nodded her approval, then gaped in astonishment as the screens broke up into electronic garbage. A sound like frying circuitry spat from all the speakers at once—from the hailing channels as well as from intraship. She almost let out a shout of surprise; but training and recognition bit it back. She knew what that was.

"Jammer," Gracias said. "We're being jammed."

"From this distance?" she demanded. "From *this distance?* That kind of signal should take"—she checked her readout—"three and some fraction minutes to get here. How do they do that?"

He didn't reply for a few seconds; he was busy restoring order to the screens. Then he said, "They've got faster-than-light drive. Scanners make ours look like toys. Why not better radio?"

"Or maybe," she put in harshly, "they started broadcasting their jammer as soon as they picked us up." In spite of her determination to be calm, she was breathing hard, sucking uncertainty and anger through her teeth. "Can you break through?"

He tried, then shook his head. "Too thick."

"Damn! Gracias, what're we going to do? If we can't warn Aster, then it's up to us. If that ship is hostile, we've got to fight it somehow."

"Not built for it," he commented. "*Aster's Hope*. About as maneuverable as a rock."

She knew. Everything about the ship had been planned with defense rather than offense in mind. She was intended, first, to survive: second, not to prematurely give anything away about her homeworld. In fact as well as in appearance, she wasn't meant as a weapon of war. And one reason for this was that the mission planners had never once considered the idea of encountering an alien (never mind hostile) ship this close to home.

She found herself wishing for different armament, more speed, and a whole lot less mass. But that couldn't be helped now. "We need to get their attention somehow," she said. "Make them cope with us before they go on." An idea struck her. "What've the scanners got on them?"

"Still not much. Size. Velocity." Then, as if by intuition, he seemed to know what she had in mind. "Shields, of course. Look like ordinary force-disruption fields."

She almost smiled. "You're kidding. No c-vector?"

"Nope."

"Then maybe—" She thought furiously. "Maybe there's something we can do. If we can slow them down, maybe do them some damage—and they can't hurt us at all—maybe they won't go on to Aster.

"Gracias, are we on a collision course with that thing?"

He glanced at her. "Not quite. Going to miss by a kilometer."

As if she were in command of *Aster's Hope*, she said, "Put us in the way."

A grin flashed through his concentration. "Yes, sir, Temple, ma'am, sir. Good idea."

At once, he started keying instructions into his com board.

While he set up the comp to adjust *Aster's Hope*'s course—and then to adjust it continuously to keep the ship as squarely as possible in the oncoming vessel's path—Temple secured herself in her momentum restraints. Less than three minutes, she thought. Three minutes to impact. For a moment, she thought Gracias was moving too slowly. But before she could say anything, he took his hands off the board and started strapping his own restraints. "Twenty seconds," he said.

She braced herself. "Are we going to feel it?"

"Inertial shift? Of course."

"No, idiot. Are we going to feel the impact?"

He shrugged. "If we hit. Nobody's ever hit a c-vector shield that hard with something that big."

Then Temple's stomach turned on its side, and the whole auxcompcon felt like it was starting into a spin.

The course adjustment was over almost immediately: at the speeds *Aster's Hope* and the alien were traveling, one kilometer was a subtle shift.

Less than two and a half minutes. If we hit. She couldn't sit there and wait for it in silence. "Are the scanners doing any better? We ought to be able to count their teeth from this range."

"Checking," he said. With a few buttons, he called a new display up onto the main screen—

—and stared at it without saying anything. His mouth hung open: his whole face was blank with astonishment.

"Gracias?" She looked at the screen for herself. With a mental effort, she tightened down the screws on her brain, forced herself to see the pattern in the numbers. Then she lost control of her voice: it went up like a yell. "Gracias?"

"Don't believe it," he murmured. "No. Don't believe it."

According to the scanners, the oncoming ship was crammed to the walls with computers and weaponry, equipment of every size and shape, mechanical and electrical energy of all kinds—and not one single living organism.

"There's nothing—" She tried to say it, but at first she couldn't. Her throat shut down, and she couldn't unlock it. She had to force a swallow past the rigid muscles. "There's nothing alive in that ship."

Abruptly, *Aster's Hope* went into a course shift that felt like it was going to pull her heart out of her chest. The alien was taking evasive action, and *Aster's Hope* was compensating.

One minute.

"That's crazy." She was almost shouting. "It comes in faster than light, and starts decelerating right at us, and jams our transmissions, and shifts course to try to keep us from running into it—and there's nobody *alive* on board? Whom do we talk to if we want to surrender?''

''Take it easy,'' Gracias said. ''One thing at a time. Artificial intelligence is feasible. Ship thinks for itself. Or on automatic. Exploration probe might—''

Another course shift cut him off. A violent inertial kick—too violent. Her head jerked to the left. Alarms went off like klaxons. *Aster's Hope* was trying to bring herself back toward collision with the other ship, trying—

The screens flashed loud warnings, danger signs as familiar to her as her name. Three of the ship's thrusters were overheating critically. One was tearing itself to pieces under the shift stress. *Aster's Hope* wasn't made for this.

She was the ship's 'nician: she couldn't let *Aster's Hope* be damaged. ''Break off!'' she shouted through the squall of the alarms. ''We can't do it!''

Gracias slapped a hand at his board, canceled the collision course.

G-stress receded. Lights on Temple's board told her about thrusters damaged, doors jammed because they'd shifted on their mounts, a locker in the meditech section sprung, a handful of cryogenic capsules gone on backup. But the alarms were cut off almost instantly.

For a second the collision warnings went into a howl. Then they stopped. The sudden silence felt louder than the alarms.

Gracias punched visual up onto the screens. He got a picture in time to see the other ship go by in a blur of metal too fast for the eye to track. From a range the scanners measured in tens of meters, the alien looked the size of a fortress—squat, squarish, enormous.

As it passed, it jabbed a bright red shaft of force at *Aster's Hope* from point-blank range.

All the screens in the auxcompcom went dark.

''God!'' Gracias gasped. ''Scanners burned out?''

That was Temple's province. She was still reeling from the shock, the knowledge that *Aster's Hope* had been fired upon; but her hands had been trained until they had a life of their own, and they knew what to do. Hardly more than a heartbeat after she understood what Gracias said, she sent in a diagnostic on the scanner circuits. The answer trailed across the screen in front of her.

"No damage," she reported.

"Then what?" He sounded flustered, groping for comprehension.

"Did you get any scan on that beam?" she returned. "Enough to analyze?" Then she explained: "Right angles to the speed of light isn't the same direction for every force. Maybe the c-vector sent this one off into some kind of wraparound field."

That was what he needed. "Right." His hands went to work on his board again.

Almost immediately, he had an answer. "Ion beam. Would've reduced us to subatomic particles without the shield. But only visual's lost. Scanners still functioning. Have visual back in a second."

"Good." She double-checked her own readouts, made sure that *Aster's Hope*'s attempts to maneuver with the alien hadn't done any urgent harm. At the same time, she reassured herself that the force of the ion beam hadn't been felt inside the shield. Then she pulled her attention back to the screens and Gracias.

"What's our friend doing now?"

He grunted, nodded up at the main screen. The comp was plotting another graph, showing the other ship's course in relation to *Aster's Hope*.

She blinked at it. That was impossible. Impossible for a ship that size moving that fast to turn that hard.

But of course, she thought with an odd sensation of craziness, there isn't anything living aboard to feel the G-stress.

"Well." She swallowed at the way her voice shook. "At least we got their attention."

Gracias tried to laugh, but it came out like a snarl. "Good for us. Now what?"

"We could try to run," she offered. "Put as much distance as possible between us and home."

He shook his head. "Won't work. They're faster."

"Besides which," she growled, "we've left a particle trail even *we* could follow all the way back to Aster. That and the incessant radio gabble— If that mechanical behemoth wants to find our homeworld, we might as well transmit a map."

He pulled back from his board, swung his seat to face her again. His expression troubled her. His eyes seemed dull, almost glazed, as if under pressure his intelligence were slowly losing its edge. "Got a choice?" he asked.

The thought that he might fail *Aster's Hope* made panic beat in her forehead; but she forced it down. "Sure," she snapped, trying to send him a spark of her own anger. "We can fight."

His eyes didn't focus on her. "Got laser cannon," he said. "Hydrogen torpedoes. Ship like that"—he nodded toward the screen—"won't have shields we can hurt. How can we fight?"

"You said they're ordinary force-disruption fields. We can break through that. Any sustained pounding can break through. That's why they didn't built *Aster's Hope* until they could do better."

He still didn't quite look at her. Enunciating carefully, he said, "I don't believe that ship has shields we can hurt."

Temple pounded the edge of her console. "Damn it, Gracias! We've got to try! We can't just sit here until they get bored and decide to go do something terrible to our homeworld. If you aren't interested—" Abruptly, she leaned back in her seat, took a deep breath, and held it to steady herself. Then she said quietly, "Key com over to me. I'll do it myself."

For a minute longer, he remained the way he was, his gaze staring unfocused past her chin. Slowly, he nodded. Moving sluggishly, he turned back to his console.

But instead of keying com over to Temple, he told the comp to begin decelerating *Aster's Hope*. Losing inertia so the ship could maneuver better.

Softly, she let a sigh of relief through her teeth.

While *Aster's Hope* braked, pulling her against her momentum restraints, and the unliving alien ship continued its impossible turn, she unlocked the weaponry controls on her console. A string of lights began to indicate the status of every piece of combative equipment *Aster's Hope* carried.

It wasn't supposed to be like this, Temple thought to herself. She'd never imagined it like this. When/if the Asterin mission encountered some unexpected form of life, another space-going vessel, a planetary intelligence, the whole situation should've been different. A hard-nosed distrust was to be expected: a fear of the unknown, a desire to protect the homeworld, communication problems, wise caution. But not unprovoked assault. Not an immediate pitched battle out in the middle of nowhere, with Aster itself at issue.

Not an alien ship full of nothing but machinery? Was that the crucial point?

All right: What purpose could a ship like that serve? Exploration probe? Then it wouldn't be hostile. A defense mechanism for a theoretically secure sector of space that *Aster's Hope* had somehow violated? But they were at least fifty light-years from the nearest neighbor to Aster's star; and it was difficult to imagine an intelligence so paranoid that its conception of "territorial space" reached out this far. Some kind of automated weapon? But Aster didn't have any enemies.

None of it made any sense. And as Temple tried to sort it out, her confusion grew worse. It started her sliding into panic.

Fortunately, Gracias chose that moment to ask gruffly, "Ready? It's hauling up on us fast. Be in range in a minute."

She made an effort to control her breathing, shake the knots of panic out of her mind. "Plot an evasive course," she said, "and key it to my board." Her weapons program had to know where *Aster's Hope* was going in order to use its armament effectively.

"Why?" he asked. "Don't need evasion. Shield'll protect us."

"To keep them guessing." Her tension was plain in her voice. "And to show them we can hit them on the run. Do it."

She thought he was moving too slowly. But faster than she could've done it, he had a plot up on the main screen, showing the alien's incoming course and the shifts *Aster's Hope* was about to make.

Temple tried to wipe the sweat from her palms on her bare legs; but it didn't do much good. Snarling at the way her hands felt, she poised them over the weapons com.

Gracias's plot stayed on the main screen; but the display in front of her gave Temple visual again, and she saw the alien ship approaching like a bright metal projectile the galaxy had flung to knock *Aster's Hope* out of the heavens. Suddenly frantic, as if she believed the other ship were actually going to crush her, she started firing.

Beams of light shot at the alien from every laser port the comp could bring to bear.

Though the ship was huge, the beams focused on a single section: Temple was trying to maximize their impact. When they hit the force-disruption field, light suddenly blared all across the spectrum, sending up a rainbow of coruscation.

"Negative," Gracias reported as *Aster's Hope* wrenched into her first evasion shift. "No effect."

Her weight rammed against the restraints, the skin of her cheeks pulling, Temple punched the weapons com into continuous fire, then concentrated on holding up her head so that she could watch the visual.

As her lasers turned the alien ship's shields into a fireworks display, another bright red shaft of force came as straight as a spear at *Aster's Hope*.

Again, the screen lost visual.

But this time Gracias was ready. He got scanner plots onto the screen while visual was out of use. Temple could see her laser fire like an equation on a graph connecting *Aster's Hope* and the unliving ship. Every few seconds, a line came back the other way—an ion beam as accurate as if *Aster's Hope* were stationary. "Any effect yet?" she gasped at Gracias as another evasion shift kicked her to the other side of her seat. "We're hitting them hard. It's got to have an effect."

"Negative," he repeated. "That shield disperses force almost as fast as it comes in. Doesn't weaken."

Then the attacker went past. In seconds it would be out of reach of Temple's laser cannon.

"Cancel evasion," she snapped, keying her com out of continuous fire. "Go after them. As fast as we can. Give me a chance to aim a torpedo."

"Right," he responded. And a second later, G-stress slammed at her as all the ship's thrusters went on full power, roaring for acceleration.

Aster's Hope steadied on the alien's course and did her best to match its speed.

"Now," Temple muttered. "Now. Before they start to turn." Her hands quick on the weapons board, she primed a whole barrage of hydrogen torpedoes. Then she pulled in course coordinates from the comp. "Go." With the flat of her hand on all the launch buttons at once, she fired.

The comp automatically blinked the c-vector shield to let the torpedoes out. Fired from a source moving as fast as *Aster's Hope* was, they attained 0.95c almost immediately and went after the other ship.

Gracias didn't wait for Temple's instructions. He reversed thrust, decelerating *Aster's Hope* again to stay as far as possible from the blast when the torpedoes hit.

If they hit. The scanner plot on the main screen showed that the alien was starting to turn.

"Come on," Temple breathed. Unconsciously, she pounded her fists on the arms of her seat. "Come on. Hit that bastard. Hit."

"Impact," Gracias said as all the blips on the scanner came together.

At that instant, visual cleared. They saw a hot white ball explode like a balloon of energy rupturing in all directions at once.

Then both visual and scan went haywire for a few long seconds. The detonation of that many hydrogen torpedoes at once filled all the space around *Aster's Hope* with chaos: energy emissions on every frequency, supercharged particles phasing in and out of existence as they scanned away from the point of explosion.

"Hit him," Gracias murmured.

Temple gripped the arms of her seat, stared at the garbage on the screens. "What do you think? Can they stand up to that?"

He didn't shrug. He looked like he didn't have that much energy left.

"Can't you clear the screens? We've got to *see*."

"The comp's doing it." Then, a second later: "Here it comes."

The screens wiped themselves clear, and a new scanner plot mapped the phosphors in front of him. It showed the alien turning hard, coming back toward *Aster's Hope*.

The readout was negative. No damage.

"Oh, God," she sighed. "I don't believe it." All the strength seemed to run out of her body. She sagged against her restraints. "Now what do we do?"

He went on staring at the screens for a long moment while the attacking ship completed its turn. Then he said, "Don't know. Try for collision again?"

When she didn't say anything, he gave the problem to the comp, told it to wait until the last possible instant—considering *Aster's Hope*'s poor maneuverability—and then thrust the ship into the alien's path. After that, he keyed his board onto automatic and leaned back in his restraints. To Temple's surprise, he yawned hugely.

"Need sleep," he mumbled thickly. "Be glad when this shift's over."

Surprise and fear made her acid. "You're not thinking very clearly, Gracias." She needed him, but he seemed to be getting farther and farther away. "Do you think the mission can continue after this? What do you think the chances are that that ship's going to give up and let us go on our way? My God, there isn't even anybody *alive* over there! The whole thing is just a machine. It can stay here and pound at us for centuries, and it won't even get bored. Or it can calculate the odds on Aster's building a c-vector shield big enough to cover the whole planet—and it can just forget about us, leave us here, and go attack our homeworld, because there won't be anything we can do to stop it and Aster is *unprotected*. We don't even know what it *wants*. We—"

She might have gone on, but the comp chose that moment to heave *Aster's Hope* in front of the alien. Every thruster screaming, the ship pulled her mass into a terrible acceleration, fighting for a collision her attacker couldn't avoid. Temple felt like she was being cut to pieces by the straps holding her in her seat. She tried to cry out, but she couldn't get any air into her lungs.

Her damage readout and lights began to put on a show.

But the alien ship skipped aside and went past without being touched.

For a second, *Aster's Hope* pulled around, trying to follow her opponent. Then Gracias forced himself forward and canceled the comp's collision instructions. Instantly, the G-stress eased. The ship settled onto a new heading chosen by her inertia, the alien already turning again to come after her.

"Damn," he said softly. "Damn it."

Temple let herself rest against her restraints. We can't—, she thought dully. Can't even run into that thing. It can't hurt us. But we can't hurt it. *Aster's Hope* wasn't built to be a warship. She wasn't supposed to protect her homeworld by fighting: she was supposed to protect it by being diplomatic and cunning and distant. If the worse came to the very worst, she was supposed to protect Aster by not coming back. But this was a mission of peace, the mission of Aster's dream: the ship was never intended to fight for anything except her own survival.

"For some reason," Temple murmured into the silence of the auxcompcom, "I don't think this is what I had in mind when I joined the Service."

Gracias started to say something. The sound of frying circuitry from the speakers cut him off. It got Temple's attention like a splash of hot oil.

This time it wasn't the jammer. She saw that in the readouts jumping across the screens. It was another scanner probe, like the one that had tried to break into the comp earlier. But now it was tearing into the ship's unprotected communication hardware—the intraship speakers.

After the initial burst of static, the sounds began to change. Frying became whistles and grunts, growls and moans. For a minute she had the impression she was listening to some inconceivable alien language. But before she could call up the comp's translation programs—or ask Gracias to do it—the interference on the speakers modulated until it became a voice and words.

A voice from every speaker in the auxcompcom at once.

Words Temple and Gracias understood.

The voice sounded like a poorly calibrated voder, metallic and insensitive. But the words were distinct.

"Surrender, badlife. You will be destroyed."

The scanner probe had turned up the gain on all the speakers. The voice was so loud it seemed to rattle the auxcompcom door on its mounts.

Involuntarily, Temple gasped, "Good God. What in hell is that?"

Gracias replied unnecessarily, "The other ship. Talking to us." He sounded dull, defeated, almost uninterested.

"I *know* that," she snapped. "For God's sake, *wake up!*" Abruptly, she slapped a hand at her board, opened a radio channel. "Who are you?" she demanded into her mike. "What do you want? We're no threat to you. Our mission is peaceful. Why are you attacking us?"

The scanner plot on the main screen showed that the alien ship had already completed its turn and caught up with *Aster's Hope*. Now it was matching her course and speed, shadowing her at a distance of less than half a kilometer.

"Surrender," the speakers blared again. "You are badlife. You will be destroyed. You must surrender."

Frantic with fear and urgency, and not able to control it, Temple slapped off her mike and swung her seat to rage at Gracias, "Can't you turn that *down?* It splitting my eardrums!"

Slowly, as if he were half-asleep, he tapped a few buttons on his console. Blinking at the readouts, he murmured, "Hardware problem. Scanner probe's stronger than the comp's line voltage. Have to reduce gain manually." Then he widened his eyes at something that managed to surprise him even in his stunned state. "Only speakers affected are in here. This room. Bastard knows exactly where we are. And every circuit around us."

That didn't make sense. It made so little sense that it caught her attention, focused her in spite of her panic. "Wait a minute," she said. "They're only using *these* speakers?

The ones in this room? How do they know we're in here? Gracias, there are 392 people aboard. How can they possibly know you and I are the only ones awake?"

"You must surrender," the speakers squalled again. "You cannot flee. You have no speed. You cannot fight. Your weapons are puny. When your shields are broken, you will be helpless. Your secrets will be lost. Only surrender can save your lives."

She keyed her mike again. "No. You're making a mistake. We're no threat to you. Who are you? What do you want?"

"Death," the speakers replied. "Death for all life. Death for all worlds. You must surrender."

Gracias closed his eyes. Without looking at what he was doing, he moved his hands on the board, got visual back up on the main screen. The screen showed the alien ship sailing like a skyborne fort an exact distance from *Aster's Hope*. It held its position so precisely that it looked motionless. It seemed so close Temple thought she could have hit it with a rock.

"Maybe," Gracias sighed, "they don't know we're the only ones awake."

She didn't understand what he was thinking, but she caught at it as if it were a lifeline. "What do you mean?"

He didn't open his eyes. "Cryogenically frozen," he said. "Vital signs so low the monitors can hardly read them. Capsules are just equipment. And the comp's encrypted. Maybe that scanner probe thinks we're the only life-forms here."

She caught her breath. "If that's true—" Ideas reeled through her head. "They probably want us to surrender because they can't figure out our shields. And because they want to know what we're doing, just the two of us in this big ship. It might be suicide for them to go on to Aster without knowing the answers to questions like that. And while they're

trying to find out how to break down our shields, the
probably stay right there.

"Gracias," she said, her heart pounding with unreason
hope, "how long would it take you to repro the comp
project a c-vector field at that ship? We're stationary
relation to each other. We can use our field generator
weapon."

That got his eyes open. When he rolled his head to the
to face her, he looked sick. "How long will it take you,"
asked, "to rebuild the generator for that kind of projecti
And what will we use for shields while you're working?"

He was right: she knew it as soon as he said it. But th
had to be something they could do, *had* to be. They coul
just sail across the galactic void for the next few thous
years while their homeworld was destroyed behind them.

There had to be *something* they could do.

The speakers started trumpeting again. "Badlife, you h
been warned. The destruction of your ship will now be
You must surrender to save your lives."

Badlife, Temple wondered crazily to herself. What d
that mean, *badlife?* Is the ship some kind of automatic wea
gone berserk, shooting around the galaxy exterminating w
it calls badlife?

How is it going to destroy *Aster's Hope?*

She didn't have to wait long to find out. Almost imm
ately, she felt a heavy metallic thunk vibrate through the s
that held her seat to the floor. A fraction of an instant late
small flash of light from somewhere amidships on the atta
ing vessel showed that a projectile weapon had been fired

Then alarms began to howl, and the damage readouts
Temple's board began to spit intimations of disaster.

Training took over through her panic. Her hands danced
the console, gleaning data. "We've been hit." Through
shield. "Some kind of projectile." *Through the c-vec
shield.* "It's breached the hull." All three layers of the shi

metal skin. ''I don't know what it was, but it's punched a hole all the way to the outer-shell wall.''

Gracias interrupted her. ''How big's the hole?''

''About a meter square.'' She went back to the discipline of her report. ''The comp is closing pressure doors, isolating the breach. Damage is minor—we've lost one heat exchanger for the climate control. But if they do that again, they might hit something more vital.'' Trusting the c-vector shields, *Aster's Hope*'s builders hadn't tried to make her particularly hard to damage in other ways.

The alien ship did it again. Another tearing thud as the projectile hit. Another small flash of light from the attacker. More alarms. Temple's board began to look like it was monitoring a madhouse.

''The same place,'' she said, fighting a rising desire to scream. ''It's pierced outer-shell. Atmosphere loss is trivial. The comp is closing more pressure doors.'' She tapped commands into the console. ''Extrapolating the path of those shots, I'm closing all the doors along the way.'' Then she called up a damage estimate on the destructive force of the projectiles. ''Two more like that will breach one of the mid-shell cryogenic chambers. We're going to start losing people.''

And if the projectiles went on pounding the same place, deeper and deeper into the ship, they would eventually reach the c-vector generator.

It was true: *Aster's Hope* was going to be destroyed.

''Gracias, what is it? This is supposed to be impossible. How are they doing it to us?''

''Happening too fast to scan.'' In spite of his torpor, he already had all the answers he needed up on his screen. ''Faster-than-light projectile. Flash shows after impact. Vaporize us if we didn't have the shields. C-vector brings it down to space-normal speed. But then it's inside the field. Ship wasn't built for this.''

A faster— For a moment her brain refused to understand the words. A faster-than-light projectile. And when it hit the shield, just enough of its energy went off at right angles to the speed of light to slow it down. Not enough to stop it.

As if in mockery, the speakers began to blast again. "Your ship is desired intact. Surrender. Your lives will be spared. You will be granted opportunity to serve as goodlife."

So exasperated she hardly knew what she was doing, Temple slapped open a radio channel. "Shut up!" she shouted across the black space between *Aster's Hope* and the alien. "Stop shooting! Give us a chance to think! How can we surrender if you don't give us a chance to think?"

Gulping air, she looked at Gracias. She felt wild and didn't know what to do about it. His eyes were dull, low-lidded: he might've been going to sleep. Sick with fear, she panted at him, "Do something! You're the ship's 'puter. You're supposed to take care of her. You're supposed to have ideas. *They can't do this to my ship!*"

Slowly—too slowly—he turned toward her. His neck hardly seemed strong enough to hold his head up. "Do what? Shield's all we've got. Now it isn't any good. That"—he grimaced—"that thing—has everything. Nothing we can do."

Furiously, she ripped off her restraints, heaved out of her seat so she could go to him and shake him. "There has to be something we can do!" she shouted into his face. "We're human! That thing's nothing but a pile of microchips and demented programming. We're more than it is! Don't surrender! *Think!*"

For a moment he stared at her. Then he let out an empty laugh. "What good's being human? Doesn't help. Only intelligence and power count. Those machines have intelligence. Maybe more than we do. More advanced than we are. And a lot more powerful." Dully, he repeated, "Nothing we can do."

In response, Temple wanted to rage at him: We can refuse

to give up! We can keep fighting! We're not beaten as long as we're stubborn enough to keep fighting! But as soon as she thought that, she knew she was wrong. There was nothing in life as stubborn as a machine doing what it was told.

"Intelligence and power aren't all that count," she protested, trying urgently to find what she wanted, something she could believe in, something that would pull Gracias out of his defeat. "What about emotion? That ship can't care about anything. What about love?"

When she said that, his expression crumpled. Roughly, he put his hands over his face. His shoulders knotted as he struggled with himself.

"Well, then," she went on, too desperate to pull back, "we can use the self-destruct. Kill *Aster's Hope*"—the bare idea choked her, but she forced it out—"to keep them from finding out how the shield generator works. Altruism. That's something they don't have."

Abruptly, Gracias wrenched his hands down from his face, pulled them into fists, pounded them on the arms of his seat. "Stop it," he whispered. "*Stop* it. Machines are altruistic. Don't care about themselves at all. Only thing they can't do is feel bad when what they want is taken away. Any second now, they're going to start firing again. We're dead, and there's nothing we can do about it, *nothing*. Stop breaking my heart."

His anger and rejection should have hurt her. But he was awake and alive, and his eyes were on fire in the way she loved. Suddenly, she wasn't alone: he'd come back from his dull horror. "Gracias," she said softly. "Gracias." Possibilities were moving in back of her brain, ideas full of terror and hope, ideas she was afraid to say out loud. "We can wake everybody up. See if anybody else can think of anything. Put it to a vote. Let the mission make its own decision.

"Or we can—"

What she was thinking scared her out of her mind, but she

told him what it was, anyway. Then she let him yell at her until he couldn't think of any more arguments against it.

After all, they had to save Aster.

Her part of the preparations was simple enough. She left him in the auxcompcom and took the nearest shaft down to the inner-shell. First she visited a locker to get her tools and a magnetic sled. Then she went to the central command center.

In the cencom, she keyed a radio channel. Hoping the alien was listening, she said, "I'm Temple. My partner is crazy—he wants to fight. I want to surrender. I'll have to kill him. It won't be easy. Give me some time. I'm going to disable the shields."

She took a deep breath, forced herself to sigh. Could a mechanical alien understand a sigh? "Unfortunately, when the shields go down, it's going to engage an automatic self-destruct. That I can't disable. So don't try to board the ship. You'll get blown to pieces. I'll come out to you.

"I want to be goodlife, not badlife. To prove my good faith, I'm going to bring with me a portable generator for the c-vector field we use as shields. You can study it, learn how it works. Frankly, you need it." The alien ship could probably hear the stress in her voice, so she made an extra effort to sound sarcastic. "You'd be dead by now if we weren't on a peace mission. We know how to break down your shields—we just don't have the firepower."

There. She clicked off the transmitter. Let them think about that for a while.

From the cencom, she opened one of the access hatches and took her tools and mag-sled down into the core of *Aster's Hope*, where most of the ship's vital equipment operated—the comp banks, the artificial gravity inducer, the primary life-support systems, the c-vector generator.

While she worked, she didn't talk to Gracias. She wanted to know how he was doing; but she already knew the intraship communication lines weren't secure from the alien's scanner probe.

In a relatively short time—she was *Aster's Hope*'s 'nician and knew what she was doing—she had the ship's self-destruct device detached from its comp links and loaded onto the mag-sled. That device (called "the black box" by the mission planners) was no more than half Temple's size, but it was a fully functional c-vector generator, capable from its own energy cells of sending the entire ship off at right angles to the speed of light, even if the rest of *Aster's Hope* were inoperative. With the comp links disconnected, Gracias couldn't do anything to destroy the ship; but Temple made sure the self-destruct's radio trigger was armed and ready before she steered the mag-sled up out of the core.

This time when she left the cencom, she took a shaft up to the mid-shell chamber where she and Gracias had their cryogenic capsules. He wasn't there yet. While she waited for him, she went around the room and disconnected all the speakers. She hoped her movements might make her look from a distance like one furtive life-form preparing an ambush for another.

He was slow in coming. The delay made her fret. Was it possible that he had lapsed back into half-somnolent panic? Or had he changed his mind—decided she was crazy? He'd yelled at her as if she were asking him to help her commit suicide. What if he—?

The door whooshed open, and Gracias came into the chamber almost at a run. "Have to hurry," he panted. "Only got fifteen minutes before the shield drops."

His face looked dark and bruised and fierce, as if he'd spent the time she was away from him hitting himself with his fists. For a second, Temple caught a glimpse of just how terrible what she was asking him to do was.

Ignoring the need for haste, she went to him, put her arms

around him, hugged him hard. "Gracias," she breathed, "it's going to work. Don't look at me like that."

He returned her embrace so roughly he made her gasp. But almost immediately he let her go. "Keep your suit radio open," he rasped while he pushed past her and moved to his capsule. "If you go off, the comp will take over. Blow you out of space." Harshly, he pulled himself over the edge into the bed of the capsule. "Two-stage code," he continued. "First say my name." His eyes burned blackly in their sockets, savage with pain and fear. "If that works, say 'Aster.' If it *doesn't* work, say 'Aster.' Whatever happens. Ship doesn't deserve to die in her sleep."

As if he were dismissing her, he reclined in the capsule and folded his arms over his chest.

But when she went to him to say good-bye, he reached out urgently and caught her wrist. "Why?" he asked softly. "Why are we doing it this way?"

Oh, Gracias. His desperation hurt her. "Because this is the only way we can persuade them not to blow up *Aster's Hope*—or come storming aboard—when we let down the shields."

His voice hissing between his clenched teeth, he asked, "Why can't I come with you?"

Tears she couldn't stop ran down her cheeks. "They'll be more likely to trust me if they think I've killed you. And somebody has to stay here. To decide what to do if this all goes wrong. These are the jobs we've been trained for."

For a long moment he faced her with his dark distress. Then he let go of her arm. "Comp'll wake me up when you give the first code."

She was supposed to be hurrying. She could hardly bear to leave him; but she forced herself to kiss him quickly, then step back and engage the lid of his capsule. Slowly, the lid closed down over him until it sealed. The gas that prepared his body for freezing filled the capsule. But he went on staring out at her, darkly, hotly, until the inside of the lid frosted opaque.

Ignoring the tears that streaked her face, she left him. The sled floating on its magnetic field ahead of her, she went to the shaft and rode up to outer-shell, as close as she could safely get to the point where the faster-than-light projectiles had breached *Aster's Hope*'s hull. From there she steered the mag-sled into the locker room beside the air lock that gave access to the nearest exterior port.

In the locker room she put on her suit. Because everything depended on it, she tested the suit's radio unit circuits four times. Then she engaged the suit's pressure seals and took the mag-sled into the air lock.

Monitored automatically by the comp, she cycled the air lock to match the null atmosphere/gravity in the port. After that, she didn't need the mag-sled anymore. With hardly a minute to spare, she nudged the black box out into the high metal cave of the port and keyed the controls to open the port doors.

The doors slid back, leaving her face to face with the naked emptiness of space.

At first she couldn't see the alien ship: everything outside the port was too dark. But *Aster's Hope* was still less than half a light-year from home; and when Temple's eyes adjusted to the void, she found that Aster's sun sent out enough illumination to show the attacking vessel against the background of the stars.

It appeared too big and fatal for her to hurt.

But after the way Gracias had looked at her in farewell, she couldn't bear to hesitate. This had to be done. As soon as the alarm went off in the port—and all over *Aster's Hope*—warning the ship that the shields were down, she cleared her throat, forced her taut voice into use.

"All right," she said into the radio. "I've done it. I've killed my partner. I've shut down the shields. I want you to keep your promise. Save my life. I'm coming out. If we're within a hundred kilometers of the ship when the automatic self-destruct goes, we'll go with it.

"I've got the portable field generator with me. I can show you how to use it. I can teach you how to make it. You've got to keep your promise."

She didn't wait for an answer: she didn't expect one. The only answer she'd received earlier was a cessation of the shooting. That was enough. All she had to do was get close to the alien ship.

Grimly, she tightened her grip on one handle of the black box and fired her suit's small thrusters to impel herself and her burden past the heavy doors out into the dark.

Automatically, the comp closed the doors after her, shutting her out.

For an instant her own smallness almost overwhelmed her. No Asterin had been where she was now: outside her ship half a light-year from home. All of her training had been in comfortable orbit around Aster, the planet acting as a balance to the immensity of space. And there had been light! Here there were only the gleams and glitters emitted by *Aster's Hope*'s cameras and scanners—and the barely discernible bulk of the alien, its squat lines only less dark than the black heavens.

But she knew that if she let herself think that way, she would go mad. Gritting her teeth, she focused her attention—and her thrusters—toward the enemy.

Now everything depended on whether the alien knew there were people alive aboard *Aster's Hope*. Whether the alien had been able to analyze or deduce all the implications of the c-vector shield. And whether she could get away.

The size of the other vessel made the distance appear less than it was; but after a while she was close enough to see a port opening in the side of the ship.

Then—so suddenly that she flinched and broke into a sweat—a voice came over her suit radio.

"You will enter the dock open before you. It is heavily shielded and invulnerable to explosion. You will remain in the dock with your device. If this is an attempt at treachery, you will be destroyed by your own weapon.

"If you are goodlife, you will be spared. You will remain with your device while you dismantle it for inspection. When its principles are understood, you will be permitted to answer other questions."

"Thanks a whole bunch," she muttered in response. But she didn't let herself slow down or shy away. Instead, she went straight toward the open port until the dock was yawning directly in front of her.

Then she put to the test the repro Gracias had done on the comp.

What she had to do was so risky, so unreasonably dangerous, that she did it almost without thinking about it, as if she'd been doing things like that all her life.

Aiming her thrusters right against the side of the black box, she fired them so that the box was kicked hard and fast into the mouth of the dock and her own momentum in that direction was stopped. There she waited until she saw the force field that shielded the dock drag the box to a stop, grip it motionless. Then she shouted into her radio as if the comp were deaf, "Gracias!"

On that code, *Aster's Hope* put out a tractor beam and snatched her away from the alien.

It was a small industrial tractor beam, the kind used first in the construction of *Aster's Hope*, then in the loading of cargo. It was far too small and finely focused to have any function as a weapon. But it was perfect for quickly moving an object the size of Temple in her suit across the distance between the two ships.

Timing was critical, but she made that decision also almost

without thinking about it. As the beam rushed her toward *Aster's Hope*, she shouted into the radio, "Aster!" And on that code, her ship simultaneously raised its c-vector shields and triggered the black box. She was inside the shield for the last brief instants while the alien was still able to fire at her.

Later, she and Gracias saw that the end of their attacker had been singularly unspectacular. Still somewhat groggy from his imposed nap, he met her in the locker room to help her take off her suit; but when she demanded urgently, "What happened? Did it work?" he couldn't answer her because he hadn't checked; he'd come straight to the locker from his capsule when the comp had awakened him. So they ran together to the nearest auxcompcom to find out if they were safe.

They were. The alien ship was nowhere within scanner range. Wherever it had gone, it left no trace or trail.

So he replayed the visual and scanner records, and they saw what happened to a vessel when a c-vector field was projected onto it.

It simply winked out of existence.

After that, she felt like celebrating. In fact, there was a particular kind of celebration she had in mind. But when she let him know what she was thinking, he pushed her gently away. "In a few minutes," he said. "Got work to do."

"What work?" she protested. "We just saved the world—and they don't even know it. We deserve a vacation for the rest of the trip."

He nodded, but didn't move away from the comp console.

"What work?" she repeated.

"Course change," he said. He looked like he was trying not to grin. "Going back to Aster."

"What?" He surprised her so much that she shouted at him without meaning to. "You're aborting the mission? Just like that? What the hell do you think you're doing?"

For a moment he did his best to scowl thunderously. Then the grin took over. ''Now we know faster-than-light is possible,'' he said. ''Just need more research. So why spend a thousand years sleeping across the galaxy. Why not go home, do the research—start again when we can do what that ship did.''

He looked at her. ''Makes sense?''

She was grinning. ''Makes sense.''

When he was done with the comp, he got even with her for spilling ice cream on him.

SALVADOR

by Lucius Shepard

We see a lot of science fiction laid in the far future—and sometimes closer such as the next century. But here is one that is laid in the appallingly near future, tomorrow, the day after tomorrow, next year—or we sincerely hope never.

Three weeks before they wasted Tecolutla, Dantzler had his baptism of fire. The platoon was crossing a meadow at the foot of an emerald-green volcano, and being a dreamy sort, he was idling along, swatting tall grasses with his rifle barrel and thinking how it might have been a first-grader with crayons who had devised this elementary landscape of a perfect cone rising into a cloudless sky, when cap-pistol noises sounded on the slope. Someone screamed for the medic, and Dantzler dove into the grass, fumbling for his ampules. He slipped one from the dispenser and popped it under his nose, inhaling frantically; then, to be on the safe side, he popped another—"A double helpin' of martial arts," as DT would say—and lay with his head down until the drugs had worked their magic. There was dirt in his mouth, and he was very afraid.

Gradually his arms and legs lost their heaviness, and his heart rate slowed. His vision sharpened to the point that he could see not only the pinpricks of fire blooming on the slope, but also the figures behind them, half-obscured by brush. A bubble of grim anger welled up in his brain, hardened by a fierce resolve, and he started moving toward the volcano. By the time he reached the base of the cone, he was all rage and reflexes. He spent the next forty minutes spinning acrobatically through the thickets, spraying shadows with bursts of his M-18; yet part of his mind remained distant from the action, marveling at his efficiency, at the comic-strip enthusiasm he felt for the task of killing. He shouted at the men he shot, and he shot them many more times than was necessary, like a child playing soldier.

"Playin' my ass!" DT would say. "You just actin' natural."

DT was a firm believer in the ampules; though the official line was that they contained tailored RNA compounds and pseudoendorphins modified to an inhalant form, he held the opinion that they opened a man up to his inner nature. He was big, black, with heavily muscled arms and crudely stamped features, and he had come to the Special Forces direct from prison, where he had done a stretch for attempted murder; the palms of his hands were covered by jail tattoos—a pentagram and a horned monster. The words DIE HIGH were painted on his helmet. This was his second tour in Salvador, and Moody—who was Dantzler's buddy—said the drugs had addled DT's brains, that he was crazy and gone to hell.

"He collects trophies," Moody had said. "And not just ears like they done in 'Nam."

When Dantzler had finally gotten a glimpse of the trophies, he had been appalled. They were kept in a tin box in DT's pack and were nearly unrecognizable; they looked like withered brown orchids. But despite his revulsion, despite the fact that he was afraid of DT, he admired the man's capacity for survival and had taken to heart his advice to rely on the drugs.

On the way back down the slope, they discovered a live casualty, an Indian kid about Dantzler's age, nineteen or twenty. Black hair, adobe skin, and heavy-lidded brown eyes. Dantzler, whose father was an anthropologist and had done field work in Salvador, figured him for a Santa Ana tribesman; before leaving the States, Dantzler had pored over his father's notes, hoping this would give him an edge, and had learned to identify the various regional types. The kid had a minor leg wound and was wearing fatigue pants and a faded COKE ADDS LIFE T-shirt. This T-shirt irritated DT no end.

"What the hell you know 'bout Coke?" he asked the kid as they headed for the chopper that was to carry them deeper into Morazan Province. "You think it's funny or somethin'?" He whacked the kid in the back with his rifle butt, and when they reached the chopper, he slung him inside and had him sit by the door. He sat beside him, tapped out a joint from a pack of Kools, and asked, "Where's Infante?"

"Dead," said the medic.

"Shit!" DT licked the joint so it would burn evenly. "Goddamn beaner ain't no use 'cept somebody else know Spanish."

"I know a little," Dantzler volunteered.

Staring at Dantzler, DT's eyes went empty and unfocused. "Naw," he said. "You don't know no Spanish."

Dantzler ducked his head to avoid DT's stare and said nothing; he thought he understood what DT meant, but he ducked away from the understanding as well. The chopper bore them aloft, and DT lit the joint. He let the smoke out his nostrils and passed the joint to the kid, who accepted gratefully.

"*Que sabor!*" he said, exhaling a billow; he smiled and nodded, wanting to be friends.

Dantzler turned his gaze to the open door. They were

flying low between the hills, and looking at the deep bays of shadow in their folds acted to drain away the residue of the drugs, leaving him weary and frazzled. Sunlight poured in, dazzling the oil-smeared floor.

"Hey, Dantzler!" DT had to shout over the noise of the rotors. "Ask him whass his name!"

The kid's eyelids were drooping from the joint, but on hearing Spanish he perked up; he shook his head, though, refusing to answer. Dantzler smiled and told him not to be afraid.

"Ricardo Quu," said the kid.

"Kool!" said DT with false heartiness. "Thass my brand!" He offered his pack to the kid.

"*Gracias, no.*" The kid waved the joint and grinned.

"Dude's named for a godamn cigarette," said DT disparagingly, as if this were the height of insanity.

Dantzler asked the kid if there were more soldiers nearby, and once again received no reply; but, apparently sensing in Dantzler a kindred soul, the kid leaned forward and spoke rapidly, saying that his village was Santander Jimenez, that his father was—he hesitated—a man of power. He asked where they were taking him. Dantzler returned a stony glare. He found it easy to reject the kid, and he realized later this was because he had already given up on him.

Latching his hands behind his head, DT began to sing—a wordless melody. His voice was discordant, barely audible above the rotors; but the tune had a familiar ring, and Dantzler soon placed it. The theme from "Star Trek." It brought back memories of watching TV with his sister, laughing at the low-budget aliens and Scotty's Actors' Equity accent. He gazed out the door again. The sun was behind the hills, and the hillsides were unfeatured blurs of dark green smoke. Oh, God, he wanted to be home, to be anywhere but Salvador! A couple of the guys joined in the singing at DT's urging, and as the volume swelled, Dantzler's emotion peaked. He was on the verge of tears, remembering tastes and sights, the way his girl Jeanine had smelled, so clean and fresh, not reeking of sweat and perfume like the whores around Ilopango—finding all this substance in the banal touchstone of his culture and the illusions of the hillsides rushing past. Then Moody tensed beside him, and he glanced up to learn the reason why.

In the gloom of the chopper's belly, DT was as unfeatured as the hills—a black presence ruling them, more the leader of a coven than a platoon. The other two guys were singing their lungs out, and even the kid was getting into the spirit of things. "*Musica!*" he said at one point, smiling at everybody, trying to fan the flame of good feeling. He swayed to the rhythm and essayed a "la-la" now and again. But no one else was responding.

The singing stopped, and Dantzler saw that the whole platoon was staring at the kid, their expressions slack and dispirited.

"Space!" shouted DT, giving the kid a little shove. "The final frontier!"

The smile had not yet left the kid's face when he toppled out the door. DT peered after him; a few seconds later, he smacked his hand against the floor and sat back, grinning. Dantzler felt like screaming, the stupid horror of the joke was so at odds with the languor of his homesickness. He looked to the others for reaction. They were sitting with their heads down, fiddling with trigger guards and pack straps, studying their bootlaces, and seeing this, he quickly imitated them.

Morazan Province was spook country. Santa Ana spooks. Flights of birds had been reported to attack pistols; animals appeared at the perimeters of campsites and vanished when you shot at them; dreams afflicted everyone who ventured there. Dantzler could not testify to the birds and animals, but he did have a recurring dream. In it the kid DT had killed was pinwheeling down through a golden fog, his T-shirt visible against the roiling backdrop, and sometimes a voice would boom out of the fog, saying, "You are killing my son." No, no, Dantzler would reply; it wasn't me, and besides, he's already dead. Then he would wake covered with sweat, groping for his rifle, his heart racing.

But the dream was not an important terror, and he assigned it no significance. The land was far more terrifying. Pine-forested ridges that stood out against the sky like fringes of electrified hair; little trails winding off into thickets and petering out, as if what they led to had been magicked away; gray rock faces along which they were forced to walk, hopelessly exposed to ambush. There were innumerable booby traps set by the guerrillas, and they lost several men to rockfalls. It was the emptiest place of Dantzler's experience. No people, no animals, just a few hawks circling the solitudes between the ridges. Once in a while they found tunnels, and these they blew with the new gas grenades; the gas ignited the rich concentrations of hydrocarbons and sent flame sweeping through the entire system. DT would praise whoever had discovered the tunnel and would estimate in a loud voice how many beaners they had "refried." But Dantzler knew they were traversing pure emptiness and burning empty holes. Days, under debilitating heat, they humped the mountains, traveling seven, eight, even ten klicks up trails so steep that frequently the feet of the guy ahead of you would be on a level with your face; nights, it was cold, the darkness absolute, the silence so profound that Dantzler imagined he could hear the great humming vibration of the earth. They might have been anywhere or nowhere. Their fear was nourished by the isolation, and the only remedy was "martial arts."

Dantzler took to popping the pills without the excuse of combat. Moody cautioned him against abusing the drugs, citing rumors of bad side effects and DT's madness; but even he was using them more and more often. During basic training, Dantzler's D.I. had told the boots that the drugs were available only to the Special Forces, that their use was optional; but there had been too many instances of lackluster battlefield performance in the last war, and this was to prevent a recurrence.

"The chickenshit infantry should take 'em," the D.I. had said. "You bastards are brave already. You're born killers, right?"

"Right, sir!" they had shouted.

"What are you?"

"Born killers, sir!"

But Dantzler was not a born killer; he was not even clear as to how he had been drafted, less clear as to how he had been manipulated into the Special Forces, and he had learned that nothing was optional in Salvador, with the possible exception of life itself.

The platoon's mission was reconnaissance and mop-up. Along with other Special Forces platoons, they were to secure Morazan prior to the invasion of Nicaragua; specifically, they were to proceed to the village of Tecolutla, where a Sandinista patrol had recently been spotted, and following that, they were to join up with the First Infantry and take part in the offensive against León, a provincial capital just across the Nicaraguan border. As Dantzler and Moody walked together, they frequently talked about the offensive, how it would be good to get down into flat country; occasionally they talked about the possibility of reporting DT, and once, after he had led them on a forced night march, they toyed with the idea of killing him. But most often they discussed the ways of the Indians and the land, since this was what had caused them to become buddies.

Moody was slightly built, freckled, and red-haired; his eyes had the "thousand-yard stare" that came from too much war. Dantzler had seen winos with such vacant, lusterless stares. Moody's father had been in 'Nam, and Moody said it had been worse than Salvador because there had been no real commitment to win; but he thought Nicaragua and Guatemala might be the worst of all, especially if the Cubans sent in troops as they had threatened. He was adept at locating tunnels and detecting booby traps, and it was for this reason Dantzler had cultivated his friendship. Essentially a loner, Moody had resisted all advances until learning of Dantzler's father; thereafter he had buddied up, eager to hear about the field notes, believing they might give him an edge.

"They think the land has animal traits," said Dantzler one day as they climbed along a ridgetop. "Just like some kinds of fish look like plants or sea bottom, parts of the land look like plain ground, jungle . . . whatever. But when you enter them, you find you've entered the spirit world, the world of the *Sukias*."

"What's *Sukias*?" asked Moody.

"Magicians." A twig snapped behind Dantzler, and he spun around, twitching off the safety of his rifle. It was only Hodge—a lanky kid with the beginnings of a beer gut. He stared hollow-eyed at Dantzler and popped an ampule.

Moody made a noise of disbelief. "If they got magicians, why ain't they winnin'? Why ain't they zappin' us off the cliffs?"

"It's not their business," said Dantzler. "They don't believe in messing with worldly affairs unless it concerns them directly. Anyway, these places—the ones that look like normal land but aren't—they're called . . ." He drew a blank on the name. "*Aya*-something. I can't remember. But they have different laws. They're where your spirit goes to die after your body dies."

"Don't they got no Heaven?"

"Nope. It just takes longer for your spirit to die, and so it goes to one of these places that's between everything and nothing."

"Nothin'," said Moody disconsolately, as if all his hopes

for an afterlife had been dashed. "Don't make no sense to have spirits and not have no Heaven."

"Hey," said Dantzler, tensing as wind rustled the pine boughs. "They're just a bunch of damn primitives. You know what their sacred drink is? Hot chocolate! My old man was a guest at one of their funerals, and he said they carried cups of hot chocolate balanced on these little red towers and acted like drinking it was going to wake them to the secrets of the universe." He laughed, and the laughter sounded tinny and psychotic to his own ears. "So you're going to worry about fools who think hot chocolate's holy water?"

"Maybe they just like it," said Moody. "Maybe somebody dyin' just give 'em an excuse to drink it."

But Dantzler was no longer listening. A moment before, as they emerged from pine cover onto the highest point of the ridge, a stony scarp open to the winds and providing a view of rumpled mountains and valleys extending to the horizon, he had popped an ampule. He felt so strong, so full of righteous purpose and controlled fury, it seemed only the sky was around him, that he was still ascending, preparing to do battle with the gods themselves.

Tecolutla was a village of whitewashed stone tucked into a notch between two hills. From above, the houses—with their black windows and doorways—looked like an unlucky throw of dice. The streets ran uphill and down, diverging around boulders. Bougainvilleas and hibiscuses speckled the hillsides, and there were tilled fields on the gentler slopes. It was a sweet, peaceful place when they arrived, and after they had gone it was once again peaceful; but its sweetness had been permanently banished. The reports of Sandinistas had proved accurate, and though they were casualties left behind to recuperate, DT had decided their presence called for extreme measures. Fu gas, frag grenades, and such. He had fired an M-60 until the barrel melted down, and then had manned the flamethrower. Afterward, as they rested atop the next ridge, exhausted and begrimed, having radioed in a chopper for resupply, he could not get over how one of the houses he had torched had resembled a toasted marshmallow.

"Ain't that how it was, man?" he asked, striding up and down the line. He did not care if they agreed about the house; it was a deeper question he was asking, one concerning the ethics of their actions.

"Yeah," said Dantzler, forcing a smile. "Sure did."

DT grunted with laughter. "You *know* I'm right, don'tcha man?"

The sun hung directly behind his head, a golden corona rimming a black oval, and Dantzler could not turn his eyes away. He felt weak and weakening, as if threads of himself were being spun loose and sucked into the blackness. He popped three ampules prior to the firefight, and his experience of Tecolutla had been a kind of mad whirling dance through the streets, spraying erratic bursts that appeared to be writing weird names on the walls. The leader of the Sandinistas had worn a mask—a gray face with a surprised hole of a mouth and pink circles around the eyes. A ghost face. Dantzler had been afraid of the mask and had poured round after round into it. Then, leaving the village, he had seen a small girl standing beside the shell of the last house, watching them, her colorless rag of a dress tattering in the breeze. She had been a victim of that malnutrition disease, the one that paled your skin and whitened your hair and left you retarded. He could not recall the name of the disease—things like names were slipping away from him—nor could he believe anyone had survived, and for a moment he had thought the spirit of the village had come out to mark their trail.

That was all he could remember of Tecolutla, all he wanted to remember. But he knew he had been brave.

* * *

Four days later, they headed up into a cloud forest. It was the dry season, but dry season or not, blackish gray clouds always shrouded these peaks. They were shot through by ugly glimmers of lightning, making it seem that malfunctioning neon signs were hidden beneath them, advertisements for evil. Everyone was jittery, and Jerry LeDoux—a slim, dark-haired Cajun kid—flat-out refused to go.

"It ain't reasonable," he said. "Be easier to go through the passes."

"We're on recon, man! You think the beaners be waitin' in the passes, wavin' their white flags?" DT whipped his rifle into firing position and pointed it at LeDoux. "C'mon, Louisiana man. Pop a few, and you feel different."

As Le Doux popped the ampules, DT talked to him.

"Look at it this way, man. This is your big adventure. Up there it be like all them animals shows on the tube. The savage kingdom, the unknown. Could be like Mars or somethin'. Monsters and shit, with big red eyes and tentacles. You wanna miss that, man? You wanna miss bein' the first grunt on Mars?"

Soon LeDoux was raring to go, giggling at DT's rap.

Moody kept his mouth shut, but he fingered the safety of his rifle and glared at DT's back. When DT turned to him, however, he relaxed. Since Tecolutla he had grown taciturn, and there seemed to be a shifting of lights and darks in his eyes, as if something were scurrying back and forth behind them. He had taken to wearing banana leaves on his head, arranging them under his helmet so the frayed ends stuck out the sides like strange green hair. He said this was camouflage, but Dantzler was certain it bespoke some secretive, irrational purpose. Of course DT had noticed Moody's spiritual erosion, and as they prepared to move out, he called Dantzler aside.

"He done found someplace inside his head that feel good

to him," said DT. "He's tryin' to curl up into it, and once he do that he ain't gon' be responsible. Keep an eye on him."

Dantzler mumbled his assent, but was not enthused.

"I know he your fren', man, but that don't mean shit. Not the way things are. Now me, I don't give a damn 'bout you personally. But I'm your brother-in-arms, and thass somethin' you can count on . . . y'understand."

To Dantzler's shame, he did understand.

They had planned on negotiating the cloud forest by nightfall, but they had underestimated the difficulty. The vegetation beneath the clouds was lush—thick, juicy leaves that mashed underfoot, tangles of vines, trees with slick, pale bark and waxy leaves—and the visibility was only about fifteen feet. They were gray wraiths passing through grayness. The vague shapes of the foliage reminded Dantzler of fancifully engraved letters, and for a while he entertained himself with the notion that they were walking among the half-formed phrases of a constitution not yet manifest in the land. They barged off the trail, losing it completely, becoming veiled in spider webs and drenched by spills of water; their voices were oddly muffled, the tag ends of words swallowed up. After seven hours of this, DT reluctantly gave the order to pitch camp. They set electric lamps around the perimeter so they could see to string the jungle hammocks; the beam of light illuminated the moisture in the air, piercing the murk with jeweled blades. They talked in hushed tones, alarmed by the eerie atmosphere. When they had done with the hammocks, DT posted four sentries—Moody, LeDoux, Dantzler, and himself. Then they switched off the lamps.

It grew pitch-dark, and the darkness was picked out by plips and plops, the entire spectrum of dripping sounds. To Dantzler's ears they blended into a gabbling speech. He imagined tiny Santa Ana demons talking about him, and to stave off paranoia he popped two ampules. He continued to pop them, trying to limit himself to one every half hour; but he was uneasy, unsure where to train his rifle in the dark, and he exceeded his limit. Soon it began to grow light again, and he assumed that more time had passed than he had thought. That often happened with the ampules—it was easy to lose yourself in being alert, in the wealth of perceptual detail available to your sharpened senses. Yet on checking his watch, he saw it was only a few minutes after two o'clock. His system was too inundated with the drugs to allow panic, but he twitched his head from side-to-side in tight little arcs to determine the source of the brightness. There did not appear to be a single source; it was simply that filaments of the cloud were gleaming, casting a diffuse golden glow, as if they were elements of a nervous system coming to life. He started to call out, then held back. The others must have seen the light, and they had given no cry; they probably had a good reason for their silence. He scrunched down flat, pointing his rifle out from the campsite.

Bathed in the golden mist, the forest had acquired an alchemic beauty. Beads of water glittered with gemmy brilliance; the leaves and vines and bark were gilded. Every surface shimmered with light . . . everything except a fleck of blackness hovering between two of the trunks, its size gradually increasing. As it swelled in his vision, he saw it had the shape of a bird, its wings beating, flying toward him from an inconceivable distance—inconceivable, because the dense vegetation did not permit you to see very far in a straight line, and yet the bird was growing larger with such slowness that it must have been coming from a long way off. It was not really flying, he realized; rather, it was as if the forest were painted on a piece of paper, as if someone were holding a lit match behind it and burning a hole, a hole that maintained the shape of a bird as it spread. He was transfixed, unable to react. Even when it had blotted out half the light, when he lay before it no bigger than a mote in relation to its huge span, he could not move or squeeze the trigger.

And then the blackness swept over him. He had the sensation of being borne along at incredible speed, and he could no longer hear the dripping of the forest.

"Moody!" he shouted. "DT!"

But the voice that answered belonged to neither of them. It was hoarse, issuing from every part of the surrounding blackness, and he recognized it as the voice of his recurring dream.

"You are killing my son," it said. "I have led you here, to this *ayahuamaco*, so he may judge you."

Dantzler knew to his bones the voice was that of the *Sukia* of the village of Santander Jimenez. He wanted to offer a denial, to explain his innocence, but all he could manage was, "No." He said it tearfully, hopelessly, his forehead resting on his rifle barrel. Then his mind gave a savage twist, and his soldiery self regained control. He ejected an ampule from his dispenser and popped it.

The voice laughed—malefic, damning laughter whose vibrations shuddered Dantzler. He opened up with the rifle, spraying fire in all directions. Filigrees of golden holes appeared in the blackness, tendrils of mist coiled through them. He kept on firing until the blackness shattered and fell in jagged sections toward him. Slowly. Like shards of black glass dropping through water. He emptied the rifle and flung himself flat, shielding his head with his arms, expecting to be sliced into bits; but nothing touched him. At last he peeked between his arms; then—amazed, because the forest was now a uniform lustrous yellow—he rose to his knees. He scraped his hand on one of the crushed leaves beneath him, and blood welled from the cut. The broken fibers of the leaf was as stiff as wires. He stood, a giddy trickle of hysteria leaking up from the bottom of his soul. It was no forest, but a building of solid gold worked to resemble a forest—the sort of conceit that might have been fabricated for the child of an emperor. Canopied by golden leaves, columned by slender golden trunks, carpeted by golden grasses. The water beads were diamonds. All the gleam and glitter soothed his apprehension; here was something out of a myth, a habitat for princesses and wizards and dragons. Almost gleeful, he turned to the campsite to see how the others were reacting.

Once, when he was nine years old, he had sneaked into the attic to rummage through the boxes and trunks, and he had run across an old morocco-bound copy of *Gulliver's Travels*. He had been taught to treasure old books, and so he had opened it eagerly to look at the illustrations, only to find that the centers of the pages had been eaten away, and there, right in the heart of the fiction, was a nest of larvae. Pulpy, horrid things. It had been an awful sight, but one unique in his experience, and he might have studied those crawling scraps of life for a very long time if his father had not interrupted. Such a sight was now before him, and he was numb with it.

They were all dead. He should have guessed they would be; he had given no thought to them while firing his rifle. They had been struggling out of their hammocks when the bullets hit, and as a result, they were hanging half-in, half-out, their limbs dangling, blood pooled beneath them. The veils of golden mist made them look dark and mysterious and malformed, like monsters killed as they emerged from their cocoons. Dantzler could not stop staring, but he was shrinking inside himself. It was not his fault. That thought kept swooping in and out of a flock of less-acceptable thoughts; he wanted to stay put, to be true, to alleviate the sick horror he was beginning to feel.

"What's your name?" asked a girl's voice behind him.

She was sitting on a stone about twenty feet away. Her hair was a tawny shade of gold, her skin a half-tone lighter, and her dress was cunningly formed out of the mist. Only her eyes were real. Brown, heavy-lidded eyes—they were at variance with the rest of her face, which had the fresh, unaffected beauty of an American teenager.

"Don't be afraid," she said, and patted the ground, inviting him to sit beside her.

He recognized the eyes, but it was no matter. He badly needed the consolation she could offer; he walked over and sat down. She let him lean his head against her thigh.

"What's your name?" she repeated.

"Dantzler," he said. "John Dantzler." And then he added, "I'm from Boston. My father's. . . ." It would be too difficult to explain about anthropology. "He's a teacher."

"Are there many soldiers in Boston?" She stroked his cheek with a golden finger.

The caress made Dantzler happy. "Oh, no," he said. "They hardly know there's a war going on."

"This is true?" she said, incredulous.

"Well, they *do* know about it, but it's just news on the TV to them. They've got more pressing problems. Their jobs, families."

"Will you let them know about the war when you return home?" she asked. "Will you do that for me?"

Dantzler had given up hope of returning home, of surviving, and her assumption that he would do both acted to awaken his gratitude. "Yes," he said fervently. "I will."

"You must hurry," she said. "If you stay in the *ayahuamaco* too long, you will never leave. You must find the way out. It is a way not of directions or trails, but of events."

"Where is this place?" he asked, suddenly aware of how much he had taken it for granted.

She shifted her leg away, and if he had not caught himself on the stone, he would have fallen. When he looked up, she had vanished. He was surprised that her disappearance did not alarm him; in reflex he slipped out a couple of ampules, but after a moment's reflection he decided not to use them. It was impossible to slip them back into the dispenser, so he tucked them into the interior webbing of his helmet for later. He doubted he would need them, though. He felt strong, competent, and unafraid.

Dantzler stepped carefully between the hammocks, not wanting to brush against them; it might have been his imagination, but they seemed to be bulged down lower than before, as if death had weighed out heavier than life. That heaviness was in the air, pressuring him. Mist rose like golden steam from the corpses, but the sight no longer affected him—perhaps because the mist gave the illusion of being their souls. He picked up a rifle with a full magazine and headed off into the forest.

The tips of the golden leaves were sharp, and he had to ease past them to avoid being cut; but he was at the top of his form, moving gracefully, and the obstacles barely slowed his pace. He was not even anxious about the girl's warning to hurry; he was certain the way out would soon present itself. After a minute or so, he heard voices, and after another few seconds, he came to a clearing divided by a stream, one so perfectly reflecting that its banks appeared to enclose a wedge of golden mist. Moody was squatting to the left of the stream, staring at the blade of his survival knife and singing under his breath—a wordless melody that had the erratic rhythm of a trapped fly. Beside him lay Jerry LeDoux, his throat slashed from ear to ear. DT was sitting on the other side of the stream; he had been shot just above the knee, and though he had ripped up his shirt for bandages and tied off the leg with a tourniquet, he was not in good shape. He was sweating, and the gray chalky pallor infused his skin. The entire scene had the weird vitality of something that had materialized in a magic mirror, a bubble of reality enclosed within a gilt frame.

DT heard Dantzler's footfalls and glanced up. "Waste him!" he shouted, pointing at Moody.

Moody did not turn from contemplation of the knife. "No,"

he said, as if speaking to someone whose image was held in the blade.

"Waste him, man!" screamed DT. "He killed LeDoux!"

"Please," said Moody to the knife. "I don't want to."

There was blood clotted on his face, more blood on the banana leaves sticking out of his helmet.

"Did you kill Jerry?" asked Dantzler; while he addressed the question to Moody, he did not relate to him as an individual, only as part of a design whose message he had to unravel.

"Jesus Christ! Waste him!" DT smashed his fist against the ground in frustration.

"O.K.," said Moody. With an apologetic look, he sprang to his feet and charged Dantzler, swinging the knife.

Emotionless, Dantzler stitched a line of fire across Moody's chest; he went sideways into the bushes and down.

"What the hell was you waitin' for!" DT tried to rise, but winced and fell back. "Damn! Don't know if I can walk."

"Pop a few," Dantzler suggested mildly.

"Yeah. Good thinkin', man," DT fumbled for his dispenser.

Dantzler peered into the bushes to see where Moody had fallen. He felt nothing, and this pleased him. He was weary of feeling.

DT popped an ampule with a flourish, as if making a toast, and inhaled. "Ain't you gon' to do some, man?"

"I don't need them," said Dantzler. "I'm fine."

The stream interested him; it did not reflect the mist, as he had supposed, but was itself a seam of the mist.

"How many you think they was?" asked DT.

"How many what?"

"Beaners, man! I wasted three or four after they hit us, but I couldn't tell how many they was."

Dantzler considered this in light of his own interpretation of events and Moody's conversation with the knife. It made sense. A Santa Ana kind of sense.

"Beats me," he said. "But I guess there's less than there used to be."

DT snorted. "You got *that* right!" He heaved to his feet and limped to the edge of the stream. "Gimme a hand across."

Dantzler reached out to him, but instead of taking his hand, he grabbed his wrist and pulled him off-balance. DT teetered on his good leg, then toppled and vanished beneath the mist. Dantzler had expected him to fall, but he surfaced instantly, mist clinging to his skin. Of course, thought Dantzler; his body would have to die before his spirit would fall.

"What you doin', man?" DT was more disbelieving than enraged.

Dantzler planted a foot in the middle of his back and pushed him down until his head was submerged. DT bucked and clawed at the foot and managed to come to his hands and knees. Mist slithered from his eyes, his nose, and he choked out the words ". . . kill you. . . ." Dantzler pushed him down again; he got into pushing him down and letting him up, over and over. Not so as to torture him. Not really. It was because he had suddenly understood the nature of the *ayahuamaco*'s laws, that they were approximations of normal laws, and he further understood that his actions had to approximate those of someone jiggling a key in a lock. DT was the key to the way out, and Dantzler was jiggling him, making sure all the tumblers were engaged.

Some of the vessels in DT's eyes had burst, and the whites were occluded by films of blood. When he tried to speak, mist curled from his mouth. Gradually his struggles subsided; he clawed runnels in the gleaming yellow dirt of the bank and shuddered. His shoulders were knobs of black land floundering in a mystic sea.

For a long time after DT sank from view, Dantzler stood beside the stream, uncertain of what was left to do and unable to remember a lesson he had been taught. Finally, he shouldered his rifle and walked away from the clearing. Morning had broken, the mist had thinned, and the forest had regained its usual coloration. But he scarcely noticed these changes, still troubled by his faulty memory. Eventually, he let it slide—it would all come clearer sooner or later. He was just happy to be alive. After a while he began to kick the stones as he went, and to swing his rifle in a carefree fashion against the weeds.

When the First Infantry poured across the Nicaraguan border and wasted León, Dantzler was having a quiet time at the VA hospital in Ann Arbor, Michigan; and at the precise moment the bulletin was flashed nationwide, he was sitting in the lounge, watching the American League playoffs between Detroit and Texas. Some of the patients ranted at the interruption, while others shouted them down, wanting to hear the details. Dantzler expressed no reaction whatsoever. He was solely concerned with being a model patient; however, noticing that one of the staff was giving him a clinical stare, he added his weight on the side of the baseball fans. He did not want to appear too controlled. The doctors were as suspicious of that sort of behavior as they were of its contrary. But the funny thing was—at least it was funny to Dantzler—that his feigned annoyance at the bulletin was an exemplary proof of his control, his expertise at moving through life the way he had moved through the golden leaves of the cloud forest. Cautiously, gracefully, efficiently. Touching nothing, and being touched by nothing. That was the lesson he had learned—to be as perfect a counterfeit of a man as the *ayahuamaco* had been of the land; to adopt the various stances of a man, and yet, by virtue of his distance from things human, to be all the more prepared for the onset of crisis or a call to action. He saw nothing aberrant in this; even the doctors would admit that men were little more than organized pretense. If he was different from other men, it was only that he had a deeper awareness of the principles on which his personality was founded.

When the battle of Managua was joined, Dantzler was living at home. His parents had urged him to go easy in readjusting to civilian life, but he had immediately gotten a job as a management trainee in a bank. Each morning he would drive to work and spend a controlled, quiet eight hours; each night he would watch TV with his mother, and before going to bed, he would climb to the attic and inspect the trunk containing his souvenirs of war—helmet, fatigues, knife, boots. The doctors had insisted he face his experiences, and this ritual was his way of following their instructions. All in all, he was quite pleased with his progress, but he still had problems. He had not been able to force himself to venture out at night, remembering too well the darkness in the cloud forest, and he had rejected his friends, refusing to see them or answer their calls—he was not secure with the idea of friendship. Further, despite his methodical approach to life, he was prone to a nagging restlessness, the feeling of a chore left undone.

One night his mother came into his room and told him that an old friend, Phil Curry, was on the phone. "Please talk to him, Johnny," she said. "He's been drafted, and I think he's a little scared."

The word "drafted" struck a responsive chord in Dantzler's soul, and after brief deliberation, he went downstairs and picked up the receiver.

"Hey," said Phil. "What's the story, man? Three months, and you don't even give me a call."

"I'm sorry," said Dantzler. "I haven't been feeling so hot."

"Yeah, I understand." Phil was silent a moment. "Listen, man. I'm leavin', y'know, and we're havin' a big send-off at Sparky's. It's goin' on right now. Why don't you come down?"

"I don't know."

"Jeanine's here, man. Y'know, she's still crazy 'bout you, talks 'bout you alla time. She don't go out with nobody."

Dantzler was unable to think of anything to say.

"Look," said Phil, "I'm pretty weirded out by this soldier shit. I hear it's pretty bad down there. If you got anything you can tell me 'bout what it's like, man, I'd 'preciate it."

Dantzler could relate to Phil's concern, his desire for an edge, and besides, it felt right to go. Very right. He would take some precautions against the darkness.

"I'll be there," he said.

It was a foul night, spitting snow, but Sparky's parking lot was jammed. Dantzler's mind was flurried like the snow, crowded like the lot—thoughts whirling in, jockeying for position, melting away. He hoped his mother would not wait up, he wondered if Jeanine still wore her hair long, he was worried because the palms of his hands were unnaturally warm. Even with the car windows rolled up, he could hear loud music coming from inside the club. Above the door the words SPARKY'S ROCK CITY were being spelled out a letter at a time in red neon, and when the spelling was complete, the letter flashed off and on and a golden neon explosion bloomed around them. After the explosion, the entire sign went dark for a split second, and the big ramshackle building seemed to grow large and merge with the black sky. He had an idea it was watching him, and he shuddered—one of those sudden lurches downward of the kind that take you just before you fall asleep. He knew the people inside did not intend him any harm, but he also knew that places have a way of changing people's intent, and he did not want to be caught off guard. Sparky's might be such a place, might be a huge black presence camouflaged by neon, its true substance one with the abyss of the sky, the phosphorescent snowflakes jittering in his headlights, the wind keening through the side vent. He would have liked very much to drive home and forget about his promise to Phil; however, he felt a responsibility to explain about the war. More than a responsibility, an evangelistic urge. He would tell them about the kid falling out of the chopper, the white-haired girl in Tecolutla, the emptiness. God, yes! How you went down chock-full of ordinary American thoughts and dreams, memories of smoking weed and chasing tail and hanging out and freeway flying with a case of something cold, and how you smuggled back a human-shaped container of pure Salvadorian emptiness. Primo grade. Smuggled it back to the land of silk and money, of mindfuck video games and topless tennis matches and fast-food solutions to the nutritional problem. Just a taste of Salvador would banish all those trivial obsessions. Just a taste. It would be easy to explain.

Of course, some things beggared explanation.

He bent down and adjusted the survival knife in his boot so the hilt would not rub against his calf. From his coat pocket he withdrew the two ampules he had secreted in his helmet that long-ago night in the cloud forest. As the neon explosion flashed once more, glimmers of gold coursed along their shiny surfaces. He did not think he would need them; his hand was steady, and his purpose was clear. But to be on the safe side, he popped them both.

PRESS ENTER■

by John Varley

Computer stories there are aplenty in the SF magazines and novels of this day, for the time of the computer has come and the silicon chip has opened the door to robotics and access to all knowledge. Here is such a story, quite up to date, and quite believable. You never know what the fellow next door may be up to. Perhaps, under his own roof, he is really planning to be the master of all the world?

"This is a recording. Please do not hang up until—"

I slammed the phone down so hard it fell onto the floor. Then I stood there, dripping wet and shaking with anger. Eventually, the phone started to make that buzzing noise they make when a receiver is off the hook. It's twenty times as loud as any sound a phone can normally make, and I always wondered why. As though it was such a terrible disaster. "Emergency! Your telephone is off the hook!!!"

Phone answering machines are one of the small annoyances of life. Confess, do you really *like* talking to a machine? But what had just happened to me was more than a petty irritation. I had just been called by an automatic dialing machine.

They're fairly new. I'd been getting about two or three such calls a month. Most of them come from insurance companies. They give you a two-minute spiel and then a number to call if you are interested. (I called back, once, to give them a piece of my mind, and was put on hold, complete with Muzak.) They use lists. I don't know where they get them.

I went back to the bathroom, wiped water droplets from the plastic cover of the library book, and carefully lowered myself back into the water. It was too cool. I ran more hot water and was just getting my blood pressure back to normal when the phone rang again.

So I sat there through fifteen rings, trying to ignore it.

Did you ever try to read with the phone ringing?

On the sixteenth ring I got up. I dried off, put on a robe, walked slowly and deliberately into the living room. I stared at the phone for a while.

On the fiftieth ring I picked it up.

"This is a recording. Please do not hang up until the message has been completed. This call originates from the house of your next-door neighbor, Charles Kluge. It will repeat every ten minutes. Mister Kluge knows he has not been the best of neighbors, and apologizes in advance for the inconvenience. He requests that you go immediately to his house. The key is under the mat. Go inside and do what needs to be done. There will be a reward for your services. Thank you."

Click. Dial tone.

I'm not a hasty man. Ten minutes later, when the phone rang again, I was still there thinking it over. I picked up the receiver and listened carefully.

It was the same message. As before, it was not Kluge's

voice. It was something synthesized, with all the human warmth of a Speak'n'Spell.

I heard it out again, and cradled the receiver when it was done.

I thought about calling the police. Charles Kluge had lived next door to me for ten years. In that time I may have had a dozen conversations with him, none lasting longer than a minute. I owed him nothing.

I thought about ignoring it. I was still thinking about that when the phone rang again. I glanced at my watch. Ten minutes. I lifted the receiver and put it right back down.

I could disconnect the phone. It wouldn't change my life radically.

But in the end I got dressed and went out the front door, turned left, and walked toward Kluge's property.

My neighbor across the street, Hal Lanier, was out mowing the lawn. He waved to me, and I waved back. It was about seven in the evening of a wonderful August day. The shadows were long. There was the smell of cut grass in the air. I've always liked that smell. About time to cut my own lawn, I thought.

It was a thought Kluge had never entertained. His lawn was brown and knee-high and choked with weeds.

I rang the bell. When nobody came I knocked. Then I sighed, looked under the mat, and used the key I found there to open the door.

"Kluge?" I called out as I stuck my head in.

I went along the short hallway, tentatively, as people do when unsure of their welcome. The drapes were drawn, as always, so it was dark in there, but in what had once been the living room ten television screens gave more than enough light for me to see Kluge. He sat in a chair in front of a table, with his face pressed into a computer keyboard and the side of his head blown away.

* * *

Hal Lanier operates a computer for the L.A.P.D., so I told him what I had found and he called the police. We waited together for the first car to arrive. Hal kept asking if I'd touched anything, and I kept telling him no, except for the front door knob.

An ambulance arrived without the siren. Soon there were police all over, and neighbors standing out in their yards or talking in front of Kluge's house. Crews from some of the television stations arrived in time to get pictures of the body, wrapped in a plastic sheet, being carried out. Men and women came and went. I assumed they were doing all the standard police things, taking fingerprints, collecting evidence. I would have gone home, but had been told to stick around.

Finally I was brought in to see Detective Osborne, who was in charge of the case. I was led into Kluge's living room. All the television screens were still turned on. I shook hands with Osborne. He looked me over before he said anything. He was a short guy, balding. He seemed very tired until he looked at me. Then, though nothing really changed in his face, he didn't look tired at all.

"You're Victor Apfel?" he asked. I told him I was. He gestured at the room. "Mister Apfel, can you tell if anything has been taken from this room?"

I took another look around, approaching it as a puzzle.

There was a fireplace and there were curtains over the windows. There was a rug on the floor. Other than those items, there was nothing else you would expect to find in a living room.

All the walls were lined with tables, leaving a narrow aisle down the middle. On the tables were monitor screens, keyboards, disc drives—all the glossy bric-a-brac of the new age. They were interconnected by thick cables and cords. Beneath the tables were still more computers, and boxes full of electronic items. Above the tables were shelves that reached the ceiling and were stuffed with boxes of tapes, discs, cartridges

. . . there was a word for it which I couldn't recall just then. It was software.

"There's no furniture, is there? Other than that . . ."

He was looking confused.

"You mean there was furniture here before?"

"How would I know?" Then I realized what the misunderstanding was. "Oh. You thought I'd been here before. The first time I ever set foot in this room was about an hour ago."

He frowned, and I didn't like that much.

"The medical examiner says the guy had been dead about three hours. How come you came over when you did, Victor?"

I didn't like him using my first name, but didn't see what I could do about it. And I knew I had to tell him about the phone call.

He looked dubious. But there was one easy way to check it out, and we did that. Hal and Osborne and I and several others trooped over to my house. My phone was ringing as we entered.

Osborne picked it up and listened. He got a very sour expression on his face. As the night wore on, it just got worse and worse.

We waited ten minutes for the phone to ring again. Osborne spent the time examining everything in my living room. I was glad when the phone rang again. They made a recording of the message, and we went back to Kluge's house.

Osborne went into the back yard to see Kluge's forest of antennas. He looked impressed.

"Mrs. Madison down the street thinks he was trying to contact Martians," Hal said, with a laugh. "Me, I just thought he was stealing HBO." There were three parabolic dishes. There were six tall masts, and some of those things you see on telephone company buildings for transmitting microwaves.

Osborne took me to the living room again. He asked me

to describe what I had seen. I didn't know what good that would do, but I tried.

"He was sitting in that chair, which was here in front of this table. I saw the gun on the floor. His hand was hanging down toward it."

"You think it was suicide?"

"Yes, I guess I did think that." I waited for him to comment, but he didn't. "Is that what you think?"

He sighed. "There wasn't any note."

"They don't always leave notes," Hal pointed out.

"No, but they do often enough that my nose starts to twitch when they don't." He shrugged. "It's probably nothing."

"That phone call," I said. "That might be a kind of suicide note."

Osborne nodded. "Was there anything else you noticed?"

I went to the table and looked at the keyboard. It was made by Texas Instruments, model TI-99/4A. There was a large bloodstain on the right side of it, where his head had been resting.

"Just that he was sitting in front of this machine." I touched a key, and the monitor screen behind the keyboard immediately filled with words. I quickly drew my hand back, then stared at the message there.

PROGRAM NAME: GOODBYE REAL WORLD
DATE: 8/20
CONTENTS: LAST WILL AND TESTAMENT; MISC. FEATURES
PROGRAMMER: "CHARLES KLUGE"

TO RUN
PRESS ENTER■

The black square at the end flashed on and off. Later I learned it was called a cursor.

Everyone gathered around. Hal, the computer expert, explained how many computers went blank after ten minutes of no activity, so the words wouldn't be burned into the television screen. This one had been green until I touched it, then displayed black letters on a blue background.

"Has this console been checked for prints?" Osborne asked. Nobody seemed to know, so Osborne took a pencil and used the eraser to press the ENTER key.

The screen cleared, stayed blue for a moment, then filled with little ovoid shapes that started at the top of the screen and descended like rain. There were hundreds of them in many colors.

"Those are pills," one of the cops said, in amazement. "Look, that's gotta be a Quaalude. There's a Nembutal." Other cops pointed out other pills. I recognized the distinctive red stripe around the center of a white capsule that had to be a Dilantin. I had been taking them every day for years.

Finally the pills stopped falling, and the damn thing started to play music at us. "Nearer My God To Thee," in three-part harmony.

A few people laughed. I don't think any of us thought it was funny—it was creepy as hell listening to that eerie dirge—but it sounded like it had been scored for pennywhistle, calliope, and kazoo. What could you do but laugh?

As the music played, a little figure composed entirely of squares entered from the left of the screen and jerked spastically toward the center. It was like one of those human figures from a video game, but not as detailed. You had to use your imagination to believe it was a man.

A shape appeared in the middle of the screen. The "man" stopped in front of it. He bent in the middle, and something that might have been a chair appeared under him.

"What's that supposed to be?"

"A computer. Isn't it?"

It must have been, because the little man extended his

arms, which jerked up and down like Liberace at the piano. He was typing. The words appeared above him.

SOMEWHERE ALONG THE LINE I MISSED SOMETHING. I SIT HERE, NIGHT AND DAY, A SPIDER IN THE CENTER OF A COAXIAL WEB, MASTER OF ALL I SURVEY . . . AND IT IS NOT ENOUGH. THERE MUST BE MORE.

ENTER YOUR NAME HERE■

"Jesus Christ," Hal said. "I don't believe it. An interactive suicide note."

"Come on, we've got to see the rest of this."

I was nearest the keyboard, so I leaned over and typed my name. But when I looked up, what I had typed was VICT9R.

"How do you back this up?" I asked.

"Just enter it," Osborne said. He reached around me and pressed enter.

DO YOU EVER GET THAT FEELING, VICT9R? YOU HAVE WORKED ALL YOUR LIFE TO BE THE BEST THERE IS AT WHAT YOU DO, AND ONE DAY YOU WAKE UP TO WONDER WHY YOU ARE DOING IT? THAT IS WHAT HAPPENED TO ME.

DO YOU WANT TO HEAR MORE, VICT9R? Y/N■

The message rambled from that point. Kluge seemed to be aware of it, apologetic about it, because at the end of each forty or fifty-word paragraph the reader was given the Y/N option.

I kept glancing from the screen to the keyboard, remembering Kluge slumped across it. I thought about him sitting here alone, writing this.

He said he was despondent. He didn't feel like he could go on. He was taking too many pills (more of them rained down the screen at this point), and he had no further goal. He had done everthing he set out to do. We didn't understand what he meant by that. He said he no longer existed. We thought that was a figure of speech.

ARE YOU A COP, VICT9R? IF YOU ARE NOT, A COP WILL BE HERE SOON. SO TO YOU OR THE COP: I WAS NOT SELLING NARCOTICS. THE DRUGS IN MY BEDROOM WERE FOR MY OWN PERSONAL USE. I USED A LOT OF THEM. AND NOW I WILL NOT NEED THEM ANYMORE.

PRESS ENTER■

Osborne did, and a printer across the room began to chatter, scaring the hell out of all of us. I could see the carriage zipping back and forth, printing in both directions, when Hal pointed at the screen and shouted.

"Look! Look at that!"

The compugraphic man was standing again. He faced us. He had something that had to be a gun in his hand, which he now pointed at his head.

"Don't do it!" Hal yelled.

The little man didn't listen. There was a denatured gunshot sound, and the little man fell on his back. A line of red dripped down the screen. Then the green background turned to blue, the printer shut off, and there was nothing left but the little black corpse lying on its back and the word ★★DONE★★ at the bottom of the screen.

I took a deep breath, and glanced at Osborne. It would be an understatement to say he did not look happy.

"What's this about drugs in the bedroom?" he said.

* * *

We watched Osborne pulling out drawers in dressers and bedside tables. He didn't find anything. He looked under the bed, and in the closet. Like all the other rooms in the house, this one was full of computers. Holes had been knocked in walls for the thick sheaves of cables.

I had been standing near a big cardboard drum, one of several in the room. It was about thirty gallon capacity, the kind you ship things in. The lid was loose, so I lifted it. I sort of wished I hadn't.

"Osborne," I said. "You'd better look at this."

The drum was lined with a heavy-duty garbage bag. And it was two-thirds full of Quaaludes.

They pried the lids off the rest of the drums. We found drums of amphetamines, of Nembutals, of Valium. All sorts of things.

With the discovery of the drugs a lot more police returned to the scene. With them came the television camera crews.

In all the activity no one seemed concerned about me, so I slipped back to my own house and locked the door. From time to time I peeked out the curtains. I saw reporters interviewing the neighbors. Hal was there, and seemed to be having a good time. Twice crews knocked on my door, but I didn't answer. Eventually they went away.

I ran a hot bath and soaked in it for about an hour. Then I turned the heat up as high as it would go and got in bed, under the blankets.

I shivered all night.

Osborne came over about nine the next morning. I let him in. Hal followed, looking very unhappy. I realized they had been up all night. I poured coffee for them.

"You'd better read this first," Osborne said, and handed me the sheet of computer printout. I unfolded it, got out my glasses, and started to read.

It was in that awful dot-matrix printing. My policy is to

throw any such trash into the fireplace, un-read, but I made an exception this time.

It was Kluge's will. Some probate court was going to have a lot of fun with it.

He stated again that he didn't exist, so he could have no relatives. He had decided to give all his worldly property to somebody who deserved it.

But who was deserving? Kluge wondered. Well, not Mr. and Mrs. Perkins, four houses down the street. They were child abusers. He cited court records in Buffalo and Miami, and a pending case locally.

Mrs. Radnor and Mrs. Polonski, who lived across the street from each other five houses down, were gossips.

The Anderson's oldest son was a car thief.

Marian Flores cheated on her high school algebra tests.

There was a guy nearby who was diddling the city on a freeway construction project. There was one wife in the neighborhood who made out with door-to-door salesmen, and two having affairs with men other than their husbands. There was a teenage boy who got his girlfriend pregnant, dropped her, and bragged about it to his friends.

There were no fewer than nineteen couples in the immediate area who had not reported income to the IRS, or who had padded their deductions.

Kluge's neighbors in back had a dog that barked all night.

Well, I could vouch for the dog. He'd kept me awake often enough. But the rest of it was *crazy!* For one thing, where did a guy with two hundred gallons of illegal narcotics get the right to judge his neighbors so harshly? I mean, the child abusers were one thing, but was it right to tar a whole family because their son stole cars? And for another . . . how did he *know* some of this stuff?

But there was more. Specifically, four philandering husbands. One was Harold "Hal" Lanier, who for three years had been seeing a woman named Toni Jones, a co-worker at the L.A.P.D. Data Processing facility. She was pressuring him for a divorce; he was "waiting for the right time to tell his wife."

I glanced up at Hal. His red face was all the confirmation I needed.

Then it hit me. What had Kluge found out about *me?*

I hurried down the page, searching for my name. I found it in the last paragraph.

". . . for thirty years Mr. Apfel has been paying for a mistake he did not even make. I won't go so far as to nominate him for sainthood, but by default—if for no other reason—I hereby leave all deed and title to my real property and the structure thereon to Victor Apfel."

I looked at Osborne, and those tired eyes were weighing me.

"But I don't *want* it!"

"Do you think this is the reward Kluge mentioned in the phone call?"

"It must be," I said. "What else could it be?"

Osborne sighed, and sat back in his chair. "At least he didn't try to leave you the drugs. Are you still saying you didn't know the guy?"

"Are you accusing me of something?"

He spread his hands. "Mister Apfel, I'm simply asking a question. You're never one hundred percent sure in a suicide. Maybe it was a murder. If it was, you can see that, so far, you're the only one we know of that's gained by it."

"He was almost a stranger to me."

He nodded, tapping his copy of the computer printout. I looked back at my own, wishing it would go away.

"What's this . . . mistake you didn't make?"

I was afraid that would be the next question.

"I was a prisoner of war in North Korea," I said.

Osborne chewed that over for a while.

"They brainwash you?"

"Yes." I hit the arm of my chair, and suddenly had to be up and moving. The room was getting cold. "No. I don't . . . there's been a lot of confusion about that word. Did they 'brainwash' me? Yes. Did they succeed? Did I offer a confession of my war crimes and denounce the U.S. Government? No."

Once more, I felt myself being inspected by those deceptively tired eyes.

"You still seem to have . . . strong feelings about it."

"It's not something you forget."

"Is there anything you want to say about it?"

"It's just that it was all so . . . no. No, I have nothing further to say. Not to you, not to anybody."

"I'm going to have to ask you more questions about Kluge's death."

"I think I'll have my lawyer present for those." Christ. Now I am going to have to get a lawyer. I didn't know where to begin.

Osborne just nodded again. He got up and went to the door.

"I was ready to write this one down as a suicide," he said. "The only thing that bothered me was there was no note. Now we've got a note." He gestured in the direction of Kluge's house, and started to look angry.

"This guy not only writes a note, he programs the fucking thing into his computer, complete with special effects straight out of Pac-Man.

"Now, I know people do crazy things. I've seen enough of them. But when I heard the computer playing a hymn, that's when I knew this was murder. Tell you the truth, Mr. Apfel, I don't think you did it. There must be two dozen motives for murder in that printout. Maybe he was blackmailing people around here. Maybe that's how he bought all those machines. And people with that amount of drugs usually die violently. I've got a lot of work to do on this one, and I'll find who did it." He mumbled something about not leaving town, and that he'd see me later, and left.

"Vic . . ." Hal said. I looked at him.

"About that printout," he finally said. "I'd appreciate it . . . well, they said they'd keep it confidential. If you know what I mean." He had eyes like a basset hound. I'd never noticed that before.

"Hal, if you'll just go home, you have nothing to worry about from me."

He nodded, and scuttled for the door.

"I don't think any of that will get out," he said.

It all did, of course.

It probably would have even without the letters that began arriving a few days after Kluge's death, all postmarked Trenton, New Jersey, all computer-generated from a machine no one was ever able to trace. The letters detailed the matters Kluge had mentioned in his will.

I didn't know about any of that at the time. I spent the rest of the day after Hal's departure lying in my bed, under the electric blanket. I couldn't get my feet warm. I got up only to soak in the tub or to make a sandwich.

Reporters knocked on the door but I didn't answer. On the second day I called a criminal lawyer—Martin Abrams, the first in the book—and retained him. He told me they'd probably call me down to the police station for questioning. I told him I wouldn't go, popped two Dilantin, and sprinted for the bed.

A couple of times I heard sirens in the neighborhood. Once I heard a shouted argument down the street. I resisted the temptation to look. I'll admit I was a little curious, but you know what happened to the cat.

I kept waiting for Osborne to return, but he didn't. The

days turned into a week. Only two things of interest happened in that time.

The first was a knock on my door. This was two days after Kluge's death. I looked through the curtains and saw a silver Ferrari parked at the curb. I couldn't see who was on the porch, so I asked who it was.

"My name's Lisa Foo," she said. "You asked me to drop by."

"I certainly don't remember it."

"Isn't this Charles Kluge's house?"

"That's next door."

"Oh. Sorry."

I decided I ought to warn her Kluge was dead, so I opened the door. She turned around and smiled at me. It was blinding.

Where does one start in describing Lisa Foo? Remember when newspapers used to run editorial cartoons of Hirohito and Tojo, when the *Times* used the word "Jap" without embarrassment? Little guys with faces wide as footballs, ears like jug handles, thick glasses, two big rabbity buck teeth, and pencil-thin moustaches . . .

Leaving out only the moustache, she was a dead ringer for a cartoon Tojo. She had the glasses, and the ears, and the teeth. But her teeth had braces, like piano keys wrapped in barbed wire. And she was five-eight or five-nine and couldn't have weighed more than a hundred and ten. I'd have said a hundred, but added five pounds each for her breasts, so improbably large on her scrawny frame that all I could read of the message on her T-shirt was "POCK LIVE." It was only when she turned sideways that I saw the esses before and after.

She thrust out a slender hand.

"Looks like I'm going to be your neighbor for a while," she said. "At least until we get that dragon's lair next door straightened out." If she had an accent, it was San Fernando Valley.

"That's nice."

"Did you know him? Kluge, I mean. Or at least that's what he called himself."

"You don't think that was his name?"

"I doubt it. 'Klug' means clever in German. And it's hacker slang for being tricky. And he sure was a tricky bugger. Definitely some glitches in the wetware." She tapped the side of her head meaningfully. "Viruses and phantoms and demons jumping out every time they try to key in, Software rot, bit buckets overflowing onto the floor . . ."

She babbled on in that vein for a time. It might as well have been Swahili.

"Did you say there were demons in his computers?"

"That's right."

"Sounds like they need an exorcist."

She jerked her thumb at her chest and showed me another half-acre of teeth.

"That's me. Listen, I gotta go. Drop in and see me anytime."

The second interesting event of the week happened the next day. My bank statement arrived. There were three deposits listed. The first was the regular check from the V.A., for $487.00. The second was for $392.54, interest on the money my parents had left me fifteen years ago.

The third deposit had come in on the twentieth, the day Charles Kluge died. It was for $700,083.04.

A few days later Hal Lanier dropped by.

"Boy, what a week," he said. Then he flopped down on the couch and told me all about it.

There had been a second death on the block. The letters had stirred up a lot of trouble, especially with the police going house to house questioning everyone. Some people had confessed to things when they were sure the cops were closing in on them. The woman who used to entertain salesmen while her husband was at work had admitted her infidelity, and the guy had shot her. He was in the County Jail. That was the worst incident, but there had been others, from fistfights to rocks thrown through windows. According to Hal, the IRS was thinking of setting up a branch office in the neighborhood, so many people were being audited.

I thought about the seven hundred thousand and eighty-three dollars.

And four cents.

I didn't say anything, but my feet were getting cold.

"I suppose you want to know about me and Betty," he said, at last. I didn't. I didn't want to hear *any* of this, but I tried for a sympathetic expression.

"That's all over," he said, with a satisfied sigh. "Between me and Toni, I mean. I told Betty all about it. It was real bad for a few days, but I think our marriage is stronger for it now." He was quiet for a moment, basking in the warmth of it all. I had kept a straight face under worse provocation, so I trust I did well enough then.

He wanted to tell me all they'd learned about Kluge, and he wanted to invite me over for dinner, but I begged off on both, telling him my war wounds were giving me hell. I just about had him to the door when Osborne knocked on it. There was nothing to do but let him in. Hal stuck around, too.

I offered Osborne coffee, which he gratefully accepted. He looked different. I wasn't sure what it was at first. Same old tired expression . . . no, it wasn't. Most of that weary look had been either an act or a cop's built-in cynicism. Today it was genuine. The tiredness had moved from his face to his shoulders, to his hands, to the way he walked and the way he slumped in the chair. There was a sour aura of defeat around him.

"Am I still a suspect?" I asked.

"You mean should you call your lawyer? I'd say don't bother. I checked you out pretty good. That will ain't gonna hold up, so your motive is pretty half-assed. Way I figure it, every coke dealer in the Marina had a better reason to snuff Kluge than you." He sighed. "I got a couple questions. You can answer them or not."

"Give it a try."

"You remember any unusual visitors he had? People coming and going at night?"

"The only visitors I *ever* recall were deliveries. Post office. Federal Express, freight companies . . . that sort of thing. I suppose the drugs could have come in any of those shipments."

"That's what we figure, too. There's no way he was dealing nickel and dime bags. He must have been a middle man. Ship it in, ship it out." He brooded about that for a while, and sipped his coffee.

"So are you making any progress?" I asked.

"You want to know the truth? The case is going in the toilet. We've got too many motives, and not a one of them that works. As far as we can tell, nobody on the block had the slightest idea Kluge had all that information. We've checked bank accounts and we can't find evidence of blackmail. So the neighbors are pretty much out of the picture. Though if he were alive, most people around here would like to kill him *now*."

"Damn straight," Hal said.

Osborne slapped his thigh. "If the bastard was alive, *I'd* kill him," he said. "But I'm beginning to think he never *was* alive."

"I don't understand."

"If I hadn't seen the goddam body . . ." He sat up a little straighter. "He said he didn't exist. Well, he practically didn't. PG&E never heard of him. He's hooked up to their lines and a meter reader came by every month, but they never billed him for a single kilowatt. Same with the phone company. He had a whole exchange in that house that was *made* by the phone company, and delivered by them, and installed by them, but they have no record of him. We talked to the guy who hooked it all up. He turned in his records, and the computer swallowed them. Kluge didn't have a bank account anywhere in California, and apparently he didn't need one. We've tracked down a hundred companies that sold things to him, shipped them out, and then either marked his account paid or forgot they ever sold him anything. Some of them have check numbers and account numbers in their books, for accounts or even *banks* that don't exist."

He leaned back in his chair, simmering at the perfidy of it all.

"The only guy we've found who ever heard of him was the guy who delivered his groceries once a month. Little store down on Sepulveda. They don't have a computer, just paper receipts. He paid by check. Wells Fargo accepted them and the checks never bounced. But Wells Fargo never heard of him."

I thought it over. He seemed to expect something of me at this point, so I made a stab at it.

"He was doing all this by computers?"

"That's right. Now, the grocery store scam I understand, almost. But more often than not, Kluge got right into the basic programming of the computers and wiped himself out. The power company was never paid, by check or any other way, because as far as they were concerned, they weren't selling him anything.

"No government agency has ever heard of him. We've checked him with everybody from the post office to the CIA."

"Kluge was probably an alias, right?" I offered.

"Yeah. But the FBI doesn't have his fingerprints. We'll

find out who he was, eventually. But it doesn't get us any closer to whether or not he was murdered."

He admitted there was pressure to simply close the felony part of the case, label it suicide, and forget it. But Osborne would not believe it. Naturally, the civil side would go on for some time, as they attempted to track down all Kluge's deceptions.

"It's all up to the dragon lady," Osborne said. Hal snorted.

"Fat chance," Hal said, and muttered something about boat people.

"That girl? She's still over there? Who is she?"

"She's some sort of giant brain from Cal Tech. We called out there and told them we were having problems, and she's what they sent." It was clear from Osborne's face what he thought of any help she might provide.

I finally managed to get rid of them. As they went down the walk I looked over at Kluge's house. Sure enough, Lisa Foo's silver Ferrari was sitting in his driveway.

I had no business going over there. I knew that better than anyone.

So I set about preparing my evening meal. I made a tuna casserole—which is not as bland as it sounds, the way I make it—put it in the oven and went out to the garden to pick the makings for a salad. I was slicing cherry tomatoes and thinking about chilling a bottle of wine when it occurred to me that I had enough for two.

Since I never do anything hastily, I sat down and thought it over for a while. What finally decided me was my feet. For the first time in a week, they were warm. So I went to Kluge's house.

The front door was standing open. There was no screen. Funny how disturbing that can look, the dwelling wide open and unguarded. I stood on the porch and leaned in, but all I could see was the hallway.

"Miss Foo?" I called. There was no answer.

The last time I'd been here I had found a dead man. I hurried in.

Lisa Foo was sitting on a piano bench before a computer console. She was in profile, her back very straight, her brown legs in lotus position, her fingers poised at the keys as words sprayed rapidly onto the screen in front of her. She looked up and flashed her teeth at me.

"Somebody told me your name was Victor Apfel," she said.

"Yes. Uh, the door was open . . ."

"It's hot," she said, reasonably, pinching the fabric of her shirt near her neck and lifting it up and down like you do when you're sweaty. "What can I do for you?"

"Nothing, really." I came into the dimness, and stumbled on something. It was a cardboard box, the large flat kind used for delivering a jumbo pizza.

"I was just fixing dinner, and it looks like there's plenty for two, so I was wondering if you . . ." I trailed off, as I had just noticed something else. I had thought she was wearing shorts. In fact, all she had on was the shirt and a pair of pink bikini underpants. This did not seem to make her uneasy.

". . . would you like to join me for dinner?"

Her smile grew even broader.

"I'd love to," she said. She effortlessly unwound her legs and bounced to her feet, then brushed past me, trailing the smells of perspiration and sweet soap. "Be with you in a minute."

I looked around the room again but my mind kept coming back to her. She liked Pepsi with her pizza; there were dozens of empty cans. There was a deep scar on her knee and upper thigh. The ashtrays were empty . . . and the long muscles of her calves bunched strongly as she walked. Kluge must have smoked, but Lisa didn't, and she had fine, downy hairs in the small of her back just visible in the green computer light. I heard water running in the bathroom sink, looked at a yellow notepad covered with the kind of penmanship I hadn't seen in decades, and smelled soap and remembered tawny brown skin and an easy stride.

She appeared in the hall, wearing cut-off jeans, sandals, and a new T-shirt. The old one had advertised BURROUGHS OFFICE SYSTEMS. This one featured Mickey Mouse and Snow White's Castle and smelled of fresh bleached cotton. Mickey's ears were laid back on the upper slopes of her incongruous breasts.

I followed her out the door. Tinkerbell twinkled in pixie dust from the back of her shirt.

"I like this kitchen," she said.

You don't really look at a place until someone says something like that.

The kitchen was a time capsule. It could have been lifted bodily from an issue of *Life* in the early fifties. There was the hump-shouldered Frigidaire, of a vintage when that word had been a generic term, like kleenex or coke. The counter tops were yellow tile, the sort that's only found in bathrooms these days. There wasn't an ounce of Formica in the place. Instead of a dishwasher I had a wire rack and a double sink. There was no electric can opener, Cuisinart, trash compacter, or microwave oven. The newest thing in the whole room was a fifteen-year-old blender.

I'm good with my hands. I like to repair things.

"This bread is terrific," she said.

I had baked it myself. I watched her mop her plate with a crust, and she asked if she might have seconds.

I understand cleaning one's plate with bread is bad manners. Not that I cared; I do it myself. And other than that, her manners were impeccable. She polished off three helpings of my casserole and when she was done the plate hardly needed washing. I had a sense of ravenous appetite barely held in check.

She settled back in her chair and I re-filled her glass with white wine.

"Are you sure you wouldn't like some more peas?"

"I'd bust." She patted her stomach contentedly. "Thank you so much, Mister Apfel. I haven't had a home-cooked meal in ages."

"You can call me Victor."

"I just love American food."

"I didn't know there was such a thing. I mean, not like Chinese or . . . you *are* American, aren't you?" She just smiled. "What I mean—"

"I know what you meant, Victor. I'm a citizen, but not native-born. Would you excuse me for a moment? I know it's impolite to jump right up, but with these braces I find I have to brush *instantly* after eating."

I could hear her as I cleared the table. I ran water in the sink and started doing the dishes. Before long she joined me, grabbed a dish towel, and began drying the things in the rack, over my protests.

"You live alone here?" she asked.

"Yes. Have ever since my parents died."

"Ever married? If it's none of my business, just say so."

"That's all right. No, I never married."

"You do pretty good for not having a woman around."

"I've had a lot of practice. Can I ask you a question?"

"Shoot."

"Where are you from? Taiwan?"

"I have a knack for languages. Back home, I spoke pidgin American, but when I got here I cleaned up my act. I also speak rotten French, illiterate Chinese in four or five varieties, gutter Vietnamese, and enough Thai to holler, 'Me wanna see American Consul, pretty-damn-quick, you!' "

I laughed. When she said it, her accent was thick.

"I been here eight years now. You figured out where home is?"

"Vietnam?" I ventured.

"The sidewalks of Saigon, fer shure. Or Ho Chi Minh's Shitty, as the pajama-heads re-named it, may their dinks rot off and their butts be filled with jagged punjee-sticks. Pardon my French."

She ducked her head in embarrassment. What had started out light had turned hot very quickly. I sensed a hurt at least as deep as my own, and we both backed off from it.

"I took you for a Japanese," I said.

"Yeah, ain't it a pisser? I'll tell you about it some day. Victor, is that a laundry room through that door there? With an electric washer?"

"That's right."

"Would it be too much trouble if I did a load?"

It was no trouble at all. She had seven pairs of faded jeans, some with the legs cut away, and about two dozen T-shirts. It could have been a load of boys' clothing except for the frilly underwear.

We went into the back yard to sit in the last rays of the setting sun, then she had to see my garden. I'm quite proud of it. When I'm well, I spend four or five hours a day working out there, year-round, usually in the morning hours. You can do that in southern California. I have a small greenhouse I built myself.

She loved it, though it was not in its best shape. I had spent most of the week in bed or in the tub. As a result, weeds were sprouting here and there.

"We had a garden when I was little," she said. "And I spent two years in a rice paddy."

"That must be a lot different than this."

"Damn straight. Put me off rice for *years*."

She discovered an infestation of aphids, so we squatted

down to pick them off. She had that double-jointed Asian peasant's way of sitting that I remembered so well and could never imitate. Her fingers were long and narrow, and soon the tips of them were green from squashed bugs.

We talked about this and that. I don't remember quite how it came up, but I told her I had fought in Korea. I learned she was twenty-five. It turned out we had the same birthday, so some months back I had been exactly twice her age.

The only time Kluge's name came up was when she mentioned how she liked to cook. She hadn't been able to at Kluge's house.

"He has a freezer in the garage full of frozen dinners." she said. "He had one plate, one fork, one spoon, and one glass. He's got the best microwave oven on the market. And that's *it*, man. Ain't nothing else in his kitchen at *all*." She shook her head, and executed an aphid. "He was one weird dude."

When her laundry was done it was late evening, almost dark. She loaded it into my wicker basket and we took it out to the clothesline. It got to be a game. I would shake out a T-shirt and study the picture or message there. Sometimes I got it, and sometimes I didn't. There were pictures of rock groups, a map of Los Angeles, Star Trek tie-ins . . . a little of everything.

"What's the L5 Society?" I asked her.

"Guys that want to build these great big farms in space. I asked 'em if they were gonna grow rice, and they said they didn't think it was the best crop for zero gee, so I bought the shirt."

"How many of these things do you have?"

"Wow, it's gonna be four or five hundred. I usually wear 'em two or three times and then put them away."

I picked up another shirt, and a bra fell out. It wasn't the kind of bra girls wore when I was growing up. It was very sheer, though somehow functional at the same time.

"You like, Yank?" Her accent was very thick. "You oughtta see my sister!"

I glanced at her, and her face fell.

"I'm sorry, Victor," she said. "You don't have to blush." She took the bra from me and clipped it to the line.

She must have mis-read my face. True, I had been embarrassed, but I was also pleased in some strange way. It had been a long time since anybody had called me anything but Victor or Mr. Apfel.

The next day's mail brought a letter from a law firm in Chicago. It was about the seven hundred thousand dollars. The money had come from a Delaware holding company which had been set up in 1933 to provide for me in my old age. My mother and father were listed as the founders. Certain long-term investments had matured, resulting in my recent windfall. The amount in my bank was *after* taxes.

It was ridiculous on the face of it. My parents had never had that kind of money. I didn't want it. I would have given it back if I could find out who Kluge had stolen it from.

I decided that, if I wasn't in jail this time next year, I'd give it all to some charity. Save the Whales, maybe, or the L5 Society.

I spent the morning in the garden. Later I walked to the market and bought some fresh ground beef and pork. I was feeling good as I pulled my purchases home in my fold-up wire basket. When I passed the silver Ferrari I smiled.

She hadn't come to get her laundry. I took it off the line and folded it, then knocked on Kluge's door.

"It's me. Victor."

"Come on in, Yank."

She was where she had been before, but decently dressed this time. She smiled at me, then hit her forehead when she saw the laundry basket. She hurried to take it from me.

"I'm sorry, Victor. I meant to get this—"

"Don't worry about it," I said. "It was no trouble. And it gives me the chance to ask if you'd like to dine with me again."

Something happened to her face which she covered quickly. Perhaps she didn't like "American" food as much as she professed to. Or maybe it was the cook.

"Sure, Victor, I'd love to. Let me take care of this. And why don't you open those drapes? It's like a tomb in here."

She hurried away. I glanced at the screen she had been using. It was blank, but for one word: intercourse-p. I assumed it was a typo.

I pulled the drapes open in time to see Osborne's car park at the curb. Then Lisa was back, wearing a new T-shirt. This one said A CHANGE OF HOBBIT, and had a picture of a squat, hairy-footed creature. She glanced out the window and saw Osborne coming up the walk.

"I say, Watson," she said. "It's Lestrade of the Yard. Do show him in."

That wasn't nice of her. He gave me a suspicious glance as he entered. I burst out laughing. Lisa sat on the piano bench, poker-faced. She slumped indolently, one arm resting near the keyboard.

"Well, Apfel," Osborne started. "We've finally found out who Kluge really was."

"Patrick William Gavin," Lisa said.

Quite a time went by before Osborne was able to close his mouth. Then he opened it right up again.

"How the hell did you find that out?"

She lazily caressed the keyboard beside her.

"Well, of course I got it when it came into your office this morning. There's a little stoolie program tucked away in your computer that whispers in my ear every time the name Kluge is mentioned. But I didn't need that. I figured it out five days ago."

"Then why the . . . why didn't you tell me?"

"You didn't ask me."

They glared at each other for a while. I had no idea what events had led up to this moment, but it was quite clear they didn't like each other even a little bit. Lisa was on top just now, and seemed to be enjoying it. Then she glanced at her screen, looked surprised, and quickly tapped a key. The word that had been there vanished. She gave me an inscrutable glance, then faced Osborne again.

"If you recall, you brought me in because all your own guys were getting was a lot of crashes. This system was brain-damaged when I got here, practically catatonic. Most of it was down and your guys couldn't get it up." She had to grin at that.

"You decided I couldn't do any worse than your guys were doing. So you asked me to try and break Kluge's codes without frying the system. Well, I did it. All you had to do was come by and interface and I would have downloaded N tons of wallpaper right in your lap."

Osborne listened quietly. Maybe he even knew he had made a mistake.

"What did you get? Can I see it now?"

She nodded, and pressed a few keys. Words started to fill her screen, and one close to Osborne. I got up and read Lisa's terminal.

It was a brief bio of Kluge/Gavin. He was about my age, but while I was getting shot at in a foreign land, he was cutting a swath through the infant computer industry. He had been there from the ground up, working at many of the top research facilities. It surprised me that it had taken over a week to identify him.

"I compiled this anecdotally," Lisa said, as we read. "The first thing you have to realize about Gavin is that he exists nowhere in any computerized information system. So I called people all over the country—interesting phone system he's got, by the way; it generates a new number for each call, and you can't call back or trace it—and started asking who the top people were in the fifties and sixties. I got a lot of names. After that, it was a matter of finding out who no longer existed in the files. He faked his death in 1967. I located one account of it in a newspaper file. Everybody I talked to who had known him knew of his death. There is a paper birth certificate in Florida. That's the only other evidence I found of him. He was the only guy so many people in the field knew who left no mark on the world. That seemed conclusive to me."

Osborne finished reading, then looked up.

"All right, Ms. Foo. What else have you found out?"

"I've broken some of his codes. I had a piece of luck, getting into a basic rape-and-plunder program he'd written to attack *other* people's programs, and I've managed to use it against a few of his own. I've unlocked a file of passwords with notes on where they came from. And I've learned a few of his tricks. But it's the tip of the iceberg."

She waved a hand at the silent metal brains in the room.

"What I haven't gotten across to anyone is just what this *is*. This is the most devious electronic weapon ever devised. It's armored like a battleship. It has to be; there's a lot of very slick programs out there that grab an invader and hang on like a terrier. If they ever got this far Kluge could deflect them. But usually they never even knew they'd been burgled. Kluge'd come in like a cruise missile, low and fast and twisty. And he'd route his attack through a dozen cut-offs.

"He had a lot of advantages. Big systems these days are heavily protected. People use passwords and very sophisticated codes. But Kluge helped *invent* most of them. You need a damn good lock to keep out a locksmith. He helped *install* a lot of the major systems. He left informants behind, hidden in the software. If the codes were changed, the computer *itself* would send the information to a safe system that

Kluge could tap later. It's like you buy the biggest, meanest, best-trained watchdog you can. And that night, the guy who *trained* the dog comes in, pats him on the head, and robs you blind."

There was a lot more in that vein. I'm afraid that when Lisa began talking about computers, ninety percent of my head shut off.

"I'd like to know something, Osborne," Lisa said.

"What would that be?"

"What is my status here? Am I supposed to be solving your crime for you, or just trying to get this system back to where a competent user can deal with it?"

Osborne thought it over.

"What worries me," she added, "is that I'm poking around in a lot of restricted data banks. I'm worried about somebody knocking on the door and handcuffing me. *You* ought to be worried, too. Some of these agencies wouldn't like a homicide cop looking into their affairs."

Osborne bridled at that. Maybe that's what she intended.

"What do I have to do?" he snarled. "Beg you to stay?"

"No. I just want your authorization. You don't have to put it in writing. Just say you're behind me."

"Look. As far as L.A. County and the State of California are concerned, this house doesn't exist. There is no lot here. It doesn't appear in the assessor's records. This place is in a legal limbo. If anybody can authorize you to use this stuff, it's me, because I believe a murder was committed in it. So you just keep doing what you've been doing."

"That's not much of a commitment," she mused.

"It's all you're going to get. Now, what else have you got?"

She turned to her keyboard and typed for a while. Pretty soon a printer started, and Lisa leaned back. I glanced at her screen. It said: osculate posterior-p. I remembered that osculate meant kiss. Well, these people have their own language. Lisa looked up at me and grinned.

"Not you," she said, quietly. *"Him."*

I hadn't the faintest notion of what she was talking about.

Osborne got his printout and was ready to leave. Again, he couldn't resist turning at the door for final orders.

"If you find anything to indicate he didn't commit suicide, let me know."

"Okay. He didn't commit suicide."

Osborne didn't understand for a moment.

"I want proof."

"Well, I have it, but you probably can't use it. He didn't write that ridiculous suicide note."

"How do you know that?"

"I knew that my first day here. I had the computer list the program. Then I compared it to Kluge's style. No *way* he could have written it. It's tighter'n a bug's ass. Not a spare line in it. Kluge didn't pick his alias for nothing. You know what it means?"

"Clever," I said.

"Literally. But it means . . . a Rube Goldberg device. Something overly complex. Something that works, but for the wrong reason. You 'kluge around' bugs in a program. It's the hacker's vaseline."

"So?" Osborne wanted to know.

"So Kluge's programs were really crocked. They were full of bells and whistles he never bothered to clean out. He was a genius, and his programs worked, but you wonder why they did. Routines so bletcherous they'd make your skin crawl. Real crufty bagbiters. But good programming's so rare, even his diddles were better than most people's super-moby hacks."

I suspect Osborne understood about as much of that as I did.

"So you base your opinion on his programming style."

"Yeah. Unfortunately, it's gonna be ten years or so before

that's admissable in court, like graphology or fingerprints. But if you know anything about programming you can look at it and see it. Somebody else wrote that suicide note—somebody damn good, by the way. That program called up his last will and testament as a sub-routine. And he definitely *did* write that. It's got his fingerprints all over it. He spent the last five years spying on the neighbors as a hobby. He tapped into military records, school records, work records, tax files and bank accounts. And he turned every telephone for three blocks into a listening device. He was one hell of a snoop."

"Did he mention anywhere why he did that?" Osborne asked.

"I think he was more than half crazy. Possibly he was suicidal. He sure wasn't doing himself any good with all those pills he took. But he was preparing himself for death, and Victor was the only one he found worthy of leaving it all to. I'd have *believed* he committed suicide if not for that note. But he didn't write it. I'll swear to that."

We eventually got rid of him, and I went home to fix the dinner. Lisa joined me when it was ready. Once more she had a huge appetite.

I fixed lemonade and we sat on my small patio and watched evening gather around us.

I woke up in the middle of the night, sweating. I sat up, thinking it out, and I didn't like my conclusions. So I put on my robe and slippers and went over to Kluge's.

The front door was open again. I knocked anyway. Lisa stuck her head around the corner.

"Victor? Is something wrong?"

"I'm not sure," I said. "May I come in?"

She gestured, and I followed her into the living room. An open can of Pepsi sat beside her console. Her eyes were red as she sat on her bench.

"What's up?" she said, and yawned.

"You should be asleep, for one thing," I said.

She shrugged, and nodded.

"Yeah. I can't seem to get in the right phase. Just now I'm in day mode. But Victor, I'm used to working odd hours, and long hours, and you didn't come over here to lecture me about that, did you?"

"No. You say Kluge was murdered."

"He didn't write his suicide note. That seems to leave murder."

"I was wondering why someone would kill him. He never left the house, so it was for something he did here with his computers. And now you're . . . well, I don't know *what* you're doing, frankly, but you seem to be poking into the same things. Isn't there a danger the same people will come after you?"

"People?" She raised an eyebrow.

I felt helpless. My fears were not well-formed enough to make sense.

"I don't know . . . you mentioned agencies . . ."

"You notice how impressed Osborne was with that? You think there's some kind of conspiracy Kluge tumbled to, or you think the CIA killed him because he found out too much about something, or—"

"I don't know, Lisa. But I'm worried the same thing could happen to you."

Surprisingly, she smiled at me.

"Thank you so much, Victor. I wasn't going to admit it to Osborne, but I've been worried about that, too."

"Well, what are you going to do?"

"I want to stay here and keep working. So I gave some thought to what I could do to protect myself. I decided there wasn't anything."

"Surely there's something."

"Well, I got a gun, if that's what you mean. But think about it. Kluge was offed in the middle of the day. Nobody saw anybody enter or leave the house. So I asked myself, who can walk into a house in broad daylight, shoot Kluge, program that suicide note, and walk away, leaving no traces he'd ever been there?"

"Somebody very good."

"Goddam good. So good there's not much chance one little gook's gonna be able to stop him if he decides to waste her."

She shocked me, both by her words and by her apparent lack of concern for her own fate. But she had said she was worried.

"Then you have to stop this. Get out of here."

"I won't be pushed around that way," she said. There was a tone of finality to it. I thought of things I might say, and rejected them all.

"You could at least . . . lock your front door," I concluded, lamely.

She laughed, and kissed my cheek.

"I'll do that, Yank. And I appreciate your concern. I really do."

I watched her close the door behind me, listened to her lock it, then trudged through the moonlight toward my house. Halfway there I stopped. I could suggest she stay in my spare bedroom. I could offer to stay with her at Kluge's.

No, I decided. She would probably take that the wrong way.

I was back in bed before I realized, with a touch of chagrin and more than a little disgust at myself, that she had every reason to take it the wrong way.

And me exactly twice her age.

I spent the morning in the garden, planning the evening's menu. I have always liked to cook, but dinner with Lisa had rapidly become the high point of my day. Not only that, I was already taking it for granted. So it hit me hard, around noon, when I looked out the front and saw her car gone.

I hurried to Kluge's front door. It was standing open. I made a quick search of the house. I found nothing until the master bedroom, where her clothes were stacked neatly on the floor.

Shivering, I pounded on the Laniers' front door. Betty answered, and immediately saw my agitation.

"The girl at Kluge's house," I said. "I'm afraid something's wrong. Maybe we'd better call the police."

"What happened?" Betty asked, looking over my shoulder. "Did she call you? I see she's not back yet."

"Back?"

"I saw her drive away about an hour ago. That's quite a car she has."

Feeling like a fool, I tried to make nothing of it, but I caught a look in Betty's eye. I think she'd have liked to pat me on the head. It made me furious.

But she'd left her clothes, so surely she was coming back.

I kept telling myself that, then went to run a bath, as hot as I could stand it.

When I answered the door she was standing there with a grocery bag in each arm and her usual blinding smile on her face.

"I wanted to do this yesterday but I forgot until you came over, and I know I should have asked first, but then I wanted to surprise you, so I just went to get one or two items you didn't have in your garden and a couple of things that weren't in your spice rack . . ."

She kept talking as we unloaded the bags in the kitchen. I said nothing. She was wearing a new T-shirt. There was a big V, and under it a picture of a screw, followed by a hyphen and a small case "p." I thought it over as she babbled on. V, screw-p. I was determined not to ask what it meant.

"Do you like Vietnamese cooking?"

I looked at her, and finally realized she was very nervous.

"I don't know," I said. "I've never had it. But I like Chinese, and Japanese, and Indian. I like to try new things." The last part was a lie, but not as bad as it might have been. I do try new recipes, and my tastes in food are catholic. I didn't expect to have much trouble with southeast Asian cuisine.

"Well, when I get through you *still* won't know," she laughed. "My momma was half-Chinese. So what you're gonna get here is a mongrel meal." She glanced up, saw my face, and laughed.

"I forgot. You've been to Asia. No, Yank, I ain't gonna serve any dog meat."

There was only one intolerable thing, and that was the chopsticks. I used them for as long as I could, then put them aside and got a fork.

"I'm sorry," I said. "Chopsticks happen to be a problem for me."

"You use them very well."

"I had plenty of time to learn how."

It was very good, and I told her so. Each dish was a revelation, not quite like anything I had ever had. Toward the end, I broke down halfway.

"Does the V stand for victory?" I asked.

"Maybe."

"Beethoven? Churchill? World War Two?"

She just smiled.

"Think of it as a challenge, Yank."

"Do I frighten you, Victor?"

"You did at first."

"It's my face, isn't it?"

"It's a generalized phobia of Orientals. I suppose I'm a racist. Not because I want to be."

She nodded slowly, there in the dark. We were on the patio again, but the sun had gone down a long time ago. I can't recall what we had talked about for all those hours. It had kept us busy, anyway.

"I have the same problem," she said.

"Fear of Orientals?" I had meant it as a joke.

"Of Cambodians." She let me take that in for a while, then went on. "When Saigon fell, I fled to Cambodia. It took me two years with stops when the Khmer Rouge put me in labor camps. I'm lucky to be alive, really."

"I thought they called it Kampuchea now."

She spat. I'm not even sure she was aware she had done it.

"It's the People's Republic of Syphilitic Dogs. The North Koreans treated you very badly, didn't they, Victor?"

"That's right."

"Koreans are pus suckers." I must have looked surprised, because she chuckled.

"You Americans feel so guilty about racism. As if you had invented it and nobody else—except maybe the South Africans and the Nazis—had ever practiced it as heinously as you. And you can't tell one yellow face from another, so you think of the yellow race as one homogeneous block. When in fact Orientals are among the most racist peoples on the earth. The Vietnamese have hated the Cambodians for a thousand years. The Chinese hate the Japanese. The Koreans hate everybody. And *everybody* hates the 'ethnic Chinese.' The Chinese are the Jews of the east."

"I've heard that."

She nodded, lost in her own thoughts.

"And I hate all Cambodians," she said, at last. "Like you, I don't wish to. Most of the people who suffered in the camps were Cambodians. It was the genocidal leaders, the

Pol Pot scum, who I should hate." She looked at me. "But sometimes we don't get a lot of choice about things like that, do we, Yank?"

The next day I visited her at noon. It had cooled down, but was still warm in her dark den. She had not changed her shirt.

She told me a few things about computers. When she let me try some things on the keyboard I quickly got lost. We decided I needn't plan on a career as a computer programmer.

One of the things she showed me was called a telephone modem, whereby she could reach other computers all over the world. She "interfaced" with someone at Stanford who she had never met, and who she knew only as "Bubble Sorter." They typed things back and forth at each other.

At the end, Bubble Sorter wrote "bye-p." Lisa typed T.

"What's T?" I asked.

"True. Means yes, but yes would be too straightforward for a hacker."

"You told me what a byte is. What's a bye-p?"

She looked up at me seriously.

"It's a question. Add p to a word, and make it a question. So bye-p means Bubble Sorter was asking if I wanted to log out. Sign off."

I thought that over.

"So how would you translate 'osculate posterior-p'?"

" 'You wanna kiss my ass?' But remember, that was for Osborne."

I looked at her T-shirt again, then up to her eyes, which were quite serious and serene. She waited, hands folded in her lap.

Intercourse-p.

"Yes," I said. "I would."

She put her glasses on the table and pulled her shirt over her head.

* * *

We made love in Kluge's big waterbed.

I had a certain amount of performance anxiety—it had been a long, *long* time. After that, I was so caught up in the touch and smell and taste of her that I went a little crazy. She didn't seem to mind.

At last we were done, and bathed in sweat. She rolled over, stood, and went to the window. She opened it, and a breath of air blew over me. Then she put one knee on the bed, leaned over me, and got a pack of cigarettes from the bedside table. She lit one.

"I hope you're not allergic to smoke," she said.

"No. My father smoked. But I didn't know you did."

"Only afterwards," she said, with a quick smile. She took a deep drag. "Everybody in Saigon smoked, I think." She stretched out on her back beside me and we lay like that, soaking wet, holding hands. She opened her legs so one of her bare feet touched mine. It seemed enough contact. I watched the smoke rise from her right hand.

"I haven't felt warm in thirty years," I said. "I've been hot, but I've never been warm. I feel warm now."

"Tell me about it," she said.

So I did, as much as I could, wondering if it would work this time. At thirty years remove, my story does not sound so horrible. We've seen so much in that time. There were people in jails at that very moment, enduring conditions as bad as any I encountered. The paraphernalia of oppression is still pretty much the same. Nothing physical happened to me that would account for thirty years lived as a recluse.

"I *was* badly injured," I told her. "My skull was fractured. I still have . . . problems from that. Korea can get very cold, and I was never warm enough. But it was the other stuff. What they call brainwashing now.

"We didn't know what it was. We couldn't understand that even after a man had told them all he knew they'd keep on at us. Keeping us awake. Disorienting us. Some guys signed confessions, made up all sorts of stuff, but even that wasn't enough. They'd just keep at you.

"I never did figure it out. I guess I couldn't understand an evil that big. But when they were sending us back and some of the prisoners wouldn't go . . . they really didn't *want* to go, they really believed . . ."

I had to pause there. Lisa sat up, moved quietly to the end of the bed, and began massaging my feet.

"We got a taste of what the Vietnam guys got, later. Only for us it was reversed. The G.I.'s were heroes, and the prisoners were . . ."

"You didn't break," she said. It wasn't a question.

"No, I didn't."

"That would be worse."

I looked at her. She had my foot pressed against her flat belly, holding me by the heel while her other hand massaged my toes.

"The country was shocked," I said. "They didn't understand what brainwashing was. I tried telling people how it was. I thought they were looking at me funny. After a while, I stopped talking about it. And I didn't have anything else to talk about.

"A few years back the Army changed its policy. Now they don't expect you to withstand psychological conditioning. It's understood you can say anything or sign anything."

She just looked at me, kept massaging my foot, and nodded slowly. Finally she spoke.

"Cambodia was hot," she said. "I kept telling myself when I finally got to the U.S. I'd live in Maine or someplace, where it snowed. And I did go to Cambridge, but I found out I didn't like snow."

She told me about it. The last I heard, a million people had died over there. It was a whole country frothing at the mouth and snapping at anything that moved. Or like one of those sharks you read about that, when its guts are ripped out, bends in a circle and starts devouring itself.

She told me about being forced to build a pyramid of severed heads. Twenty of them working all day in the hot sun finally got it ten feet high before it collapsed. If any of them stopped working, their own heads were added to the pile.

"It didn't mean anything to me. It was just another job. I was pretty crazy by then. I didn't start to come out of it until I got across the Thai border."

That she had survived it at all seemed a miracle. She had gone through more horror than I could imagine. And she had come through it in much better shape. It made me feel small. When I was her age, I was well on my way to building the prison I have lived in ever since. I told her that.

"Part of it is preparation," she said, wryly. "What you expect out of life, what your life has been so far. You said it yourself. Korea was new to you. I'm not saying I was ready for Cambodia, but my life up to that point hadn't been what you'd call sheltered. I hope you haven't been thinking I made a living in the streets by selling apples."

She kept rubbing my feet, staring off into scenes I could not see.

"How old were you when your mother died?"

"She was killed during Tet, 1968. I was ten."

"By the Viet Cong?"

"Who knows? Lot of bullets flying, lot of grenades being thrown."

She sighed, dropped my foot, and sat there, a scrawny Buddha without a robe.

"You ready to do it again, Yank?"

"I don't think I can, Lisa. I'm an old man."

She moved over me and lowered herself with her chin just below my sternum, settling her breasts in the most delicious place possible.

"We'll see," she said, and giggled. "There's an alternative sex act I'm pretty good at, and I'm pretty sure it would make you a young man again. But I haven't been able to do it for about a year on account of these." She tapped her braces. "It'd be sort of like sticking it in a buzz saw. So now I do this instead. I call it 'touring the silicone valley.' " She started moving her body up and down, just a few inches at a time. She blinked innocently a couple times, then laughed.

"At last, I can see you," she said. "I'm awfully myopic."

I let her do that for a while, then lifted my head.

"Did you say silicone?"

"Uh-huh. You didn't think they were real, did you?"

I confessed that I had.

"I don't think I've ever been so happy with anything I ever bought. Not even the car."

"Why did you?"

"Does it bother you?"

It didn't, and I told her so. But I couldn't conceal my curiosity.

"Because it was safe to. In Saigon I was always angry that I never developed. I could have made a good living as a prostitute, but I was always too tall, too skinny, and too ugly. Then in Cambodia I was lucky. I managed to pass for a boy some of the time. If not for that I'd have been raped a lot more than I was. And in Thailand I knew I'd get to the West one way or another, and when I got there, I'd get the best car there was, eat anything I wanted any time I wanted to, and purchase the best tits money could buy. You can't imagine what the West looks like from the camps. A place where you can buy tits!"

She looked down between them, then back at my face.

"Looks like it was a good investment," she said.

"They do seem to work okay," I had to admit.

We agreed that she would spend the nights at my house. There were certain things she had to do at Kluge's, involving equipment that had to be physically loaded, but many things she could do with a remote terminal and an armload of software. So we selected one of Kluge's best computers and about a dozen peripherals and installed her at a cafeteria table in my bedroom.

I guess we both knew it wasn't much protection if the people who got Kluge decided to get her. But I know I felt better about it, and I think she did, too.

The second day she was there a delivery van pulled up outside, and two guys started unloading a king-size waterbed. She laughed and laughed when she saw my face.

"Listen, you're not using Kluge's computers to—"

"Relax, Yank. How'd you think I could afford a Ferrari?"

"I've been curious."

"If you're really good at writing software you can make a lot of money. I own my own company. But every hacker picks up tricks here and there. I used to run a few Kluge scams, myself."

"But not anymore?"

She shrugged. "Once a thief, always a thief, Victor. I told you I couldn't make ends meet selling my bod."

Lisa didn't need much sleep.

We got up at seven, and I made breakfast every morning. Then we would spend an hour or two working in the garden. She would go to Kluge's and I'd bring her a sandwich at noon, then drop in on her several times during the day. That was for my own peace of mind; I never stayed more than a minute. Sometime during the afternoon I would shop or do household chores, then at seven one of us would cook dinner. We alternated. I taught her "American" cooking, and she taught me a little of everything. She complained about the lack of vital ingredients in American markets. No dogs, of course, but she claimed to know great ways of preparing monkey, snake, and rat. I never knew how hard she was pulling my leg, and didn't ask.

After dinner she stayed at my house. We would talk, make love, bathe.

She loved my tub. It is about the only alteration I have made in the house, and my only real luxury. I put it in—having to expand the bathroom to do so—in 1975, and never regretted it. We would soak for twenty minutes or an hour, turning the jets and bubblers on and off, washing each other, giggling like kids. Once we used bubble bath and made a mountain of suds four feet high, then destroyed it, splashing water all over the place. Most nights she let me wash her long black hair.

She didn't have any bad habits—or at least none that clashed with mine. She was neat and clean, changing her clothes twice a day and never so much as leaving a dirty glass on the sink. She never left a mess in the bathroom. Two glasses of wine was her limit.

I felt like Lazarus.

Osborne came by three times in the next two weeks. Lisa met him at Kluge's and gave him what she had learned. It was getting to be quite a list.

"Kluge once had an account in a New York bank with nine *trillion* dollars in it," she told me after one of Osborne's visits. "I think he did it just to see if he could. He left it in for one day, took the interest and fed it to a bank in the Bahamas, then destroyed the principal. Which never existed anyway."

In return, Osborne told her what was new on the murder investigation—which was nothing—and on the status of Kluge's property, which was chaotic. Various agencies had sent people out to look the place over. Some FBI men came, wanting to take over the investigation. Lisa, when talking about computers, had the power to cloud men's minds. She did it first by explaining exactly what she was doing, in terms so abstruse that no one could understand her. Sometimes that was enough. If it wasn't, if they started to get tough, she just moved out of the driver's seat and let them try to handle Kluge's contraption. She let them watch in horror as dragons leaped out of nowhere and ate up all the data on a disc, then printed "You Stupid Putz!" on the screen.

"I'm cheating them," she confessed to me. "I'm giving them stuff I *know* they're gonna step in, because I already stepped in it myself. I've lost about forty percent of the data Kluge had stored away. But the others lose a hundred percent. You ought to see their faces when Kluge drops a logic bomb into their work. That second guy threw a three thousand printer clear across the room. Then tried to bribe me to be quiet about it."

When some federal agency sent out an expert from Stanford, and he seemed perfectly content to destroy everything in sight in the firm belief that he was *bound* to get it right sooner or later, Lisa showed him how Kluge entered the IRS main computer in Washington and neglected to mention how Kluge had gotten out. The guy tangled with some watchdog program. During his struggles, it seemed he had erased all the tax records from the letter S down into the W's. Lisa let him think that for half an hour.

"I thought he was having a heart attack," she told me. "All the blood drained out of his face and he couldn't talk. So I showed him where I had—with my usual foresight—arranged for that data to be recorded, told him how to put it back where he found it, and how to pacify the watchdog. He couldn't get out of that house fast enough. Pretty soon he's gonna realize you *can't* destroy that much information with anything short of dynamite because of the backups and the limits of how much can be running at any one time. But I don't think he'll be back."

"It sounds like a very fancy video game," I said.

"It is, in a way. But it's more like Dungeons and Dragons. It's an endless series of closed rooms with dangers on the other side. You don't dare take it a step at a time. You take it a *hundredth* of a step at a time. Your questions are like, 'Now this isn't a question, but if it entered my mind to *ask* this question—which I'm not about to do—concerning what might happen if I looked at this door here—and I'm not touching it, I'm not even in the next room—what do you suppose you might do?' And the program crunches on that, decides if you fulfilled the conditions for getting a great big cream pie in the face, then either throws it or allows as how it *might* just move from step A to step A Prime. Then you say, 'Well, maybe I *am* looking at that door.' And sometimes the program says 'You looked, you looked, you dirty crook!' And the fireworks start."

Silly as all that sounds, it was very close to the best explanation she was ever able to give me about what she was doing.

"Are you telling everything, Lisa?" I asked her.

"Well, not *every*thing. I didn't mention the four cents."

Four cents? Oh my god.

"Lisa, I didn't want that. I didn't ask for it, I wish he'd never—"

"Calm down, Yank. It's going to be all right."

"He kept records of all that, didn't he?"

'That's what I spend most of my time doing. Decoding his records."

"How long have you known?"

"About the seven hundred thousand dollars? It was in the first disc I cracked."

"I just want to give it back."

She thought that over, and shook her head.

"Victor, it'd be more dangerous to get rid of it now than it would be to keep it. It was imaginary money at first. But now it's got a history. The IRS thinks it knows where it came from. The taxes are paid on it. The State of Delaware is convinced that a legally chartered corporation disbursed it. An Illinois law firm has been paid for handling it. Your bank has been paying you interest on it. I'm not saying it would be impossible to go back and wipe all that out, but I wouldn't like to try. I'm good, but I don't have Kluge's touch."

"How could he *do* all that? You say it was imaginary money. That's not the way I thought money worked. He could just pull it out of thin air?"

Lisa patted the top of her computer console, and smiled at me.

"This is money, Yank," she said, and her eyes glittered.

At night she worked by candlelight so she wouldn't disturb me. That turned out to be my downfall. She typed by touch, and needed the candle only to locate software.

So that's how I'd go to sleep every night, looking at her slender body bathed in the glow of the candle. I was always reminded of melting butter dripping down a roasted ear of corn. Golden light on golden skin.

Ugly, she had called herself. Skinny. It was true she was thin. I could see her ribs when she sat with her back impossibly straight, her tummy sucked in, her chin up. She worked in the nude these days, sitting in lotus position. For long periods she would not move, her hands lying on her thighs, then she would poise, as if to pound the keys. But her touch was light, almost silent. It looked more like yoga than programming. She said she went into a meditative state for her best work.

I had expected a bony angularity, all sharp elbows and knees. She wasn't like that. I had guessed her weight ten pounds too low, and still didn't know where she put it. But she was soft and rounded, and strong beneath.

No one was ever going to call her face glamorous. Few would even go so far as to call her pretty. The braces did that, I think. They caught the eye and held it, drawing attention to that unsightly jumble.

But her skin was wonderful. She had scars. Not as many as I had expected. She seemed to heal quickly, and well.

I thought she was beautiful.

I had just completed my nightly survey when my eye was caught by the candle. I looked at it, then tried to look away.

Candles do that sometimes. I don't know why. In still air, with the flame perfectly vertical, they begin to flicker. The flame leaps up then squats down, up and down, up and down, brighter and brighter in regular rhythm, two or three beats to the second—

—and I tried to call out to her, wishing the candle would stop its regular flickering, but already I couldn't speak—

—I could only gasp, and I tried once more, as hard as I could, to yell, to scream, to tell her not to worry, and felt the nausea building . . .

I tasted blood. I took an experimental breath, did not find the smells of vomit, urine, feces. The overhead lights were on.

Lisa was on her hands and knees leaning over me, her face very close. A tear dropped on my forehead. I was on the carpet, on my back.

"Victor, can you hear me?"

I nodded. There was a spoon in my mouth. I spit it out.

"What happened? Are you going to be all right?"

I nodded again, and struggled to speak.

"You just lie there. The ambulance is on its way."

"No. Don't need it."

"Well, it's on its way. You just take it easy and—"

"Help me up."

"Not yet. You're not ready."

She was right. I tried to sit up, and fell back quickly. I took deep breaths for a while. Then the doorbell rang.

She stood up and started to the door. I just managed to get my hand around her ankle. Then she was leaning over me again, her eyes as wide as they would go.

"What is it? What's wrong now?"

"Get some clothes on," I told her. She looked down at herself, surprised.

"Oh. Right."

She got rid of the ambulance crew. Lisa was a lot calmer after she made coffee and we were sitting at the kitchen table. It was one o'clock, and I was still pretty rocky. But it hadn't been a bad one.

I went to the bathroom and got the bottle of Dilantin I'd hidden when she moved in. I let her see me take one.

"I forgot to do this today," I told her.

"It's because you hid them. That was stupid."

"I know." There must have been something else I could have said. It didn't please me to see her look hurt. But she was hurt because I wasn't defending myself against her attack, and that was a bit too complicated for me to dope out just after a grand mal.

"You can move out if you want to," I said. I was in rare form.

So was she. She reached across the table and shook me by the shoulders. She glared at me.

"I won't take a lot more of that kind of shit," she said, and I nodded, and began to cry.

She let me do it. I think that was probably best. She could have babied me, but I do a pretty good job of that myself.

"How long has this been going on?" she finally said. "Is that why you've stayed in your house for thirty years?"

I shrugged. "I guess it's part of it. When I got back they operated, but it just made it worse."

"Okay. I'm mad at you because you didn't tell me about

it, so I didn't know what to do. I want to stay, but you'll have to tell me how. Then I won't be mad anymore."

I could have blown the whole thing right there. I'm amazed I didn't. Through the years I'd developed very good methods for doing things like that. But I pulled through when I saw her face. She really did want to stay. I didn't know why, but it was enough.

"The spoon was a mistake," I said. "If there's time, and if you can do it without risking your fingers, you could jam a piece of cloth in there. Part of a sheet, or something. But nothing hard." I explored my mouth with a finger. "I think I broke a tooth."

"Serves you right," she said. I looked at her, and smiled, then we were both laughing. She came around the table and kissed me, then sat on my knee.

"The biggest danger is drowning. During the first part of the seizure, all my muscles go rigid. That doesn't last long. Then they all start contracting and relaxing at random. It's *very* strong."

"I know. I watched, and I tried to hold you."

"Don't do that. Get me on my side. Stay behind me, and watch out for flailing arms. Get a pillow under my head if you can. Keep me away from things I could injure myself on." I looked her square in the eye. "I want to emphasize this. Just *try* to do all those things. If I'm getting too violent, it's better you stand off to the side. Better for both of us. If I knock you out, you won't be able to help me if I start strangling on vomit."

I kept looking at her eyes. She must have read my mind, because she smiled slightly.

"Sorry, Yank. I am not freaked out. I mean, like, it's totally gross, you know, and it barfs me out to the max, you could—"

"—gag me with a spoon, I know. Okay, right, I know I was dumb. And that's about it. I might bite my tongue or the inside of my cheek. Don't worry about it. There is one more thing."

She waited, and I wondered how much to tell her. There wasn't a lot she could do, but if I died on her I didn't want her to feel it was her fault.

"Sometimes I have to go to the hospital. Sometimes one seizure will follow another. If that keeps up for too long, I won't breathe, and my brain will die of oxygen starvation."

"That only takes about five minutes," she said, alarmed.

"I know. It's only a problem if I start having them frequently, so we could plan for it if I do. But if I don't come out of one, start having another right on the heels of the first, or if you can't detect any breathing for three or four minutes, you'd better call an ambulance."

"Three or four minutes? You'd be dead before they got here."

"It's that or live in a hospital. I don't like hospitals."

"Neither do I."

The next day she took me for a ride in her Ferrari. I was nervous about it, wondering if she was going to do crazy things. If anything, she was too slow. People behind her kept honking. I could tell she hadn't been driving long from the exaggerated attention she put into every movement.

"A Ferrari is wasted on me, I'm afraid," she confessed at one point. "I never drive it faster than fifty-five."

We went to an interior decorator in Beverly Hills and she bought a low-watt gooseneck lamp at an outrageous price.

I had a hard time getting to sleep that night. I suppose I was afraid of having another seizure, though Lisa's new lamp wasn't going to set it off.

Funny about seizures. When I first started having them, everyone called them fits. Then, gradually, it was seizures, until fits began to sound dirty.

I guess it's a sign of growing old, when the language changes on you.

There were rafts of new words. A lot of them were for things that didn't even exist when I was growing up. Like software. I always visualized a limp wrench.

"What got you interested in computers, Lisa?" I asked her.

She didn't move. Her concentration when sitting at the machine was pretty damn good. I rolled onto my back and tried to sleep.

"It's where the power is, Yank." I looked up. She had turned to face me.

"Did you pick it all up since you got to America?"

"I had a head start. I didn't tell you about my Captain, did I?"

"I don't think you did."

"He was strange. I knew that. I was about fourteen. He was an American, and he took an interest in me. He got me a nice apartment in Saigon. And he put me in school."

She was studying me, looking for a reaction. I didn't give her one.

"He was surely a pedophile, and probably had homosexual tendencies, since I looked so much like a skinny little boy."

Again the wait. This time she smiled.

"He was good to me. I learned to read well. From there on, anything is possible."

"I didn't actually ask you about your Captain. I asked why you got interested in computers."

"That's right. You did."

"Is it just a living?"

"It started that way. It's the future, Victor."

"God knows I've read that enough times."

"It's true. It's already here. It's power, if you know how to use it. You've seen what Kluge was able to do. You can make money with one of these things. I don't mean earn it, I mean *make* it, like if you had a printing press. Remember Osborne mentioned that Kluge's house didn't exist? Did you think what that means?"

"That he wiped it out of the memory banks."

"That was the first step. But the lot exists in the county plat books, wouldn't you think? I mean, this country hasn't *entirely* given up paper."

"So the county really does have a record of that house."

"No. That page was torn out of the records."

"I don't get it. Kluge never left the house."

"Oldest way in the world, friend. Kluge looked through the L.A.P.D. files until he found a guy known as Sammy. He sent him a cashier's check for a thousand dollars, along with a letter saying he could earn twice that if he'd go to the hall of records and do something. Sammy didn't bite, and neither did McGee, or Molly Unger. But Little Billy Phipps did, and he got a check just like the letter said, and he and Kluge had a wonderful business relationship for many years. Little Billy drives a new Cadillac now, and hasn't the faintest notion who Kluge was or where he lived. It didn't matter to Kluge how much he spent. He just pulled it out of thin air."

I thought that over for a while. I guess it's true that with enough money you can do just about anything, and Kluge had all the money in the world.

"Did you tell Osborne about Little Billy?"

"I erased the disc, just like I erased your seven hundred thousand. You never know when you might need somebody like Little Billy."

"You're not afraid of getting into trouble over it?"

"Life is risk, Victor. I'm keeping the best stuff for myself. Not because I intend to use it, but because if I ever needed it badly and didn't have it, I'd feel like such a fool."

She cocked her head and narrowed her eyes, which made them practically disappear.

"Tell me something, Yank. Kluge picked you out of all

your neighbors because you'd been a Boy Scout for thirty years. How do you react to what I'm doing?"

"You're cheerfully amoral, and you're a survivor, and you're basically decent. And I pity anybody who gets in your way."

She grinned, stretched, and stood up.

" 'Cheerfully amoral.' I like that." She sat beside me, making a great sloshing in the bed. "You want to be amoral again?"

"In a little bit." She started rubbing my chest. "So you got into computers because they were the wave of the future. Don't you ever worry about them . . . I don't know, I guess it sounds corny . . . do you think they'll take over?"

"Everybody thinks that until they start to use them," she said. "You've got to realize just how stupid they are. Without programming they are good for nothing, literally. Now, what I do believe is that the people who *run* the computers will take over. They already have. That's why I study them."

"I guess that's not what I meant. Maybe I can't say it right."

She frowned. "Kluge was looking into something. He'd been eavesdropping in artificial intelligence labs, and reading a lot of neurological research. I think he was trying to find a common thread."

"Between human brains and computers?"

"Not quite. He was thinking of computers and neurons. Brain cells." She pointed to her computer. "That thing, or any other computer, is light-years away from being a human brain. It can't generalize, or infer, or categorize, or invent. With good programming it can appear to do some of those things, but it's an illusion.

"There's an old speculation about what would happen if we finally built a computer with as many transistors as the human brain has neurons. Would there be a self-awareness? I think that's baloney. A transistor isn't a neuron, and a quintillion of them aren't any better than a dozen.

"So Kluge—who seems to have felt the same way—started looking into the possible similarities between a neuron and an 8-bit computer. That's why he had all that consumer junk sitting around his house, those Trash-80's and Atari's and TI's and Sinclair's, for chrissake. He was used to *much* more powerful instruments. He ate up the home units like candy."

"What did he find out?"

"Nothing, it looks like. An 8-bit unit is more complex than a neuron, and no computer is in the same galaxy as an organic brain. But see, the words get tricky. I said an Atari is more complex than a neuron, but it's hard to really compare them. It's like comparing a direction with a distance, or a color with a mass. The units are different. Except for one similarity."

"What's that?"

"The connections. Again, it's different, but the concept of networking is the same. A neuron is connected to a lot of others. There are trillions of them, and the way messages pulse through them determines what we are and what we think and what we remember. And with that computer I can reach a million others. It's bigger than the human brain, really, because the information in that network is more than all humanity could cope with in a million years. It reaches from Pioneer Ten, out beyond the orbit of Pluto, right into every living room that has a telephone in it. With that computer you can tap tons of data that has been collected but nobody's even had the time to look at.

"That's what Kluge was interested in. The old 'critical mass computer' idea, the computer that becomes aware, but with a new angle. Maybe it wouldn't be the size of the computer, but the *number* of computers. There used to be thousands of them. Now there's millions. They're putting them in cars. In wristwatches. Every home has several, from the simple timer on a microwave oven up to a video game or home terminal. Kluge was trying to find out if critical mass could be reached that way."

"What did he think?"

"I don't know. He was just getting started." She glanced down at me. "But you know what, Yank? I think you've reached critical mass while I wasn't looking."

"I think you're right." I reached for her.

Lisa liked to cuddle. I didn't, at first, after fifty years of sleeping alone. But I got to like it pretty quickly.

That's what we were doing when we resumed the conversation we had been having. We just lay in each others' arms and talked about things. Nobody had mentioned love yet, but I knew I loved her. I didn't know what to do about it, but I would think of something.

"Critical mass," I said. She nuzzled my neck, and yawned.

"What about it?"

"What would it be like? It seems like it would be such a vast intelligence. So quick, so omniscient. God-like."

"Could be."

"Wouldn't it . . . run our lives? I guess I'm asking the same questions I started off with. Would it take over?"

She thought about it for a long time.

"I wonder if there would be anything to take over. I mean, why should it care? How could we figure what its concerns would be? Would it want to be worshipped, for instance? I doubt it. Would it want to 'rationalize all human behavior, to eliminate all emotion,' as I'm sure some sci-fi film computer must have told some damsel in distress in the 'fifties.

"You can use a word like awareness, but what does it mean? An amoeba must be aware. Plants probably are. There may be a level of awareness in a neuron. Even in an integrated circuit chip. We don't even know what our own awareness really is. We've never been able to shine a light on it, dissect it, figure out where it comes from or where it goes when we're dead. To apply human values to a thing like this hypothetical computer-net consciousness would be pretty stupid. But I don't see how it could interact with human awareness at all. It might not even notice us, any more than we notice cells in our bodies, or neutrinos passing through us, or the vibrations of the atoms in the air around us."

So she had to explain what a neutrino was. One thing I always provided her with was an ignorant audience. And after that, I pretty much forgot about our mythical hyper-computer.

"What about your Captain?" I asked, much later.

"Do you really want to know, Yank?" she mumbled, sleepily.

"I'm not afraid to know."

She sat up and reached for her cigarettes. I had come to know she sometimes smoked them in times of stress. She had told me she smoked after making love, but that first time had been the only time. The lighter flared in the dark. I heard her exhale.

"My Major, actually. He got a promotion. Do you want to know his name?"

"Lisa, I don't want to know any of it if you don't want to tell it. But if you do, what I want to know is did he stand by you."

"He didn't marry me, if that's what you mean. When he knew he had to go, he said he would, but I talked him out of it. Maybe it was the most noble thing I ever did. Maybe it was the most stupid.

"It's no accident I look Japanese. My grandmother was raped in '42 by a Jap soldier of the occupation. She was Chinese, living in Hanoi. My mother was born there. They went south after Dien Bien Phu. My grandmother died. My mother had it hard. Being Chinese was tough enough, but being half Chinese and half Japanese was worse. My father was half French and half Annamese. Another bad combination. I never knew him. But I'm sort of a capsule history of Vietnam."

The end of her cigarette glowed brighter once more.

"I've got one grandfather's face and the other grandfather's height. With tits by Goodyear. About all I missed was some American genes, but I was working on that for my children.

"When Saigon was falling I tried to get to the American Embassy. Didn't make it. You know the rest, until I got to Thailand, and when I finally got Americans to notice me, it turned out my Major was still looking for me. He sponsored me over here, and I made it in time to watch him die of cancer. Two months I had with him, all of it in the hospital."

"My god." I had a horrible thought. "That wasn't the war, too, was it? I mean, the story of your life—"

"—is the rape of Asia. No, Victor. Not that war, anyway. But he was one of those guys who got to see atom bombs up close, out in Nevada. He was too Regular Army to complain about it, but I think he knew that's what killed him."

"Did you love him?"

"What do you want me to say? He got me out of hell."

Again the cigarette flared, and I saw her stub it out.

"No," she said. "I didn't love him. He knew that. I've never loved anybody. He was very dear, very special to me. I would have done almost anything for him. He was fatherly to me." I felt her looking at me in the dark. "Aren't you going to ask how old he was?"

"Fiftyish," I said.

"On the nose. Can I ask you something?"

"I guess it's your turn."

"How many girls have you had since you got back from Korea?"

I held up my hand and pretended to count on my fingers.

"One," I said, at last.

"How many before you went?"

"One. We broke up before I left for the war."

"How many in Korea?"

"Nine. All at Madame Park's jolly little whorehouse in Pusan."

"So you've made love to one white and ten Asians. I bet none of the others were as tall as me."

"Korean girls have fatter cheeks, too. But they all had your eyes."

She nuzzled against my chest, took a deep breath, and sighed.

"We're a hell of a pair, aren't we?"

I hugged her, and her breath came again, hot on my chest. I wondered how I'd lived so long without such a simple miracle as that.

"Yes. I think we really are."

Osborne came by again about a week later. He seemed subdued. He listened to the things Lisa had decided to give him without much interest. He took the printout she handed him, and promised to turn it over to the departments that handled those things. But he didn't get up to leave.

"I thought I ought to tell you, Apfel," he said, at last. "The Gavin case has been closed."

I had to think a moment to remember Kluge's real name had been Gavin.

"The coroner ruled suicide a long time ago. I was able to keep the case open quite a while on the strength of my suspicions." He nodded toward Lisa. "And on what she said about the suicide note. But there was just no evidence at all."

"It probably happened quickly," Lisa said. "Somebody caught him, tracked him back—it can be done; Kluge was lucky for a long time—and did him the same day."

"You don't think it was suicide?" I asked Osborne.

"No. But whoever did it is home free unless something new turns up."

"I'll tell you if it does," Lisa said.

"That's something else," Osborne said. "I can't authorize you to work over there anymore. The county's taken possession of house and contents."

"Don't worry about it," Lisa said, softly.

There was a short silence as she leaned over to shake a cigarette from the pack on the coffee table. She lit it, exhaled, and leaned back beside me, giving Osborne her most inscrutable look. He sighed.

"I'd hate to play poker with you, lady," he said. "What do you mean, 'Don't worry about it'?"

"I bought the house four days ago. And its contents. If anything turns up that would help you re-open the murder investigation, I will let you know."

Osborne was too defeated to get angry. He studied her quietly for a while.

"I'd like to know how you swung that."

"I did nothing illegal. You're free to check it out. I paid good cash money for it. The house came onto the market. I got a good price at the Sheriff's sale."

"How'd you like it if I put my best men on the transaction? See if they can dig up some funny money? Maybe fraud. How about I get the F.B.I. in to look it all over?"

She gave him a cool look.

"You're welcome to. Frankly, Detective Osborne, I could have stolen that house, Griffith Park, and the Harbor Freeway and I don't think you could have caught me."

"So where does that leave me?"

"Just where you were. With a closed case, and a promise from me."

"I don't like you having all that stuff, if it can do the things you say it can do."

"I didn't expect you would. But that's not your department, is it? The county owned it for a while, through simple confiscation. They didn't know what they had, and they let it go."

"Maybe I can get the Fraud detail out here to confiscate your software. There's criminal evidence on it."

"You could try that," she agreed.

They stared at each other for a while. Lisa won. Osborne rubbed his eyes and nodded. Then he heaved himself to his feet and slumped to the door.

Lisa stubbed out her cigarette. We listened to him going down the walk.

"I'm surprised he gave up so easy," I said. "Or did he? Do you think he'll try a raid?"

"It's not likely. He knows the score."

"Maybe you could tell it to me."

"For one thing, it's not his department, and he knows it."

"Why did you buy the house?"

"You ought to ask *how*."

I looked at her closely. There was a gleam of amusement behind the poker face.

"Lisa. What did you do?"

"That's what Osborne asked himself. He got the right answer, because he understands Kluge's machines. And he knows how things get done. It was no accident that house going on the market, and no accident I was the only bidder. I used one of Kluge's pet councilmen."

"You bribed him?"

She laughed, and kissed me.

"I think I finally managed to shock you, Yank. That's gotta be the biggest difference between me and a native-born American. Average citizens don't spend much on bribes over here. In Saigon, everybody bribes."

"Did you bribe him?"

"Nothing so indelicate. One has to go in the back door over here. Several entirely legal campaign contributions appeared in the accounts of a State Senator, who mentioned a certain situation to someone, who happened to be in the position to do legally what I happened to want done.'' She looked at me askance. ''Of *course* I bribed him, Victor. You'd be amazed to know how cheaply. Does that bother you?''

''Yes,'' I admitted. ''I don't like bribery.''

''I'm indifferent to it. It happens, like gravity. It may not be admirable, but it gets things done.''

''I assume you covered yourself.''

''Reasonably well. You're never entirely covered with a bribe, because of the human element. The councilman might geek if they got him in front of a grand jury. But they won't, because Osborne won't pursue it. That's the second reason he walked out of here without a fight. *He* knows how the world wobbles, he knows what kind of force I now possess, and he knows he can't fight it.''

There was a long silence after that. I had a lot to think about, and I didn't feel good about most of it. At one point Lisa reached for the pack of cigarettes, then changed her mind. She waited for me to work it out.

''It is a terrific force, isn't it,'' I finally said.

''It's frightening,'' she agreed. ''Don't think it doesn't scare me. Don't think I haven't had fantasies of being superwoman. Power is an awful temptation, and it's not easy to reject. There's so much I could do.''

''Will you?''

''I'm not talking about stealing things, or getting rich.''

''I didn't think you were.''

''This is political power. But I don't know how to wield it . . . it sounds corny, but to use it for good. I've seen so much evil come from good intentions. I don't think I'm wise enough to do any good. And the chances of getting torn up like Kluge did are large. But I'm not wise enough to walk away from it. I'm still a street urchin from Saigon, Yank. I'm smart enough not to use it unless I have to. But I can't give it away, and I can't destroy it. Is that stupid?''

I didn't have a good answer for that one. But I had a bad feeling.

My doubts had another week to work on me. I didn't come to any great moral conclusions. Lisa knew of some crimes, and she wasn't reporting them to the authorities. That didn't bother me much. She had at her fingertips the means to commit more crimes, and that bothered me a lot. Yet I really didn't think she planned to do anything. She was smart enough to use the things she had only in a defensive way—but with Lisa that could cover a lot of ground.

When she didn't show up for dinner one evening, I went over to Kluge's and found her busy in the living room. A nine-foot section of shelving had been cleared. The discs and tapes were stacked on a table. She had a big plastic garbage can and a magnet the size of a softball. I watched her wave a tape near the magnet, then toss it in the garbage can, which was almost full. She glanced up, did the same operation with a handful of discs, then took off her glasses and wiped her eyes.

''Feel any better now, Victor?'' she asked.

''What do you mean? I feel fine.''

''No you don't. And I haven't felt right, either. It hurts me to do it, but I have to. You want to go get the other trash can?''

I did, and helped her pull more software from the shelves.

''You're not going to wipe it all, are you?''

''No. I'm wiping records, and . . . something else.''

''Are you going to tell me what?''

''There are things it's better not to know,'' she said, darkly.

* * *

I finally managed to convince her to talk over dinner. She had said little, just eating and shaking her head. But she gave in.

"Rather dreary, actually," she said. "I've been probing around some delicate places the last couple days. These are places Kluge visited at will, but they scare the hell out of me. Dirty places. Places where they know things I thought I'd like to find out."

She shivered, and seemed reluctant to go on.

"Are you talking about military computers? The CIA?"

"The CIA is where it starts. It's the easiest. I've looked around at NORAD—that's the guys who get to fight the next war. It makes me shiver to see how easy Kluge got in there. He cobbled up a way to start World War Three, just as an exercise. That's one of the things we just erased. The last two days I was nibbling around the edges of the big boys. The Defense Intelligence Agency and the National Security . . . something. DIA and NSA. Each of them is bigger than the CIA. Something knew I was there. Some watchdog program. As soon as I realized that I got out quick, and I've spent the last five hours being sure it didn't follow me. And now I'm sure, and I've destroyed all that, too."

"You think they're the ones who killed Kluge?"

"They're surely the best candidates. He had tons of their stuff. I know he helped design the biggest installations at NSA, and he'd been poking around in there for years. One false step is all it would take."

"Did you get it all? I mean, are you sure?"

"I'm sure they didn't track me. I'm not sure I've destroyed all the records. I'm going back now to take a last look."

"I'll go with you."

We worked until well after midnight. Lisa would review a tape or a disc, and if she was in any doubt, toss it to me for the magnetic treatment. At one point, simply because she was unsure, she took the magnet and passed it in front of an entire shelf of software.

It was amazing to think about it. With that one wipe she had randomized billions of bits of information. Some of it might not exist anywhere else in the world. I found myself confronted by even harder questions. Did she have the right to do it? Didn't knowledge exist for everyone? But I confess I had little trouble quelling my protests. Mostly I was happy to see it go. The old reactionary in me found it easier to believe There Are Things We Are Not Meant To Know.

We were almost through when her monitor screen began to malfunction. It actually gave off a few hisses and pops, so Lisa stood back from it for a moment, then the screen started to flicker. I stared at it for a while. It seemed to me there was an image trying to form in the screen. Something three-dimensional. Just as I was starting to get a picture of it I happened to glance at Lisa, and she was looking at me. Her face was flickering. She came to me and put her hands over my eyes.

"Victor, you shouldn't look at that."

"It's okay," I told her. And when I said it, it was, but as soon as I had the words out I knew it wasn't. And that is the last thing I remembered for a long time.

I'm told it was a very bad two weeks. I remember very little of it. I was kept under high dosage of drugs, and my few lucid periods were always followed by a fresh seizure.

The first thing I recall clearly was looking up at Doctor Stuart's face. I was in a hospital bed. I later learned it was in Cedars-Sinai, not the Veteran's Hospital. Lisa had paid for a private room.

Stuart put me through the usual questions. I was able to answer them, though I was very tired. When he was satisfied as to my condition he finally began to answer some of my questions. I learned how long I had been there, and how it had happened.

"You went into consecutive seizures," he confirmed. "I don't know why, frankly. You haven't been prone to them for a decade. I was thinking you were well under control. But nothing is ever really stable, I guess."

"So Lisa got me here in time."

"She did more than that. She didn't want to level with me at first. It seems that after the first seizure she witnessed she read everything she could find. From that day, she had a syringe and a solution of Valium handy. When she saw you couldn't breathe she injected you with 100 milligrams, and there's no doubt it saved your life."

Stuart and I had known each other a long time. He knew I had no prescription for Valium, though we had talked about it the last time I was hospitalized. Since I lived alone, there would be no one to inject me if I got in trouble.

He was more interested in results than anything else, and what Lisa did had the desired results. I was still alive.

He wouldn't let me have any visitors that day. I protested, but soon was asleep. The next day she came. She wore a new T-shirt. This one had a picture of a robot wearing a gown and mortarboard, and said "Class of 11111000000." It turns out that was 1984 in binary notation.

She had a big smile and said "Hi, Yank!" and as she sat on the bed I started to shake. She looked alarmed and asked if she should call the doctor.

"It's not that," I managed to say. "I'd like it if you just held me."

She took off her shoes and got under the covers with me. She held me tightly. At some point a nurse came in and tried to shoo her out. Lisa gave her profanities in Vietnamese, Chinese, and a few startling ones in English, and the nurse left. I saw Doctor Stuart glance in later.

I felt much better when I finally stopped crying. Lisa's eyes were wet, too.

"I've been here every day," she said. "You look awful, Victor."

"I feel a lot better."

"Well, you look better than you did. But your doctor says you'd better stick around another couple of days, just to make sure."

"I think he's right."

"I'm planning a big dinner for when you get back. You think we should invite the neighbors?"

I didn't say anything for a while. There were so many things we hadn't faced. Just how long could it go on between us? How long before I got sour about being so useless? How long before she got tired of being with an old man? I don't know just when I had started to think of Lisa as a permanent part of my life. And I wondered how I could have thought that.

"Do you want to spend more years waiting in hospitals for a man to die?"

"What do you want, Victor? I'll marry you if you want me to. Or I'll live with you in sin. I prefer sin, myself, but if it'll make you happy—"

"I don't know why you want to saddle yourself with an epileptic old fart."

"Because I love you."

It was the first time she had said it. I could have gone on questioning—bringing up her Major again, for instance—but I had no urge to. I'm very glad I didn't. So I changed the subject.

"Did you get the job finished?"

She knew which job I was talking about. She lowered her voice and put her mouth close to my ear.

"Let's don't be specific about it here, Victor. I don't trust any place I haven't swept for bugs. But, to put your mind at ease, I did finish, and it's been a quiet couple of weeks. No one is any wiser, and I'll never meddle in things like that again."

I felt a lot better. I was also exhausted. I tried to conceal my yawns, but she sensed it was time to go. She gave me one more kiss, promising many more to come, and left me.

It was the last time I ever saw her.

At about ten o'clock that evening Lisa went into Kluge's kitchen with a screwdriver and some other tools and got to work on the microwave oven.

The manufacturers of those appliances are very careful to insure they can't be turned on with the door open, as they emit lethal radiation. But with simple tools and a good brain it is possible to circumvent the safety interlocks. Lisa had no trouble with them. About ten minutes after she entered the kitchen she put her head in the oven and turned it on.

It is impossible to say how long she held her head in there. It was long enough to turn her eyeballs to the consistency of boiled eggs. At some point she lost voluntary muscle control and fell to the floor, pulling the microwave down with her. It shorted out, and a fire started.

The fire set off the sophisticated burglar alarm she had installed a month before. Betty Lanier saw the flames and called the fire department as Hal ran across the street and into the burning kitchen. He dragged what was left of Lisa out onto the grass. When he saw what the fire had done to her upper body, and in particular her breasts, he threw up.

She was rushed to the hospital. The doctors there amputated one arm and cut away the frightful masses of vulcanized silicone, pulled all her teeth, and didn't know what to do about the eyes. They put her on a respirator.

It was an orderly who first noticed the blackened and

bloody T-shirt they had cut from her. Some of the message was unreadable, but it began, "I can't go on this way anymore . . ."

There is no other way I could have told all that. I discovered it piecemeal, starting with the disturbed look on Doctor Stuart's face when Lisa didn't show up the next day. He wouldn't tell me anything, and I had another seizure shortly after.

The next week is a blur. I remember being released from the hospital, but I don't remember the trip home. Betty was very good to me. They gave me a tranquilizer called Tranxene, and it was even better. I ate them like candy. I wandered in a drugged haze, eating only when Betty insisted, sleeping sitting up in my chair, coming awake not knowing where or who I was. I returned to the prison camp many times. Once I recall helping Lisa stack severed heads.

When I saw myself in the mirror, there was a vague smile on my face. It was Tranxene, caressing my frontal lobes. I knew that if I was to live much longer, me and Tranxene would have to become very good friends.

I eventually became capable of something that passed for rational thought. I was helped along somewhat by a visit from Osborne. I was trying, at that time, to find reasons to live, and wondered if he had any.

"I'm very sorry," he started off. I said nothing. "This is on my own time," he went on. "The department doesn't know I'm here."

"Was it suicide?" I asked him.

"I brought along a copy of the . . . the note. She ordered it from a shirt company in Westwood, three days before the . . . accident."

He handed it to me, and I read it. I was mentioned, though not by name. I was "the man I love." She said she couldn't cope with my problems. It was a short note. You can't get too much on a T-shirt. I read it through five times, then handed it back to him.

"She told you Kluge didn't write his note. I tell you she didn't write this."

He nodded reluctantly. I felt a vast calm, with a howling nightmare just below it. Praise Tranxene.

"Can you back that up?"

"She saw me in the hospital shortly before she died. She was full of life and hope. You say she ordered the shirt three days before. I would have felt that. And that note is pathetic. Lisa was never pathetic."

He nodded again.

"Some things I want to tell you. There were no signs of a struggle. Mrs. Lanier is sure no one came in the front. The crime lab went over the whole place and we're sure no one was in there with her. I'd stake my life on the fact that no one entered or left that house. Now, *I* don't believe it was suicide, either, but do you have any suggestions?"

"The NSA," I said.

I explained about the last things she had done while I was still there. I told him of her fear of the government spy agencies. That was all I had.

"Well, I guess they're the ones who could do a thing like that, if anyone could. But I'll tell you, I have a hard time swallowing it. I don't know why, for one thing. Maybe you believe those people kill, like you and I'd swat a fly." His look made it into a question.

"I don't know what I believe."

"I'm not saying they wouldn't kill for national security, or some such shit. But they'd have taken the computers, too. They wouldn't have left her alone, they wouldn't even have let her *near* that stuff after they killed Kluge."

"What you're saying makes sense."

He muttered on about it for quite some time. Eventually I

offered him some wine. He accepted thankfully. I considered joining him—it would be a quick way to die—but did not. He drank the whole bottle, and was comfortably drunk when he suggested we go next door and look it over one more time. I was planning on visiting Lisa the next day, and knew I had to start somewhere building myself up for that, so I agreed to go with him.

We inspected the kitchen. The fire had blackened the counters and melted some linoleum, but not much else. Water had made a mess of the place. There was a brown stain on the floor which I was able to look at with no emotion.

So we went back to the living room, and one of the computers was turned on. There was a short message on the screen.

IF YOU WISH TO KNOW MORE
PRESS ENTER■

"Don't do it," I told him. But he did. He stood, blinking solemnly, as the words wiped themselves out and a new message appeared.

YOU LOOKED

The screen started to flicker and I was in my car, in darkness, with a pill in my mouth and another in my hand. I spit out the pill, and sat for a moment, listening to the old engine ticking over. In my other hand was the plastic pill bottle. I felt very tired, but opened the car door and shut off the engine. I felt my way to the garage door and opened it. The air outside was fresh and sweet. I looked down at the pill bottle and hurried into the bathroom.

When I got through what had to be done there were a dozen pills floating in the toilet that hadn't even dissolved. There were the wasted shells of many more, and a lot of other stuff I won't bother to describe. I counted the pills in the bottle, remembered how many there had been, and wondered if I would make it.

I went over to Kluge's house and could not find Osborne. I was getting tired, but I made it back to my house and stretched out on the couch to see if I would live or die.

The next day I found the story in the paper. Osborne had gone home and blown out the back of his head with his revolver. It was not a big story. It happens to cops all the time. He didn't leave a note.

I got on the bus and rode out to the hospital and spent three hours trying to get in to see Lisa. I wasn't able to do it. I was not a relative and the doctors were quite firm about her having no visitors. When I got angry they were as gentle as possible. It was then I learned the extent of her injuries. Hal had kept the worst from me. None of it would have mattered, but the doctors swore there was nothing left in her head. So I went home.

She died two days later.

She had left a will, to my surprise. I got the house and contents. I picked up the phone as soon as I learned of it, and called a garbage company. While they were on the way I went for the last time into Kluge's house.

The same computer was still on, and it gave the same message.

PRESS ENTER■

I cautiously located the power switch, and turned it off. I had the garbage people strip the place to the bare walls.

I went over my own house very carefully, looking for anything that was even the first cousin to a computer. I threw out the radio. I sold the car, and the refrigerator, and the stove, and the blender, and the electric clock. I drained the waterbed and threw out the heater.

Then I bought the best propane stove on the market, and hunted a long time before I found an old icebox. I had the garage stacked to the ceiling with firewood. I had the chimney cleaned. It would be getting cold soon.

One day I took the bus to Pasadena and established the Lisa Foo Memorial Scholarship fund for Vietnamese refugees and their children. I endowed it with seven hundred thousand eighty-three dollars and four cents. I told them it could be used for any fied of study except computer science. I could tell they thought me eccentric.

And I really thought I was safe, until the phone rang.

I thought it over for a long time before answering it. In the end, I knew it would just keep on going until I did. So I picked it up.

For a few seconds there was a dial tone, but I was not fooled. I kept holding it to my ear, and finally the tone turned off. There was just silence. I listened intently. I heard some of those far-off musical tones that live in phone wires. Echoes of conversations taking place a thousand miles away. And something infinitely more distant and cool.

I do not know what they have incubated out there at the NSA. I don't know if they did it on purpose, or if it just happened, or if it even has anything to do with them, in the end. But I know it's out there, because I heard its soul breathing on the wires. I spoke very carefully.

"I do not wish to know any more," I said. "I won't tell anyone anything. Kluge, Lisa, and Osborne all committed suicide. I am just a lonely man, and I won't cause you any trouble."

There was a click, and a dial tone.

* * *

Getting the phone taken out was easy. Getting them to remove all the wires was a little harder, since once a place is wired they expect it to be wired forever. They grumbled, but when I started pulling them out myself, they relented, though they warned me it was going to cost.

PG&E was harder. They actually seemed to believe there was a regulation requiring each house to be hooked up to the grid. They were willing to shut off my power—though hardly pleased about it—but they just weren't going to take the wires away from my house. I went up on the roof with an axe and demolished four feet of eaves as they gaped at me. Then they coiled up their wires and went home.

I threw out all my lamps, all things electrical. With hammer, chisel, and handsaw I went to work on the drywall just above the baseboards.

As I stripped the house of wiring I wondered many times why I was doing it. Why was it worth it? I couldn't have very many more years before a final seizure finished me off. Those years were not going to be a lot of fun.

Lisa had been a survivor. She would have known why I was doing this. She had once said I was a survivor, too. I survived the camp. I survived the death of my mother and father and managed to fashion a solitary life. Lisa survived the death of just about everything. No survivor expects to live through it all. But while she was alive, she would have worked to stay alive.

And that's what I did. I got all the wires out of the walls, went over the house with a magnet to see if I had missed any metal, then spent a week cleaning up, fixing the holes I had knocked in the walls, ceiling, and attic. I was amused trying to picture the real-estate agent selling this place after I was gone.

It's a great little house, folks. No electricity . . .

* * *

Now I live quietly, as before.

I work in my garden during most of the daylight hours. I've expanded it considerably, and even have things growing in the front yard now.

I live by candlelight, and kerosene lamp. I grow most of what I eat.

It took a long time to taper off the Tranxene and the Dilantin, but I did it, and now take the seizures as they come. I've usually got bruises to show for it.

In the middle of a vast city I have cut myself off. I am not part of the network growing faster than I can conceive. I don't even know if it's dangerous, to ordinary people. It noticed me, and Kluge, and Osborne. And Lisa. It brushed against our minds like I would brush away a mosquito, never noticing I had crushed it. Only I survived.

But I wonder.

It would be very hard . . .

Lisa told me how it can get in through the wiring. There's something called a carrier wave that can move over wires carrying household current. That's why the electricity had to go.

I need water for my garden. There's just not enough rain here in southern California, and I don't know how else I could get the water.

Do you think it could come through the pipes?

THE ALIENS WHO KNEW, I MEAN, *EVERYTHING*

by George Alec Effinger

You could take this story seriously if you wanted to. Or you could take it as an elaborate joke by this author, known for his sardonic humor. The fact is that we all think we know our likes and dislikes and that we know better than the other fellow. Fortunately we have all learned that this is a matter of personal opinions. But does that apply to a benevolent intelligent people from another world, a people who, as the title says, really did know what was best?

I was sitting at my desk, reading a report on the brown pelican situation, when the secretary of state burst in. "Mr. President," he said, his eyes wide, "the aliens are here!" Just like that. "The aliens are here!" As if I had any idea what to do about them.

"I see," I said. I learned early in my first term that "I see" was one of the safest and most useful comments I could possibly make in any situation. When I said "I see," it indicated that I had digested the news and was waiting intelligently and calmly for further data. That knocked the ball back into my advisers' court. I looked at the secretary of state expectantly. I was all prepared with my next utterance, in the event that he had nothing further to add. My next utterance would be, "Well?" That would indicate that I was on top of the problem, but that I couldn't be expected to make an executive decision without sufficient information, and that he should have known better than to burst into the Oval Office unless he had that information. That's why we had protocol; that's why we had proper channels; that's why I had advisers. The voters out there didn't want me to make decisions without sufficient information. If the secretary didn't have anything more to tell me, he shouldn't have burst in in the first place. I looked at him awhile longer. "Well?" I asked at last.

"That's about all we have at the moment," he said uncomfortably. I looked at him sternly for a few seconds, scoring a couple of points while he stood there all flustered. I turned back to the pelican report, dismissing him. I certainly wasn't going to get all flustered. I could think of only one president in recent memory who was ever flustered in office, and we all know what happened to him. As the secretary of state closed the door to my office behind him, I smiled. The aliens were probably going to be a bitch of a problem eventually, but it wasn't my problem yet. I had a little time.

But I found that I couldn't really keep my mind on the pelican question. Even the president of the United States has *some* imagination, and if the secretary of state was correct, I was going to have to confront these aliens pretty damn soon. I'd read stories about aliens when I was a kid, I'd seen all sorts of aliens in movies and television, but these were the first aliens who'd actually stopped by for a chat. Well, I wasn't going to be the first American president to make a fool of himself in front of visitors from another world. I was going to be briefed. I telephoned the secretary of defense. "We must have some contingency plans drawn up for this," I told him. "We have plans for every other possible situation."

This was true; the Defense Department has scenarios for such bizarre events as the rise of an imperialist fascist regime in Liechtenstein or the spontaneous depletion of all the world's selenium.

"Just a second, Mr. President," said the secretary. I could hear him muttering to someone else. I held the phone and stared out the window. There were crowds of people running around hysterically out there. Probably because of the aliens. "Mr. President?" came the voice of the secretary of defense. "I have one of the aliens here, and he suggests that we use the same plan that President Eisenhower used."

I closed my eyes and sighed. I hated it when they said stuff like that. I wanted information, and they told me these things knowing that I would have to ask four or five more questions just to understand the answer to the first one. "You have an alien with you?" I said in a pleasant enough voice.

"Yes, sir. They prefer not to be called 'aliens.' He tells me he's a 'nuhp.' "

"Thank you, Luis. Tell me, why do you have an al— Why do you have a nuhp and I don't"

Luis muttered the question to his nuhp. "He says it's because they wanted to go through proper channels. They learned about all that from President Eisenhower."

"Very good, Luis." This was going to take all day, I could see that; and I had a photo session with Mick Jagger's granddaughter. "My second question, Luis, is what the hell does he mean by 'the same plan that President Eisenhower used'?"

Another muffled consultation. "He says that this isn't the first time that the nuhp have landed on Earth. A scout ship with two nuhp aboard landed at Edwards Air Force Base in 1954. The two nuhp met with President Eisenhower. It was apparently a very cordial occasion, and President Eisenhower impressed the nuhp as a warm and sincere old gentleman. They've been planning to return to Earth ever since, but they've been very busy, what with one thing and another. President Eisenhower requested that the nuhp not reveal themselves to the people of Earth in general, until our government decided how to control the inevitable hysteria. My guess is that the government never got around to that, and when the nuhp departed, the matter was studied and then shelved. As the years passed, few people were even aware that the first meeting ever occurred. The nuhp have returned now in great numbers, expecting that we'd have prepared the populace by now. It's not their fault that we haven't. They just sort of took it for granted that they'd be welcome."

"Uh-huh," I said. That was my usual utterance when I didn't know what the hell else to say. "Assure them that they are, indeed, welcome. I don't suppose the study they did during the Eisenhower administration was ever completed. I don't suppose there really is a plan to break the news to the public."

"Unfortunately, Mr. President, that seems to be the case."

"Uh-huh," That's Republicans for you, I thought. "Ask your nuhp something for me, Luis. Ask him if he knows what they told Eisenhower. They must be full of outer-space wisdom. Maybe they have some ideas about how we should deal with this."

There was yet another pause. "Mr. President, he says all they discussed with Mr. Eisenhower was his golf game. They helped to correct his putting stroke. But they are definitely full of wisdom. They know all sorts of things. My nuhp—that is, his name is Hurv—anyway, he says that they'd be happy to give you some advice."

"Tell him that I'm grateful, Luis. Can they have someone meet with me in, say, half an hour?"

"There are three nuhp on their way to the Oval Office at this moment. One of them is the leader of their expedition, and one of the others is the commander of their mother ship."

"Mother ship?" I asked.

"You haven't seen it? It's tethered on the Mall. They're real sorry about what they did to the Washington Monument. They say they can take care of it tomorrow."

I just shuddered and hung up the phone. I called my secretary. "There are going to be three—"

"They're here now, Mr. President."

I sighed. "Send them in." And that's how I met the nuhp. Just as President Eisenhower had.

They were handsome people. Likeable, too. They smiled and shook hands and suggested that photographs be taken of the historic moment, so we called in the media; and then I had to sort of wing the most important diplomatic meeting of my entire political career. I welcomed the nuhp to Earth. "Welcome to Earth," I said, "and welcome to the United States."

"Thank you," said the nuhp I would come to know as Pleen. "We're glad to be here."

"How long do you plan to be with us?" I hated myself when I said that, in front of the Associated Press and UPI and all the network news people. I sounded like a room clerk at a Holiday Inn.

"We don't know, exactly," said Pleen. "We don't have to be back to work until a week from Monday."

"Uh-huh," I said. Then I just posed for pictures and kept my mouth shut. I wasn't going to say or do another goddamn thing until my advisors showed up and started advising.

Well, of course, the people panicked. Pleen told me to expect that, but I had figured it out for myself. We've seen too many movies about visitors from space. Sometimes they come with a message of peace and universal brotherhood and just the inside information mankind has been needing for thousands of years. More often, though, the aliens come to enslave and murder us because the visual effects are better, and so when the nuhp arrived, everyone was all prepared to hate them. People didn't trust their good looks. People were suspicious of their nice manners and their quietly tasteful clothing. When the nuhp offered to solve all our problems for us, we all said, sure, solve our problems—*but at what cost?*

That first week, Pleen and I spent a lot of time together, just getting to know one another and trying to understand what the other one wanted. I invited him and Commander Toag and the other nuhp bigwigs to a reception at the White House. We had a church choir from Alabama singing gospel music, and a high school band from Michigan playing a medley of favorite collegiate fight songs, and talented clones of the original stars nostalgically re-creating the Steve and Eydie Experience, and an improvisational comedy troupe from Los Angeles or someplace, and the New York Philharmonic under the baton of a twelve-year-old girl genius. They played Beethoven's Ninth Symphony in an attempt to impress the nuhp with how marvelous Earth culture was.

Pleen enjoyed it all very much. "Men are as varied in their expressions of joy as we nuhp," he said, applauding vigorously. "We are all very fond of human music. We think Beethoven composed some of the most beautiful melodies we've ever heard, anywhere in our galactic travels."

I smiled. "I'm sure we are all pleased to hear that," I said.

"Although the Ninth Symphony is certainly not the best of his work."

I faltered in my clapping. "Excuse me?" I said.

Pleen gave me a gracious smile. "It is well known among us that Beethoven's finest composition is his Piano Concerto No. 5 in E-flat major."

I let out my breath. "Of course, that's a matter of opinion. Perhaps the standards of the nuhp—"

"Oh, no," Pleen hastened to assure me, "taste does not enter into it at all. The Concerto No. 5 is Beethoven's best, according to very rigorous and definite critical principles.

And even that lovely piece is by no means the best music ever produced by mankind."

I felt just a trifle annoyed. What could this nuhp, who came from some weirdo planet God alone knows how far away, from some society with not the slightest connection to our heritage and culture, what could this nuhp know of what Beethoven's Ninth Symphony aroused in our human souls? "Tell me, then, Pleen," I said in my ominously soft voice, "what *is* the best human musical composition?"

"The score from the motion picture *Ben-Hur*, by Miklos Rózsa," he said simply. What could I do but nod my head in silence? It wasn't worth starting an interplanetary incident over.

So from fear our reaction to the nuhp changed to distrust. We kept waiting for them to reveal their real selves; we waited for the pleasant masks to slip off and show us the true nightmarish faces we all suspected lurked beneath. The nuhp did not go home a week from Monday, after all. They liked Earth, and they liked us. They decided to stay a little longer. We told them about ourselves and our centuries of trouble; and they mentioned, in an offhand nuhp way, that they could take care of a few little things, make some small adjustments, and life would be a whole lot better for everybody on Earth. They didn't want anything in return. They wanted to give us these things in gratitude for our hospitality: for letting them park their mother ship on the Mall and for all the free refills of coffee they were getting all around the world. We hesitated, but our vanity and our greed won out. "Go ahead," we said, "make our deserts bloom. Go ahead, end war and poverty and disease. Show us twenty exciting new things to do with leftovers. Call us when you're done."

The fear changed to distrust; but soon the distrust changed to hope. The nuhp made the deserts bloom, all right. They asked for four months. We were perfectly willing to let them have all the time they needed. They put a tall fence all around the Namib and wouldn't let anyone in to watch what they were doing. Four months later, they had a big cocktail party and invited the whole world to see what they'd accomplished. I sent the secretary of state as my personal representative. He brought back some wonderful slides: the vast desert had been turned into a bontanical miracle. There were miles and miles of flowering plants now, instead of the monotonous dead sand and gravel sea. Of course, the immense garden contained nothing but hollyhocks, many millions of hollyhocks. I mentioned to Pleen that the people of Earth had been hoping for a little more in the way of variety, and something just a trifle more practical, too.

"What do you mean, 'practical'?" he asked.

"You know," I said, "food."

"Don't worry about food," said Pleen. "We're going to take care of hunger pretty soon."

"Good, good. But hollyhocks?"

"What's wrong with hollyhocks?"

"Nothing," I admitted.

"Hollyhocks are the single prettiest flower grown on Earth."

"Some people like orchids," I said. "Some poeple like roses."

"No," said Pleen firmly. "Hollyhocks are it. I wouldn't kid you."

So we thanked the nuhp for a Namibia full of hollyhocks and stopped them before they did the same thing to the Sahara, the Mojave, and the Gobi.

On the whole, everyone began to like the nuhp, although they took just a little getting used to. They had very definite opinions about everything, and they wouldn't admit that what they had were *opinions*. To hear a nuhp talk, he had a direct line to some categorical imperative that spelled everything out in terms that were unflinchingly black and white. Hollyhocks were the best flowers. Alexander Dumas was the greatest novelist. Powder blue was the prettiest color. Melancholy was the most ennobling emotion. *Grand Hotel* was the finest movie. The best car ever built was the 1956 Chevy Bel Air, but it had to be aqua and white. And there just wasn't room for discussion: the nuhp made these pronouncements with the force of divine revelation.

I asked Pleen once about the American presidency. I asked him who the Nuhp thought was the best president in our history. I felt sort of like the Wicked Queen in "Snow White." Mirror, mirror, on the wall. I didn't really believe Pleen would tell me that I was the best president, but my heart pounded while I waited for his answer; you never know, right? To tell the truth, I expected him to say Washington, Lincoln, Roosevelt, or Akiwara. His answer surprised me: James K. Polk.

"Polk?" I asked. I wasn't even sure I could recognize Polk's portrait.

"He's not the most familiar," said Pleen, "but he was an honest if unexciting president. He fought the Mexican War and added a great amount of territory to the United States. He saw every bit of his platform become law. He was a good, hardworking man who deserves a better reputation."

"What about Thomas Jefferson?" I asked.

Pleen just shrugged. "He was O.K., too, but he was no James Polk."

My wife, the First Lady, became very good friends with the wife of Commander Toag, whose name was Doim. They often went shopping together, and Doim would make suggestions to the First Lady about fashion and hair care. Doim told my wife which rooms in the White House needed redecoration, and which charities were worthy of official support. It was Doim who negotiated the First Lady's recording contract, and it was Doim who introduced her to the Philadelphia cheese steak, one of the nuhp's favorite treats (although they asserted that the best cuisine on Earth was Tex-Mex).

One day, Doim and my wife were having lunch. They sat at a small table in a chic Washington restaurant, with a couple of dozen Secret Service people and nuhp security agents disguised elsewhere among the patrons. "I've noticed that there seem to be more nuhp here in Washington every week." said the First Lady.

"Yes," said Doim, "new mother ships arrive daily. We think Earth is one of the most pleasant planets we've ever visited."

"We're glad to have you, of course," said my wife, "and it seems that our people have gotten over their initial fears."

"The hollyhocks did the trick," said Doim.

"I guess so. How many nuhp are there on Earth now?"

"About five or six million, I'd say."

The First Lady was startled. "I didn't think it would be that many."

Doim laughed. "We're not just here in America, you know. We're all over. We really like Earth, Although, of course, Earth isn't absolutely the best planet. Our own home, Nupworld, is still Number One; but Earth would certainly be on any Top Ten list."

"Uh-huh." (My wife has learned many important oratorical tricks from me.)

"That's why we're so glad to help you beautify and modernize your world."

"The hollyhocks were nice," said the First Lady. "But when are you going to tackle the really vital questions?"

"Don't worry about that," said Doim, turning her attention to her cottage cheese salad.

"When are you going to take care of world hunger?"

"Pretty soon. Don't worry."

"Urban blight?"

"Pretty soon."

"Man's inhumanity to man?"

Doim gave my wife an impatient look. "We haven't even

been here for six months yet. What do you want, miracles? We've already done more than your husband accomplished in his entire first term."

"Hollyhocks," muttered the First Lady.

"I heard that," said Doim. "The rest of the universe absolutely *adores* hollyhocks. We can't help it if humans have no taste."

They finished their lunch in silence, and my wife came back to the White House fuming.

That same week, one of my advisers showed me a letter that had been sent by a young man in New Mexico. Several nuhp had moved into a condo next door to him and had begun advising him about the best investment possibilities (urban respiratory spas), the best fabrics and colors to wear to show off his coloring, the best holo system on the market (the Esmeraldas F-64 with hex-phased Libertad screens and a Ruby Challenger argon solipsizer), the best place to watch sunsets (the revolving restaurant on top of the Weyerhauser Building in Yellowstone City), the best wines to go with everything (too numerous to mention—send SASE for list), and which of the two women he was dating to marry (Candi Marie Esterhazy). "Mr. President," said the bewildered young man, "I realize that we must be gracious hosts to our benefactors from space, but I am having some difficulty keeping my temper. The nuhp are certainly knowledgeable and willing to share the benefits of their wisdom, but they don't even wait to be asked. If they were people, regular human beings who lived next door, I would have punched their lights out by now. Please advise. And hurry: they are taking me downtown next Friday to pick out an engagement ring and new living room furniture. I don't even *want* new living room furniture!"

Luis, my secretary of defense, talked to Hurv about the ultimate goals of the nuhp. "We don't have any goals," he said. "We're just taking it easy."

"Then why did you come to Earth?" asked Luis.

"Why do you go bowling?"

"I don't go bowling."

"You should," said Hurv. "Bowling is the most enjoyable thing a person can do."

"What about sex?"

"Bowling *is* sex. Bowling is a symbolic form of intercourse, except you don't have to bother about the feelings of some other person. Bowling is sex without guilt. Bowling is what people have wanted down through all the millennia: sex without the slightest responsibility. It's the very distillation of the essence of sex. Bowling is sex without fear and shame."

"Bowling is sex without pleasure," said Luis.

There was a brief silence. "You mean," said Hurv, "that when you put that ball right into the pocket and see those pins explode off the alley, you don't have an orgasm?"

"Nope," said Luis.

"*That's* your problem, then. I can't help you there, you'll have to see some kind of therapist. It's obvious this subject embarrasses you. Let's talk about something else."

"Fine with me," said Luis moodily. "When are we going to receive the real benefits of your technological superiority? When are you going to unlock the final secrets of the atom? When are you going to free mankind from drudgery?"

"What do you mean, 'technological superiority'?" asked Hurv.

"There must be scientific wonders beyond our imagining aboard your mother ships."

"Not so's you'd notice. We're not even so advanced as you people here on Earth. We've learned all sorts of wonderful things since we've been here."

"What?" Luis couldn't imagine what Hurv was trying to say.

"We don't have anything like your astonishing bubble memories or silicon chips. We never invented anything comparable to the transistor, even. You know why the mother ships are so big?''

''My God.''

''That's right,'' said Hurv, ''vacuum tubes. All our spacecraft operate on vacuum tubes. They take up a hell of a lot of space. And they burn out. Do you know how long it takes to find the goddamn tube when it burns out? Remember how people used to take bags of vacuum tubes from their television sets down to the drugstore to use the tube tester? Think of doing that with something the size of our mother ships. And we can't just zip off into space when we feel like it. We have to let a mother ship warm up first. You have to turn the key and let the thing warm up for a couple of minutes, *then* you can zip off into space. It's a goddamn pain in the neck.''

''I don't understand,'' said Luis, stunned. ''If your technology is so primitive, how did you come here? If we're so far ahead of you, we should have discovered your planet, instead the other way around.''

Hurv gave a gentle laugh. ''Don't pat yourself on the back, Luis. Just because your electronics are better than ours, you aren't necessarily superiors in any way. Look, imagine that you humans are a man in Los Angeles with a brand-new Trujillo and we are a nuhp in New York with a beat-up old Ford. The two fellows start driving toward St. Louis. Now, the guy in the Trujillo is doing 120 on the interstates, and the guy in the Ford is putting along at 55; but the human in the Trujillo stops in Vegas and puts all of his gas money down the hole of a blackjack table, and the determined little nuhp cruises along for days until at least he reaches his goal. It's all a matter of superior intellect and the will to succeed. Your people talk a lot about going to the stars, but you just keep putting your money into other projects, like war and popular music and international athletic events and resurrecting the fashions of previous decades. If you wanted to go into space, you would have.''

"But we *do* want to go."

"Then we'll help you. We'll give you the secrets. And you can explain your electronics to our engineers, and together we'll build wonderful new mother ships that will open the universe to both humans and nuhp."

Luis let out his breath. "Sounds good to me," he said.

Everyone agreed that this looked better than hollyhocks. We all hoped that we could keep from kicking their collective asses long enough to collect on that promise.

When I was in college, my roommate in my sophomore year was a tall, skinny guy named Barry Rintz. Barry had wild, wavy black hair and a sharp face that looked like a handsome, normal face that had been sat on and folded in the middle. He squinted a lot, not because he had any defect in his eyesight, but because he wanted to give the impression that he was constantly evaluating the world. This was true. Barry could tell you the actual and market values of any object you happen to come across.

We had a double date one football weekend with two girls from another college in the same city. Before the game, we met the girls and took them to the university's art museum, which was pretty large and owned an impressive collection. My date, a pretty elementary ed. major named Brigid, and I wandered from gallery to gallery, remarking that our tastes in art were very similar. We both like the Impressionists, and we both like Surrealism. There were a couple of little Renoirs that we admired for almost half an hour, and then we made a lot of silly sophomore jokes about what was happening in the Magritte and Dali and de Chirico paintings.

Barry and his date, Dixie, ran across us by accident as all four of us passed through the sculpture gallery. "There's a terrific Seurat down there," Brigid told her girlfriend.

"Seurat," Barry said. There was a lot of amused disbelief in his voice.

"I like Seurat," said Dixie.

"Well, of course," said Barry, "there's nothing really *wrong* with Seurat."

"What do you mean by that?"

"Do you know F. E. Church?" he asked.

"Who?" I said.

"Come here." He practically dragged us to a gallery of American paintings. F. E. Church was a remarkable American landscape painter (1826–1900) who achieved an astonishing and lovely luminance in his works. "Look at that light!" cried Barry. "Look at that space! Look at that air!"

Brigid glanced at Dixie. "Look at that air?" she whispered.

It was a fine painting and we all said so, but Barry was insistent. F. E. Church was the greatest artist in American history, and one of the best the world has ever known. "I'd put him right up there with Van Dyck and Canaletto."

"Canaletto?" said Dixie. "The one who did all those pictures of Venice?"

"Those skies!" murmured Barry ecstatically. He wore the drunken expression of the satisfied voluptuary.

"Some people like paintings of puppies or naked women," I offered. "Barry likes light and air."

We left the museum and had lunch. Barry told us which things on the menu were worth ordering, and which things were an abomination. He made us all drink an obscure imported beer from Ecuador. To Barry, the world was divided up into masterpieces and abominations. It made life so much simpler for him, except that he never understood why his friends could never tell one from the other.

At the football game, Barry compared our school's quarterback to Y. A. Tittle. He compared the other team's punter to Ngoc Van Vinh. He compared the halftime show to the Ohio State band's Script Ohio formation. Before the end of the third quarter, it was very obvious to me that Barry was going to have absolutely no luck at all with Dixie. Before the clock ran out in the fourth quarter, Brigid and I had made whispered plans to dump the other two as soon as possible and sneak away by ourselves. Dixie would probably find an excuse to ride the bus back to her dorm before suppertime. Barry, as usual, would spend the evening in our room, reading *The Making of the President 1996*.

On other occasions Barry would lecture me about subjects as diverse as American Literature (the best poet was Edwin Arlington Robinson, the best novelist James T. Farrell), animals (The only correct pet was the golden retriever), clothing (in anything other than a navy blue jacket and gray slacks a man was just asking for trouble), and even hobbies (Barry collected military decorations of czarist Imperial Russia. He wouldn't talk to me for days after I told him my father collected barbed wire).

Barry was a wealth of information. He was the campus arbiter of good taste. Everyone knew that Barry was the man to ask.

But no one ever did. We all hated his guts. I moved out of our dorm room before the end of the fall semester. Shunned, lonely, and bitter Barry Rintz wound up as a guidance counselor in a high school in Ames, Iowa. The job was absolutely perfect for him; few people are so lucky in finding a career.

If I didn't know better, I might have believed that Barry was the original advance spy for the nuhp.

When the nuhp had been on Earth for a full year, they gave us the gift of interstellar travel. It was surprisingly inexpensive. The nuhp explained their propulsion system, which was cheap and safe and adaptable to all sorts of other earthbound applications. The revelations opened up an entirely new area of scientific speculation. Then the nuhp taught us their navigational methods, and about the "shortcuts" they had discovered in space. People called them space warps, although technically speaking, the shortcuts had nothing to do with Einsteinian theory or curved space or anything like that. Not many humans understood what the nuhp were talking about, but that didn't make very much difference. The nuhp didn't understand the shortcuts, either; they just used them. The matter was presented to us like a Thanksgiving turkey on a platter. We bypassed the whole business of cautious scientific experimentation and leaped right into commercial exploitation. Mitsubishi of La Paz and Martin Marietta used nuhp schematics to begin construction of three luxury passenger ships, each capable of transporting a thousand tourists anywhere in our galaxy. Although man had yet to set foot on the moons of Jupiter, certain selected travel agencies began booking passage for a grand tour of the dozen nearest inhabited worlds.

Yes, it seemed that space was teeming with life, humanoid life on planets circling half the G-type stars in the heavens. "We've been trying to communicate with extraterrestrial intelligence for decades," complained one Soviet scientist. "Why haven't they responded?"

A friendly nuhp merely shrugged "Everybody's trying to communicate out there," he said. "Your messages are like Publishers Clearing House mail to them." At first, that was a blow to our racial pride, but we got over it. As soon as we joined the interstellar community, they'd begin to take us more seriously. And the nuhp had made that possible.

We were grateful to the nuhp, but that didn't make them any easier to live with. They were still insufferable. As my second term as president came to an end, Pleen began to advise me about my future career. "Don't write a book," he told me (after I had already written the first two hundred pages of a *A President Remembers*). "If you want to be an elder statesman, fine; but keep a low profile and wait for the people to come to you."

"What am I supposed to do with my time, then?" I asked.

"Choose a new career," Pleen said. "You're not all that old. Lots of people do it. Have you considered starting a mail-order business? You can operate it from your home. Or go back to school and take courses in some subject that's always interested you. Or become active in church or civic projects. Find a new hobby: raising hollyhocks or collecting military decorations."

"Pleen," I begged, "just leave me alone."

He seemed hurt. "Sure, if that's what you want." I regretted my harsh words.

All over the country, all over the world, everyone was having the same trouble with the nuhp. It seemed that so many of them had come to Earth, every human had his own personal nuhp to make endless suggestions. There hadn't been so much tension in the world since the 1992 Miss Universe contest, when the most votes went to No Award.

That's why it didn't surprise me very much when the first of our own mother ships returned from its 28-day voyage among the stars with only 276 of its 1,000 passengers still aboard. The other 724 had remained behind on one lush, exciting, exotic, friendly world or another. These planets had one thing in common: they were all populated by charming, warm, intelligent, humanlike people who had left their own home worlds after being discovered by the nuhp. Many races lived together in peace and harmony on these planets, in spacious cities newly built to house the fed-up expatriates. Perhaps these alien races had experienced the same internal jealousies and hatreds we human beings had known for so long, but no more. Coming together from many planets throughout our galaxy, these various peoples dwelt contentedly beside each other, united by a single common adversion: their dislike for the nuhp.

Within a year of the launching of our first interstellar ship, the population of Earth had declined by 0.5 percent. Within two years, the population had fallen by almost 14 million. The nuhp were too sincere and too eager and too sympathetic to fight with. That didn't make them any less tedious. Rather than make a scene, most people just up and left. There were plenty of really lovely worlds to visit, and it didn't cost very much, and the opportunities in space were unlimited. Many people who were frustrated and disappointed on Earth were able to build new and fulfilling lives for themselves on planets that until the nuhp arrived, we didn't even know existed.

The nuhp knew this would happen. It had already happened dozens, hundreds of times in the past, wherever their mother ships touched down. They had made promises to us and they had kept them, although we couldn't have guessed just how things would turn out.

Our cities were no longer decaying warrens imprisoning the improverished masses. The few people who remained behind could pick and choose among the best housing. Landlords were forced to reduce rents and keep properties in perfect repair just to attract tenants.

Hunger was ended when the ratio of consumers to food producers dropped drastically. Within ten years, the population of Earth was cut in half, and was still falling.

For the same reason, poverty began to disappear. There were plenty of jobs for everyone. When it became apparent that the nuhp weren't going to compete for those jobs, there were more opportunities than people to take advantage of them.

Discrimination and prejudice vanished almost overnight. Everyone cooperated to keep things running smoothly despite the large-scale emigration. The good life was available to everyone, and so resentments melted away. Then, too, whatever enmity people still felt could be focused solely on the nuhp; the nuhp didn't mind, either. They were oblivious to it all.

I am now the mayor and postmaster of the small human community of New Dallas, here on Thir, the fourth planet of a star known in our old catalog as Struve 2398. The various alien races we encountered here call the star by another name, which translates into "God's Pineal." All the aliens here are extremely helpful and charitable, and there are few nuhp.

All through the galaxy, the nuhp are considered the messengers of peace. Their mission is to travel from planet to planet, bringing reconciliation, prosperity, and true civilization. There isn't an intelligent race in the galaxy that doesn't love the nuhp. We all recognize what they've done and what they've given us.

But if the nuhp started moving in down the block, we'd be packed and on our way somewhere else by morning.

BLOODCHILD

by Octavia E. Butler

Out there among the myriad worlds that bear life, we will probably find many very different from that of Earth, or so we like to think. But our own planet has such tremendously varied living species that it may be quite difficult to find something out there that does not in some way utilize biological systems that have their parallels right here too. Here is a story that might be a bit strong for those with weak stomachs, but it is not unthinkable.

My last night of childhood began with a visit home. T'Gatoi's sisters had given us two sterile eggs. T'Gatoi gave one to my mother, brother, and sisters. She insisted that I eat the other one alone. It didn't matter. There was still enough to leave everyone feeling good. Almost everyone. My mother wouldn't take any. She sat, watching everyone drifting and dreaming without her. Most of the time she watched me.

I lay against T'Gatoi's long, velvet underside, sipping from my egg now and then, wondering why my mother denied herself such a harmless pleasure. Less of her hair would be gray if she indulged now and then. The eggs prolonged life, prolonged vigor. My father, who had never refused one in his life, had lived more than twice as long as he should have. And toward the end of his life, when he should have been slowing down, he had married my mother and fathered four children.

But my mother seemed content to age before she had to. I saw her turn away as several of T'Gatoi's limbs secured me closer. T'Gatoi liked our body heat, and took advantage of it whenever she could. When I was little and at home more, my mother used to try to tell me how to behave with T'Gatoi—how to be respectful and always obedient because T'Gatoi was the Tlic government official in charge of the Preserve, and thus the most important of her kind to deal directly with Terrans. It was an honor, my mother said, that such a person had chosen to come into the family. My mother was at her most formal and severe when she was lying.

I had no idea why she was lying, or even what she was lying about. It *was* an honor to have T'Gatoi in the family, but it was hardly a novelty. T'Gatoi and my mother had been friends all my mother's life, and T'Gatoi was not interested in being honored in the house she considered her second home. She simply came in, climbed onto one of her special couches and called me over to keep her warm. It was impossible to be formal with her while lying against her and hearing her complain as usual that I was too skinny.

"You're better," she said this time, probing me with six or seven of her limbs. "You're gaining weight finally. Thinness is dangerous." The probing changed subtly, became a series of caresses.

"He's still too thin," my mother said sharply.

T'Gatoi lifted her head and perhaps a meter of her body off the couch as though she were sitting up. She looked at my mother and my mother, her face lined and old-looking, turned away.

"Lien, I would like you to have what's left of Gan's egg."

"The eggs are for the children," my mother said.

"They are for the family. Please take it."

Unwillingly obedient, my mother took it from me and put it to her mouth. There were only a few drops left in the now-shrunken, elastic shell, but she squeezed them out, swallowed them, and after a few moments some of the lines of tension began to smooth from her face.

"It's good," she whispered. "Sometimes I forget how good it is."

"You should take more," T'Gatoi said. "Why are you in such a hurry to be old?"

My mother said nothing.

"I like being able to come here," T'Gatoi said. "This place is a refuge because of you, yet you won't take care of yourself."

T'Gatoi was hounded on the outside. Her people wanted more of us made available. Only she and her political faction stood between us and the hordes who did not understand why there was a Preserve—why any Terran could not be courted, paid, drafted, in some way made available to them. Or they did understand, but in their desperation, they did not care. She parceled us out to the desperate and sold us to the rich and powerful for their political support. Thus, we were necessities, status symbols, and an independent people. She oversaw the joining of families, putting an end to the final remnants of the earlier system of breaking up Terran families to suit impatient Tlic. I had lived outside with her. I had seen the desperate eagerness in the way some people looked at me. It was a little frightening to know that only she stood between us and that desperation that could so easily swallow us. My mother would look at her sometimes and say to me, "Take care of her." And I would remember that she too had been outside, had seen.

Now T'Gatoi used four of her limbs to push me away from

her onto the floor. "Go on, Gan," she said. "Sit down there with your sisters and enjoy not being sober. You had most of the egg. Lien, come warm me."

My mother hesitated for no reason that I could see. One of my earliest memories is of my mother stretched alongside T'Gatoi, talking about things I could not understand, picking me up from the floor and laughing as she sat me on one of T'Gatoi's segments. She ate her share of eggs then. I wondered when she had stopped, and why.

She lay down now against T'Gatoi, and the whole left row of T'Gatoi's limbs closed around her, holding her loosely, but securely. I had always found it comfortable to lie that way but, except for my older sister, no one else in the family liked it. They said it made them feel caged.

T'Gatoi meant to cage my mother. Once she had, she moved her tail slightly, then spoke. "Not enough egg, Lien. You should have taken it when it was passed to you. You need it badly now."

T'Gatoi's tail moved once more, its whip motion so swift I wouldn't have seen it if I hadn't been watching for it. Her sting drew only a single drop of blood from my mother's bare leg.

My mother cried out—probably in surprise. Being stung doesn't hurt. Then she sighed and I could see her body relax. She moved languidly into a more comfortable position within the cage of T'Gatoi's limbs. "Why did you do that?" she asked, sounding half asleep.

"I could not watch you sitting and suffering any longer."

My mother managed to move her shoulders in a small shrug. "Tomorrow," she said.

"Yes. Tomorrow you will resume your suffering—if you must. But for now, just for now, lie here and warm me and let me ease your way a little."

"He's still mine, you know," my mother said suddenly.

"Nothing can buy him from me." Sober, she would not have permitted herself to refer to such things.

"Nothing," T'Gatoi agreed, humoring her.

"Did you think I would sell him for eggs? For long life? My son?"

"Not for anything," T'Gatoi said stroking my mother's shoulders, toying with her long, graying hair.

I would like to have touched my mother, shared that moment with her. She would take my hand if I touched her now. Freed by the egg and the sting, she would smile and perhaps say things long held in. But tomorrow, she would remember all this as a humiliation. I did not want to be part of a remembered humiliation. Best just to be still and know she loved me under all the duty and pride and pain.

"Xuan Hoa, take off her shoes," T'Gatoi said. "In a little while I'll sting her again and she can sleep."

My older sister obeyed, swaying drunkenly as she stood up. When she had finished, she sat down beside me and took my hand. We had always been a unit, she and I.

My mother put the back of her head against T'Gatoi's underside and tried from that impossible angle to look up into the broad, round face. "You're going to sting me again?"

"Yes. Lien."

"I'll sleep until tomorrow noon."

"Good. You need it. When did you sleep last?"

My mother made a wordless sound of annoyance. "I should have stepped on you when you were small enough," she muttered.

It was an old joke between them. They had grown up together, sort of, though T'Gatoi had not, in my mother's lifetime, been small enough for any Terran to step on. She was nearly three times my mother's present age, yet would still be young when my mother died of age. But T'Gatoi and my mother had met as T'Gatoi was coming into a period of rapid development—a kind of Tlic adolescence. My mother was only a child, but for a while they developed at the same rate and had no better friends than each other.

T'Gatoi had even introduced my mother to the man who became my father. My parents, pleased with each other in spite of their very different ages, married as T'Gatoi was going into her family's business—politics. She and my mother saw each other less. But sometimes before my older sister was born, my mother promised T'Gatoi one of her children. She would have to give one of us to someone, and she preferred T'Gatoi to some stranger.

Years passed. T'Gatoi traveled and increased her influence. The Preserve was hers by the time she came back to my mother to collect what she probably saw as her just reward for her hard work. My older sister took an instant liking to her and wanted to be chosen, but my mother was just coming to term with me and T'Gatoi liked the idea of choosing an infant and watching and taking part in all the phases of development. I'm told I was first caged within T'Gatoi's many limbs only three minutes after my birth. A few days later, I was given my first taste of egg. I tell Terrans that when they ask whether I was ever afraid of her. And I tell it to Tlic when T'Gatoi suggests a young Terran child for them and they, anxious and ignorant, demand an adolescent. Even my brother who had somehow grown up to fear and distrust the Tlic could probably have gone smoothly into one of their families if he had been adopted early enough. Sometimes, I think for his sake he should have been. I looked at him, stretched out on the floor across the room, his eyes open, but glazed as he dreamed his egg dream. No matter what he felt toward the Tlic, he always demanded his share of egg.

"Lien, can you stand up?" T'Gatoi asked suddenly.

"Stand?" my mother said. "I thought I was going to sleep."

"Later. Something sounds wrong outside." The cage was abruptly gone.

"What?"

"Up, Lien!"

My mother recognized her tone and got up just in time to avoid being dumped on the floor. T'Gatoi whipped her three meters of body off her couch, toward the door, and out at full speed. She had bones—ribs, a long spine, a skull, four sets of limbbones per segment. But when she moved that way, twisting, hurling herself into controlled falls, landing running, she seemed not only boneless, but aquatic—something swimming through the air as though it were water. I loved watching her move.

I left my sister and started to follow her out the door, though I wasn't very steady on my own feet. It would have been better to sit and dream, better yet to find a girl and share a waking dream with her. Back when the Tlic saw us as not much more than convenient big warm-blooded animals, they would pen several of us together, male and female, and feed us only eggs. That way they could be sure of getting another generation of us no matter how we tried to hold out. We were lucky that didn't go on long. A few generations of it and we would have *been* little more than convenient big animals.

"Hold the door open, Gan," T'Gatoi said. "And tell the family to stay back."

"What is it?" I asked.

"N'Tlic."

I shrank back against the door. "Here? Alone?"

"He was trying to reach a call box, I suppose." She carried the man past me, unconscious, folded like a coat over some of her limbs. He looked young—my brother's age perhaps—and he was thinner than he should have been. What T'Gatoi would have called dangerously thin.

"Gan, go to the call box," she said. She put the man on the floor and began stripping off his clothing.

I did not move.

After a moment, she looked up at me, her sudden stillness a sign of deep impatience.

"Send Qui," I told her. "I'll stay here. Maybe I can help."

She let her limbs begin to move again, lifting the man and pulling his shirt over his head. "You don't want to see this," she said. "It will be hard. I can't help this man the way his Tlic could."

"I know. But send Qui. He won't want to be of any help here. I'm at least willing to try."

She looked at my brother—older, bigger, stronger, certainly more able to help her here. He was sitting up now, braced against the wall, staring at the man on the floor with undisguised fear and revulsion. Even she could see that he would be useless.

"Qui, go!" she said.

He didn't argue. He stood up, swayed briefly, then steadied, frightened sober.

"This man's name is Bram Lomas," she told him, reading from the man's arm band. I fingered my own arm band in sympathy. "He needs T'Khotgif Teh. Do you hear?"

"Bram Lomas, T'Khotgif Teh," my brother said. "I'm going." He edged around Lomas and ran out the door.

Lomas began to regain consciousness. He only moaned at first and clutched spasmodically at a pair of T'Gatoi's limbs. My younger sister, finally awake from her egg dream, came close to look at him, until my mother pulled her back.

T'Gatoi removed the man's shoes, then his pants, all the while leaving him two of her limbs to grip. Except for the final few, all her limbs were equally dexterous. "I want no argument from you this time, Gan," she said.

I straightened. "What shall I do?"

"Go out and slaughter an animal that is at least half your size."

"Slaughter? But I've never—"

She knocked me across the room. Her tail was an efficient weapon whether she exposed the sting or not.

I got up, feeling stupid for having ignored her warning, and went into the kitchen. Maybe I could kill something with a knife or an ax. My mother raised a few Terran animals for the table and several thousand local ones for their fur. T'Gatoi would probably prefer something local. An achti, perhaps. Some of those were the right size, though they had about three times as many teeth as I did and a real love of using them. My mother, Hoa, and Qui could kill them with knives. I had never killed one at all, had never slaughtered any animal. I had spent most of my time with T'Gatoi while my brother and sisters were learning the family business. T'Gatoi had been right. I should have been the one to go to the call box. At least I could do that.

I went to the corner cabinet where my mother kept her larger house and garden tools. At the back of the cabinet there was a pipe that carried off waste water from the kitchen—except that it didn't any more. My father had rerouted the waste water before I was born. Now the pipe could be turned so that one half slid around the other and a rifle could be stored inside. This wasn't our only gun, but it was our most easily accessible one. I would have to use it to shoot one of the biggest of the achti. Then T'Gatoi would probably confiscate it. Firearms were illegal in the Preserve. There had been incidents right after the Preserve was established—Terrans shooting Tlic, shooting N'Tlic. This was before the joining of families began, before everyone had a personal stake in keeping the peace. No one had shot a Tlic in my lifetime or my mother's, but the law still stood—for our protection, we were told. There were stories of whole Terran families wiped out in reprisal back during the assassinations.

I went out to the cages and shot the biggest achti I could find. It was a handsome breeding male and my mother would not be pleased to see me bring it in. But it was the right size, and I was in a hurry.

I put the achti's long, warm body over my shoulder—glad that some of the weight I'd gained was muscle—and took it to the kitchen. There, I put the gun back in its hiding place. If T'Gatoi noticed the achti's wounds and demanded the gun, I would give it to her. Otherwise, let it stay where my father wanted it.

I turned to take the achti to her, then hesitated. For several seconds, I stood in front of the closed door wondering why I was suddenly afraid. I knew what was going to happen. I hadn't seen it before but T'Gatoi had shown me diagrams, and drawings. She had made sure I knew the truth as soon as I was old enough to understand it.

Yet I did not want to go into that room. I wasted a little time chosing a knife from the carved, wooden box in which my mother kept them. T'Gatoi might want one, I told myself, for the tough, heavily furred hide of the achti.

"Gan!" T'Gatoi called, her voice harsh with urgency.

I swallowed. I had not imagined a simple moving of the feet could be so difficult. I realized I was trembling and that shamed me. Shame impelled me through the door.

I put the achti down near T'Gatoi and saw that Lomas was unconscious again. She, Lomas, and I were alone in the room, my mother and sisters probably sent out so they would not have to watch. I envied them.

But my mother came back into the room as T'Gatoi seized the achti. Ignoring the knife I offered her, she extended claws from several of her limbs and slit the achti from throat to anus. She looked at me, her yellow eyes intent. "Hold this man's shoulders, Gan."

I stared at Lomas in panic, realizing that I did not want to touch him, let alone hold him. This would not be like shooting an animal. Not as quick, not as merciful, and, I hoped, not as final, but there was nothing I wanted less than to be part of it.

My mother came forward. "Gan, you hold his right side," she said. "I'll hold his left." And if he came to, he would throw her off without realizing he had done it. She was a tiny woman. She often wondered aloud how she had produced, as she said, such "huge" children.

"Never mind," I told her, taking the man's shoulders. "I'll do it."

She hovered nearby.

"Don't worry," I said. "I won't shame you. You don't have to stay and watch."

She looked at me uncertainly, then touched my face in a rare caress. Finally, she went back to her bedroom.

T'Gatoi lowered her head in relief. "Thank you, Gan," she said with courtesy more Terran than Tlic. "That one . . . she is always finding new ways for me to make her suffer."

Lomas began to groan and make choked sounds. I had hoped he would stay unconscious. T'Gatoi put her face near his so that he focused on her.

"I've stung you as much as I dare for now," she told him. "When this is over, I'll sting you to sleep and you won't hurt any more."

"Please," the man begged. "Wait . . ."

"There's no more time, Bram. I'll sting you as soon as it's over. When T'Khotgif arrives she'll give you eggs to help you heal. It will be over soon."

"T'Khotgif!" the man shouted, straining against my hands.

"Soon, Bram." T'Gatoi glanced at me, then placed a claw against his abdomen slightly to the right of the middle, just below the last rib. There was movement on the right side—tiny, seemingly random pulsations moving his brown flesh, creating a concavity here, a convexity there, over and over until I could see the rhythm of it and knew where the next pulse would be.

Lomas's entire body stiffened under T'Gatoi's claw, though she merely rested it against him as she wound the rear section of her body around his legs. He might break my grip, but he would not break hers. He wept helplessly as she used his pants to tie his hands, then pushed his hands above his head so that I could kneel on the cloth between them and pin them in place. She rolled up his shirt and gave it to him to bite down on.

And she opened him.

His body convulsed with the first cut. He almost tore himself away from me. The sounds he made . . . I had never heard such sounds come from anything human. T'Gatoi seemed to pay no attention as she lengthened and deepened the cut, now and then pausing to lick away blood. His blood vessels contracted, reacting to the chemistry of her saliva, and the bleeding slowed.

I felt as though I were helping her torture him, helping her consume him. I knew I would vomit soon, didn't know why I hadn't already. I couldn't possibly last until she was finished.

She found the first grub. It was fat and deep red with his blood—both inside and out. It had already eaten its own egg case, but apparently had not yet begun to eat its host. At this stage, it would eat any flesh except its mother's. Let alone, it would have gone on excreting the poisons that had both sickened and alerted Lomas. Eventually it would have begun to eat. By the time it ate its way out of Lomas's flesh, Lomas would be dead or dying—and unable to take revenge on the thing that was killing him. There was always a grace period between the time the host sickened and the time the grubs began to eat him.

T'Gatoi picked up the writhing grub carefully, and looked at it, somehow ignoring the terrible groans of the man.

Abruptly, the man lost consciousness.

"Good," T'Gatoi looked down at him. "I wish you Terrans

could do that at will." She felt nothing. And the thing she held . . .

It was limbless and boneless at this stage, perhaps fifteen centimeters long and two thick, blind and slimy with blood. It was like a large worm. T'Gatoi put it into the belly of the achti, and it began at once to burrow. It would stay there and eat as long as there was anything to eat.

Probing through Lomas' flesh, she found two more, one of them smaller and more vigorous. "A male!" she said happily. He would be dead before I would. He would be through his metamorphosis and screwing everything that would hold still before his sisters even had limbs. He was the only one to make a serious effort to bite T'Gatoi as she placed him in the achti.

Paler worms oozed to visibility in Lomas's flesh. I closed my eyes. It was worse than finding something dead, rotting, and filled with tiny animal grubs. And it was far worse than any drawing or diagram.

"Ah, there are more," T'Gatoi said, plucking out two long, thick grubs. You may have to kill another animal, Gan. Everything lives inside you Terrans."

I had been told all my life that this was a good and necessary thing Tlic and Terran did together—a kind of birth. I had believed it until now. I knew birth was painful and bloody, no matter what. But this was something else, something worse. And I wasn't ready to see it. Maybe I never would be. Yet I couldn't *not* see it. Closing my eyes didn't help.

T'Gatoi found a grub still eating its egg case. The remains of the case were still wired into a blood vessel by their own little tube or hook or whatever. That was the way the grubs were anchored and the way they fed. They took only blood until they were ready to emerge. Then they ate their stretched, elastic egg cases. Then they ate their hosts.

T'Gatoi bit away the egg case, licked away the blood. Did

she like the taste? Did childhood habits die hard—or not die at all?

The whole procedure was wrong, alien. I wouldn't have thought anything about her could seem alien to me.

"One more, I think," she said. "Perhaps two. A good family. In a host animal these days, we would be happy to find one or two alive." She glanced at me. "Go outside, Gan, and empty your stomach. Go now while the man is unconscious."

I staggered out, barely made it. Beneath the tree just beyond the front door, I vomited until there was nothing left to bring up. Finally, I stood shaking, tears streaming down my face. I did not know why I was crying, but I could not stop. I went farther from the house to avoid being seen. Every time I closed my eyes I saw red worms crawling over redder human flesh.

There was a car coming toward the house. Since Terrans were forbidden motorized vehicles except for certain farm equipment, I knew this must be Lomas's Tlic with Qui and perhaps a Terran doctor. I wiped my face on my shirt, struggled for control.

"Gan," Qui called as the car stopped. "What happened?" He crawled out of the low, round, Tlic-convenient car door. Another Terran crawled out the other side and went into the house without speaking to me. The doctor. With his help and a few eggs, Lomas might make it.

"T'Khotgif Teh?" I said.

The Tlic driver surged out of her car, reared up half her length before me. She was paler and smaller than T'Gatoi—probably born from the body of an animal. Tlic from Terran bodies were always larger as well as more numerous.

"Six young," I told her. "Maybe seven, all alive. At least one male."

"Lomas?" she said harshly. I liked her for the question

and the concern in her voice when she asked it. The last coherent thing he had said was her name.

"He's alive," I said.

She surged away to the house without another word.

"She's been sick," my brother said, watching her go. "When I called, I could hear people telling her she wasn't well enough to go out even for this."

I said nothing. I had extended courtesy to the Tlic. Now I didn't want to talk to anyone. I hoped he would go in—out of curiosity if nothing else.

"Finally found out more than you wanted to know, eh?"

I looked at him.

"Don't give me one of *her* looks," he said. "You're not her. You're just her property."

One of her looks. Had I picked up even an ability to imitate her expressions?

"What'd you do, puke?" He sniffed the air. "So now you know what you're in for."

I walked away from him. He and I had been close when we were kids. He would let me follow him around when I was home and sometimes T'Gatoi would let me bring him along when she took me into the city. But something had happened when he reached adolescence. I never knew what. He began keeping out of T'Gatoi's way. Then he began running away—until he realized there was no "away." Not in the Preserve. Certainly not outside. After that he concentrated on getting his share of every egg that came into the house, and on looking out for me in a way that made me all but hate him—a way that clearly said, as long as I was all right, he was safe from the Tlic.

"How was it, really?" he demanded, following me.

"I killed an achti. The young ate it."

"You didn't run out of the house and puke because they ate an achti."

"I had . . . never seen a person cut open before." That

was true, and enough for him to know. I couldn't talk about the other. Not with him.

"Oh," he said. He glanced at me as though he wanted to say more, but he kept quiet.

We walked, not really headed anywhere. Toward the back, toward the cages, toward the fields.

"Did he say anything?" Qui asked. "Lomas, I mean."

Who else would he mean? "He said 'T'Khotgif.' "

Qui shuddered. "If she had done that to me, she'd be the last person I'd call for."

"You'd call for her. Her sting would ease your pain without killing the grubs in you."

"You think I'd care if they died?"

No. Of course he wouldn't. Would I?

"Shit!" He drew a deep breath. "I've seen what they do. You think this thing with Lomas was bad? It was nothing."

I didn't argue. He didn't know what he was talking about.

"I saw them eat a man," he said.

I turned to face him. "You're lying!"

"*I saw them eat a man.*" He paused. "It was when I was little. I had been to the Hartmund house and I was on my way home. Halfway here, I saw a man and a Tlic and the man was N'Tlic. The ground was hilly. I was able to hide from them and watch. The Tlic wouldn't open the man because she had nothing to feed the grubs. The man couldn't go any farther and there were no houses around. He was in so much pain he told her to kill him. He begged her to kill him. Finally, she did. She cut his throat. One swipe of one claw. I saw the grubs eat their way out, then burrow in again, still eating."

His words made me see Lomas's flesh again, parasitized, crawling. "Why didn't you tell me that?" I whispered.

He looked startled, as though he'd forgotten I was listening. "I don't know."

"You started to run away not long after that, didn't you?"

"Yeah. Stupid. Running inside the Preserve. Running in a cage."

I shook my head, said what I should have said to him long ago. "She wouldn't take you, Qui. You don't have to worry."

"She would . . . if anything happened to you."

"No. She'd take Xuan Hoa. Hoa . . . wants it." She wouldn't if she had stayed to watch Lomas.

"They don't take women," he said with contempt.

"They do sometimes." I glanced at him. "Actually, they prefer women. You should be around them when they talk among themselves. They say women have more body fat to protect the grubs. But they usually take men to leave the women free to bear their own young."

"To provide the next generation of host animals," he said, switching from contempt to bitterness.

"It's more than that!" I countered. Was it?

"If it were going to happen to me, I'd want to believe it was more, too."

"It *is* more!" I felt like a kid. Stupid argument.

"Did you think so while T'Gatoi was picking worms out of that guy's guts?"

"It's not supposed to happen that way."

"Sure it is. You weren't supposed to see it, that's all. And his Tlic was supposed to do it. She could sting him unconscious and the operation wouldn't have been as painful. But she'd still open him, pick out the grubs, and if she missed even one, it would poison him and eat him from the inside out."

There was actually a time when my mother told me to show respect for Qui because he was my older brother. I walked way, hating him. In his way, he was gloating. He was safe and I wasn't. I could have hit him, but I didn't think I would be able to stand it when he refused to hit back, when he looked at me with contempt and pity.

He wouldn't let me get away. Longer-legged, he swung

ahead of me and made me feel as though I were following him.

"I'm sorry," he said.

I strode on, sick and furious.

"Look, it probably won't be that bad with you. T'Gatoi likes you. She'll be careful."

I turned back toward the house, almost running from him.

"Has she done it to you yet?" he asked, keeping up easily. "I mean, you're about the right age for implantation. Has she—"

I hit him. I didn't know I was going to do it, but I think I meant to kill him. If he hadn't been bigger and stronger, I think I would have.

He tried to hold me off, but in the end, had to defend himself. He only hit me a couple of times. That was plenty. I don't remember going down, but when I came to, he was gone. It was worth the pain to be rid of him.

I got up and walked slowly toward the house. The back was dark. No one was in the kitchen. My mother and sisters were sleeping in their bedrooms—or pretending to.

Once I was in the kitchen, I could hear voices—Tlic and Terran from the next room. I couldn't make out what they were saying—didn't want to make it out.

I sat down at my mother's table, waiting for quiet. The table was smooth and worn, heavy and well-crafted. My father had made it for her just before he died. I remembered hanging around underfoot when he built it. He didn't mind. Now I sat leaning on it, missing him. I could have talked to him. He had done it three times in his long life. Three clutches of eggs, three times being opened and sewed up. How had he done it? How did anyone do it?

I got up, took the rifle from its hiding place, and sat down again with it. It needed cleaning, oiling.

All I did was load it.

"Gan?"

She made a lot of little clicking sounds when she walked on bare floor, each limb clicking in succession as it touched down. Waves of little clicks.

She came to the table, raised the front half of her body above it, and surged onto it. Sometimes she moved so smoothly she seemed to flow like water itself. She coiled herself into a small hill in the middle of the table and looked at me.

"That was bad," she said softly. "You should not have seen it. It need not be that way."

"I know."

"T'Khotgif—Ch'Khotgif now—she will die of her disease. She will not live to raise her children. But her sister will provide for them, and for Bram Lomas." Sterile sister. One fertile female in every lot. One to keep the family going. That sister owed Lomas more than she could ever repay.

"He'll live then?"

"Yes."

"I wonder if he would do it again."

"No one would ask him to do that again."

I looked into the yellow eyes, wondering how much I saw and understood there, and how much I only imagined. "No one ever asks us," I said. "You never asked me."

She moved her head slightly. "What's the matter with your face?"

"Nothing. Nothing important." Human eyes probably wouldn't have noticed the swelling in the darkness. The only light was from one of the moons, shining through a window across the room.

"Did you use the rifle to shoot the achti?"

'Yes."

"And do you mean to use it to shoot me?"

I stared at her, outlined in moonlight—coiled, graceful body. "What does Terran blood taste like to you?"

She said nothing.

"What are you?" I whispered. "What are we to you?"

She lay still, rested her head on her topmost coil. "You know me as no other does," she said softly. "You must decide."

"That's what happened to my face," I told her.

"What?"

"Qui goaded me into deciding to do something. It didn't turn out very well." I moved the gun slightly, brought the barrel up diagonally under my own chin. "At least it was a decision I made."

"As this will be."

"Ask me, Gatoi."

"For my children's lives?"

She would say something like that. She knew how to manipulate people, Terran and Tlic. But not this time.

"I don't want to be a host animal," I said. "Not even yours."

It took her a long time to answer. "We use almost no host animals these days," she said. "You know that."

"You use us."

"We do. We wait long years for you and teach you and join our families to yours." She moved restlessly. "You know you aren't animals to us."

I stared at her, saying nothing.

"The animals we once used began killing most of our eggs after implantation long before your ancestors arrived," she said softly. "You know these things, Gan. Because your people arrived, we are relearning what it means to be a healthy, thriving people. And your ancestors, fleeing from their homeworld, from their own kind who would have killed or enslaved them—they survived because of us. We saw them as people and gave them the Preserve when they still tried to kill us as worms.

At the word "Worms" I jumped. I couldn't help it, and she couldn't help noticing it.

"I see," she said quietly. "Would you really rather die than bear my young, Gan?"

I didn't answer.

"Shall I go to Xuan Hoa?"

"Yes!" Hoa wanted it. Let her have it. She hadn't had to watch Lomas. She'd be proud. . . . Not terrified.

T'Gatoi flowed off the table onto the floor, startling me almost too much.

"I'll sleep in Hoa's room tonight," she said. "And sometime tonight or in the morning, I'll tell her."

This was going too fast. My sister. Hoa had had almost as much to do with raising me as my mother. I was still close to her—not like Qui. She could want T'Gatoi and still love me.

"Wait! Gatoi!"

She looked back, then raised nearly half her length off the floor and turned it to face me. "These are adult things, Gan. This is my life, my family!"

"But she's . . . my sister."

"I have done what you demanded. I have asked you!"

"But—"

"It will be easier for Hoa. She has always expected to carry other lives inside her."

Human lives. Human young who would someday drink at her breasts, not at her veins.

I shook my head. "Don't do it to her, Gatoi." I was not Qui. It seemed I could become him, though, with no effort at all. I could make Xuan Hoa my shield. Would it be easier to know that red worms were growing in her flesh instead of mine?

"Don't do it to Hoa," I repeated.

She stared at me, utterly still.

I looked away, then back at her. "Do it to me."

I lowered the gun from my throat and she leaned forward to take it.

"No," I told her.

"It's the law," she said.

"Leave it for the family. One of them might use it to save my life someday."

She grasped the rifle barrel, but I wouldn't let go. I was pulled into a standing position over her.

"Leave it here!" I repeated. "If we're not your animals, if these are adult things, accept the risk. There is risk, Gatoi, in dealing with a partner."

It was clearly hard for her to let go of the rifle. A shudder went through her and she made a hissing sound of distress. It occurred to me that she was afraid. She was old enough to have seen what guns could do to people. Now her young and this gun would be together in the same house. She did not know about our other guns. In this dispute, they did not matter.

"I will implant the first egg tonight," she said as I put the gun away. "Do you hear, Gan?"

Why else had I been given a whole egg to eat while the rest of the family was left to share one? Why else had my mother kept looking at me as though I were going away from her, going where she could not follow? Did T'Gatoi imagine I hadn't known?

"I hear."

"Now!" I let her push me out of the kitchen, then walked ahead of her toward my bedroom. The sudden urgency in her voice sounded real. "You would have done it to Hoa tonight!" I accused.

"I must do it to someone tonight."

I stopped in spite of her urgency and stood in her way. "Don't you care who?"

She flowed around me and into my bedroom. I found her waiting on the couch we shared. There was nothing in Hoa's room that she could have used. She would have done it to Hoa on the floor. The thought of her doing it to Hoa at all disturbed me in a different way now, and I was suddenly angry.

Yet I undressed and lay down beside her. I knew what to do, what to expect. I had been told all my life. I felt the familiar sting, narcotic, mildly pleasant. Then the blind probing of her ovipositor. The puncture was painless, easy. So easy going in. She undulated slowly against me, her muscles forcing the egg from her body into mine. I held on to a pair of her limbs until I remembered Lomas holding her that way. Then I let go, moved inadvertently, and hurt her. She gave a low cry of pain and I expected to be caged at once within her limbs. When I wasn't, I held on to her again, feeling oddly ashamed.

"I'm sorry," I whispered.

She rubbed my shoulders with four of her limbs.

"Do you care?" I asked. "Do you care that it's me?"

She did not answer for some time. Finally, "You were the one making choices tonight, Gan. I made mine long ago."

"Would you have gone to Hoa?"

"Yes. How could I put my children into the care of one who hates them?"

"It wasn't . . . hate."

"I know what it was."

"I was afraid."

Silence.

"I still am." I could admit it to her here, now.

"But you came to me . . . to save Hoa."

"Yes." I leaned my forehead against her. She was cool velvet, deceptively soft. "And to keep you for myself," I said. It was so. I didn't understand it, but it was so.

She made a soft hum of contentment. "I couldn't believe I had made such a mistake with you," she said. "I chose you. I believed you had grown to choose me."

"I had, but . . ."

"Lomas."

"Yes."

"I have never known a Terran to see a birth and take it well. Qui has seen one, hasn't he?"

"Yes."

"Terrans should be protected from seeing."

I didn't like the sound of that—and I doubted that it was possible. "Not protected," I said. "Shown. Shown when we're young kids, and shown more than once. Gatoi, no Terran ever sees a birth that goes right. All we see is N'Tlic—pain and terror and maybe death."

She looked down at me. "It is a private thing. It has always been a private thing."

Her tone kept me from insisting—that and the knowledge that if she changed her mind, I might be the first public example. But I had planted the thought in her mind. Chances were it would grow, and eventually she would experiment.

"You won't see it again," she said. "I don't want you thinking any more about shooting me."

The small amount of fluid that came into me with her egg relaxed me as completely as a sterile egg would have, so that I could remember the rifle in my hands and my feelings of fear and revulsion, anger and despair. I could remember the feelings without reviving them. I could talk about them.

"I wouldn't have shot you," I said. "Not you." She had been taken from my father's flesh when he was my age.

"You could have," she insisted.

"Not you." She stood between us and her own people, protecting, interweaving.

"Would you have destroyed yourself?"

I moved carefully, uncomfortably. "I could have done that. I nearly did. That's Qui's 'away.' I wonder if he knows."

"What?"

I did not answer.

"You will live now."

"Yes." *Take care of her*, my mother used to say. Yes.

"I'm healthy and young," she said. "I won't leave you as Lomas was left—alone, N'Tlic. I'll take care of you."

THE COMING OF THE GOONGA

by Gary W. Shockley

Scientists tell us that the laws of chemistry and physics are universal and that if we venture to other planets we will still find that what we know about those natural laws will be valid. Quite probably so. But what about psychology and sociology? How universal would such mentalist sciences be? Or would the courses of alien intelligences be such that we might find ourselves ignorant of the most elemental ways? Here is a marvelously strange story of an intelligent alien species with the very serious problem of fending off an invasion from outer space.

It is the Crepuscular Greatdawn, time when the twin suns track together above the Spire Mounts and the double shadows grow long. In the Orange Basin near Calep there are close-knit shadows of precise geometry not to be found elsewhere. We hide beyond their stretch and contemplate their source, the spot where a shortseason ago the pods fell, and where in a few days the industrious aliens fashioned their fabulous base. On murknights when the echo-cloud blots out the twin suns, we can see three dashing stars. These we know to be their mother ships.

They are truly great builders, they who call themselves "human."

Our zeromaster Batinka predicts a good year. This is disconcerting to us, for it is the remarkable talent of a zeromaster always to be wrong. Early in her long reign Batinka scribed long lists of animal viscera; later, suffering chokeblossom fever, she spent days scribing, "Spare the Treader of the Painted Leaf"; later still she scribed a line so perfectly straight that we could see no deviation for a hundredflop. These and other prophecies, if such they be, defeat our understanding. These we ballast with the years and let sink to haunt our inner minds. But Batinka is topical and clear when she mentions "visitors from the mountain of the sky." Many close friendships will develop between our kinds, she says, and all will profit from our cooperative ventures. This is a prophecy indeed for the outer mind, and it fills us with trepidation.

Among the frozen and sharp-edged shadows there is one that is neither, which distorts wildly across the others till its tip nearly touches our concealment. The one they call Lola walks near the outskirts of the base. She stops when she comes upon the one they call Roxanne. Faintly we hear the mingling of their voices.

We have our own names for these two. Lola we call Awakener because our Watchers wake us when she appears (we have instructed them to do so). She knows no schedule, is apt to rise at any hour to go prowling through the night. This she did a few hours ago and walked eastward through the jezelles to the edge of our ancestral slicks. We are ever fascinated by the way she touches things, peers at them close up with her device, and remarks upon them to her wrist. Sometimes she collects the things she studies, putting them in collapsible bubbles. But she is ever careful not to disturb what she suspects is ours. The humans know of our presence and our intelligence, but Awakener alone respects us. She has given us a name: slinkies. It is a better one than yeddeenians, which we call ourselves. I use it always now.

Her function remains unclear. She speaks often with the cooks, pointing to the things she has collected, but at greater length she speaks to those crouched in constant vigil over complex implements. We think that she is a foodsmith, though her small skin pores suggest a weathersnapper.

The other, the one they call Roxanne, we call Loud Giant. She is taller by a head than Awakener and certainly much taller than we, and her voice carries above the moontoad's. But the basis for her name goes further, to the nature of her exploits. For she will start a war with our kind. Noisy, devastating, it will bring death to four of every five slinkies. This I know because those times have come and gone, this being written after the fact. I use the present tense to describe the past, because I must. It is my curse, but also my blessing, for it sustains me. Tha present is my salvation.

Our Watchers sometimes venture into the base in the cloaked hours to peer through the transparent membranes. Some have even entered the structures. They tell us knowingly of the soft-soil mound where Loud Giant and Awakener lie together, unsheathed, like fevered jungle mudsquabs. This memory arouses my jealousy and calls to mind Loud Giant's own at the time: while she gives all her love to Awakener, Awakener gives hers to many—to Janice, Sarah, Roger, Bill. . . . Loud Giant once made Bill's face bleed and threatened the others. But it gained her nothing; Awakener would not speak to her for a stark moon. Now they are friends once more and have spent this morning together.

We, the slinkies, can understand Loud Giant's jealousy. We are monogamists with few exceptions. We take one mate for life, another for death. This does not mean we despise Awakener for her ways. Indeed, she is loved by all, watched by all, as much the favorite of our kind as of theirs.

Awakener, as I am saying, pauses to speak with Loud Giant. We, working some distance away under cover of huehair and weewoochuntz, admire the agility of her many-jointed body (today her carapace is seaform blue with flecks of silver) and sense joy in her every gesture. Though she is not slinkie, there is a richness of expression about her that strikes us as very beauti—

"Op!" the conjuremaster Pedeet barks my name. I shake free of entrancement and see that inattention has let the goonga grow restless. (Awakener calls our goongas "bagpipes," but I prefer our name.) It is trying to belly out. That would kink its eight long snouts or dislodge the slender hollow reeds we have fitted in their ends. Jentzoot and Kamin prod it from this urge while I apply myself to fondling. Soon it quivers with only one wish. I communicate this fact to the pointers, who load; then I slip about to the glands. I am pleasantly surprised to have a clear view of Loud Giant and Awakener as I fondle and squeeze.

The seconds become vivid. Awakener is laughing, has finished a gesture, must talk louder than she would like because of the hums and rattles of nearby machinery. Beyond the shadows where we of the goonga patrol lurk, these sounds are nearly lost. We hear instead the stridencies of the winged lamoor, the bray of the dozerwomp, the chatter-clark of rocksips . . . and the coming of the goonga.

The latter is a sharp "whoof," almost a thunderclap, and the goonga's fierce compaction sends me sprawling. But not for an instant do I lose sight of the pair.

Awakener is not at first responsive to the faint jarring that afflicts her. She talks a moment longer before seeing the alarm registering upon Loud Giant's face. Only then does she look down upon her own body and see the eight fibrillances piercing her chest and stomach, pinning her against the structure behind. She squints, perhaps seeing the tiny wellings of blood at the entry points. Her eyes go wide, her mouth is open and silently working. It is then that she moves and in this way chooses her moment to expire. . . .

It is the Painting Season, time to suggest to nature a new attire. As in past seasons I choose the zigzag leaf. Always have I felt that it lacks something in shape and venation. After all, the zigzag trees that shadow the Evernight deserve the finest of calling cards. For two week I labor over it, dyeing it, trimming its irregular outline, adding ribs and veins and the faintest hint of spots. I take it to the nature festival where everyone shows their renderings of leaf, bark, stone, grass, moss, and even skyscape. Afterward we return our suggestions to the field for nature to consider. And next year we will see how she has judged them.

Loud Giant catches Awakener as she twists and sags with seafoam carapace bursting red. Their shadows sharply retreat as one escorts the other to the ground, to a sleep from which Awakener will never awaken; and there, rocking her in her arms, Loud Giant suddenly looks up with trouncelot eyes. She looks out, toward our position. And she bellows. She bellows and is running at us. Awakener extinguishes her own shadow in a final sprawl that turns the bottom of her left boot toward us. There we can see my painted leaf.

Long ago Batinka wrote, "Spare the Treader of the Painted Leaf," and we did not know its meaning. Now we do, and, though buried by a score of years, that behest must now be honored, must now be disobeyed. We are sorry, Awakener. We are truly sorry.

I try to coax the goonga back to its underground safe haven. The conjuremaster, the pointers, and the prodders have fled, lacking my compassion, or perhaps I their wits. Suddenly Loud Giant stands over me, a rock uplifted beside her red-tasseled head. The moment is uncertain; she emotes fiercely: "I will kill every last one of you! Do you understand? Every last one! Tell the rest. Tell them they will all die by my hand. Tell them!'' She hurls the rock far over my head, turns and retraces her steps.

How can one not be impressed by the suddenness, the singleness, the utterness of her decision? Among my kind, to commit oneself even briefly to a course of action is rare, and regardless of its overall merit it deserves the highest praise—for it suggests zeromaster blood. It is, I think, at this moment, as I sit watching the guttering retreat of Loud Giant's fierce long shadows, that I begin to love her.

We will meet again, many times, over the course of the war, which will span three years and see our kind's steady retreat across the Great Sinking Ocherlands, through the Desert Crystallith, over the Shaglands of Ordorn, and back again. Near the midpoint of the war we will meet near the Shaddocks of Trite and there I will be killed. And a year later, at war's end, a similar fate will find her. Of such things are great tragedies written. Yet this is not as it seems; this will not be tragedy. Nor do I scribe the horrors of war, of which there were certainly many. Nor a grand heroic epic to please the minions. My perspective is different. I perceive and live the war as an elaborate courtship, elegant in its rituals, uncompromising in its expressions of love. As such will I describe it. Only when it serves my purpose will I delve into the finer aspects of war. Let me now begin to tell the things that were and have become.

There is confusion and dismay among our droves as the humans, led by Loud Giant and others, venture into our territories and begin the slaughter. We wait for our zeromaster to instruct us. In ten days our number in the Enumerated Lands is halved, and we fear for the survival of our species. It is then that our zeromaster's words reach us: ''Surrender to an enemy whose weapons speak louder than yours; do not prolong the inevitable defeat; do not expend lives in a lost cause." With these words we are committed to winning the war.

There are fifty-seven in the drove to which I humbly belong. The first major skirmish is ours, at Hasson Cove near the Windgate. I, a fondler among many, lead us to slaughter with my staggering incompetence. I bring my goonga to discharge too quickly, so that it spends the fibrillances at the enemy's feet, serving to warn rather than to harm. Near me is Geesha, the one that I then love. She works her goonga expertly and still works it as I flee. She does not survive the skirmish. Later, upon the Feeding Quakemoss east of the Quenchant, my conjuremaster disciplines me for my impatience. I accept the splinters without protest, though I know my behavior was soundly inspired. Loud Giant was leading her troops. I feared she would fall in the first volley. That must not happen. Not yet—not till we are closer to the Evernight.

It is six skirmishes later that our retreat brings us through the low Ocherlands, where it is convenient for us to pay the Manuscriptors of Evernight a formal visit. Most are in the mating coves, and their passionate grappling/signaling for an instant strikes me as countless pairs of human hands swinging boom-weapons about to fire, to pierce us with lances we can never find—invisilances, we call them. But my imagination wanders far afield. We pass by the mating coves and come to the nutrient glades. There we see what the Manuscriptors have scrawled that day.

Some who read this may be human. For those I should digress. We, the slinkies, do not bury our dead. Once we shared that ritual with you, but no more. We take our dead to the outer glades and feed each to a single healthy full-grown squab who has failed to run the Labyrinth. A squab that runs the Labyrinth has already consumed a higher intelligence, and it is not good to join it with a second. The squab remains a squab; its basic needs remain its basic needs. But should one supply it with all that it requires, placing it upon a glade of nutrient, its primitive intelligence relaxes enough to let the other flicker through. The only physical manifestation the slinkie mind can effect is control over the crawlpath. It is in this way—through the written word—that our dead communicate with us. The present tense must prevail, for the squab is a creature of the present moment, and to use the past tense is to disturb its sense of well-being, which leads to suppression.

The first message reaching us from one new to the Evernight will be an afterwish. If it is deemed reasonable, and possible, those closest to the deceased must grant it. Should we of the first life want to communicate something to a Manuscriptor, we write upon the nutrient with a concentrate of the same and place the squab at the proper end. The slinkie mind and the squab itself have poor eyesight, but while the squab inexorably follows the concentrate, the slinkie mind can read words from its motion.

Today we hope to learn from those who perished in recent battles. Standing beneath a zigzag tree that contributes a generous swath of shade to the Evernight, I peer out upon the chaotic lines of those who died in terror and die not recover. Less salient are the long tedious epic poems indulged in by so many dead warriors. Still others are tiny neat scribbles, sorrowful repentances of misspent lives.

Vidor of Tazambe, a fondler like myself, whose goonga proved unresponsive, reveals something of significance. She has seen our fibrillances hit the silver human carapaces and crumble, leaving only dents. And she has seen our fibrillances strike and shatter the clear bubbles of their heads. A controversy over strategy arises. Some believe it best to trim back the goonga's four snouts so that they will grow back branched, and do so again, bringing to sixteen the weapons provided by each, and in this way increase the chances of striking the clear bubbles of the enemy. But others fear that the firepower going to each fibrillance will be diminished beyond effectiveness. They prefer a radically different tack: amputate all but one snout and infect the goongas with lungmites. These will kill the goongas in two years' time, but in the interim the goongas' lung capacity will quadruple, and the firepower of the single fibrillance will be prodigious. This scheme draws equal controversy; it will be half a year before the goongas see service, and the war is now. A compromise is achieved, a long-range battle plan formalized. Our droves will begin a great retreat that is not retreat, a wide circle through many territories, each containing goongas tended differently. In the last—in the Mad Steppes abutting the Shaglands of Ordorn—the great mite-ridden one-snouted goongas will be left to mature. And if the war still rages when we complete our circle, they will be our final weapons, and the Mad Steppes our last stand.

Seated on the root of a zigzag tree, dissatisfied and oppressed by its canopy of leaves, I notice and draw attention to a totally random scribble along the south edge of the nutrient glade. We trace it back for several hours to where its intelligence first waned. From that scription we identify the one who has died the second and final death. It is Batinka. Early into a fierce war we are left without a zeromaster.

I play a prominent role in a long succession of battles. When we would defend the pass at Languishing Rock in Craterspin Valley, I drug the conjuremasters with weirdclover so that they summon up sandscrews and rockleeches instead of goongas. At Misty Crevice and Dire Canyon east of the Running Forest, it is the goongas that I drug, so that they rise indifferent to all caresses. On the pebbled plains of Skyspawn I sneeze in such a fashion that my fellows mistake it as the signal, while the enemy is yet a thousandflop distant. And in the Desert Crystallith. I gather woppingglows and rig their release at the direst moment, so that the goongas about to discharge do not, but instead flee before the wild-flicker.

I am tormented by my actions and the slaughter they bring upon my kind. We are now too distant from the Evernight; those who die are denied the second life. Yet I do it. I do it and watch in horror as my love for Loud Giant is tenfold increased by each slinkie falling before her. For I see this as an expression of her supreme devotion to the memory of Awakener. And if I would have so great a lover, I must show an equal devotion.

It is said that prolonged anxiety speeds up the maturational processes. This must be so, for though barely a tripleyear in age, I spontaneously bud a son in the saltspray of Weeping Meadow. I name him Spont and send him away with the wounded, to be educated by the eminent linguist Zalsor, who was my mentor. It is my hope that he will not see any part of the war.

We, the surviving, combine many of our diminished droves and complete the outward swing of our great circle. The occasion is marked by a crushing defeat near the Shaddocks of Trite. Our drove lags and does not arrive till after the battle is lost. The southern Evernight is but a day's journey farther; there is hope of a second life for those who have perished here. Thus are we deadgathering in the hour of the echo-cloud when the swogboles all about lift their fiery sheaths to a faint whisper. In another instant we shudder before prodigious booms; everywhere slinkies fall. The enemy is upon us. I have been fondling a goonga as part of the guard detail, keeping it ever at the ready. Now the conjuremaster commands us to our task. The pointers load and aim at five charging humans. The foremost figure is tall, with red tassels nearly filling her clear bubble. It is Loud Giant. Too late do I try to undo my work; here the goongas are oversensitive, and even now mine discharges. I look on in horror as the onrushers falter together as if over a tripvine—all but one. Loud Giant charges onward, grim with the memory of Awakener. For an instant I watch the pointers fleeing to either side and wonder if perhaps they miss her intentionally, and if I am not alone in my abiding love for her. But if this is so, they do not plan as carefully as I—I, who am like the zeromaster in my determination, and who must certainly have a drop at least of that royal blood. They will not purchase her love. They will not.

I slap the goonga and whine melodiously to warn it of danger. It slips down through doughy humus, sending up to me slow bubbles like soft goodbyes. I am struck by the thought that the goongas may be as capable of loving slinkies as I am of loving a human. Beside me the conjuremaster tries to flipflop away but is wounded and cannot. Humans are charging from all sides now, but none so fast as Loud Giant. It is at this moment that I accept the invisilance through the spewovum that kills me.

There is a way by which Manuscriptors can read each other's works. In the deepnight, when the squab's control is least, the slinkie mind can use the squab's keen sense of smell to locate and trace another's path. This is how I am able to follow the war. Those now joining our ranks in the nutrient glade reveal to us that it goes ever worse. Indeed, we learn that adjacent wildglades are being tamed to accommodate our growing numbers. Renderings of each successive battle come to us. Most are so richly embroidered that we cannot believe any portion of them. Some are detailed accounts of atrocity and defeat and cannot be doubted. There are those who would have us believe that Loud Giant is dead. I will not believe this. I refuse to believe this.

We read of catastrophe at Tumbler's Heap, where the goongas are plentiful but the fibrillances misplaced; of Peninsula Sway, where the downdraft of a human airship distorts the groundwaves so that the pointers miss their targets; of Lesser Emberdusk, where a hundred slinkies discover that the goongas have chosen the direst moment for their unfathomable bedrock migration. . . .

The seasons come and go in this fashion until there arrive

upon our banks (we sense rather than see) a great many slinkies. One flipflops down beside me, and I realize it is Spont, my son. He writes in the nutrient, and soon I read of the completion of the circuit and the fierce battle of Ordorn, where our kind makes its final stand. The monstrous one-snouted goongas prove formidable weapons. The lungmite infection has impressed upon their systems the need to survive, to reproduce. The slightest touch brings discharge; the slightest wait reenables it. The fibrillances thus impelled know no obstacle; they split trees, shatter rocks, and kill humans. Many, many humans. The battle of Ordorn ends with the humans repulsed, the pods returning to the sky, and the three dashing stars winking out. The battle of Ordorn is the end of the war.

The slinkies have let me read of it first, knowing that it was my painted leaf that set the stage for the war. I suspect that most of them know also of my afterwish. And I wonder . . . There is a scent about my son that is not entirely slinkie; he carries a wild squab. This he places next to me and we touch. I am ecstatic. My slinkie friends have honored my afterwish, for Loud Giant lives the second life beside me.

I worry that it will not work out between us. A squab, after all, is very particular when choosing a lifelong mate. Even now the squab that holds Loud Giant glides away. It will take time, I reassure myself. Such things take time.

We suffer a new crisis with the war's end. Batinka's final prophecy now stands satisfied. The future stretches before us like the Evernight. Though we barely skirt its edge, already we are lost. We need someone to direct us. We need, alas, a new zeromaster. Finding one is never easy. They are a rare breed—the blindly irrational, the incorrigibly ignorant. The ones who seldom read another trail . . . the solitary minds that wander alone . . . incessant, introverted scribblers . . .

Upon a time we sought the rule of erudites, but such was

their openmindedness that they could not choose a clear path for us. We floundered through the centuries, victims of uncertainty, till we tried zeromaster rule. A zeromaster must be brilliantly ignorant. A zeromaster will not hesitate to point us in a wrong direction. We then need only to take the opposite way.

We have a new zeromaster at last. It is, of course, Loud Giant. But there is a problem. Her language is not ours, and while the human spoken language comes easily to us, that which they write does not fit our minds. Four of our greatest living linguists gather to study the human documents we have gathered from the war. Zalsor, my onetime mentor and now my son's, heads the group. One member soon grows so distressed at the difficulties that he kills himself. Zalsor herself will do likewise at a later time, but with great magnanimity. The language is slowly, painstakingly learned, and there comes a day when Zalsor deems the linguists ready. They descend to read the zeromaster's solitary scrawl and find it entirely incomprehensible.

The seasons roll onward, and though the war has ended, we remain in turmoil, for we do not know our direction.

It is again the Painting Season, the time to appeal to nature for improvements in its attire. I can no longer participate, being a Manuscriptor of the Evernight, but my son can, and he carries on my quest for a better zigzag leaf. He brings his leaf to me before going to the festival. He puts it in the path of my squab so that the latter must crawl over it. In this way I sense its structure and hue. It is nothing like mine. My son does not appreciate my orange tints, my gray flecking of the edges, or the symmetry of my venation. Instead he goes for tinseled edging, fine close-set stripes that distort with knots along their length, and an intricate asymmetrical venation like that in rampoid eyes.

His leaf is better.

I scribe that he should return to tell me of the festival. This he does, but he does not come alone. The banks are heavy with slinkies, and we, the Manuscriptors of Evernight, read of the festival with shock. No awards are given this year because Zalsor, our foremost linguist, lifts a baby goonga, arouses it, and takes three shafts in the invidex. She does it for the good of all, in the hope that as a Manuscriptor she will know the zeromaster's scribble, for we must learn our path.

It is a week before Zalsor acclimates and resumes her work in Evernight. Wherever we scent Loud Giant's passage, Zalsor's soon follows. And then there comes a day when Zalsor scribbles a translation:

"My kind will not give up! More will come. More, and still more! And they will slaughter every last one of you!"

The message reaches us in different ways. Those on the bank, those in the first life, see it immediately; we of the Evernight must read the scribble one by one. But eventually we all know. And at the news, we rejoice.

I must now stop writing. The day draws to an end, and Loud Giant approaches. I think at last she wants me to go with her deep into the mating cove, where we will squirm together, unsheathed, like two humans on a soft-soil mound.

MEDRA

by Tanith Lee

One of Tanith Lee's most fascinating novels is called The Silver Metal Lover *and a graphic arts version of this is to appear soon while a cinematic version has been optioned by Hollywood. Although this story is entirely separate from that novel, it does have within it a character who could be called The Golden Metallic Lover. Although this is his story, it is also very much that of she who awaited him.*

I

At the heart of a deserted and partly ruined city, an old hotel rose up eighty-nine stories into the clear sunset air. The hotel was not necessarily the tallest structure left in the city. It had been a very modern metropolis; many of its buildings were of great height. But it had happened that several of the blocks surrounding the hotel plaza had fallen, for one reason or another. Now the tiered, white architecture, like a colossal wedding cake, was visible from almost any vantage of the city, and from miles away, across the dusty dry plains of the planet beyond, the hotel could be seen.

This planet's sunset took a number of hours, and was quite beautiful. The hotel seemed softened in the filmy, rosy light. Its garlands and sprays of ornamentation, long-blunted by the wind, had over the years become the nesting-places of large climbing lizards. During the hours of sunfall, they would emerge, crawling up and down the stem of the building, past the empty windows behind which lay empty rooms. Their armor blinked gold, their gargoyle faces stared away over the vistas of the city whose tall abandoned blocks flashed goldenly back at them. The big lizards were not foolish enough to mistake these sky-scrapers for anything alive. The only live thing, aside from themselves and occasional white skeletal birds which flew over, lived on the eighty-ninth floor. Sometimes, the lizards saw the live thing moving about inside two layers of glass, and sometimes the throb of machineries, or music, ran down the limb of the hotel, so the stones trembled, and the lizards, clinging, trembled, listening with their fan-like swivelled ears.

Medra lived on the eighty-ninth floor. Through the glass portals she was frequently visible—a young Earth woman, by appearance, with coal-black hair that fell to her waist. She had a classical look, a look of calmness and restraint. Much of the day, and often for long intervals of the night, she would sit or lie perfectly still. She would not seem to move, not the flicker of a finger or quiver of an eyelid. It was just possible, after intense study, to see her breathing.

At such times, which actually occupied her on an average for perhaps twenty-seven hours in every thirty-six-hour diurnal-nocturnal planetary period, Medra—lying motionless—experienced curious mental states. She would, mentally, travel a multiplicity of geographies, physical and non-physical, over mountains, under oceans, even across and among galaxies. Through the flaming peripheries of stars she had passed, and through the cold reaches of a space where the last worlds hung tiny as specks of moisture on the window-panes of her rooms. Endless varieties of creatures came and went on the paths of Medra's cerebral journeys. Creatures of landscape, waterscape, airscape, and of the gaplands between the suns. Cities and other tumuli evolved and disappeared as simply as the forests and cultivation which ran towards her and away. She had a sense that all these visions concerned and incorporated her. That she wove something into them, from herself, if she did not actually form them, and so was a part of her own weaving, and of them. She threaded them all with love, lacking any fear, and when they drifted behind her she knew a moment's pang of gentle loss. But solely for that moment. It was only when she "woke" that Medra felt a true bereavement.

Her eyes would open. She would look around her. She would presently get up and walk about her apartment, which the hotel mechanisms kept for her scrupulously.

All the rooms were comfortable, and two or three were elegant. A hot-house with stained-glass walls projected from one side of the building. Enormous plants bloomed and fruited. There was a bathroom with a sunken bath of marble, in which it was feasible to swim. The literature and music, the art and theatre of many worlds were plenteously represented. At the touch of a button, food of exquisite quality—in its day, the hotel had been renowned through twenty solar systems—would be served to Medra from out of the depths below.

She herself never went downstairs. Years ago, now and then, she had done so. She had walked the dusty riverbeds of the streets, or, getting into one of the small hover-cars, gone gliding between the walls, past the blank windows, over the bridges—and back again. At night, she had sat eighty-nine floors down on the hotel's decorated porch, sipping coffee or sherbet. The planet's stars were lustrous and thickly scattered. Slaves to their generators, a few lights still quickened in the city when sunset faded. She did not trouble to pretend that any life went on in those distant lighted buildings. Sometimes one of the lizards would steal up to her. They were very cautious, despite their size. She caressed those that came close enough and would allow it. But the lizards did not need her and, "waking," she did not understand them.

In recent years, she stayed at the top of her tower. There was no purpose in leaving her apartment. She accepted this.

But every so often, "waking," opening her eyes, sensing loss, she wept. She was alone and lonely. She felt the pain of it always, although always differently—sharp as a razor, insistent as a needle, dull as a healing bruise. "I'm alone," she said. Looking out from the balconied heights, she saw the lizards moving endlessly up and down. She saw the city and the dust haze far off which marked the plains beyond. The weaving of her dreams was her solace. But not enough.

"Alone," said Medra in a soft, tragic voice. She turned her back to the window.

And so missed a new golden spark that dazzled wildly over the sunset air, and the white feather of vapor which followed it down.

Jaxon landed his shuttle about half a mile from the city's outskirts. He emerged into the long sunset fully armed and, from force of habit, set the vessel's monitors on defensive. There was, almost certainly, nothing to defend against, out here. The planet had been thoroughly scanned by the mothership on the way in.

Jaxon began to stroll down to the city. He was an adventurer who would work for hire if the pay was good. What had tempted him to this outcast place, well-removed from the pioneer worlds and trade routes that generally supplied his living, was the connivance of a freelance captain whose ship now hung overhead. They had met in some dive on the rim of Lyra, Jaxon a figure of gold as he always was, but gold somewhat spoiled by the bloody nose and black eye gained at an adjacent fight.

"So thanks for saving my skin. What do you want?" The captain showed him an old star-map and indicated a planet. "Why?" said Jaxon. The captain explained. It was, at that juncture, only a story, but stories sometimes led to facts. It would seem that a century before, a machine of colossal energy had been secreted on this small world. The planetary colony was promptly evacuated on the excuse of unstabilized earthquake activity. A whole city was abandoned. No one went there any more. Out of bounds and off the current maps, the planet had by now been overlooked, forgotten. Only the story of the machine remained, and finally surfaced.

Very well, Jaxon would assume the captain wished that someone (Jaxon) would investigate. What capacity did the hidden machine have? There must be safeguards on it, which were? "It's presumably a war-machine. That's why it's been dumped. Whoever gets hold of it will be able to call the shots." ("Oh, nice," said Jaxon sarcastically, bleeding in his free drink.) "On the other hand, it may be nothing. But we'd like to follow the rumor up, without sticking our necks out too far."

"So you want to stick my neck out too far instead." The captain detailed the fee. Jaxon thought about it. It was not until he was aboard the ship that he asked again: "You still haven't given me specific answers to my two specific questions. What does this machine do? How's it protected?"

"All right. This is apocryphal, maybe. I heard it's an unraveller." Which was the slang name for something that had been a nightmare for decades, was condemned by all solar and galactic governments, could not, in any case, exist.

Jaxon said, "By which we're talking about a Matter-Displacement-Destructor?"

"Yes. And here's the punchline. Be ready to laugh. The only safeguard on the damn thing is one lone woman in a white hotel."

Legends abounded in space, birthed in bars and backlands,

carried like seeds by the crazier shipping, planted in fertile minds, normally born to be nothing. But Jaxon, who had scented something frenetic behind the deal, was ultimately granted the whole truth. The freelance captain was a ruse. The entire run was government based, the mission—to find and destroy that machine, if it existed. Anything else was a cover. A quasi-pirate on a joyride, a notorious adventurer looking for computer treasure—that was all it was to be. If the powers who had hidden the machine learned its fate and made a fuss, the event must fail to become a galactic confrontation. You didn't go to war because you'd been ripped off by a cat-burglar.

"Alternatively, someone may pulverize the cat-burglar."

"Or it may all be nothing. Tall stories. Lies. A storm in a teacup."

"You ever seen a storm in a teacup?" asked Jaxon. "I did, once. A trick some character pulled in a bar one night. It made a hell of a mess of the bar."

As he entered the city, framed between the sky-touching pylons of the bridge Jaxon saw the hotel.

He stood and looked at it, and thought about the idea of one woman guarding there an MDD chaos device that could literally claw the fabric of everything—planets, suns, space itself—apart. If any of it were so, she would have to be a robot, or robot-android. He had a scanner of his own, concealed in the plain gold ring he always wore. This would tell him exactly what she was, if she existed, from a distance of three hundred feet.

One of the hover-cars swam by. Jaxon hailed it and got in. It carried him swiftly towards the eccentric old hotel. At two hundred feet, Jaxon consulted the ring. It told him promptly the woman did indeed exist and, as expected, exactly what she was. Her name had been planet-registered in the past; it was Medra. She was not a robot, an android, or even (present analysis) biologically tampered with. She was a young woman.

She had black springing hair, pale amber skin, dark amber eyes. She weighed—"Just wait," said Jaxon. "More important, what about implants?" But there were no implants. The car was now only thirty feet from the building, and rising smoothly as an elevator up the floors, sixty, sixty-nine, seventy—"Check again," said Jaxon. The lizards glared at him with bulging eyes as he passed them, but he had already checked those—there were over two thousand of them dwelling in and on the building. They were saurian, unaggressive, obliquely intelligent, harmless, and nonmechanic. A bird flew over, a couple of hundred feet up. "And check *that*," snapped Jaxon, scowling at the lizards. But it was only a bird.

Seventy-nine, eighty, eighty-nine—And the car stopped.

Jaxon beheld the woman called Medra. She was standing at a window, gazing out at him through a double thickness of glass. Her eyes were glorious, and wide.

Jaxon leaned forward, smiling, and mouthed: *Can I come in?*

He was made of gold. Golden skin, yellow-golden eyes, golden fleece of hair. The semi-uniform he wore was also of a tawny gleaming material. He seemed to blind what looked at him.

Medra retreated from the window and pressed the switch which let up the pressurized bubble over the balcony. The man stepped gracefully from the car to the balustrade and over. The bubble closed down again. Medra thought, should she leave him there, trapped and safe, an interesting specimen? But his presence was too powerful, and besides the inner glass was rather fragile and might be broken. She permitted the pane to rise, and golden Jaxon walked through into her room.

The selection of opening gambits was diverse. He had already decided what would be the most effective.

"Good evening," said Jaxon. "I gather the name by which you know yourself is Medra, M-E-D-R-A. Mine is usually Jaxon, J-A-X-O-N. I have been called other things. Your suite is charming. Is the service still good here? I'll bet it is. And the climate must be pleasant. How do you get on with the lizards?" He moved forward as he spoke. The woman did not back away. She met his eyes and waited. He paused when he was a couple of feet from her. "And the machine," he said, "where is that?"

She said, "Which machine? There are several."

"Now, you know which machine. Not the machine that makes the bed or tosses the salad or puts the music on. Not the city computer that keeps the cars running, or the generators that work the lights in the stores."

"There's nothing else," she said.

"Yes there is. Or why are you here?"

"Why am I—?" She looked at him in astonishment.

All this time the ring was sending its tiny impulses through his skin, his finger joint, messages he had long ago learned to read quickly and imperceptibly. She is not lying. She is shocked by this arrival and so reacting unemotionally; presently emotion will break through. Her pulse ticks at this and this, rising now, faster. But she is not lying. (Brain-handled, then, not to know?) Possibly. Pulse rising, faster, and faster.

"—I'm here," she said, she gave a shaken little laugh, "because I stayed behind. That's all. The planet's core is unstable. We were told to leave. But I elected—to stay here. I was born here, you see. And all my family died here. My father was the architect who designed the hotel. I grew up in the hotel. When the ships lifted off I didn't go with them. There was nowhere else to go to. Nowhere else, no one else . . . How eccentric, to want to remain. But the earthquake activity—it's not so dangerous as they said. A few mild tremors. The hotel is stabilized, although the other buildings sometime- Only six months ago, one of the blocks across the plaza collapsed—a column of dust going up for half an hour. I'm talking too much,'' she said. ''I haven't seen another human being for—I can't remember—I suppose—ten years?'' The last was a question, as if he knew better than she and would tell her. She put her hands over her eyes and began to fall very slowly forwards. Jaxon caught her, and held her as she lay in his arms weeping. (No lies. Valid. Emotional impulse verified: The ring stung and tickled its information through to him.) It was also a long time for him, since he had held any woman *this* way. He savored it abstractedly, his thoughts already tracking in other directions, after other deductions. As if in the distance he took pleasure in the warm scent of her, the softness of her dark witch's hair; pleasure in comforting her.

II

There was time, all the time a world could give. For once, no one and nothing urging him to hurry. The only necessity was to be sure. And from the beginning he was sure enough, it was only a matter of proving that sureness, being certain of a certainty. Aside from the miniaturized gadgets he always carried with him, there were his own well-tuned senses. Jaxon knew, inside ten minutes, that there was nothing here remotely resembling the powerful technology of a fabled MDD. In other words, no key to nemesis. The government ship continued to cruise and to scan far overhead, tracking the hollows of the hills, the deep places underground, the planet's natural penthouses and basements. And he, striding through the city, riding through it in the ever-ready little cars, picked up no resonance of anything.

Yet, there was something. Something strange, which did not fit.

Or was that only his excuse for remaining here a fraction longer?

The first evening, as the sunset began at last to dissolve in night, she had said to him, "You're here, I don't know why. I don't understand you at all. But we'll have champagne. We'll open the ballroom." And when he grimaced with amusement she said, "Oh, be kind to us. Be kind to the hotel. It's pining for a guest."

And it was true, the hotel came alive at the touch of switches. It groomed and readied itself and put on a jewelry of lights. In the ballroom, they ate off the fine service, every plate, cup, napkin and knife printed and embossed with the hotel's blazon. They drank from crystal goblets, and danced, on the crystal floor, the lazy sinuous contemporary dances of ten years ago, while music played down on them like a fountain. Sophisticated beyond his self-appointed station, Jaxon was not embarrassed or at a loss with any of this. Medra became a child again, or a very young girl. This had been her physical youth, which was happy, before—before the outsiders had come with their warnings, the death of the city, the going away of the ships and of everything.

But she was not a child. And though in her way she had the innocence of a very young girl, she was still a woman, moving against him when they danced, brushed by sequins from the lights. He was mostly accustomed to another kind of woman, hard, wise, sometimes even intellectual, the casual courtings, makings, and foregone departures amid the liquor-palaces he frequented on-planet, or in the great liners of deep space. This does not mean he had only ever known such women as these. There had been love affairs once or twice—that is, affairs of love. And Medra, her clever mind and her sweetness coming alive through the stimulus of this proximity—he was not immune to any of that. Nor to the obvious fact that, with a sort of primal cunning, she had trusted him, since she could do nothing else.

And for Medra? She fell in love with him the moment she saw him. It was inevitable, and she, recognizing the cliché and the truth which underlay the cliché, and not being a fool, did not deny it.

After the first night, a first date, waited on and worshipped by the reborn glory of the hotel, they parted, went each to an allotted suite of rooms. As Jaxon revelled like a golden shark in the great bathroom, drew forth old brandies and elixirs from cabinets, eventually set up the miniaturized communicator and made contact with the ship, reporting nothing—as all this occurred, Medra lay on her bed, still clothed in her dancing dress, dreaming awake. The waking dream seemed superior to any other dream of stars and oceans and altitudes. The man who had entered her world—her planet, the planet of her awareness—he was now star, sun, ocean, and high sky-held peak. When she fell asleep, she merely slept, and in her sleep, dreamed of him.

Then the days began, extended warm days. Picnics in the ruins, where the dust made both carpet and parasol. Or lunches in the small number of restaurants which would respond, like the hotel, to a human request. Together, they walked the city, explored its emptied libraries, occasionally finding some taped or crated masterpiece, which in the turmoil of evacuation had been overlooked. In the stores, the mannequins, the solar cadillacs, had combined to form curious sculptures of mutation.

Jaxon accompanied her everywhere, testing, on the lookout, alert for anything that would indicate the presence of the item he sought, or had come seeking. But the other level of him was totally aware of Medra. She was no longer in the distance. Every day she moved nearer. The search had become a backdrop, a prelude.

Medra wandered through the abandoned city, refinding it. She was full of pity and nostalgia. She had come to realize she would be going away. Although nothing had been said, she knew that when he left he would take her with him.

The nights were warm, but with a cooler, more fragrant warmth. The lizards came into the lighted plaza before the hotel, staring, their ears raised and opened like odd flowers. They fed from Medra's hands, not because they needed to, but because they recognized her, and she offered them food. It was almost a tradition between them. They enjoyed, but did not require the adventure. Jaxon they avoided.

Medra and Jaxon patrolled the nighttime city. (A beacon, the hotel glowed from many vantages.) In other high places, the soft wind blowing between them and the star-encrusted dark, he would put his arm around her and she would lean on him. He told her something of his life. He told her things that generally he entrusted to no one. Black things. Things he accepted in himself but took no pride in. He was testing her again, seeing now how she would respond to these facts; she did not dismiss them, she did not grow horrified and shut them out. She was coming to understand him after all, through love. He knew she loved him. It was not a matter of indifference to him. It crossed his mind he would not leave her here when he left the planet. In some other place, less rarified than this one, they would be far better able, each of them, to judge what was between them.

In the end, one night, travelling together in the elevator up towards the top floors of the hotel, Jaxon told her this: "The business I had here is settled. I'm leaving tomorrow."

Although she knew he would not go without her, even so she thought in this instant that of course he would go without her.

"I shall turn out all the lights," she said simply. "As your ship takes you away, you'll see a shadow spread across the city."

"You can watch that too," he said. "There's plenty of

room in a shuttle for both of us. Unless you want to bring any of those damn lizards along.''

The ritual completed, they moved together, not any more to comfort, or to dance. Not as a test. He kissed her, and she returned his kiss.

They reached the eighty-ninth floor, and went into her apartment. On the bed where she had slept, and wandered among galaxies, slept and dreamed of him, they made love. About the bright whirlwind of this act, the city stood still as a stopped clock. The hotel was just a pillar of fire, with fiery gargoyles hotly frozen on its sides, and one solitary nova burning on the eighty-ninth floor.

III

A couple of hours before sunrise, Jaxon left his lover, Medra, sleeping. He returned to his rooms on the seventy-fourth floor and operated the communicator. He gave details to the mothership of his time of return. He told the government officer who manned the intercom that there would be a passenger on the shuttle. The officer was open-faced and noncommittal of tone, not discouraging. ''She's the last of the colony,'' said Jaxon, reasonably, insidiously threatening. There would be no trouble over it. The story of the MDD had been run to ground and could be exploded. Spirits would be high, and Jaxon in favor. Maybe rich, for a short while. She would like that, the harmony money would produce for her, not the raw essentials of cash. . . .

Having switched off and dismantled the communicator into its compact travelling form, Jaxon lay back on his bed. He thought about the woman fifteen stories above him, five minutes away. He thought about her as noncommittally and easily as the young man on the ship's bridge. But nevertheless, or perhaps sequentially, a wave of desire came in on him. Jaxon was about to leave the bed and go back to her, when he heard the door open and a whisper of silk. Medra had come to him.

She walked towards him slowly. Her face was very serious and composed. In the dimness of the one low lamp he had kept alight, her black hair gathered up the shadows and draped her with them. She was, no less than he, like a figure from a myth. No less than he. More so than he. And then he saw—with a start of adrenalin that brought him to his feet—that the one low lamp was shining *through* her.

"What," he said, putting his hand to the small gun by the bed—uselessly—"is going on? A real ghost, or just an inefficient hologram? Where are you really, Medra? If you *are* Medra."

"Yes," she said. The voice was exactly hers, the same voice which, a handful of hours ago, had answered his in passion and insistence. "I'm Medra. Truly Medra. Not a hologram. I must approximate. Will you countenance an astral projection—the subconscious, free of the body?"

"Oh, fine. And the body? Let's not forget that. I'm rather fond of your body, Medra. Where is it?"

"Upstairs. Asleep. Very deeply asleep. A form of ultra-sleep it's well used to."

"If you're playing some game, why not tell me the rules?"

"Yes, I know how dangerous you are. *I* know, better than I do, that is, my physical self. I'm sorry," the translucent image of Medra said to him, most politely. "It can only be done this way. Please listen. You'll find that you do grasp everything I say to you. On some level, you've known all the time. The inner mind is always stronger and more resilient than the thinking process we have, desperately, termed the brain."

He sat down on the bed again. He allowed her to go on. At some point, he let the gun slide from his hand.

Afterwards, for the brief while that he remembered, he

seemed to have heard everything in her voice, a conversation or dialogue. It was not improbable that she had hypnotized him in some manner, an aid to his acceptance.

She understood (*she*, this essence of Medra), why he had come to the planet, and the nature of the machine he had been pursuing. The legend of an MDD was merely that. Such a device did not, anywhere, exist. However, the story had its roots in a fact far more ambivalent and interesting. The enormous structure of the universe, like any vast tapestry, rubbed and used and much plundered, had come with the centuries to contain particular areas of weakness. In such spots, the warp and woof began to fray, to come apart—*fundamentally*. Rather than a mechanical destruction which could be caused to engender calamity, the macrocosm itself, wearing thin, created calamity spontaneously. Of course, this giving way of atoms was a threat both local and, in the long term, all-encompassing. A running tear in such a fabric—there could be only one solution. That every rent be mended, and thereafter monitored, watchfully held together; for eternity, if need be. Or at least until the last sentient life of the physical universe was done with it.

"You must picture then," she said, "guardians. Those who will remain at their posts for all time, as time is known to us. Guardians who, by a vast mathematical and esoteric weaving, constantly repair and strengthen the tissue of cosmic life. No, they are not computers. What upholds a living thing must itself be *alive*. We are of many galactic races. We guard many gates. This planet is one such gate, and I am one such guardian."

"You're a woman, an Earth woman," he recalled saying.

"Yes. I was born here, in the Terran colony, the daughter of an architect who designed one of the most glamorous hotels in twenty systems. When they came—those who search out the guardians are also sentient creatures, of course—they discovered that my brain, my intellectual processes, were suitable for this task. So they trained me. Here is one more reality: Extended to its full range, the mind of a human being is greater, more complex, capable of more astounding feats, than any mechanism mankind has or will ever design. *I* am the computer you searched for, Jaxon. Not a force of chaos, but a blueprint for renewal and safety. For this reason I remained, for this reason I always must remain. Those who were evacuated were given a memory, a whole table of excellent reasons for leaving. You, also, will be given a reason. I will give it to you. There'll be no regrets. Despite all the joy you've brought me."

"I didn't arrive here alone," he said. "The sky up there is full of suspicious characters who may not believe—"

"Yes. They'll believe whatever you tell them. I've seen to it they will."

"Good God. So what are you? A human machine, the slave of some—"

"No slave. In the beginning I was offered a choice. I chose—this. But also to forget, as you will forget."

"You're still a woman, not—"

"Both. And yes, in her forgetfulness, sometimes the woman despairs and is bitterly sad. 'Awake,' she doesn't know what she is. Only 'sleeping,' she knows. Always to know, to know when 'awake,' carries implications of power I don't trust myself with. Occasional sadness is better."

"Perhaps I don't accept any of this."

"Yes," she said. "All of it. As always happens. Dear love, you're not the first to alleviate my physical loneliness. When the time is right, I call and I'm answered. Who do you think drew you here?"

He swore. She laughed.

She said, "Don't be appalled. This episode is full of charm and amusement. Thank you again, so very much. Good-bye."

And she was gone. Into the air. The opening of the door, the whisper of material, they had been reassurances, and a ploy. He told himself he had been tricked. His nerves rioted with an impression of traps and subterfuge, but then these instincts quietened and the sullen protests ceased. It must be as she had said, on some level he did know and had accepted. There had been a joke once, God's a woman—

He fell asleep, sitting on the bed.

Jaxon drove the shuttle up into the pure air of sunrise, then beyond the sunrise into the inky night of space. He left it all behind him, the planet, the city, the hotel, and the woman. He felt bad about leaving her, but he had foreseen the pit before his feet. Living as she had, she would be a little mad, and certainly more than a little dependent. There was no room in his life for that; he would not be able to deal with it. Her fey quality had delighted him, but it was no grounds for perpetuity. Eventually she would have clung and he would have sloughed her in anger. It might have been expressive anger at that, beyond a cruel word, a cruel blow, and the hospitals were makeshift in the areas he most frequented. She wasn't for him, and it was better to finish on a note of pathos than in that kind of mess. Ships came by, she had told him. Someone else would rescue her, or not.

"Which woman?" he said to the captain of the mothership. "Fine. She didn't want to leave after all. Come on, you got what you wanted, I did your work for you. Now elaborate on the fee."

He had left her sleeping. Her hair had spread across the pillows, black breakers and rivulets of hair. Eyes like dark red amber closed by two petals of lids. He thought of the facades of empty buildings, the glitter of meaningless lights, the lizards who did not talk to her. He thought of the hothouse of colored glass. He had a memory of strange wild dreams she had mentioned to him, which took the place of life. She was a difficult woman, not a woman to be lived with, and if loved, only for a little while. *I am half sick of shadows*, she said to him now, in his mind's ear. But that was a line from some antique poem of Earth, wasn't it? Somehow he didn't believe the phantom words. Those shadows were very real for Medra.

In the deserted, partly ruined city, on the eighty-ninth floor of the white hotel, Medra wept.

She wept with a terrible hurt, with despair, in her anguish of loss. And with shame. For she had trusted and moved forward openly, without camouflage, and the blow had crashed against her, breaking her, crippling her—as it seemed to her—forever. She had been misled. Everything had contrived to mislead her. His smile, his words, gestures of politeness and lust, meaning nothing. Even her planet had deceived her. The way in which the sunlight fell on particular objects, the way music sounded. The leaves that towered in the hot-house had misled her with their scent. And she, she was guilty too. Hope is a punishable offense. The verdict is always death; one more death of the heart.

Medra wept.

Later she wandered her rooms. And she considered, with a practical regard, the means to her absolute death. There were medicines which would ensure a civilized exit. Or cruder implements. She could even die in agony, if she wished, as if to curse with her pain's savageness the one who had betrayed her.

But all violent measures require energy, and she felt herself drained. Her body, a bell, rang with misery. After a prolonged stasis of insomnia, there was no other refuge but sleep.

Medra slept.

She slept, and so . . . she *slept*. Down, down, deeper and deeper, further and further. The chains of her physical needs, her pulses, sighs, hormones, were left behind as the golden shards of the city had been left behind, and as she herself had been left, by one she had decided to love. Then her brain, fully cognizant, trained, motivated, keyed to vast concepts and extraordinary parallels, then her *brain* woke up.

Medra moved outwards now, like a sky-flying bird, her wings bearing her strongly. Into the vistas, into the sheens and shades, murmurs and orchestrations. She travelled through a multiplicty of geographies, over mountains, under oceans, galaxies—

Through the periphery of suns she passed, the cold reaches of space. She wove the tapestry and was the tapestry. The pictures filled her with happiness. The universe was her lover. Here, then, in the mystery, the weaver heard some far-off echo, diminishing. She thought, It must stay between the glass. She saw herself, part of a pattern, and elsewhere, random, her life. She said to it, kindly, You are my solace, but you are not enough. The stars flowed by her, and her brain fashioned their fires and was fashioned by them. She thought: But this—*this* is enough.